END STATE

James T. Emry

Grosvenor House
Publishing Limited

This book is published by
Grosvenor House Publishing Ltd
Link House
140 The Broadway, Tolworth, Surrey, KT6 7HT.
www.grosvenorhousepublishing.co.uk

A CIP record for this book
is available from the British Library

Paperback ISBN 978-1-83615-519-5
eBook ISBN 978-1-83615-520-1

Acknowledgements

The author would like to thank Sarah Palmer and Forrest Levin for their help in the publication of this novel.

If you travel to any country in the world that has had a civil conflict over the last 50 years and find someone over the age of 70, ask them a simple question, *did you ever expect your country to fall apart like it has done?* The answer will always be the same, *not in a million years.*

This has been the experience of a great many people in countries and regions as diverse as Iraq, Afghanistan, Libya, Syria, the former Yugoslavia, Yemen, and many other countries besides. It will also quite likely be the experience one day for a great many people presently living in the UK, the great majority of whom believe that the UK is a stable nation. It isn't.

PART ONE

CHAPTER ONE

April, 1994. Anlong Veng, Cambodia

The Khmer fighter sat on his haunches, partly propped against the outside wall of the small guard block with his bare feet splayed apart and linen shirt yellowing from exposure to the tropical heat and rain. His hands remained firmly on the stock of the AK-47, held vertically in front of him with the butt in the gravel. He stared obliquely across the compound as three white men marched in from the surrounding jungle, the rain starting to beat down more heavily. The three, in their olive green shirts and broad-rimmed tropical hats, stopped just beyond the guard block and turned round to face the half-open door.

The humidity was always greatest in April, and Sergeant Declan Gale, despite nearly two months of training and acclimatisation, was sweating waterfalls. His pale, clammy skin, dark red hair, and impressive physique marked him out completely from the small, wiry Khmer fighters positioned around the compound and even from the other two British soldiers sent to mentor the Khmer Rouge unit. They were smaller, not quite so muscular, but well-bronzed after the rigorous in-country training. All three looked well-prepared for the work ahead.

As they stood waiting, the jungle seemed strangely quiet. That was something they all knew would soon change with the impending spring offensive by the Royal Cambodian Army.

'Declan Gale,' called a voice from inside the guard house. Gale straightened, stood to attention, marched into the hut and saluted the figure sitting behind the desk. There was no furniture in the room other than the desk and the chair the British officer was sitting on. The officer was almost completely bald and in his mid-forties. He looked up from his notes.

'Stand easy, Gale. Glad to see you finally made it. You'll be here six months. You have already been briefed about the training you'll be giving to these men. One of them will show you to your quarters where you'll find your kit. Do you have any questions for me?'

'No, sir.'

'Well then, it just remains for me to welcome you on board. This place will take a bit of getting used to but judging by your career so far, you can more than handle it.'

'Thank you, sir.'

With that, Gale stood to attention, saluted, stepped back and wheeled round to his right.

'One other thing, Gale.'

'Sir?'

'There's no saluting here of any kind and I'm not a sir. Do you understand?'

'Yes. No saluting.'

'That'll be all,' the officer stated without looking up from his desk.

~~~

January, 2020. Al Hamisi TV Channel, Middle East

The man, his face shrouded by a Shemagh, spoke eloquently in a cut-glass English public school accent as if he was delivering a lecture. The only part of his face still visible was his eyes.

Life is just a collection of experiences, but life itself is about spiritual awakening. That means that all the objects we collect in life are meaningless. Material possessions have no real meaning. Only actions and reactions have meaning. That's why so many corrupt countries around the world are about to fall apart, as they have spent so much time pursuing material existence, they have missed the bigger spiritual picture. People thought that consumerism would keep them happy, but it doesn't. Humans have spiritual needs.

A good metaphor is the corporation that constantly tries to use hard selling techniques above all else. Eventually, it will die as a business as people naturally turn away. Human beings are not robots and never will be; they are spiritual beings and all will eventually learn this. However, while most people inevitably turn away from that way of life, many politicians never change their ways. They still think they can spread their disastrous political ideologies. They don't understand that no one is listening any more, especially in their own countries. Their houses are built on nothing but sand and are about to collapse.

This is what's happening right across the world. People are turning off and trying something different: civil conflict, the overthrow of corrupt political elites, and breaking the chains that hold them back. One corrupt state after another has been exposed for their lies, cowardice, and hypocrisy. Their corrupt political and legal systems have only ever functioned to protect the elite, never the mass of people within those states. And now those high-ranking and corrupt self-servers, who have been despised by generations for lining their pockets while millions of innocents have suffered and died, are being
~~~

dealt the hand of justice. Soon, we will be taking our activities into the very heart of these failing states. We will destroy them. More importantly, we will create a new way of life, Inshallah.

The camera panned away revealing two similar figures, each either side of the speaker, and a hooded man on his knees in front of them with his hands tied in front of him. The speaker was holding a scimitar-shaped blade which he then drew up and pointed at the camera.

~~~

Present Day. London

As he leaned against the bar of the Holloway pub waiting to be served, Declan Gale reflected that no one really knows what they are supposed to do in life, and most of us just take an educated guess and go for it. He also pondered the notion that no one can predict the extent of resistance that life throws back at us as it attempts to blight our plans to do well in our chosen enterprises.

He then reflected that this can have one of two consequences. It can force us to change our own career paths, or it can turn us round completely, even altering our value systems. Some would call this an awakening, others failure.

Declan also knew that he had spent the last few years trying to fathom his own life and had tried his hand at all kinds of things since leaving the British Army, without yet finding his chosen path. He waited for the barman to finish pouring the second pint of beer and looked up at the TV screen above the bar. It was almost silent but carried the images of another harrowing attack by militants somewhere in the world, the sound of the other Friday evening drinkers drowning out most of the reportage.

While Declan was under no illusions that at nearly forty-nine years of age he had so far failed to find a decent career, he was also aware that he wasn't actively seeking one. But he'd realised something else, something that didn't occur to most other people, that this was probably as good as it gets. Freedom for him had come in the form of lapsed desire. And as long as abject poverty was kept at bay, then the future wouldn't deepen any sense of personal crisis, or fear of penury for that matter. He may have gone for a low denominator in life, but it wasn't the lowest.

That was the trick; perhaps it was just his trick. His way of turning off and tuning out, with no real career, no longer any marriage, and no stress. That meant no heart attack when he realised he could no longer pay a mortgage or provide for a family.

However, he had begun to question his own integrity. He had left Northern Ireland in 1988 and joined the British Army as an infantryman. After more
~~~

than two decades' service he got divorced for the second time and for the next few years he worked for various construction companies, having used some of his army settlement to pay for a degree course in building studies. The latest recession had put paid to new construction starts and, after getting a small redundancy package, he decided to work for his cousin Jez. He was still fit enough to work on site having kept his frame lean and well-toned. This was unlike the hirsute Jez, who spent much of his time in a site office, had bad posture, and was quite overweight. But, despite looking after himself, Declan wasn't sure where life was taking him.

Integrity was a word that he had played games with all his life and one that he had never really understood. This attitude might have fostered a dangerous level of conceit on his part, but it had become sealed by a grudging acceptance of his own feelings of indifference. It was this indifference that had also helped him deal with some of the acts of evil he had encountered in life. That was perhaps his main defence mechanism against pain.

The barman lifted the two pints of IPA over the counter and placed them on the bar top in front of Declan, next to a bag of salted peanuts.

'There you go. That's eight pounds ninety in total.'

Declan handed a ten pound note over, got his change, and then lifted the pints, still with one eye on the TV screen. He turned gingerly to avoid the punters behind him and made his way to the table where his cousin, Jez, was waiting. He placed the round of drinks on the table and Jez looked up at him, raising his eyebrows enough for Declan to notice.

'We are exceptional,' Declan stated loudly and methodically.

'We are what?' replied Jez.

'I'll spell it out for you: E.X.C.E.P.T.I.O.N.A.L.'

'What's that got to do with the price of a bag of nuts, Dec?'

'Ah, Jez, I forgot them again!'

'I'm as sure as Istanbul has dogs.'

Declan turned back towards the bar and, as he walked away, shouted back, 'So, does Istanbul have a dog problem then, Jez?'

On Declan's return Jez seemed to be in a reflective mood, pointing up at the TV screen and commenting, *I think what we're talking about here Dec is the end of the good times. That's what's really happening; the world economy is being attacked.* Jez stared at his IPA as he spoke.

He and his brother, Gavin, had left Northern Ireland not long after Declan but had taken very different paths in life, training as civil and mechanical engineers respectively and then starting their own small construction business. It had been hard, twenty-five years of trying to win tenders, gradually garnering enough contracts to pay off the initial bank loan. Jez now owned the freehold of their business premises, and he was looking at expanding.

He could see Declan fitting into the business one day, but he was never very sure what his cousin actually wanted out of life. He therefore only ever offered him short contracts, mainly on the demolition side of the business. Gavin was his younger brother by six years. Their father was the slightly younger brother of Declan's father.

Declan nodded and sipped his pint, tilting his head slightly to look at the distant TV screen. In his soldiering years Declan had seen a lot of violence, much of it whilst serving in Iraq and Afghanistan. The media was now the main source of insecurity, a visual reminder of all the bad times.

Jez stopped talking and stared into space. While Declan didn't wish to add to the conversation, he equally didn't want to appear rude. All he wanted was a calm, relaxing evening. But his thoughts then suddenly turned to his son, a teenager who lived in Australia with his second ex-wife, Fiona, in Adelaide.

He looked at Jez and put his pint down before stuttering a reply, 'I think all any of this means is the end of the financial supremacy of the United States, Jez, that's all. Their empire was probably over a long time ago, a bit like the British, but maybe they don't see it that way.'

Jez looked up, grinning before replying, 'You really are an intellectual, Dec. You were always trying to get one over on me when we were kids.'

'Hah! That old chestnut,' Declan replied, smiling.

'It's true. You left Belfast at the right time.'

What was true was that Jez himself had been lucky, getting the higher education that many could only dream of at that time. Declan, on the other hand, had seen the worst of both worlds with a youth disturbed by the Troubles and then a lack of opportunity in his late teens. However, while he had always slightly resented not going to college, the military had given him a decent career as well as an education. He didn't regret anything in life.

After another hour of banter, he was suddenly aware that both of them had been drinking heavily all evening. Jez, perhaps noticing this, then changed the atmosphere in an abrupt and somewhat banal fashion, shouting out, 'Why am I so bloody embarrassing?'

It was meant as a rhetorical question and Declan at first chose to ignore it. However, he eventually replied after a long pause, 'It's probably just that quite a few in our wider family are genuinely embarrassing people, Jez. Not you in particular.' He paused and took a swig of his drink.

Declan then lowered his voice, adding, 'Anyhow what would you rather be; boring? I mean, let's face it, some of these people in here have the most boring accents.'

'You're right there, Dec,' Jez replied with a wink.

He then turned away and looked across the bar which was now nearly full of drinkers, mostly banking types, and most of them chatting loudly.

The financial world was obviously still thriving despite the increasing political turmoil just beyond its perimeter.

Jez then seemed to wake up again, adding, 'Maybe we're just a bunch of creatures from the black lagoon.'

'I don't even know what you're talking about but you're right. And we have to leave, right now, Jez, before we fall off our stools.'

They drained their glasses, Jez picking up his jacket with his other hand. He then put his glass down on the table and pulled on his jacket.

Through a beery snort he announced, 'You've got a point though, Dec, as it's the end of an empire really. The morons in power don't know what's hitting them, as they've always been so bloody arrogant. But the likes of you have seen a lot more than most, what with the military and all that.'

Declan looked straight at the TV screen nearest them, clips of police vans littering a barren landscape. He recognised that type of scene from various places he had served, and it made him shudder. But this was mainland Britain. They walked out of the bar.

~~~

Ches and Becker were sitting in a café on Camden Road. Ches stared at the TV monitor mounted high on the wall and poked at his breakfast disinterestedly. To an observer, it was obvious that he didn't care what was on the news.

Ches was in his early forties, nearly six feet tall, stocky, and with a face pitted by a tough upbringing in Hackney. He had done much in life, including soldiering, divorce and college, as well as a reasonable time in sales until the financial crisis of recent years. A red dragon tattoo crept up to his neck from his torso. However, for all his outward appearance, he was a placid enough man to those who knew him.

He still had some cash left over, but he needed more. Unlike most of his mates he didn't have kids and wasn't therefore paying any maintenance. But his desire to acquire as much money as possible had led him to the edge of a world of low-level crime and he was now concerned about the future.

He had known Becker for over five years, since they had both attended a vocational college in North London, for adult training. From the age of nineteen Ches had spent fourteen years in the British Army, although he never liked to admit it. He now ran his own joinery business, and the three years spent doing an NVQ had been time well spent after leaving the military. On occasion he would give Becker a job when he needed help.

Becker was quite the opposite. Ten years younger, wiry, and with a street persona that had earned him a slightly undesirable reputation around Waltham
~~~

Forest. He had given up on education and generally ran errands for local crime lords. He had no visible tattoos.

Becker looked up from his bacon and eggs and snorted, *You know Ches, please tell me I've been stupid. I mean this lot I've been working for recently; they're hanging me out to dry man. All they've done is stand back, while the rest of us do the hard work.*

Ches, in a disinterested and lowered tone of voice, replied, 'The guy in charge of all these scores; what's his name again?'

'I don't know the main man. No one will tell us his name.' Becker replied quietly, taking the hint and keeping his voice low.

'Well, that guy. He sounds like a right lump of meat, the sort who screws up everyones else's life and makes money out of it.' Ches paused, ate some toast, and then continued, 'But you wanted to do this job. It's an earner, you said.' Ches didn't really want anything to do with Becker's nocturnal activities, but he also knew that Becker was happiest when he was talking about them. For Ches, most people only resorted to armed robbery when they were dealt the worst hand in life. That could be down to a total lack of opportunity, or even some upheaval in their personal lives. This, the latest criminal to walk into Becker's life, sounded like he suffered from both.

Becker responded almost too quietly, *Yeah, it's an earner. But after these ones are over I'm going to lie low for while and stick to my own business.* He had only been running errands, driving vehicles, and making deliveries for the gang. But it was still enough to get him a long stretch in prison, and both he and Ches knew it.

'No probs pal,' Ches replied softly. 'But why don't you give me a hand with the shop work? Only if you want to, and cash of course.'

'Much appreciated, Ches. Let me know when.'

~~~

'That Kenny's a dickhead, a total nutter,' the Glaswegian shouted at the TV screen that was showing a midweek football match, Glasgow Celtic versus Galatasaray. The Islington bar was packed and the man continued to shout, regardless of those around him. 'I mean, why's he even on the pitch anyway?'

Declan Gale and his two cousins, Gavin and Jez, were standing a few feet from the bar. They stared at the shouting man momentarily before carrying on with their conversation. The screen suddenly changed, and a newscaster came on with a news bulletin reporting a British warship that was under attack in the Arabian Gulf, with a number of militants storming the vessel. There had been casualties.

'Oh man, who cares?' Gavin stated loudly. 'Get the game back on.'
~~~

Declan and Jez both shot ugly glances at Gavin.

'I suppose you're right there, Gav,' Declan replied sarcastically. 'I mean, who really gives a monkeys about people dying? The game's more important. Am I right or am I right?'

'You're so right, Dec,' Jez exclaimed. He stood up and went to get another round of drinks. Declan looked at the screen and then back at Gavin.

Gavin returned Declan's stare, and smiled, before replying, 'Apologies, Dec. I didn't mean any disrespect.'

'None taken.'

Declan slouched back into the seat as the football came back on the screen. He reflected that all three of them had been small boys growing up in Belfast with big attitudes. His was mainly because he had been bullied on account of his father being an alcoholic. He had spent his early teens bullying others to get his own back until ten days after his seventeenth birthday when his father had died. The disgusted looks of his father's two brothers, who couldn't bear to see the sight of their renegade nephew at the funeral, made him realise that he was going nowhere very quickly. He had changed his attitude almost overnight, but then quickly decided that he had to get away from the province. However, he hadn't forgotten how his uncles had blanked him at his own father's funeral.

'What a beauty, man,' the loudmouth at the bar shouted in appreciation of a Celtic goal. He fell back off his chair, narrowly avoiding Jez who was walking away and clutching three pints of lager.

~~~

Hackney.

The tall, attractive, mousy-haired blonde woman stood proudly, as she got ready to address a crowd totalling a few hundred on a cold, grey afternoon in Victoria Park. Next to her stood a shorter, grey-bearded man with thinning hair, about fifty years of age, who stared sideways at her. To an observer he appeared slightly jealous of her thirty years and good looks. Somewhat incongruously, he wore a tropical shirt with black jeans.

The man, Brandon Sinclair, was a political activist and veteran of many grassroots campaigns against alleged political corruption in the higher echelons of society. Now, as opposition to the mainstream politicians was growing, he had made it clear that he wanted more than ever for the younger generation to take over the mantle of responsibility for militant opposition while he organised his own clandestine political activities. He was stepping aside, or so he claimed.
~~~

The woman stepped forward as a chill wind swept through the crowd, whistling up into the barren trees. She then exclaimed clearly, 'Hello, everyone. My name's Jay Saxby, in case you don't know me. We're here to talk about what we're going to do to take the fight to the politicians, as well as against police violence and the corruption that's taken over our country. Indeed, we are tethered here by the Met police today. So go on, wave at the nice police. After all, they're only there to protect the paedophiles and war criminals within the ruling class, including the champagne socialists.' At this there was a general murmuring of agreement within the crowd.

Saxby continued, 'Unfortunately, too many of those in power, supported by their media friends, have got away with criminal activities of all kinds, including massive financial fraud, genocidal warfare, as well as selling weapons systems to fascist regimes around the world. And such powerful people will always get away with crimes if everyone else does nothing, and that's you and me, folks.

'However, all of us here do have one thing in common. We know that the mainstream politicians only actually represent one small group of people, the overprivileged. They've ignored what's been happening here for too long, as have the media, who consistently tell us that we all have to be good poor people and show everyone just how hard working we are. The likes write every day in their columns for the daily papers and then go scuttling back to their ivory towers in the suburbs away from the realities of this world. The reality is that this country is now a disaster zone as a result of the failed policies of the gangs of crooks that have bled this country, destroying its present and its future.'

She paused momentarily, looking around at the gathered people before continuing. 'Make no mistake, it's brave people who stop wars. They don't start them. Brave people stand up to corrupt leaders, brave people prevent conflict, and brave people stop the slaughter of innocents. We're not brave. Why? Because we haven't done anything to prevent the terrible wars perpetrated by our so-called leaders against foreign peoples over the last fifty years and we're all now paying for these bloody mistakes. So far, we haven't done anything about them, but the time has come to get together and deal with them.'

At that, there was a loud cheer from the crowd that soon became a chant, drowning everything else out. There were violent gestures towards a group of around twenty police stationed thirty metres away and seconds later, a small group had broken away from the crowd and attacked the police line. Two policemen became separated from the main group and were thrown to the ground, their assailants punching and kicking them until other police officers managed to wade in to rescue their colleagues.

However, more then joined the breakaway group, attacking the police cordon, some screaming, *Murderers!* One man surged forward, shouting, *go back to your political masters, you corrupt filth.*

As the man lifted his arm, he was struck with a baton round fired from the police line. He went down and his friends swiftly pulled him away.

The crowds grew through the afternoon, the police retreating. By early evening, the mob had grown until several thousand strong. The police set up roadblocks, but other groups got behind them and bombarded the vehicles with petrol bombs. Eventually, the police made a swift exit in whatever vehicles were left.

Brandon Sinclair had watched all this from a distance, making sure that he and his circle of followers could slip away undetected. He was happy at what he had witnessed, particularly the large numbers of people turning up to attack the police. He could see that his own opposition movement, along with various others, had now attracted many more members to the ranks in recent months, and in fact far more people than the mainstream media had ever expected.

By late evening, buildings were ablaze on routes heading into the City of London, and the crowds of militants started to splinter into smaller groups as they edged towards the West End. They attacked only premises associated with the rich, including outlets for performance cars, bespoke tailors, banks and souvenir shops. Throughout the night, as news spread of the violence, various outer areas around London became targets.

By early the following morning, the streets were lashed by rain and the winds had picked up. They drowned out the shouts of the remaining rioters to the extent that many residents thought it was just the high spirits of drunken people they could hear making their way home after a night out in London's clubs. In total, around fifty buildings were burned out, mostly on the eastern fringes of the City of London, but none of the turmoil made the national news due to reporting restrictions by the government.

~~~

Harrow, London.

'You must have fooled around a bit in the past,' Annie purred as Tactical Support Commander Chris Kane of the Metropolitan Police ran his hand over the smooth curves of her back.

He sat behind her, staring at her backside, and replied, 'I may have got around a bit in the past, but I think I've now arrived where I want to be.'

He stroked her perfect, pale, arching back. She lent on her crooked left arm and bent her head back towards him with a contented look on her freckled face, her luscious dark red hair falling across the bedspread.
~~~

'So who is it this time, more terrorists?'

'Can't tell you baby. But they're going to get it whoever they are.'

He shuffled closer and pressed behind her, pushing his erection against her contoured behind.

'You know,' he stated casually. 'There's really only one thing that appeals to me right now, but it might involve your consent.'

'I might give you it baby but only when you come back safely to me after your shift.'

She wiggled ever so slightly and moved away. He looked at his watch on the sideboard. He had thirty minutes to get to the briefing.

Kane peeled himself away from his girlfriend's prostrate form and turned onto his back, staring at the ceiling. He was the highest ranking black tactical police commander in the Met, but it made no real difference to him. He felt like a cog in the machine and a very small cog at that.

However, he had come a long way from his humble beginnings and at thirty-three years of age he didn't want to look back. It had been a hard upbringing in a small house in Hounslow, with two older sisters near the Heathrow flight path. They had all done well, mainly due to the tough Christian values of their parents. Dad still worked for a security company and had worked his way to the top. Mum was a senior geography teacher at a secondary school in nearby Uxbridge. His two sisters were both married to successful bankers.

Despite the hardships of being a Met Police Tactical Support Unit commander, he enjoyed his work. He just hated the paperwork, as well as the politics that invariably went along with it. However, with the political climate now changing for the worse, and his relationship with Annie growing ever stronger, he was anxious about the increasingly violent situation in many urban areas across the country. Senior officers had warned him about how difficult it was to balance the needs of work with a normal home life and the fact was that, so far, his career had caused several relationships to fall apart. He didn't want this one to go the same way.

He got dressed and headed over to the Tactical Support Unit HQ in North London. It was going to be a long day now that he had lost his partner Jake Hughes to the internal investigation. He had known him for just over two years, and he trusted Jake's judgement in everything except the man's ability to keep his mouth shut and accept orders, especially when they didn't seem to make sense.

Twenty minutes later he arrived on his Triumph Tiger motorbike at a dour, grey, industrial-looking building near Ealing. He got to the interview room where Jake, still a serving TSU officer, was being disciplined for the alleged assault against a fellow officer.

Chris could see that he was late as Jake was already flanked by two members of the Met's Internal Investigations Unit. After Chris had been briefed separately by the two, a skinny hairless man and an angry-looking woman, he was allowed to hear Jake respond to the accusation that he had assaulted a fellow male officer.

'We all knew he had been bullying a younger officer,' Jake exclaimed. 'He had been getting away with it for too long and was getting cocky. Maybe we all have skeletons in our cupboards but sometimes they're just that, skeletons. And sometimes claims of harrassment are just that, claims. The guy isn't telling the truth and it was really just a push and a single punch by me, that's all.'

The attending male officer interjected, 'Just calm down, Jake. We only want to hear your side of this story so please just tell us what happened in as much detail as possible.'

Jake explained the circumstances of how he came to hit the officer, whose nickname was Dizzy Davis, a character of ten years service who thought he could get away with harassing female recruits and embarrassing young male recruits in front of senior ranks. He had done so until Jake had punched him in the face two weeks before in front of a senior officer for bullying a recent addition to the unit.

Chris had known Jake long enough to be aware that the well-built ex-soldier had a short fuse. During that time he had himself been tested on occasion by Jake's hostile behaviour and he felt that this was probably the last chance for him in the TSU.

Once he had finished telling his side of the story Jake sat back in the chair and stared at Chris. The investigating officers got Chris to sign a statement and then walked out. In the canteen afterwards Chris bought coffee for both of them and then made sure they were located far away from any overly attentive ears.

Chris opened up, *You need to calm down a bit mate.*

'Why should I calm down, Chris? Commander Aley wants to wreck my career and you're telling me to calm down.'

'I'll tell you why, because they're looking at all the evidence pal, every minor altercation you ever had. They have to. And if you want this one to stick then keep going the way you are. What happened the other night is ABH and needs to be investigated. Don't mess with this; you're either in or out. It's your decision.'

Jake's eyes rolled upwards. His face had turned the colour of ash. Chris sat in silence, tapping the side of his cup.

~~~
~~~

An elongated white transit van pulled up outside the gates to the military compound in the Midlands, half-filled with men dressed in standard army combat clothing. The guard stared through the narrow opening in the gate but couldn't see their faces as they seemed to be turned outwards. The driver, also dressed in combats, was carrying a patrol sack over his shoulder as he approached the gate. He showed his ID card through the small aperture and the guard pulled the gate open. The van drove in.

The ten men stepped down from the van and the guard noticed that they were all carrying small rucksacks. From within the group one man burst forward killing the guard with rapid fire from a silenced automatic pistol. Another sprinted forward into the hut pouring rounds into the second guard.

The bulk of the group then carried on towards the central control station inside the camp, three men remaining to secure the perimeter gate they had just overpowered. Meanwhile another van pulled up at the second perimeter gate one kilometre away on the outer road. The eight men demounted quickly and overpowered the guards shooting each of them through the head. As soon as the two teams had converged on the control building, breaking through an inner set of gates, demolition charges were then placed on the intelligence facility.

Once the charges were set all the men returned, in their original formations, to the two outer gates, got back in the vehicles and sped off to a point overlooking the site, a couple of miles away. The firing devices had already had channels allocated and all that remained was for the operator to locate the correct channels for each of the two charges, one for each wing of the building.

Several seconds elapsed between each explosion which created shockwaves going up the hillside. Human nature would prevent anyone in the vicinity from venturing out for a few minutes. That gave the two vans time to speed off towards a parking area eight miles away where the men then transferred to other vehicles.

~~~

Ches and Becker were in a small café just off Camden Road staring at a TV monitor mounted high on the wall and showing a news channel and were just starting their cooked breakfasts.

Becker shook his head, stating quietly, 'I did another one last night Ches. Wish I hadn't.'

'Who was it with this time mate?' Ches replied half-heartedly. He had heard all these hard luck stories before and had little sympathy.

'Jay. Jay Saxby. It's *she* by the way.'
~~~

'You did an armed robbery with a woman?' Ches paused before adding, 'You need to get the hell out of it pal or you'll get the heat.'

Ches didn't really want anything more to do with the situation, but he was happy to talk to Becker about it. He had never actually been on the wrong side of the law and wanted his life to stay that way. He pondered the facts as he pushed a piece of toast into the scrambled egg. Not least that some people must have had such a poor deal in life that they were trapped inside a continual cycle of violence. In many ways it made little difference as Becker didn't really fall into that category and had only ever been a bit-part player, mostly for London gangs north of the river. Only recently had he been branching out with other groups. Ches had no idea who they were. All he knew was that they paid those stupid enough to run with them, regardless of what was involved.

'I'm going to lie low for while,' Becker replied. He was lying. There was another robbery planned for that weekend.

'You can give me a hand with the joinery work if you want; and it'll be cash of course.'

Becker smiled and nodded, replying, 'This time I will Ches.'

'Cool!' Ches nodded back at Becker.

The opportunity for something better in life would always be there for Becker as far as Ches was concerned.

~~~

'You know Jake there's a lot of talented people in this country but none of them are in politics.' Chris spoke as he held a cup of coffee and stared at a parliamentary debate being shown on a TV screen in the Tactical Support Unit briefing room. Jake had been allowed to resume his duties after their boss, Commander Bob Aley, had insisted the team should be brought up to strength due to manpower shortages.

'Politicians have always been failures. I wish things were different, but that's how it will always be,' Jake replied.

'To be honest, I don't really care,' Chris retorted. 'I just do my job. Who cares about politics anyway? Do you see anyone buying newspapers these days?'

'That's the point; most people have switched off. That means the extremists are gaining ground because people don't want the mainstream. This is a dangerous time.'

Chris smiled. 'Just watch it. The fact is you'll be a team leader yourself, if you don't screw up again, so show some responsibility. From what I've seen we don't actually know what we're dealing with these days. A few years ago we
~~~

thought it was just disillusioned students or a few psychos with rucksacks on transport systems. But it's not anymore. We don't know how, or where, they'll strike. There are networks everywhere and they're shifting. The politicians are looking dead on their feet and we're probably the last line in the sand.'

Chris stared into space. It felt like they were on their own much of the time, but at the same time he still respected the judgement of the senior commanders. However, he had noticed Aley's more politicised comments in recent weeks and was concerned that his boss now seemed more animated by things going on at a higher level than what was actually happening on the ground.

Chris continued, 'We've had many briefings, Jake. We're watching loads of people, admittedly, but it's nothing we can't handle. Let's stop worrying ourselves.'

Jake nodded and replied nonchalantly, *I know but I think we'll have to be more careful with how we deal with things.*

Chris replied, lowering his voice slightly. 'Some of these outfits are probably watching us.'

'I've come across that before.'

'Where was that?'

'They're probably learning our methods and how to get round them, maybe in order to hit us harder. It's what happens in urban warfare. It's what we were taught in the military, that's all.'

Chris sipped his coffee and raised an eyebrow at Jake.

~~~

Becker was sitting in the back of the rusting van waiting for the latest update on what they were doing. It was just past midnight and all he knew was that the Oxfordshire mansion they were supposed to be robbing belonged to a senior banker. It was about a mile from where they were parked by the side of woodland. According to the driver there was nothing to stop them getting into the property and taking what they wanted as the family was away. It would be simple enough.

Becker yawned and stared at the walls of the van, lit only by the light from a small camping lantern. He knew he should never have got involved again but the lure of easy money was too much for him.

He exchanged nods in the dim interior with another man opposite and then exclaimed, 'I hope this all goes OK.' He recalled the last time he had been involved with the same gang and guessed that the others also knew about the failed attempt to rob the farm, resulting in the shooting dead of three guard dogs.

'Yeah, so do I pal,' the man replied in a scouse accent.
~~~

At that point the driver shouted from the front of the van, 'Listen up you lot we're trying to work OK? Let's concentrate on the job.'

Next to the driver sat Jay Saxby. She had a UHF radio in her lap, listening to the regular updates from the men checking the area around the mansion. Another man walked up to the van and put his head through Saxby's window.

'So do we have a detailed plan with maps and info yet?' asked Saxby without looking up.

'Not exactly boss.' The man replied.

'Why? I thought we agreed on this. We should have confirmation of the layout, security system, locks and the egress routes by now. What's the problem?'

'Well, we've had a few problems. We had to revise the plan of action. Theres more security than we'd expected. That's caused a delay.'

Saxby went a different shade of red, before replying, 'How long a delay?'

'It could be another six hours.'

She rolled her eyes towards the ceiling of the van. She wanted to hit the place while it was still empty and calculated that they had a window period of no more than two days as everyone was away for the weekend. The police were generally more pre-occupied with the rioting due to the economic crisis rather than increasing local crime rates. However, Saxby knew that if they flooded the country with Tactical Support Units there could be less freedom to move around in the coming weeks, so this was the ideal window period to stage some high-level robberies.

Brandon Sinclair was sitting fifty miles away in another van. He was being updated of the logistical problems by Saxby on her mobile phone.

'You know you need to sort this out,' Sinclair stated without emotion.

'I know Brandon; we'll see what we can do,' Saxby replied.

She got out of the vehicle, gathered the men around, and said quietly, 'This isn't going anywhere guys, and we need a proper plan. We need to get this sorted.' The men looked at each other.

She continued, 'With all due respect we're not here to drink decaf cappuccinos and as usual when it all hits the fan you people are never ready. Most of you think everything will turn out rosy in the end if you just give your usual level of support but it doesn't work like that in real life.'

She paused and straightened her body to its full height and stared into the darkness before continuing, 'Well it won't do and you're all going to have to wake up. In other words, we have to be good enough to sort this out otherwise it will all be for nothing, a total waste of time. That means that if you don't want to be part of this then you have to get off right now.

If you don't want it then there's the exit. It's your choice. Make it happen now.'

Five minutes later Becker slipped out the back of the vehicle and walked off at speed into the darkness, stating that he was going for a piss to the men in the back of the van. He didn't return.

~~~

Jake and Chris were observing a building from inside an unmarked patrol car. Jake had survived the assault claim by the skin of his teeth and had been re-appointed as Chris's driver and number two. He was back where he wanted to be, in the middle of the team at the centre of surveillance work.

Chris looked aimlessly out of the vehicle. They were outside a gaming centre in Brockley and had been there for over two hours. He was getting concerned that locals would start noticing them.

He turned to Jake, stating, 'We'll have to go mate; we can't stay here any longer. Those dickheads will be in there all day.' He motioned for Jake to drive away.

Jake turned the engine on and eased the black BMW out into the traffic. They were now at the start of rush hour and Jake went on the radio.

'3 Tango. We're moving from location.'

A crackle came over the net, *Control. Confirmed.*

'I bet there's absolutely nothing happening with those boys,' Jake stated as he drove off.

Chris was thinking of Annie and bed. It was her birthday, and she had promised him a special evening. Not that an evening with her wasn't special. She could coax him out of slumber any time but tonight he wouldn't be tired, despite the fact he hadn't slept properly for the last two nights. He really didn't want anything to get in the way of his journey home.

'So, Chris is your lady at home waiting for you?' Jake asked. He smirked very slightly, both at his ability to read Chris's mind, as well as his own lack of tact.

'Mate, if only. I'm lucky if I get it twice in a month pal, especially now we've started living together.'

'Welcome to reality. Mine's up the duff. I don't know how that'll go down in the department now that my card's marked.'

'Well done mate. I'll buy you a beer, but maybe not tonight.'

'Cheers, I won't forget.'

~~~

'You know, Dec, why is it some people manage to be routinely annoying in everything they do?' Jez lamented as he sat next to Gavin and Declan in a Farringdon bar.

Jez was explaining the latest twist in his relationship with his wife at home. However, Declan and Gavin were more interested in the news on the TV screen above the bar.

'My teenage girl's just like her mother, just the same.' Jez added before glancing up at the screen. He took the hint, continuing, 'So have they made any arrests yet?'

The news story was about an attack on a government facility, but the reporters wouldn't disclose exactly where it was.

'No,' Declan replied. 'They just said some buildings got blown up and some guards got shot in the crossfire. All the attackers got away.'

'Oh well, too bad!' Jez replied, almost feigning interest.

'Do you know what's a bit odd about this?' Declan replied quickly. 'They said they took some 40mm grenades, but most of these groups wouldn't bother to get hold of that kind of thing. We had 40mm UGL in the infantry. That's underslung grenade launchers. You need the right weapons to launch them from.'

'Maybe they have,' Gavin replied.

To Jez it all sounded like a foreign language, and he just nodded at Declan. As they were watching the screen a well-known female political commentator came on and was talking about the recent upsurge in political violence across Europe. Jez sighed and got up to go and buy another round of drinks at the bar.

Declan looked up at the scenes of rioting and violence across Europe, and exclaimed, 'It seems to me like everywhere's going up in smoke.'

After a couple of minutes Jez returned and put the drinks down on the table. In an attempt to lighten the mood, he asked, 'Anyway Dec, I haven't seen you with anyone since the divorce. How's life treating you in that department?'

Declan knew what was coming but he refused to engage as he didn't want to get too embroiled in explaining his personal life. He turned his head slowly, before replying, 'I've always put friendships before relationships Jez, even when I was married. You know that.' He swallowed a quarter of his pint before continuing. 'That was probably why things didn't last to be fair. Anyway, I'm fine at the moment. What about this latest work you got for me? Cash you said.'

Jez looked at Declan and thought hard for a moment. 'Yeah, there's some work for you, but give me a week or two.'

He then took a drink and observed, 'You know if being married has ever taught me anything it's that it's not being married that makes you happy.

It's all the other friendships and relationships around it. That's what keeps us human Dec.'

Declan, who had never been one for drunken philosophizing, squinted at Jez as he replied, 'Jeez Jez! Have you been reading that Bertrand Russell again?'

Gavin laughed, interrupting, 'Now, who the hell is this Bertrand Russell?'

Both Declan and Jez laughed. Before Declan had a chance to reply Jez interjected, 'No one Gav. I'm reading a book at the moment about how we're all motivated in different ways. It's about what makes us all tick. You know about that, Dec?'

'I have no idea Jez; no idea whatsoever.' Declan had a glazed look on his face.

The bar was now busy, and just over half-full, which was, Declan thought, something that was made worse when someone like Jez was around. If a place was full, then people couldn't easily hear what others would be saying above the background noise. If it was empty, then it didn't matter. But if it was half-occupied it meant a significant number of people could hear someone's views especially when they had to talk louder than their drinking partner in order to get heard. These were things Declan had learned while serving as a surveillance and intelligence officer with the British Army and they had stuck with him over the years.

The subject of conversation soon moved on to politics.

'All we're talking about here is that the state is being attacked,' Jez stated categorically. He lifted his pint of beer to his mouth, took a sip and then grinned. 'But it's actually quite normal in historical terms and the English especially are used to it, as it's been happening down the ages. People just don't realise that political and social upheaval are just normal states for humans.'

'I think it's the end of an era,' Gavin replied. 'But a lot of people in power believe they're untouchable; that they're still powerful even when they're not.'

'You're such a bloody intellectual Gav,' Jez replied. 'I, on the other hand, didn't do so well at school. The teachers were shocking.' Jez laughed loudly. The barman looked over at them.

Declan was conscious that the three of them had been drinking heavily all evening. He felt jaded with the conversation.

'Why do we always behave like this? It's embarrassing, isn't it?' asked Gavin rhetorically. He continued, 'It's not just that we're all generally just total pissheads, but we really do all talk a load of crap don't we?'

'You're right there Gav,' Declan stated, slightly indignantly, and turned away to look across the bar which was now full of office workers, chatting loudly. Two very attractive young female city workers shot a look back at Declan. London's financial centre certainly seemed to be thriving.

'We're the trogs living in caves as far as everyone else is concerned,' Jez added.

'I don't even know what you're talking about but you're right mate,' Declan replied. 'But in fact, you two are so right that we have to leave. Right now, before we get into trouble with the bouncers.'

There was a pause as they drained their glasses. Jez then picked up his jacket, stating loudly, 'You've got a point though Gav. It's the end of an era really. Those eejits in power don't know what's hitting them, as they've always been too arrogant. They started all these wars but couldn't finish them because they're too weak. But someone like you Dec; well, you've seen a lot more than those cheating bastards ever will.'

Declan looked straight up at the TV screen above the bar. The woman had gone and there were clips of police vans on fire littered across a barren landscape. Declan recognised that type of scene from his years in the British Army and it made him shudder.

He looked at his cousins. Declan had grown sick of all the lies of his generation including how they had been safeguarding peace by going to war in Iraq and Afghanistan. He had been in both and had never felt the world was any safer as a result. Some politicians still claimed that the world had been saved from a greater calamity, but it now seemed that the world was in an even more parlous state.

For Declan survival was his only thing, not just his survival but that of his friends and family. However, it was his ability to avoid confrontation that had carried him through life. He knew that he could defuse any situation, as it was his natural skill. And his two cousins respected that quality in him.

Declan looked straight at Jez, whose eyes looked blacker than normal, probably due to the stress of running a small company and looking after a family, and stated, 'Don't worry Jez. Everything's a total mess and always has been. But we'll all survive.'

~~~

'You know Chris there seems to be an unhealthy situation out there on the streets right now and it seems to be getting worse.' Annie finished speaking and stared at Chris as he sat on the edge of the bed and put his shirt on.

'You've been watching TV again, haven't you love? It's bad for your health you know.' Chris knew he sounded patronizing, but he couldn't help it.

'It's true Chris. I'm worried about what's happening and about you.'

'Don't worry about me Annie – all I care about is that you're OK.'

He turned and winked at her as he slipped on his trousers and black TSU jacket.
~~~

'Can we at least agree on something for once?' It sounded more like pleading than anger as she slid over and hugged him.

Chris felt odd being in her bedroom. It had never bothered him before, but he was now surrounded by her objects, her way of life. Times were changing and the rules governing his life were changing. He realised that he might have to start taking care of himself, not for his own peace of mind but for hers.

While he knew that he could at least rely on his tactical team to watch his own back, events on the streets were now definitely turning a corner with attacks by militants expected on government facilities and the security services. He also knew that more casualties would soon follow. Ports, train stations, government complexes, power stations were being patrolled by armed personnel and many reservists had been called up under a civil contingency plan. The government was taking the situation seriously. He also started to wonder about some of the groups who were supposed to be under surveillance. They had gone quiet, of late.

'Go back to sleep love and I'll call later.' He put on his shoes, stood up, picked up his wallet and car keys, blew her a kiss, and walked out.

~~~

There were about twenty militant commanders from Brandon Sinclair's National Action Group gathered in the Harrow flat, amongst them Jay Saxby. She spoke first.

'Let's face it we haven't hit a single, high-profile target yet. If we really think that politicians are the enemy, shouldn't we have dealt with a few of them by now? These people are sitting targets. They've made careers out of killing innocent people and lining their pockets so it's now time to hit them even harder. Robbing rich bastards isn't enough.'

She stopped herself for a second just to look up and see the expressions on the faces around her before continuing. 'Millions of innocents across the Middle East and beyond have died over the last twenty years as a direct result of what British politicians have done. They have quite literally walked away from their crimes. It's time for them to pay and that's our job. The reason we're here is because a lot of people see this country's establishment as corrupt, and they're right about that. But nothing is being done. I don't know about you, but I can't wait to get at the politicians as well as their media allies. We simply haven't been striking hard enough and that's why we need to improve our game. We have enough money now to buy some serious equipment.'

A Geordie militant shouted out, 'Just remember that it only takes one man or woman to make a stand. It all comes down to that individual, and their
~~~

experiences, their motivations, their disillusionment. That's what this is really about.'

'Thanks for that,' Brandon Sinclair interjected. He had heard enough and jumped up while Saxby sat down quietly next to him.

Sinclair turned and, looking straight at Saxby, stated warmly, 'Thank you Jay, we should be proud that we have capable commanders like you with us. The rest of you would do well to follow her example.'

He turned to the front and, addressing the whole group, started talking methodically. 'I've no problem with what any one of us says, as we are all one body after all. But remember we're doing this for our people in this country. We're republicans who represent the working classes, black and white, whatever their religion, so don't let the media barons try and cast us as anything else. They're the real problem in all this as they will use any tactic to drag us down. Don't forget that it was their own political parties that many years ago started killing unknown numbers of civilians in other countries, as well as using the politics of divide and rule in this one to keep us all silent.' At that there was murmured approval around the table.

Sinclair carried on, but in a more assertive tone. 'You know why they did all that? Because those so-called politicians were scared of the future and they were also scared of change. We're not. All peoples and nations are our brothers and sisters, and we'll fight alongside them. We'll destroy these corrupt politicians and then take power. So there'll be no more bloody wars in the Middle East or anywhere else. We therefore have no choice. We have to take on and attack those in power.'

The group sat in silence as Sinclair continued, this time raising his fist and banging the table, shouting, 'As a nation we're all guilty of cowardice. We could have all done more to stop the illegal occupation of other lands, the killing of great numbers of innocents and the theft of their resources. But we chose not to. We have allowed our politicians to continue claiming that this country has a right to attack other nations when they haven't. Moreover, the oil and mineral supplies of those regions are for the peoples of those regions. We need to learn to live with what we have. It was our collective cowardice that brought this on as we failed to stop them, and we now have to do something about it. We have to get rid of the existing political class and replace them with something better.'

Sinclair stopped himself, looked around and then checked his agenda in front of him. Recent activities hadn't gone that well and his first objective was to get more money for the organisation. He then started to explain where and when the next actions would take place.

~~~
~~~

CHAPTER TWO

'He goes by the name of Wee Georgie, but don't worry about him.' The rotund Glaswegian exclaimed cheerfully and smiled, as he invited Brandon Sinclair into his Islington flat. He used his foot to pin the small, yapping creature back, against the wall of the corridor. Sinclair moved swiftly past and ended up outside a room at the end of the corridor where he heard a number of men talking.

The man with the dog followed on, ponderously, but finally opening the door into the room. There were five others sat down, two of them smoking. They were all in their mid to late fifties, all sporting thick beards. None of them looked up as the two men walked in, but carried on talking and playing cards, Scottish and Northern Irish accents merging.

One of those seated then stood up and waved his hands, welcoming Sinclair to their group. He shouted above the din, *OK guys, this is Brandon. He ran the logistics for the last few knocks.*

'Looks like all our boys did was turn up then,' one of the men joked. The others laughed.

Sinclair knew that no one was interested in anyone else's reasons for being there, the assumption being that if you were involved at this stage then reasons weren't really important. It was all about getting the right result, as the team had been lying low for weeks and waiting for the latest strike. They were now keen to get on with it.

He also knew that for some of the men armed robbery had been a way of life for a very long time, having started their 'careers' with armed political gangs. These men were still using the same tactics they had employed throughout the last four decades, and they worked.

For several of those in the room the enterprise wasn't just about gaining large amounts of cash, but something much bigger and more political. For them *The Troubles* had never really ended, even when the British government had finally had to seek a peace deal over Northern Ireland. Of course it was dressed up as a victory for the British people in the jargon of the day, but it was anything but.

However, for most of those in the room what was important was the outcome. The fact was, regardless of any political allegiance, committing armed robberies and selling guns, amongst other illiegal activities, had all paid fat dividends.

As far as Sinclair was concerned the team assembled in front of him had a great wealth of talent and range of skills. He had been made aware that they included amongst their ranks weapons specialists, expert drivers, mechanics, forgers, to name just a few trades. Any individual motivations were not his immediate concern.

All the men sitting around the table had one thing in common: they were old hands at keeping secrets from newcomers, as well as each other if required. Many of the old ways of doing business were now long gone but, after years of subterfuge and in-fighting, those still operating within the gangs had learned to keep their mouths firmly shut so as not to attract outside interest. In that sense it wasn't avoiding the authorities or police that mattered so much. What really mattered now was how to score as much cash as possible and that meant keeping their heads down and not involving others.

The men knew they would be working for Brandon Sinclair on a few robberies. He was the new paymaster, and they were contracted as part of his operation. They didn't care about about anyone in his political organisation. They were being paid to rob rich capitalists and line their pockets regardless of anyone else's ambitions. Hopefully the plan would work well for all parties concerned.

The men in front of him looked both professional and casual to Sinclair, which for him was a rare combination. He briefly looked at the walls in the room, and around the table, before unveiling the plans of the small ammunition storage facility that was the new target. The briefing would last thirty minutes and then he would be gone. Until the RV three days later.

~~~

'I think that guy sees himself as some kind of poet, or something like that,' Jez stated to Declan while staring at an old man singing on a stage located to one side of the bar area. They had fought their way to the front of the crowd in an Irish club in Holloway. The erstwhile crooner carried on with songs about life, love and politics.

Declan turned round and, scanning the floor, saw Gavin beckoning them both to come over to a table set in a side alcove. They got the drinks and joined him.

'Hey lads,' Gavin whispered. 'I thought I'd sit my sorry arse down to claim the table and let you boys get the beers in.'

'Yeah, we got that Gav,' Declan whispered back. He had been on his guard ever since entering the club, as he was always careful how he behaved in Irish bars in London, mainly in case he was recognised as a former British soldier. He had been lucky to avoid unwarranted attention over the years but old
~~~

habits died hard as far as he was concerned, and he wasn't taking any risks, especially as all his closest family was Catholic.

When they had been in their early twenties Declan had asked Jez to drop some white lies that he had gone to the United States and joined the United States Marine Corps. No one knew any different as Declan rarely returned home. However, Declan's whereabouts was a secret that he had maintained for many years, and keeping a low profile at all times had been his personal philosophy over the years. His mother, brother and sister had moved to England by 1995, and by then most people had stopped asking questions.

Lowering his voice Declan whispered to Jez, 'So what's up with the old guy. He's not exactly Christy Moore is he?'

Jez replied jokingly, 'Don't worry about him Dec. He'd already had too many beers before he got here. His voice will actually get better.'

Declan grinned and shook his head, looking around at the assembled gathering. They looked like the usual bunch of drinkers, crooners, site workers and bohemians, who were there for the cheap drinks rather than any high-end culture.

After twenty minutes Declan went to get the next round of drinks and whilst standing at the bar looked at the news on his Android phone. The caption read 'Raid on Ammunition Facility' and a face appeared on the screen. He thought he recognised the face but couldn't put a name to it. It was a photofit picture. There was something about the image that sent a shudder through him.

'Are you OK?' Gavin asked as Declan arrived back with the drinks.

'Don't worry, Gav,' Declan replied. 'It's nothing important.'

~~~

Jay Saxby and Mal, an ex-soldier from Hull, wandered down the Lincolnshire country lane in the cool of the May night, their night vision now functioning well enough to make out the gravel as they walked. The recent heavy rain hadn't been enough to churn up the path into the woods and they managed to follow it as far as a public footpath post.

Saxby then felt her way along a low fence to the start of a low brick wall. On hands and knees, she found the top of a metal manhole cover in the undergrowth. She got out her pocket torch and checked the extremity of the cover. A couple of pulls were enough to lift it and she and Mal flipped it over in the mud.

They looked down and saw the four dark packages stacked inside. They pulled them out and carefully put the lid back down. Back in the van they unraveled the sandbags and took off the black plastic bags which had been
~~~

woven methodically around the four Heckler and Koch MSG 90 rifles. They checked the weapons over and Saxby then banged on the wall of the cabin three times. The driver started up the engine and checked his watch.

Saxby dialed a number on her phone. 'We're on Brandon,' she stated.

'OK, Jay,' Sinclair replied crisply.

She smiled, got out of the back of the vehicle and walked round to the front where she pulled the door open and looked in, stating softly, 'We've just about enough time to get to the target.'

'Yeah, no probs,' the driver replied.

She jumped in front, shut the door, and said to the driver, 'OK, let's get on with it.'

An hour later they arrived at the target, a sprawling Derbyshire mansion. They parked up on a side lane two hundred metres from the entrance gates. It was 11:55 P.M. and silent.

The driver stayed with the UHF radio. He was to send a radio check to the rest of the team once they had got into their locations. The drill, if they were approached by anyone, would be to pretend that they were contractors.

Despite the tip-off that the place would be empty for a few days they wanted to avoid running into any security or maintenance staff, and Saxby could only afford two hours for the whole operation. Moreover, the senior politician who owned the property was known to employ ex-military staff to patrol the grounds, so the window of opportunity was further restricted. Only one of the rifles was kept at hand, loaded with a full magazine by Mal.

'Send checks,' came over the driver's headset, from Saxby. He then sent the radio check message to the three other vans, one team in each.

'On site,' they each replied.

Two teams then went towards the property on foot, with the other two in support. There were no guards, and it had already been established that the only external security was the CCTV system. Once that was disabled, they then had to get to the house alarm control panel which took about another ten minutes. Having disabled the alarms, they then turned the house over taking anything of any value. The safe was cracked and a siginificant amount of money and valuables taken.

Everything was put in the back of Saxby's van. The four vans then went off in different directions with Saxby's eventually arriving at a house near Derby. Here, Saxby, Mal and the driver deposited their haul in the lock-up at the back of the semi-detached property, including the rifles, which were now placed in a new container.

After resting there for the day they then headed to a location near to Warwick and met up with another group led by Sinclair. The target was Sir Jeffrey Hammond, who had recently been busy as an executive director of a large weapons company called Brownstone Solutions. Parts of the media had identified Hammond as one of the most corrupt energy oligarchs in the country, lining his pockets to the tune of millions of pounds while *Pensioners freeze to Death* as one tabloid newspaper had put it. That was before he turned his attention to defence procurement and the lucrative deals on offer.

Apart from being an ex-cabinet member Sir Jeffrey Hammond had been a vociferous supporter of the invasions of various Middle Eastern countries over the decades as well as those companies that had been reaping the financial benefits of military action.

Sinclair wanted the media to see that those working for him could hit more than one location in a matter of a few hours. The haul of money and valuables would be useful but getting noticed by the wider world was far more valuable in terms of the publicity it would generate.

Saxby had already checked the best means of entry into the mansion. She had surveillance photos but still wasn't totally sure about the presence of secure CCTV.

'We may as well go through the front door with our masks on, as it'll be quicker,' she said under her breath to Sinclair through the side window of the van. The rest of the team slept in the back. 'We'll be bringing ourselves into the open from the first.' Sinclair nodded and said nothing. It was Saxby's operation. She got the men out of their slumber and set off up the track towards the house.

Saxby attached a silencer to her 9mm pistol. She felt inside her smock for the two extra magazines. They shouldn't be needed, unless there were guard dogs or security people guarding the house.

Sinclair had made it clear that his and another vehicle would only be there to give support for extraction. They would not allow themselves to be compromised if things went wrong.

Saxby gave final instructions to the men as they approached. They got to the start of the track leading up to the house. Lights shone from several windows and several dogs started barking.

'We'd better get off this track and wait out,' Saxby asserted softly. They walked back down the track and fell back onto some firm ground in front of trees. Another dog barked in the distance.

After twenty minutes of waiting to see if there was any movement around the area Saxby sent two men to check the house. There was no one around but there were sirens in the distance, so they all went back quickly to the vehicles.

Saxby walked up to Sinclair's open window, stating clearly, *I think we should head. Possible security: and I'm not willing to get busted here.*

Sinclair nodded and signaled to the driver. He nodded and started the engine. The two vans were soon heading at speed away from the area.

As they drove Sinclair was thinking about another location, the Ricoh Arena in Coventry. They headed back to the house near Derby.

~~~

Chris and Jake were in the TSU control room waiting for the briefing. After a lengthy delay Commander Aley stood up. 'OK people, listen up. We don't have much time before we send you out and this time we have a group in our sights. We think we know where they're headed as we heard some chatter last night.'

'They think they know!' Chris muttered quietly to Jake. Jake lifted his eyebrows. After five more minutes of background information on the militant group the orders came out and were distributed to each team's laptop.

'Once in location you will switch to the correct frequency and then take up positions as directed in orders.'

Chris and Jake listened to the rest of the briefing and the likely list of targets. They then checked their weapons and waited for the vehicles to be cleared. All the units were heading for the same location, the Ricoh Arena Conference Centre in the East Midlands.

Two hours later Chris and his team arrived outside the entrance to the complex. Chris shouted down the armoured van, 'All right guys, I'm going to have a look in and check what's happening with the local police. Wait out.'

He jumped out, entered the arena and walked over to where another team commander, Catrina, an academy colleague, was standing.

'Hi Cat. Where's the chief?'

'Search me, Chris. Last I heard he'd ordered his guys to go off on some lost cause. Some bigwig's place was about to get done over. There was a tip-off by an ex-con, apparently had enough of the low pay and long hours. They nearly got them driving away.'

'That's a shame! Well, I suppose we'd better just take up our designated spots then?'

'Yep, guess you'd better.'

Chris started off towards the exit, all the time hearing the speech coming over the public address system by a member of an opposition political party. *We should let this failed government fall apart. They're just another bunch of self-obssessed celebrity politicians whose only concern is their own public image and not the good of this country.*

After Chris arrived back at the van Jake radioed the TSU's control office to say that they were in position. They could still just hear the centre's public address system.

'Bit rich coming from this lot,' Jake said away from his mouthpiece to Chris.
~~~

Another team was in position eighty metres away, within view, and outside another entrance gate. Jake held his arm aloft through the window in acknowledgement of a wave from the driver of the other team.

Suddenly, there was a surge in the air pressure, followed by an enormous crack. Jake felt the blast wave before anyone else in the van, which was knocked sideways slightly. The van was parked slightly sideways to the entrance and Jake could tell that the blast had come from behind them in the middle of the mainly empty car park.

Chris shouted down the van, 'Everyone stay still until I say different, there could be another one.'

Jake looked out the window and could see two bodies sprawled out on the tarmac not far from the other van and closer to the centre of the car park. He pointed them out to Chris, who nodded.

After a few more seconds Chris said, 'Ok, let's go and check out what's happened.' He opened his door and signaled for Jake to go with him, shouting back to the rest of the team, 'Everyone stay put for now.'

They quickly got to the men, both of whom were conscious and trying to get to their feet, the smouldering remains of a vehicle only eighty metres away.

'You lads, OK?' Chris shouted. Through his radio he then stated, 'All units, officers down in car park near Arena entrance. Medic, requested.'

Both the men were now moving and one replied, 'Yes boss, bit close that one but I think I'm OK.'

A number of car alarms were set off and one of the vehicles near to the destroyed car had been thrown over. Chris reasoned that it was either a badly timed detonation or it had been intended as a warning. Either way it was a close shave for the two patrolling officers.

The leader of the other team arrived at the scene. Seeing the men were OK he asked, 'Is this a diversion do you think? Or is something else about to happen?'

'You might have got it in one.' Chris replied. 'But someone had better check what's happening inside the centre.'

The officer replied quickly, *OK, but let's not get channeled. There may be another. I'll contact the control box in the West Stand.*

Chris nodded, replying, 'Make sure the EOD team get here soon. Me and Jake will head in.'

Back at the van Chris told the rest of his team to wait in support and then walked into the arena with Jake. As they walked, he asked Jake to state their locations to the control centre.

Chris hoped that the rest of the units were scanning the rest of the complex for suspect devices. He held his own position for a moment so Jake could check any reports coming in. People were still in a state of shock, some standing and looking worried. Thankfully there were neither many cars in the parking areas, nor people inside the facility, as the political party had failed to attract many people.

Chris entered the conference hall itself and then made sure the people inside were made aware of what was happening. He went to the podium and said quietly to the speaker, 'Excuse me sir, could you tell everyone to stay firm for a short while please. We just want to check the place over.'

'Of course,' came the reply.

Jake then entered and scanned the hall for any suspect packages.

Most of the delegates had already gathered by the exit doors but Chris was uncompromising, stating loudly, 'Ladies and gentlemen, we have to keep you here for the time being, as we need to assess the situation. It won't take long so please remain calm.'

The rest of the units radioed that they were checking each of their zones. Chris knew that only a clear set of orders would make them move any further.

He turned to look back through the large curtain wall windows to the world outside. There were now sirens and flashing lights. Beyond the car park was the main access road. He knew that whoever had planted the device would be long gone.

Jake appeared in front of Chris, asking pointedly, 'Boss, shall I start checking the rest of the place over?'

Chris grimaced and raised his eyebrows. 'I don't know Jake. Let's wait for forensics and let the rest do their work. We'll wait for Aley to tell us what to do next.'

Soon more teams entered the site and all areas, including the buildings, were gradually sealed down and checked for further devices. Chris told Jake to radio their own team to join the searches in the car park. All the people who had been inside the arena were accounted for.

It became clear that whoever had planted the device had decided to exit the area. It had been placed in an old Mark 4 VW Golf positioned near the access road. There weren't any casualties.

While forensics teams scanned the outside area Chris and Jake helped evacuate the delegates through gates on the other side of the arena. Many were clearly shaken, not expecting that their small political conference would be a potential target.

'We finally got a bit of the action,' Chris said under his breath to Jake, after everyone had left. They went back to the van.

'We made the news mate,' Jake stated and laughed as he looked at a TV monitor in the van. 'Anyway, my woman will be on my case when I get home.'

Chris laughed, replying, 'That bad mate?'

'Married life does that.'

'I'll buy you a comfort coffee and a doughnut later mate.'

~~~

Ches and Becker were working on some joinery items for a retail unit out of the back of Ches's rusting transit van in Stoke Newington. Becker needed to get back into some kind of legitimate business, at least in the short term, and Ches had appointed him as an apprentice joiner. As far as the tax and benefits offices were concerned Becker was now apprenticed to Ches on small retail and commercial jobs.

'I hope I don't cock this up for you,' Becker exclaimed as he measured a frame. 'At least it'll get the benefits people off my back for a time.'

Ches paused before replying, 'You know Becks I had mates who I served with. Some are builders now. I was thinking of seeking one or two out and seeing what they're up to. I could see if they've got any contacts. What do you reckon? There might be some work in it?'

'Yep, good idea,' Becker replied. 'You told me once that you had served with a mate of yours, an Irish lad. Do you remember?'

'Yeah, Declan. He was someone I knew around, a face if you know what I mean. I haven't seen him for a while now.'

Becker nodded. 'No problems Ches. Any work is good by me.'

Ches moved swiftly with a circular saw. He stopped, looked up and stated, 'Well anyway I've got more work as well coming on these fit outs if you want it.'

'As long as they pay on time,' Becker replied sarcastically.

'What are you on?'

'I was joking Ches.'

Becker was secretly scared. Now that he had left the gangs the rules of the game had changed. The likes of Saxby and Mal were unlikely to ever find out who had contacted the police. But he could never go back. He had finally burned his bridges.

~~~

The forest of columns, partly covered in scaffold boards, gradually disappeared behind them as Gavin, Declan and Jez walked along the street away from the building site in Nottingham. It was just before five in the evening and the days seemed to be getting longer with the extra hours of light.

They had been working on the refurbishment of a commercial unit near Beeston in the south of the city. Gavin and Jez were running the new cable trays and conduits as part of the first fix. Declan was there as a labourer.

'Let's find a bar, but not round here,' Jez stated. He didn't look up as he opened the door to the Land Rover, an old 110.

Ten minutes later they pulled into a large pub car park just as the news came on the radio. The main story was about the explosion in Coventry the week before. The police were not ruling out terrorism but they had few leads. The three made their way to the main restaurant bar and ordered food and drinks.

'This is the life boys, work and play,' Jez stated, almost shouting. 'It's two more days here and then onto the next site.' Jez loved his work and was only really happy when on a construction site.

They stayed until last orders and then headed back to their rooms in a city centre bed and breakfast. Declan then checked his emails, including several from old military contacts offering some kind of work, along with a link to a page on a social network site he had just joined.

He recognised one of his former mates, Ches, who had been a corporal for many years while he had been a senior NCO in the same regiment. Ches had been a decent enough soldier and, under his command, had shown a lot of promise as a junior NCO. However, that last tour in Afghanistan had been a tough one for all of them and, on his return, Ches had decided to quit soldiering.

They had then lost touch with each other mainly because Declan had been abroad after leaving the military. His subsequent divorce had rendered him penniless and depressed, something he still didn't want to admit to former comrades. The last thing he had wanted was for his old mates to see him like that. He posted a message to the group, stating *Life's now better than ever*. It was a lie.

~~~

Jake and Chris were in the Tactical Support Unit's briefing area and as usual they had arrived five minutes before Commander Aley and the rest of the teams. Jake looked at Chris and said quietly, 'I wonder at what point those idiots in command will realise just how bad things have got out there on the streets.'

'Who know's mate but we have to work as a team, whatever,' Chris replied. He was only slightly annoyed by Jake's negative attitude. 'Anyway, it appears there are now groups of militants moving around outside certain government locations. These people are trained and motivated and they are checking out government facilities. They hate politicians and that means they hate us. They're getting ready for a major series of hits, so we need to stay focused on this.'

'Have you noticed how all the foreigners are suddenly leaving by whatever route they can find,' Jake replied. 'They're like birds going home for the winter. Pretty soon there won't be anyone left to do all the rubbish jobs.'
~~~

Chris laughed mildly. He then looked up, replying with a serious expression, 'Exactly what rubbish jobs are you talking about? Would that be the ones that my own family has done over the years?'

'Sorry man,' Jake replied, 'I didn't mean to have a go at you.'

'You're so soft Jake,' Chris replied. 'I'm only pulling your piece you idiot. And anyway, how about our own one, trying to deal with these gangs of armed nutcases? Doesn't that mean anything to you?'

Jake nodded in agreement, adding, 'Yep, too right Chris.'

Commander Aley breezed into the large open plan office and started talking immediately. 'Intel has produced a list of three potential targets in the next few days. That's why the following assigned teams are going out: Red Alpha, Green Bravo, Blue Charlie, with a back-up for each, six men in each team. You'll all be with new faces, so get used to them now. I mean right now. And go over your orders until you know them off pat. No screw ups.'

Commander Aley carried on with more detailed items including vehicle assignments, radio checks, weapons and handling evidence.

'That's a bit bloody rich,' Chris said to Jake and two of his team members just after the briefing had finished. 'It's not as if we messed up last time. It was those Intel idiots that put us in the wrong part of Britain! The bomb at the Ricoh was never intended to harm anyone. The real hit was probably that politician.'

Chris could see that Commander Aley and several other senior policemen had been rattled by recent events, especially as some of the details of the attempted attack on Sir Jeffrey Hammond's home in Derbyshire were now common knowledge due to leaks. What had also been revealed was how slow the police were to respond, even after getting the tip-off.

However, the group, or groups, they were chasing after now looked increasingly organised and professional and that worried some of those who had seen the intelligence reports. Moreover, the attack in Coventry could so easily have led to a great number of casualties and it could also have been at a much bigger event. It was obvious they were being played by the militants.

Chris and his team got their kit together, left the building and moved to the unmarked vehicles. It was a series of white vans.

'Jeez!' Jake said when he saw the vans. 'We're going to be a bunch of white van men for a few days. I hope this Op isn't in Essex. We won't be able to tell our vehicles from any others over there.' The other men laughed.

Chris felt his own stress levels dissipate slightly. He was glad that he was in a team with people who could have a laugh about the situation. However, he still had a feeling of nausea in the pit of his stomach.

~~~
~~~

Declan and Gavin were in a pub on Whitecross Street in Islington. It was early evening and office workers were mingling with locals and site workers as the late sun was giving way to a cool evening. They were waiting for a call from Jez about some more site work. Above the din of the bar, the TV monitor high on the wall was covering the recent attacks on government facilities by militant groups.

Declan had a flashback to when he was serving as a young infantry section commander in Northern Ireland in the late Eighties. A chill ran through him as he recalled the events surrounding a killing in a remote farmhouse.

Gavin looked at Declan. 'Are you OK mate? Beer's not bad, is it?'

'No, I'm OK Gav,' Declan replied. 'I'll get some more in. What are you having?'

Two streets away Ches and Becker were having a meal in an almost empty café. Becker didn't appear interested in any kind of conversation as he downed his food.

'What's up with you mate?' asked Ches.

'Nada. Why, do I look like something is?'

'Yeah, you do. Did something happen?' Ches had no longer any great interest in Becker's activities but wanted him to prove he had finally broken free from the circle of cons he had been involved with.

Becker looked at Ches, replying quietly, 'Truth is mate, if I told you everything, no matter how crazy, you might not believe me.'

'Why're you being threatened?'

'No, not exactly, but I'm sick of it Ches, especially as I'm still looking over my shoulder. I don't think their last hit went well anyway.'

'I didn't see anything in any papers,' Ches paused. 'But it's none of my business.'

'A lot of these lads don't get what they're doing. They think that it's just the money. Some of them are right twisted bastards as well.' He paused. *It's just not worth the risks, and there's very little cash in it.*

'So, why do they bother?'

'Well, I guess the hoods need expertise and play hard so as to get it. Without people like me the jobs will never work. But I'm not going back to them again. They keep calling me and I wish they wouldn't. They make it sound like it's worth my while.'

Ches felt uncomfortable. His question had been designed so that Becker would react, but the situation sounded worse than he had imagined.

Becker continued, 'But I was just one of the foot soldiers.'

'Without people like you they'd never get the job done, is that it?'

'You're right. But it doesn't need to be like that.' Becker paused and spoke softly. 'You and me, we could do this for ourselves, but on a smaller scale.'

'What, extortion and robbing rich bastards?' Ches replied in a very low tone. 'You got to be kidding?'

'All we need to do is to find some decent and worthwhile targets. It won't be easy, but we do get to keep the winnings.'

'And what exactly did you have in mind?'

'We pick the richest and the most corrupt and then screw them over. No one cares anyway, and the police have given up on most of these bastards; especially the politicians who've been lining their pockets.'

'You mean a load of random hits?'

Becker nodded. Ches looked slightly confused and annoyed as Becker stared at the table.

Becker broke the silence, 'All I know is that the stakes might be high; and it's going to take a hell of a lot of legwork. But it will pay. Are you up for it?'

Ches stopped and looked around, before answering. 'I do know that you're bloody good at what you do Becks. You know security systems better than anyone else and you get them sorted quicker than anyone.'

'In and out without any bother, that's me mate,' Becker replied, a bit too loudly. 'We'll only be going after rich criminal types, don't forget that Ches. Not regular people.'

Becker sipped his tea. 'I've only ever hit a few places anyway, so I was never a main part of that group. I've heard from some of the others that the people in charge are doing it only for political reasons. They just use whoever they can get hold of for a particular job. I don't know who's paying them.'

'You still need to be careful mate. There's a lot happening out there right now mate. I'm not sure the police have the manpower to go after some of these gangs but it's the political violence that's the main problem for them, and they may already have your mugshot.'

'Yeah; I can see that Ches, but I don't care any more.'

Both men ate for a minute, before Becker continued. 'But if you fancy it let me know. It's what I'm good at after all.' He thought for a moment, ate some more, and then added, 'Maybe I should go it alone. It makes more sense. I'd then keep it all and run fewer risks.'

'But you haven't got anything behind you. Even if you could take on these other crews you have next to nothing in terms of equipment or capital.' Ches looked at the street outside the window.

'Well, once I've done a few jobs things will change,' Becker reasoned. 'It's dynamic; rolling stones and all that.'

'Sounds to me like you've already made up your mind, Becks.'

Becker looked out the window as a police van went past with its lights flashing. He held his breath and then stared blankly across the café.

~~~
~~~

'Hey lads, the next person who says they don't like my Gloria Gaynor impression is going to get it. But really, I will survive.' Jake rolled out the last three words loudly and slowly so that everyone in the restaurant could hear it. He then threw the curls of his black wig over his right shoulder. Chris banged his knife on the table. The *X* team, as they secretly called their own squad, was in a Lebanese restaurant near to Marylebone Station. They had been drinking heavily over the previous few hours and were very close to the inebriated state of *Bikini Black*, as Jake liked to call it.

Chris didn't usually take a central role at police gatherings. His general approach was to let someone like Jake shine as the centre of attention and in this instance the celebration was really for Jake's pregnant wife.

Chris hid that he was slightly jealous of the fact Jake's wife was pregnant. He realised that he now needed to move his relationship with Annie to a higher level. To that end he had spent much of his precious little spare time running through the list of things he wanted to do over the next few years, which included getting a bigger place to live, children, and some kind of promotion. He needed a plan of action as that was how his mind worked.

The other members of the team were falling around at Jake's jokes, but Chris had heard them all before. He eventually managed to find the right moment and left, reminding them all at what time to muster in the morning for a forensics brief. He hadn't taken his motorbike to work that day as he didn't like riding it when he knew he would be out for a few drinks, so he'd left it back at the flat. And anyway, it was a straight run up the Metropolitan line from Baker Street to Ruislip.

He got as far as Northwick Park when the driver announced that the train ahead had broken down. Chris cursed, having promised Annie that he would be home at a good time. Annie wasn't a demanding sort of woman, but he wanted to get out of any bad habits that he'd been drawn into over the years. Being late home from work half-drunk was one of them.

He disinterestedly thumbed through a free newspaper and stared down the carriage. Opposite was a middle-aged black woman panning her tablet, while further along on his side was a couple talking quickly and heatedly in low voices in a language Chris didn't recognise. Opposite, further along from the woman, and to her right, were two men, both early middle-aged, thick-set and balding.

He could just make out a small shape on the lapel of one, and more specifically that it was in the style of a Shamrock. The other man was looking in a brown leather diary. What caught Chris's eye was that both men were carrying narrow elongated tool bags, of the type that Chris's own father had once owned. He'd been a carpenter and spent his life on building sites around the London area, until his premature death, many years before, at the age of forty-four.

The sight of the tool bags reminded him of his own sense of loss, as well as that of his mother who had brought him and his two younger sisters up in a council flat in Hounslow, under the Heathrow flight path. She had been relieved when Chris had joined the Metropolitan Police, as it meant that he had a career and that she would hopefully not have to worry about his future. She was now immensely proud of him and made no bones about it to relatives and friends. That annoyed Chris, and she had learned over time to be more careful in revealing his workplace identity, especially to strangers.

Chris could just make out what one of the men was saying.

'Hey, Micky. We do it ourselves or not at all. OK?'

The other man just shook his head and turned his face to look down the carriage. His eyes then looked straight at Chris, and that was when Chris saw the outline of what looked like a long-barrelled pistol in the man's jacket. The man stared coldly back, and Chris averted his gaze.

Chris looked along the carriage the other way and then, when he was sure the two were not looking at him, pretended to read a newspaper while casting a sideward glance.

He may have had a long day, what with the evening festivities, but his eyes hadn't deceived him. 'What are the chances of that?' He tried to rationalise the situation.

He remembered what one police instructor had said to him about being able to react quickly and decisively when attacked. It was a strange mechanism in that once someone stopped thinking about what was happening then they would stop caring about the situation. They would then be able to deal with the consequences of any actions. That logic could be applied to almost any situation but the officer being attacked had to switch off from fear in the same instant as being attacked.

He guessed that the man opposite might own an air pistol, so he didn't jump to any conclusions. He didn't see the point of confronting them. While his instinct told him that it would be worth investigating, he would have to let it go for now. So, he buried his head further in the newspaper.

The men got off at West Harrow and Chris made a note of their appearance and what they were wearing in his notebook, as well as the time.

~~~

Ches put the two pints of lager down on the table of the Holloway pub, stating loudly, 'Be careful what you wish for mate, as you might miss the rest of your life.'

Becker ignored him, hungrily eating some crisps, whilst watching the news on the TV screen up on the wall. Every now and then he stole a look
~~~

at someone he recognised who was seated on the far side of the public bar area. It was Jay Saxby. He then made a point of staring even harder at the evening news on the TV screen above the bar, so as to avoid any eye contact with her.

He had no interest in talking to her. Although he wanted to leave the pub at the earliest opportunity, he also realised that he could use the situation to check on the identities of a few of Jay's closest crew. That was mainly so he could avoid bumping into them ever again.

He turned slightly towards Ches. He lifted his drink, deliberately catching Ches's eye, and then scowling whilst nodding, almost imperceptibly, towards Jay's table. Ches turned away from Becker's fixed stare and carried on reading the newspaper, whilst casting a sidewards glance over at the table.

Ches had never met any of Becker's associates and had also vowed never to take part in any of their activities. However, he had always been quietly impressed that Becker had enough guts to work with such people in the first place. He had put it down to quiet desperation on his friend's part, as he certainly wasn't a career criminal.

Becker didn't wish to make life any more complicated than it was already. However, regardless of the characters sitting near his table, he was still angry that he hadn't ever been fully paid for the last few jobs. But he wasn't about to ask for his money, especially after running away from the back of the van that night.

'Why did they come here tonight?' he thought, dismissing any notion that it was to do with him.

After another pint, Becker and Ches got up to go and Becker glanced over again at Jay's table. Jay wasn't there, but Becker interrupted the stare of one of the three men sitting at the table. He averted his own gaze.

Becker and Ches left the pub and walked briskly down the street, Becker glancing over his shoulder. He could see three more men approaching the pub entrance and half-recognised two of them. Luckily, they were far enough away not to see him, and he was glad to be out of the place.

"Ches, let's head up that way,' Becker stated. 'I need some cash. After that I'll buy you a kebab mate.' The two men walked up a side street.

One hour later Declan, Jez and Gavin entered the same pub. They were celebrating starting on a new construction site in London and managed to find a free table.

Jez was getting the drinks when he started talking to three young women who were chatting near him. 'So where are you ladies off to; anywhere nice?'

'Nothing spectacular; probably a club in the West End,' the oldest answered. Why are you up for it?' She giggled into her vodka, and the others joined in the chorus of giggling.

'Me? No, I'm an old sod. I'm married and all that. My mates over there might be though.' Jez gestured towards Declan and Gavin.

'Ah! You're a real sweety,' the same woman replied. 'You're trying to set your mates up; aren't you babe?'

Jez laughed quite loudly at that; so much so that Declan looked over with a smile on his face.

'Not much gets past Jez,' Declan shouted, gesturing over to the bar. The women waved back.

Gavin grinned, mainly at Jez's lack of tact. 'That's about right,' he replied loudly.

'It's not really your fault Jez,' Declan stated as Jez returned with the drinks. 'Us two may be just a couple of losers, but you've never been restrained Jez, in your whole life.'

'Excuse me,' Jez replied. 'Some of us are married already. I was just warming them up for you. You need to stop hugging columns in nightclubs.'

'What are you on man?' Declan gave Jez a jokingly stern look as he lifted his pint glass and saluted him, before adding, 'But thanks for thinking of us, old git.'

Ten minutes later the three women left the pub, waving at Jez as they walked past, and Declan went to the bar to buy the next round of drinks. He looked over at a table with five men and a woman around it. He could hear some heated exchanges, and for a moment he thought he recognised one of them. Two of the men stared hard at him.

The two men then stood up and exited the rear door, presumably for a smoke in the outside smoking area. When he returned to the table he turned to Jez, Gavin having gone to the toilets.

'Jez, you see those guys over there,' he stated. 'Well, there's more to those men than you might imagine. I think I recognise one or two of them from somewhere.'

'Let's not go there,' replied Jez, disinterestedly. He laughed. 'About those girls; I was just breaking the ice, in my own way. But you need to get over your divorce mate and move on.'

'You fell through the ice more like,' Declan replied, shaking his head.

'Jeez, I won't bother then.'

Gavin returned and, looking at Declan, observed, 'You look a bit stressed Dec, everything OK?'

Declan shook his head, smiled sarcastically, and picked up his pint. Jez grimaced.

The rest of the evening went off in an alcoholic haze and the three men fell out of the bar after midnight.

'I'm totally shattered guys,' exclaimed Declan. 'Jez, I'll sort out a cab. Gav you're OK getting back to your place, aren't you?'

'Yeah, I'm fine!' Gavin replied, looking the worst for wear of the three men.

Seconds later Declan had flagged down a cab for the fifteen-minute drive to his own flat in Kilburn. Gavin said goodbye and set off on foot. Declan recognised two of the men from the bar standing nearby. He could see that they were watching him.

He stepped into the taxi with Jez. Twenty yards further on, he stopped the driver, shouting, 'I won't be long; I just need to get some cash. Wait here.' Jez was almost asleep.

He ran at first and then walked to get within ten yards of the two men who had been watching them earlier. They were following Gavin, who had now turned down a side road.

The two men then quickened their pace. They were within a few metres of the unknowing man and Declan wasn't about to let them close in on him.

He saw one of the men take something out of his pocket with his right hand. He was drawing it back and Declan realised that he had only a few seconds at most, so he sprinted at full speed.

As the man raised the knife above Gavin's head Declan jumped up and, with his knee in the small of the man's back, he wrapped his right arm around the man's raised arm at high level. Declan's left elbow came down on the back of the man's head and, as the man crumpled to the ground, the knife fell harmlessly away.

Declan turned quickly to the other man who was clearly surprised and now standing still. Declan punched him twice in the face and the man stumbled back. He was considerably bigger than Declan who then launched at him, kicking and punching him until he couldn't get up. By now the first man was stirring on the pavement, so Declan went up to him and kicked him hard in the head.

Gavin, who had spun round, stood frozen on the spot, staring at Declan.

'What's going on Declan?' He stammered with a cracked voice.

'I don't know Gav. But I just stopped you being stabbed, pal.'

Declan didn't know whether he should call the police and decided after a short pause that it would be the best policy. He told Gavin to go back to the taxi and make sure Jez got home.

'When you've done that make sure you come back here as you'll need to give a statement as well as me. I'll make sure these two tossers don't get up, but I want to know what's going on. And by the way, maybe you should be staying at my place until this blows over. Do you understand?'

Declan interrogated the man who had the knife. He had him face down on the ground and every now and then pressed his knee into the small of his back. The man screamed and Declan told him to be quiet, or he *would get it.*

By the time the police arrived a few minutes later all they saw was that Declan had the two men tied up with their own belts with Gavin sitting on the bigger one.

However, one of the men was determined to have a go back and shouted repeatedly, 'You're bloody dead.' The Derry accent was clear enough to Declan. The knife had stayed where it had fallen as Declan didn't want his own prints on it.

'So, sir, you claim that this man had raised this knife and tried to stab your friend from behind as he was walking. That was when you forced him down to the ground.' Declan nodded as the two policemen carried out the questioning.

Luckily an old Asian man had been walking past with his dog at the time of the incident and, although he hadn't seen everything, he corroborated enough of Declan's statement for the police to believe it.

After more questioning the two men on the ground were arrested and they all went to Hornsey police station. The arresting officer turned to Declan, *Sir, could you come back to the police station at six tomorrow morning? That's if you want these two formally charged. Can you do that please?*

'Yes, of course I will,' Declan replied.

'We'll examine local CCTV to check it all out, especially that they were tailing your friend.'

'That's fine. I'll be there in the morning. Thanks, officer.'

'Oh God, I will have such a hangover, Dec,' Gavin exclaimed as they boarded a taxi home.

'At least you're still bloody alive. Do you know why they were trying to kill you?'

Declan was secretly glad that he was still quick enough to react and make a difference after all these years. After leaving the military he worked, for a short while, for a security company in the Middle East. The company had valued the gathering of information above all else. However, he was surprised that he had been able to handle himself so easily in what was barely a fight with two men on a night out in London. But he also needed to know what had just happened and why.

In the morning Declan went to the police station and made the statement. The police confirmed that CCTV had shown one of the men producing a knife from his jacket pocket as they turned the corner into the side road. They gave Declan a telephone number to call and said they would be in touch.

Declan walked out. The cold chill of the early morning was still biting, and it prompted a thought that kept invading Declan's mind, *Gavin's jacket is the same colour as mine and we're both the same height and build.*

~~~
~~~

'The way I see it we all have a choice: either years of enjoying a sane and normal existence, or years of being part of a bunch of losers who don't have anything in life and never will.' Jake was discussing with Chris why some people were attracted to a life of crime. He continued, 'It's just easier to get a job, get married, or whatever normal people do these days, and live a happy life. Why do anything else?' Jake concluded by raising his hands palms up.

Chris smiled at Jake, before replying, 'You know mate you're very good at stating the obvious, so maybe you should be in politics yourself.'

'No, I hate the bastards. I agree with the terrorists on that one! All politicians should be shot. Team GB should be run by the British Army. Let the generals have a go, as the political classes have failed.'

'Now you sound like a terrorist Jake, or, at the very least, a right wing nutter,' Chris lamented, lifting his hands up in desperation.

'No, I'm just a normal sort of guy,' Jake paused. 'But I'm not actually surprised that people are starting to fight back where the government's concerned; I mean, it's a piece of crap, isn't it?'

'Don't worry. I won't let on what you really think mate. It may affect your promotion.'

Jake laughed, snorting, 'Sod the promotion. I don't want to do this job for much longer and neither does the wife.'

'What are you looking at doing?'

'Teaching, Chris. I'm going to turn the next generation into people who don't accept the crap we had to. Things will be different in the future.'

'Good for you mate. I hope you succeed.' Chris didn't add any sarcasm to his statement. He genuinely wanted Jake to be happy. No one could do their job for long anyway. Ten years max he had told himself, but five years max he had said to Annie. But for now, he and Jake had to do their own jobs, as the rest of the team was relying on them.

Lorenzo, another TSU officer, had just finished pinning up on the main board of the briefing room a few photographs of suspected militant activists, including Brandon Sinclair and his associates. Jay Saxby was not included.

'Chris, have you come across this guy before?' Lorenzo asked, pointing towards the figure of Sinclair. 'Apparently, he has something to do with that lot who had a go at the politician recently, as well as the bombing in Coventry. Intel says they're connected somehow.'

'No, I don't recall him Lorenzo,' Chris replied. 'Why? What's the guy actually done?'

'He's called Brandon Sinclair, and he's allegedly involved in all sorts of things, including GBH and armed robbery.'

'So, why's that news to us?'

'It's really just a lead at the moment. But we're waiting on forensics for a bunch of things. I'll let you know if there's a breakthrough.'

'OK mate.'

Chris and Jake went off to the canteen. As they waited for food Chris broke the tedium. 'On Friday, Jake, in Holloway, uniform got a man who was attempting to stab someone. But something doesn't match up.'

'Why?'

'The man arrested gave his name as Craig Mahoney, but the prints are different from a previous Craig Mahoney we pulled a few years back, who would otherwise seem to be the same guy.'

'So, why's it important?'

'This one's come up plus for PE7 on his clothes. We don't know where it's from yet. We've been checking around but the stuff he had on him is similar to that used in Coventry. He claims he works in dems on building sites, but it looks very suspicious. The Coventry bomb wasn't on a timer: it was initiated remotely and there must have been a spotter.'

'That might not be a big deal. I mean PE is used in dems on sites. Have you checked that he's a site worker? If he was just trying to rob some guy after a night out on the piss, then we should make sure of his story.'

'I know that's why it's being checked out. We haven't anything yet other than the fact this is a man with an assumed ID and that he's probably been up to something.'

'I suppose it'll all come out in the wash.'

'They'll need to check the forensics again. We'll have to pin it properly.'

'Agreed!'

'There's something else mate. The guy who was pulled with him has been done in the past for firearms possession.'

'Now, that is something.'

~~~
~~~

CHAPTER THREE

Ches and Becker were in Becker's flat looking at the photo images of a fifty-something politician on the table in front of them.

Becker had done his research. 'Well, the fact is Ches, that this bastard forced several girls into prostitution before going into politics. He got them hooked on cocaine and had them working for him. Now he's a mayor, somewhere up north.'

He turned the images over, commenting, 'I've got his address and everything we need: bank details, you name it. The crew had him in their sights for a while but dropped it as they thought it was too hot. But he's definitely do-able and worth a few bob.'

'So, why're you doing it?' asked Ches, refusing to acknowledge that he was part of any potential hit.

'You mean why're we doing it?' Becker replied with an annoyed edge to his voice.

'Whatever.'

'Because we can mate,' Becker replied. 'Just you and me: less to worry about if you know what I mean. We've all the skills required. You can get through any door, and I can get round any security system, within reason. And we can handle ourselves!'

'Yeah, that's really sweet, and then we'll end up doing ten years at least.'

Becker ignored Ches's comment. 'We'll do a few jobs with little risk. And there'll be loads of cash.' He paused; *I've told a few people that I'm going to lie low.*

He continued, with added enthusiasm, 'We do as few places as possible, so we go after the easiest but take all the high value items as well as cash. We can target people like this creep, but we should also fleece him for everything else.'

'How do we do that?'

'We find out where the safes are beforehand and hit them as soon as we get into the place.'

'What happens if we don't know where they are?'

Becker shrugged. Ches sat still for a moment. He smiled, and, answering his own question, added, 'Actually, the easiest way to get info out of people is what one guy taught me in my regiment, you batter the legs, nothing else.

Hit one of the legs a few times and show them a gun, or a knife, whatever. You have to make him believe you're going to kill him anyway.'

Becker nodded and replied, 'Then you tell him that he's dead, but his family will still have a chance, but only if he gets you the cash out of his safe and all the other nooks in his house.'

'I thought you might have a few ideas.' Ches laughed.

Becker continued, 'We need to be switched on as to where the wife keeps the gems. It's not always easy to find them. They nearly always have them stashed away in the house, somewhere. It can be a real timewaster.' He tapped the side of his head.

'That's the point,' Ches replied. 'We'll have to waste some time looking.' Ches seemed to have suddenly come round to Becker's way of thinking more readily than Becker had expected.

Becker replied, somewhat guardedly, 'Sounds like we'll be deviating from the methods but who gives a damn? The police are after the main gangs. That gives us some space.'

'Yeah, I guess it does.' Ches replied. He thought for a moment. 'The only way this can work is if we do just a few random hits, so we don't leave the Old Bill any clues. No patterns.'

'Don't worry, we won't. Unlike most of the outfits I know. Also, most of them launder the cash in the most obvious way possible. We won't.'

'So, what'll we do?'

'Who knows? Sit on it. I'm not sure exactly, but we won't get caught.' Becker continued. 'I think we'll have to take it easy at first. I've also got a feeling that the police know what most of the others are up to. We'll see what happens if they get pulled in.'

'Well Becks we need some time so we can plan this properly.'

'Yeah, too right, so let's start. We need a decent lead-in time. We need to find out what we can about the place, like where things are kept, cameras, and the coming and going. I want to see what he does every day.'

'We need to know where the safe is.'

~~~

'He was, until very recently, working for some outfit called the Environmental Design and Research Establishment, based near Luton.' The forensics officer thumbed through some more papers, as he continued briefing Chris and Jake about a militant network that had been hacking into private bank accounts. 'That gave him a good cover. But we still don't have any clue as to what his identity really is, or that of his associate. They're probably both from abroad, and it's likely they've both just been hired for the job.'
~~~

'What about forensics?' Chris replied.

'Nothing yet, as the only prints are from Mr "X" and nothing has come up yet. But we've no proper leads on either of them.'

'Well, if we get one guy in a case like this the other will usually follow,' Chris replied. 'But we have to make the charges stick. Otherwise, they'll be out after six weeks.' Chris grimaced at Jake.

'You reckon they'll talk?' Jake asked.

'Let's get a stronger link first,' the forensics officer replied. 'No doubt they would have deleted everything off their hard drives, but we need to get their phones and pads. We have a team going into their bedsit in Kilburn. It seems the other guy has been sofa-surfing a lot. We only have his assumed ID and there are leads to private rentals. Always cash if you know what I mean. So far, we haven't found any bank cards or details.'

Chris thanked him and they headed off to the canteen. In the queue Jake turned to Chris. 'Have you noticed that the catering's been a bit crap recently, especially the smoothies?'

Chris picked one up and held it up to examine it. 'Must be cutbacks Jake. Anyway, there's a bit of fruit in this one.'

'Is that what it is?'

They got their lunch and sat down.

'I don't get it Chris. Why bother getting a job as a cover? It would also be less obvious to go to a smaller outfit than that, wouldn't it?'

'Not for some people. They don't see the world like that. Maybe these two are low level operators, hacking into sites wherever they can to get cash and info. They must have used the company as a front to get at bank details.'

'What the hell? Wouldn't it be easier just to go for the bigger institutions, large financial houses, that kind of thing?' Jake spooned some beans and mashed potato down his throat.

'No, actually it wouldn't. It would be too easy to trace them, and they know it.'

'And what's this place near Luton? Why work there?'

'Maybe it gave access to something we don't yet know about. It sounds like one of those slightly corrupt little government offices that have grown too much over the years, with a license to print money and all that. Maybe they found something; some way to access financial systems. I'm no expert.'

Chris ate some quiche, 'Some places employ anyone these days without any real checks in place. Anyway, we have some background now. Our job is to go and check the rest of it; go over any forensics and background checks. It should be easy.'

'Why do you say that?'

'Look at the main suspect's picture. He doesn't look like a terrorist: thin, faded shirt, old trainers, frizzy hair. He might be involved but he's only a minor operator. Or maybe a minder for the other guy, maybe even keeping him paid.'

'So, what does your average terrorist look like?'

'Not like him; that's all I can say.'

'Whatever, the cash they've stolen has been flowing towards Mr Sinclair at a phenomenal rate.'

~~~

'So, who stuck two in his chest then?' Brandon Sinclair asked irately. He then stared at Jay as they stood over the prostrate, bloodied figure. 'I said only clean kills: and only when necessary. There's blood everywhere.'

'He was going for the shotgun,' one of Jay's operators retorted, stepping forward, somewhat angrily. He continued, 'Anyway; who cares? That bastard felt some pain.' The dead man stared back at him.

Jay kicked the corpse in the side of his torso. The victim had been a senior ex-politicial figure and weapons dealer and had been active, over many years, in various misguided foreign policy interventions. It was Sinclair's stated political aim to hunt down the architects of conflict and the subsequent conflicts they spawned. Stealing from them was the icing on the cake.

The dead man had been lying low for months since being tipped off by the security services that a group was after him. He hadn't wasted any time getting prepared, hiring a team of armed ex-soldiers to protect him and his family. It hadn't been succesful.

Sinclair stepped up to the body, stating, absent-mindedly, *If he'd told us everything, we wanted to know in the first place it may have turned out a bit different for him, but as it is we'll never know all the answers.* He glared at Jay.

Several other members of the gang ransacked the house for the next fifteen minutes. 'We got everything we can boss,' one of them shouted down the Georgian stairwell.

'Check again,' Sinclair shouted back. He turned to Saxby, adding quietly, 'I bet they haven't been that thorough.'

The wife and son of the dead weapons dealer were not in the UK. Instead, they were at a house near Bordeaux. With radom politicised attacks increasing across the UK many rich politicians and businessmen had packed their loved ones off to what they regarded as safer havens. Many others were being guarded by private security companies.
~~~

Sinclair wanted his own people to stay sharp. He had never lost his his hatred for the British political and military establishment, whom he blamed for the death of some of his own family members in Northern Ireland over thirty years before. He knew he could easily lose his own life but killing British politicians, as well as their closest allies, was the immediate cause. After all, it was their meddling that had cost the lives of many more innocents, not least across the Middle East. The nightmares of people over there never seemed to cease, but Sinclair vowed they would soon become the nightmares of British politicians.

He hadn't told Saxby everything about his own aims, other than that he ultimately wanted to attack the centre of government in London. He knew that this correlated loosely with what she wanted, in that the chief architects of the wars in the Middle East were to be wiped out. Despite appearing English, she had many Shia Muslim relatives on her father's side and they had suffered terrible losses in those areas of the Middle East where there had been constant fighting due to British interventions in Syria and Iraq. She wanted justice for those responsible for these conflicts, in a similar way to Sinclair's desire for justice for the suffering of the Irish over time.

At the same time Sinclair welcomed fighters from overseas to his own cause. One contact, Conor, had put him in touch with the right people. Conor had helped to obtain forged IDs; some having taken the identities of deceased British and Irish men. One arrival, now known as Michael Reilly, was being held in police custody, for what exactly Sinclair didn't know. But he'd heard rumours that it was an attempted hit on a former British Army Intelligence Officer. The case intrigued Sinclair for various reasons.

He knew the authorities wouldn't have much on him as they hadn't been keeping track of Britain's borders for years since the soft post-Brexit agreement had been forced through. There was now an army of former terrorists and criminals masquerading as British and European nationals. The security service was therefore running to catch up all the time, and it was one reason why they were now resorting to paramilitary police tactics. But for his people to try and take out such a valued asset, even a retired one, was great publicity, if nothing else.

Of his own inner circle only Sinclair knew about Jay Saxby's true background; how her three brothers had fought for Assad in Syria, as well as against the Sunni militants and Salafists in Iraq and elsewhere. Sinclair respected her as one of his best lieutenants and he always counted Shia Muslims tested in battle as potential allies for the future. He also admired those who had fought for Hezbollah against Israel, as he felt he would be able to rely on them when it came to *End State*, as he termed the end of the British political establishment. And with or without the likes of Saxby, there would be major changes in the political landscape, he was certain of that. Not least a united Ireland.

~~~

'The real enemy has never been Al Qaeda, the Taleban or anyone else in the Middle East. It has never been any of the so-called terrorist organisations we've been told about for nearly two decades now.' The Croydon community hall was hushed as the bearded militant spoke from the front stage. It was an impromptu gathering of various groups lined up against the government. Jake looked on, some distance away at the back of the hall, having assumed the identity of a militant.

The man continued to speak. 'The real enemies are the corrupt politicians, as they're the ones who've destroyed our lives and those of our children through the wars they started and the chaos that's followed. And guess what? We're going to destroy them, once and for all. And we'll do this by any means possible.'

Jake had maintained his distance from the stage area just in case someone took note of his identity. But it was also imperative that he carried out observations on those in the hall. He edged towards the rear exit doors, which were slightly ajar, and stepped into the external yard. He rang Chris.

'Have you found anything out yet?' Chris asked bluntly.

'Not yet but I'm here at least,' Jake replied quietly.

'If you get any leads at all there let us know.'

'Will do.'

What neither man knew was that two-hundred miles away three high-ranking ex-politicians had been rounded up and taken hostage in West Yorkshire. When in power all three had supported various British interventions in the Middle East. They had each then made a lot of money as executives with defence companies over the course of a decade. The three were about to be placed in a ventilated shipping container before being shipped off to the Middle East. They would then be hooded and forced to make confessions about their crimes on camera. The speaker in the hall knew all of these things.

~~~

'So, Dec; has anything more turned up about that psycho who tried to stab Gav?' asked Jez. He and Declan were in an Islington pub.

'Well, I had a visit from a policeman,' Declan replied swiftly. 'He said the two men arrested already have police records, but they wouldn't say any more than that. They have no idea why they were trying to get Gav. The coppers don't believe it was a robbery. Maybe he said something to someone at the club. You know those places can attract some pretty weird types.'

'That was a weird evening,' replied Jez.

'You're telling me; I wish I could have done more.'

'Like what exactly?'

'Who knows? But with all this crap happening around the country nothing surprises me at the moment. Last night there were riots everywhere.'

'I know. The papers are saying there's some kind of hidden agenda behind a lot of these events.'

'I think so as well. Things like this don't just happen. I saw it often enough in Northern Ireland. There was always a political group behind the violence, or the guiding hand of an extortion racket.'

Declan and Jez stared at the bar of the Islington pub. Gavin had been due to walk in, and it wasn't like him to be late.

'I hope Gav isn't in some kind of trouble,' said Jez.

'Don't worry mate, he can look after himself.' Declan paused and looked at Jez. He knew that the attackers hadn't been after Gavin on the night of the attack, as he had been the real target. Moreover, he had recognised one of the men who had tried to stab Gavin within a few hours of the incident. He was a face from more than thirty years before from when he had been living in Northern Ireland. He still couldn't put a name on it.

Declan felt cold. The man belonged to a previous century of organised crime, killing and butchery. Declan didn't want to be reminded of that world, especially as he'd promised himself long ago that he would leave it all behind. He shook his head and shut his eyes.

~~~

'Chris, we just had a call. It was about an attempted GBH a little while back.' Tommy, one of Chris's team, was holding up the receiver of the phone.

'What's it about exactly? Can you take it?' Chris was pre-occupied with a surveillance report on a flat in Harrow.

'Apparently a man who stopped the stabbing has given a partial ID on one of the men arrested. He recalls him from some time in the past and there may be a strong lead. He's on a mobile and said he was happy to be called at any time.'

'Take his number, I'll call him back. Has anything else come up with that flat we're monitoring?'

'No, we're still on it.'
~~~

Chris turned to Jake, quietly stating, 'Well you better get your eyes on this report Jake. We'll go in soon if this carries on for much longer, but it rests on a higher authority for now.'

'OK Chris,' Jake replied.

Ten minutes later Chris dialed the number given him by Tommy. 'Hello. Is that Declan Gale?'

'Yes. Who's that?'

'I'm Sergeant Chris Kane, of the Met Police. I'm working on the investigation into the recent attempted stabbing of one of your friends; a cousin, I believe? Have you a minute to talk?'

'Fire away.'

'I heard you may have some more info on one of the men.'

'Well, I'm not totally sure about this but I had his image in my head for days after the attack and I think I came across him one time. When I was a young soldier serving in Belfast we pulled some men in for questioning after a series of attacks on the RUC. I'm sure that guy was arrested but they couldn't prove anything. He was a young lad back then, but I recognised the features. You always remember the odd ones if you know what I mean.'

'I do indeed.'

'He was totally quiet when we interviewed him. Not a single word. Not that we laid a finger on him, but quite often they were gobby, especially after a few hours. Not him though, and that's why I recall it all.'

'Do you think there would be a file anywhere in the MOD, any old records?'

'I doubt it. A lot were destroyed after the Good Friday agreement. Too much hassle, especially if they'd never been formally charged.'

'But you're certain you saw him in Northern Ireland. Do you have a rough time and place?'

Declan related a few details but with the caveat that they had made a lot of arrests and he couldn't be totally sure of anything.

'That's great Declan. Thanks a lot. Can I call you if we need more help?'

'Yes, no probs.'

As Declan put the phone down, he remembered some of the other details from those days that came flooding back into his mind like unwanted guests. There was the hooker who had been raped by a group of men and left for dead. He recalled the slash injury across her chest that had required twenty stitches. How she survived no one knew, but she ended up living in Manchester under an assumed ID. That was something he had found out through friends in the police at the time.

Like others she'd been forced into drugs and prostitution by a terrorist gang bent on raising money for *The Cause* whilst blissfully unaware that this was being undermined by the gang's own depraved lack of order and morality, at least as far as the local community had been concerned. It had also become obvious, both to Declan and the men he had served with, that after just a few months into his second tour in the province, some people, once they had got a political idea into their heads, would try and justify everything in terms of *The Cause*.

And that was the world Declan had been in. His own provincial countrymen were the enemy as far as he had been concerned and he had never been happy with trying to reason why that should be the case. However, he had come to the inevitable conclusion later in life that the situation there had been too complex to make any sense and that there were no answers. So, he had given up trying to find any.

What he had witnessed with the disfigured victims of attacks on both sides; the shattered young lives, the families still wondering what had happened to their own, had all left scars on him. He had never had the time to realise back then just how much it had affected him as an individual. Like all soldiers he had parked his personal issues in a place no one else could see. But it had got to him over the years to the extent that he could no longer dismiss such things.

He had never wanted to go back to the province, and he hadn't. By 2013 his military career was over and, with his family and cousins now all living in England, he had no reason to. He had gone to college and for the last few years he had kicked around doing the site work with his cousins, as well as claiming part of his military pension.

However, he now regarded it as an advantage that he had few strings, and that he could go anywhere and do anything. He was still young enough. Canada, the United States, New Zealand were his first thoughts; anywhere but Europe. He relaxed into a glass of whisky and felt re-assured that the law was now onto the men who had attacked Gavin; that they would positively identify them and put them away. But he then reflected on the likelihood that they were just part of a wider network.

He suddenly recalled the irony of being born at about the time *The Troubles* had officially started in Northern Ireland. They had cursed him all through his life and that curse seemed to be getting worse. *Maybe that's the real reason why my uncles thought that I'd brought them bad luck.*

~~~

Ches and Becker were standing behind the chair and its occupant. They both had their balaclavas on. Strapped to the chair was the twisted figure of a man whose hooded, semi-naked figure seemed to turn yellow in the dimmed light. It twitched almost imperceptibly, whilst the upper body slumped to the left.
~~~

The man had wet himself and the odour now permeated the whole of the outbuilding. However, the dank cool air had kept the smell to a manageable level.

'Look mate, it's not the fact you're well-connected, and that's the actual issue here.' Becker couldn't resist a joke at the man's expense. He continued, 'It's the fact that you're well disconnected, from the rest of society, at this present moment in time.' A muffled sound emanated from inside the Hessian hood.

Whilst the former mayor, Rahzeb Chowdhury, was now clearly willing to negotiate, Becker and Ches had no such intention. Their only real interest was in finding out where some of his family's great wealth was hidden.

They had given up on targeting Chowdhury in his palatial home as the place had too many cameras. Instead, they had snatched him outside the front gates and taken him to a derelict garage they had identified for the purpose a day earlier.

Chowdhury had been outed by the media for taking bribes from defence companies during the conflicts in the Middle East, whilst acting as a legal consultant to the then government. He had been the main negotiator with regards military procurement and was now loaded with blood money according to many broadsheet newspapers.

He had also provided a financial laundry service to corrupt politicians, helping some of them hide all their newly acquired fortunes, and accused of holding private parties over time where young women had been raped and abused. However, so far, he hadn't been charged with any offences, mainly because he had been protected by the same political masters he had served.

Ches took a step forward and stood in front of the chair, looking down at the figure. The man's hooded head was now tilted back, and Ches could sense that the eyes were now pleading and that his facial features had probably tightened considerably. The terrified man had, quite obviously, defecated.

'Please leave my family alone, they've had nothing to do with anything,' a muffled voice came from inside the hood.

'It's not the family we have a problem with; it's you and others like you,' Ches shouted. 'You're just another seedy little sod, who had his fingers in the till. You took whatever you wanted, you little bastard while others paid with their lives. What goes around comes around. You sent out a message to every slimy little bastard out there that it's right to take what isn't yours. You were part of the gravy train. So, what we want from you is a lot of money. We're not interested in your family, unless of course they get in our way.'

After another minute filled the dank air, Becker motioned to Ches to move outside. They walked out of the rear door, which was propped open, and into the night.

'This isn't going to work mate,' Becker exclaimed quietly.

'How's that then?' Ches replied, taken aback.

'Think about it; if he gets us the cash it won't be much. He couldn't take out more than a few thousand quid from his accounts. It's not really worth it. However, if he dies now there'll be no link back to us. We got him in the night, so no one saw us. We haven't done anything to give ourselves away. But if we try and get into his accounts we'll be screwed. It's not worth it.'

'So, you're seriously suggesting topping him. I thought the idea was to take advantage of bastards like him as the police are busy with the bombings and riots.'

'That's my point. This is the time to knock it on the head. No one is missing this bastard, except his family and a few others.'

'So, we'll be murderers. That was never part of the plan Becks.'

'Forget the plan. It's survival I'm more concerned about.'

'There must be some way of getting some cash out of him. Let's dump him somewhere after we've got something out of him and give the bugger a sporting chance. He's not seen our faces anyway. But let's go back to his house first. Trust me on this. You wanted me in on this remember? Give me a chance to get something worthwhile out of it, without killing him.'

Becker looked at his friend and nodded. 'OK mate: you only live once. But let's scare the crap out of him so he will think twice about saying anything.'

'Alright, let me do the talking.'

Ches walked back in and spoke assertively to the cowering figure. 'OK so here's what's going to happen. Tell your wife to load up a holdall with a hundred grand. Don't tell her what it's for.'

~~~

'Extremists attack again,' Gavin stated loudly.

He was sitting with Declan and Jez in a transport café at seven in the morning in Tottenham Hale, London. Reading the headlines from the newspaper in front of him, he was then cut short by Declan. *Gav, give it a rest mate. We're eating our breakfast.*

The three were working on the remodelling of a nearby industrial site. Gavin and Jez stared at Declan who was clearly thinking about something other than the job at hand. They both knew that when he was deep in thought it was time to keep quiet.

Declan eventually sensed the heavy atmosphere and added, somewhat softly, and pointing at the newspaper, 'Let's face it the politicians are all dickheads anyway. By the government's definition of what constitutes a terrorist anyone who has a grievance against the state is a terrorist, so that's most of us.'
~~~

'Well, maybe that's right but I'm past giving a damn myself; about any of it,' Jez replied. He stared into space. The air hung heavy with Jez's words.

Declan hadn't told either of them about his conversation with the police, and neither had he mentioned that he had recognised the man who had tried to attack Gavin. He didn't want them to be involved, or to know any more about the accused men and their true loyalties.

Earlier in the day events dating back to the night of the attack on Gavin had been relayed to him by Sergeant Chris Kane who had told him that the ID of one of the men hadn't tallied with their records, suggesting that he had an assumed identity. They were re-checking the man's DNA and would let him know the outcome.

~~~

Chris and Jake were sifting through some evidence relating to the gang of armed militants. Jake looked up at Chris, stating, 'Why not just charge them anyway? There's enough here to hold them for quite a while.' Chris had said that, according to forensics, it seemed almost as if the two men had wanted to get caught. He recalled that both men had turned up positive for explosives as there were traces on their arms and clothes. They were holding them for that as well as the attempted assault with a deadly weapon. However, they were only likely to formerly charge them once they had explored all possible avenues.

Jake nodded gently and, picking up one of the reports again, he flicked through it and laid it next to his cup of coffee. He then looked at Chris and asked, 'What's this, the Harrow network? What are they really up to; any ideas?'

Chris, who hadn't bothered reading any recent new evidence, shrugged, before replying, 'I can't really comment Jake. But the fact is we're not getting anywhere at the moment and there's obviously things happening out there that we're struggling to get to grips with. We need some breakthroughs.'

'I say we charge a few of them and link them with that Sinclair network. Let the news out and then see what happens. We could flush out a few more out in the meantime.'

'We can't Jake. We need more evidence before we can charge them.' Chris looked and sounded tired. He picked up another file, opened it, and stated clearly, 'With this one, that guy Declan may have handed us something. He reckons he may have seen one of them before, when he was a soldier.'

'Well, that is a lead. How long ago was that?'

'Years before, Jake. But it's hardly admissible. We would need to find out the history, and what the connection is, and what any of his mates are up to.'
~~~

'That shouldn't be too difficult.'

'We should really be turning up new evidence.' Chris had been made aware by a higher authority that certain targets were not being achieved. They needed real results, not ones from a poor source, and even though the pressure was of a political nature no one was interested in fabricating evidence.

Commander Aley walked in, shouting, 'So, have we got anything new to go on; we've had weeks turning over old stones.'

'Sir, we may have something, but we need to work on it.' Chris's lowered voice made it seem like it was worth pursuing.

What does that mean exactly?' Commander Aley's assertiveness required an immediate answer.

Jake replied loudly, and a bit too assertively, 'Well, sir, one of our potential sources has turned something up.'

'What?'

Chris replied, drily, 'The lead thinks that when he was serving in Northern Ireland as a squaddy, back in the day, he took one of the men into custody that were arrested on a recent attempted GBH. It seems there could be a link between that and a wider network.'

'How long have you known this?'

'Only a short while and we can't act until we have something firm.'

'And how do you propose going about that?'

'We're examining evidence and will follow it up. We may be able to get a team onto it soon, but we'll need your authorisation.'

'You got it. Just do it. I'll sign whatever. We need results guys, like yesterday.'

~~~
~~~

PART TWO

CHAPTER FOUR

'All the parties are guilty, not just because of the lies surrounding everything they do but because they work together against the interests of the working class.' Brandon Sinclair was addressing the crowd inside the Edmonton warehouse. There were around two hundred of his most loyal activists present. He continued, 'We're their judges and their executioners. We will avenge their crimes and punish them for the suffering they have caused.'

There were muffled sounds of approval, but these were soon drowned out by the sound of police sirens and helicopters which seemed to engulf the whole area. Sinclair and three associates ran to the rear exit doors and, while activists barricaded the front doors, they made their way out of the building, down a tunnel and under the railway line, arriving at the top of a flight of steps. They then boarded a waiting van in a corner of an industrial yard. As they drove away, they could hear shouts and screaming coming from behind them.

Sinclair stated loudly to the others in the van, 'Don't worry. We'll win this. It doesn't matter how many of us they get. We'll win and then pay them back for what they've done.'

~~~

'Jake, you haven't been watching porn on your pad again?' Chris grinned sideways at Jake.

'Come off it man. You know my missus would kill me.'

'You shouldn't do it mate. You'll get some virus on your pad and someone from high-up will find it.'

'Why? Do they watch porn as well?'

Chris laughed, replying, 'Probably. But it's your funeral mate.'

'You're a bit of a prude Chris.'

'It's my upbringing mate. My mum would kick my arse to kingdom come if I did that.'

'How would your mum know? You don't live with her now.'

'When she comes over, she checks the whole place out. You don't know her.'

'What about Annie?'
~~~

'Well, we've only just started living together. Truth, I haven't even told her what my mum's really like.'

Jake let out a stifled laugh, before replying, 'You're living dangerously mate.'

'Yeah, you think I don't know?'

Chris broke off to check his emails on his own pad. After several minutes he looked up and said, 'Hey I got something, Jake. There's another email about that attempted GBH in Holloway. It seems that the ex-soldier is willing to come over, go through it all again and make a new statement.'

'I'm beginning to think he could be more useful to us than we expected.'

'Too right, Jake; I'll have a word with Aley.' Chris forwarded the email to Commander Aley explaining that Declan Gale was to be contacted again to arrange a time for another statement. He then booked an interview room.

~~~

'The real fascists are not out there on the streets. It's the British politicians. They're the ones who've been murdering innocent people for hundreds of years. They're the real enemy.' Ches was sitting in the café in Bethnal Green. He had no choice but to listen to the man on the next table drone on to his friends about politics while he ate his breakfast.

Ches had given Becker his share of the cash from the kidnapping of Chowdhury but, so far, he hadn't been able to fence the assorted gems they had stolen from the man's wife. He realised that one of the downsides of increased police activity on the streets is that a lot of useful people go abroad or into hiding, all be it on a temporary basis.

He hadn't yet seen any reports in the newspapers about former mayors suffering ordeals at the hands of house thieves. However, he was under no illusions that he and Becker had to walk away from what they had done and never look back. He wasn't going to kill himself worrying about it, but he wouldn't be doing another robbery any time soon.

'Maybe he won't report it after all,' Ches pondered. 'Perhaps he'll be too embarrassed to tell anyone. Maybe he's done himself in!' Ches punctured an egg on his plate.

The man on the next table continued with his diatribe against the government. *The politicians are going to get it. Look at the riots. You know I've heard of armed gangs on the streets attacking rich people, especially bankers. It's about bloody time!*

The man's voice rang through the café, so much so that Ches flinched. He deliberately avoided looking over and all he really cared about was when the fence was going to turn up.
~~~

Rashid, the man Ches was waiting for, finally walked in and sat down opposite. He looked at him intently and then relaxed, asking casually, 'You know man; I got some other business around here after you. When the guy comes, you'll have to excuse me. OK?'

'No problem.' Ches had placed the items under his newspaper before Rashid had arrived, and he now pushed the package deftly towards him.

Rashid picked the items out carefully as he lifted the newspaper, placing them in a small bag under the table. He nodded approvingly. The man at the next table was now shouting.

Rashid spoke quietly, 'Let's head out, shall we? Maybe the park would be better.'

'Yep, that's fine.'

Ches finished his coffee and made his way out after Rashid.

~~~

'It seems like the natural allies of these guys are extremists of all shapes and sizes; republicans, anarchists you name it.' Commander Aley paused in his briefing to the small group of people in front of him, men and women drawn from the Tactical Support Units.

He continued. 'We're up against some kind of unholy alliance where all these militants are concerned. Some of the surveillance has given a confused picture but they're probably all working together. That includes robbing on a large scale in order to get the funds for what we believe is their actual aim, a possible attack on a government facility. We've been able to listen to some of their chatter and that's what they're saying.'

They were in a briefing room in the TSU HQ near Ealing. It was a structure that looked like any grey metal-clad unit on any industrial estate, anywhere in the world. From the street the unmarked cars could come and go and, unless you knew what was going on inside, it looked like any other business in the area. Except this one had a fully stocked armoury.

'Sir, do you think there's a link between the riots and the attacks on political figures?' asked Jake.

'Yes indeed, without any doubt. One of the main characters involved in these riots is Brandon Sinclair, and he's now been positively ID'd. He'll kill as many people as it takes to attack the government. We're getting closer and closer to him and his main associates. He's also been sighted at many riots and violent demos.'

'Sir; is it true that he's converted to Islam?' a female officer asked.

'We don't know. We do know he has links to the Middle East and that there are probably Arab fighters amongst his men. They could be remnants of the wars of the last few decades.'
~~~

'Sir, doesn't that mean we have him now?' Chris asked. 'After all we know who he is, who his associates are and what their aims are.'

'Yes; but we have no conclusive evidence other than some photos and potential DNA matches.'

'Isn't that enough?' another commander asked pointedly.

'Not to put him away for long enough and we need to get more evidence to put him away for a long time. Moreover, there's no point in taking him in at the moment. If he goes, there are plenty of others to take his place and we could stimulate support for his network as well by doing so. We need to shut the networks down and that includes the robbers and lower ranks as well as the top men. We need to keep him there so we can get all of them at a time of our choosing.'

All the while Chris was admiring Commander Aley's cool and candid delivery he was also beginning to see why Aley was in charge of the TSU. The briefings had become political exercises designed to make it look like they were making progress when they clearly weren't. Aley's air of smooth authority wasn't just down to his rank and senior position. It was mainly because he was able to deal with questions both from his own people as well as from the media.

Aley continued, 'You've all done excellent work by the way and we're starting to get real breakthroughs. We're getting a lot coming through regards the Harrow cell now and we'll make some arrests shortly. We need the rest of these networks, but Harrow may well prove to be the key to the door, even if it's only one of many groups out there causing mayhem.'

After the briefing, Commander Aley moved over to Chris and Jake's team, asking softly, 'Can you and Jake do me a favour?'

'What's that, sir?' Chris replied.

'Can you two run a couple of teams alongside your own? I think we need to be organising a few simultaneous hits and you lads are the best we have. We have the Harrow place but we've also got some of Sinclair's mates under surveillance. They're not going anywhere, and I need you both to send people out to search premises and bring people in.'

Chris was dreading this. It wasn't how he and Jake and the team operated, as they favoured their own close-support tactics over Aley's hit-and-run approach. The latter meant that a team would go in with little or no prior information and then hope for the best. And if you got nothing out of it you were left hanging. That was the opposite of the meticulous planning they usually put into their own operations.

'Can you tell me what file we'll be working out of sir?' Chris choked back the words.

'I'll get that for you later, but for now we've some aerial footage and addresses we need following up first.' With that, Aley turned briskly and then headed out of the briefing area.

~~~

'Bunch of morons in suits, that's what they are.' Declan held the pint of beer and looked through the dark and golden interior.

'Too right Dec!' replied Gavin, as he sipped his own beer.

They were staring at the TV monitor high up on the bar room wall. The news items related to three former British politicians who had been kidnapped in the Middle East. They now appeared on a Middle Eastern TV channel chained to beds and dressed in orange jumpsuits.

'I don't care if those warmongering bastards get it,' Jez added. 'What goes around comes around.' He shook his head as he lifted his pint glass.

'Well said Jez, many would agree with you,' Declan replied. After a pause he added, 'That copper got back to me.'

'What happened?' asked Jez.

'Seems like our friend still hasn't said anything but he's come up positive on forensics for something serious. They got him now. He isn't going anywhere; too much evidence.'

'You're kidding me,' Gavin replied angrily. 'No one ever got back to me about why they tried to jump me.'

'I know Gav,' Declan replied sheepishly. 'It was probably a mistaken identity. They meant to jump someone else, but were too pissed and thought you were them.'

Declan knew that they had seen him in the pub, and believed it was him walking along the road instead of Gavin. He could never tell Gavin that the person they thought they were jumping was himself and not Gavin.

This had been confirmed to Declan by a TSU officer after a successful interrogation of one of the assailants had eventually revealed the actual target. There were good reasons Declan didn't want Gavin or Jez to know what had been going on. His time undercover in Northern Ireland had created some lifelong enemies and he always knew that they could some day catch up with him.

He glanced at Gavin, content in the knowledge that none of his close family or friends would ever know what he had actually been doing during his military career. But he still had a sinking feeling that events might run away from him

Declan spluttered, 'I got to make a call guys.'
~~~

Gavin and Jez nodded as they stared blankly at the TV screen.

~~~

'Look mate, if we can both get through life without actually killing anyone then we've done OK in my view.' Ches was standing on the Millenium Bridge and looking downstream as he spoke on his mobile phone to Becker. 'By the way I got your money Becks. Those stones were worth something you'll be pleased to know. And I have another job lined up.'

'Wow, you really are taking to this. Don't forget it was my idea we went solo.'

'Don't you mean duo?' Ches joked.

'Whatever. What's it this time?'

'I figured that we don't want to set patterns. No this one's a bit special. I'll let you know soon enough.'

'Mate, we need to be a bit careful. We need to play it safe.'

'Fine, but it depends on what you mean by safe.'

'I think we should stay low for a while and leave it for a few weeks.'

'OK. But I'll let you know what I had in mind. It's not what you think.'

'Yeah, but like you said we don't want to set patterns. Let's leave it for a little while and have a good break.'

'OK. I'll be in touch about the cash. I'll drop it off at your mum's flat. I'll say it's some of your personal stuff that you left one night. I'll stick the cash in a washbag and leave it in the holdall. Tell your mum not to wash it, will you?'

'Yeah OK but let me know when you're dropping it off and I'll be there. I've got to go and see her soon anyway, so we'll sort it out that way.'

'Will do mate.'

In the back of Ches's mind was the need to keep some distance from other people and not reveal what they were up to. He recalled what an old army mate had once said that it's easy to be one of the lads but not so easy to be someone in firm control of a situation.

~~~

Declan instinctively looked over his shoulder as he made his way down the back street in Burley, Leeds. He had gone to Yorkshire to check up on an old comrade from his first regiment, from the time he was a young corporal in Northern Ireland.

'This has to be the place.'

He hadn't seen Greig for eight years, but they had been best mates, as serving soldiers, and stayed friends once they had left the military. Greig had gone on to train reservists in Yorkshire but still kept in touch with Declan, when he could, mainly through social media.

'Hey! You old bast'd,' Greig shouted, as the two men embraced on the back terrace doorstep. Declan followed him into the house. Greig soon put two cups of coffee on the kitchen table.

After they had exchanged news, with Declan explaining the recent attempted assault in Holloway, Greig became more guarded towards Declan, stating, 'You know Dec, I've a wife and two kids here. I don't want to attract any characters if you know what I mean.'

'You won't mate. I've only come here to have a chat.'

'You could have done that on the phone Dec. If anyone's after you they might trace you here.'

'I don't think so. The Met Police have got the main guys in custody.'

'Exactly: only the main guys! There must be others out there, psychotic, some of them. You know what I'm saying.'

'Greig I wouldn't put you or your family in any danger, you know that.'

'So, why're you here Dec?'

'The security services in London are talking about my time in Belfast, and wherever, and they require some leads. They're into various groups from the past they think could be behind some of the things that are going down. They think some of it could be just a smoke screen for something much bigger.'

Declan stopped as Greig rolled a cigarette. 'Do you remember anyone Greig? Or anyone that might give me some more names?'

Greig looked at Declan, lit the cigarette and then puffed some smoke in his direction. 'Well, the files have gone from those days. They were incinerated. These friends of yours down south will have little evidence left, even if some of those characters are at large again.' He paused for another lug on the cigarette. 'Seems like we're needed after all; the likes of you and me.'

They both laughed sarcastically, Declan responding, 'Jeez, so much for Good Friday and all that. Look where it got us! It's not just them though. Some people in the Met reckon hardcore terrorists are behind an extremist network.'

'You know that wouldn't surprise me. We both know that a lot of the ones we came across were trained in the Middle East.' Greig paused and looked at Declan before continuing, 'So you need some more names then? Tell you what give me a few days, and I reckon I can come up with something, it might not be that great, but it will be something.'

'Cheers Greig. I was right. I can rely on you.'

~~~
~~~

The elderly politician got up to address an almost empty House of Commons. It was the last day of parliamentary activity before the summer recess and the debate was over the worsening security situation.

Despite his age the wizened looking man spoke clearly. 'Isn't it about time the PM and his cabinet now got on top of this situation? We have towns and cities burning, armed gangs on the streets, ex-politicians being kidnapped, three of whom are still missing. And what precisely are you doing about all this?'

There was a sad chorus of 'Hear, hear,' from the few in the chamber as the Deputy Prime Minister got up to speak.

'Unfortunately, the PM is on a trade mission in Qatar right now but I'm endeavouring to receive an update on the most recent events.'

Laughter emanated from the benches and the man tried to continue, 'But make no mistake, we are on top of this situation. We will not surrender to those who threaten the very foundations of our society.'

The Shadow Home Secretary stood up to reply, 'We should therefore assume that the Deputy PM doesn't read the newspapers? The headlines read thus: *Rough Justice for the Corrupt* and *PM fiddles while London burns*, so it's hardly a supportive media.'

One opposition MP stood up, shouting, 'When will you wake up? You're despised by the people of this country. Some are calling this a revolution. Whatever it is you've lost control of the situation.'

Another opposition member joined in the chorus, 'The government is clearly no longer in charge of vast swathes of this country. There aren't enough armed police and security units and there aren't enough soldiers to patrol many key areas. This is all because of the cutbacks. This must be the most incompetent administration ever.'

The Deputy Prime Minister interrresponded, 'The honourable gentlemen must recall that we inherited an economy left in tatters by the previous government and the security services are in a parlous state due to the actions of your own party whilst it was in power. There's no money left to train any new troops or police officers. And even if there were, few people are interested in joining.'

'And how is that surprising?' a female opposition MP shouted, without standing. She continued, 'No one sees the point of serving a corrupt establishment. not after so many years of failed policies.' Loud jeers came from various parts of the chamber.

At their HQ Chris and Jake watched the proceedings in the House of Commons on a TV monitor in the staff room, as they chatted and drank coffee.

'I heard from my man this morning Jake,' Chris began. 'I think we owe him some expenses.'

'Maybe we should give him a job. He's doing more than anyone else to help pull some of the psychos in.'

'I've already told Aley we need him on board. Anyway, it seems one of his old pals up inYorkshire has produced a list from memory of likely lads from the bad old days. It's based on a list that had been written down and filed away but was subsequently lost.'

'How many names?'

'Over a hundred.'

'For pity's sake are we going to have to pull them all in?'

'No, some are dead anyway. Some are in the United States and can stay there. But we'll need to check a number of them. And the boss has given us another team to get on with that task. I'll brief them later.'

'Is there anything else?'

'He said he might have some more leads, but he needs more time. That's enough for now anyway. But we have something on one of these high-profile robberies. That slimy bastard of a mayor up north; you know the one the media were onto for sex parties or whatever it was.'

'Oh yeah: that guy.'

'Well, it seems he was tied up and robbed blind a few weeks ago. No one knew about it because he was too ashamed to admit it. It seems that the police thought it may have been a prank at first and maybe even staged by a newspaper. But it wasn't. They were organised criminals, and they fenced the family jewellery. It's worth over three hundred grand.'

'Not bad for a day's work.'

'Too right, and it seems that's not all. The Met has got some of the stones. An undercover guy in Dalston I think.'

'Why're you telling me?'

'It's you and me that are going to check it out.'

~~~

Ches and Becker walked out of Grantham station having got off the train from Kings Cross. It was 8:30 P.M. on a Thursday evening in early summer and the air was dry, made cooler by the brisk breeze. They made their way along the main road at the front of the station.

Ches seemed almost too keen to carry out another hit so soon after the last. He hadn't said anything to Becker but there was now an atmosphere between them that wasn't going away.

They were in Lincolnshire to visit Danny; an old friend of Ches. Danny worked locally and had a Polish girlfriend called Rosa who worked as a housekeeper for a local TV presenter. Ches's idea was to use her to get inside
~~~

a large celebrity mansion as it was full of cash and valuables. The celebrity was a flamboyant gay man who liked staging raucous parties at his home.

Becker, who had only been given a few details, asked pointedly, 'Ches, have you any idea where the safe is located at all?'

Ches grunted and then replied, somewhat annoyed, 'Give us a chance Becks; we only just got here. I'll tell you later.'

Becker looked away and shook his head.

Ches added, more positively, 'Let's head into town. We'll have a few beers and then crash at Danny's place. He won't be in but Rosa's around.'

Four hours later the two fell out of a town centre bar and stumbled up the hill. They got to Danny's ground floor flat and collapsed onto the sofa.

'So at least let me know where this job is?' asked Becker.

'It's here mate; or near here,' Ches replied drowsily. 'I told you; he's a minor celebrity, works in TV, I think. Apparently, there's a safe under his swimming pool.'

'Great, so how the hell are we going to get into that?'

'I'm only kidding you.' Ches laughed loudly. 'There's one up on the first floor. It's a mansion and we can check out any cameras while we're there. There's a party tomorrow night. Seems the guy's parties are a bit wild; lots of other gay chaps in fancy dress, that kind of thing. Rosa says there's not much security and they throw cash around all the time, like snorting Charlie with a fifty note.'

Becker laughed, but still sensed problems with Ches's proposal. 'Those sorts of places are like little forts Ches. Let's face it they'll have loads of CCTV, probably linked straight into the police. We'll be on You Tube if we're not careful.'

'Who said that we'd break into anything? Rosa looks after the place, and she has a key to the room with the safe. She can let us straight in and we'd be there as guests at a house party. She told Danny that the safe is never locked as the guy doesn't really give a monkey's armpit about security. We just have to be a bit clever, that's all.'

'So, what do you propose?'

'Keep it simple, that's what. The host will be stoned by twelve. So, what I reckon is that we get in as gay guests, in fancy dress like everyone else, and sack the place while everyone's off their heads on coke and spritzers. Rosa will be there, but we'll keep our distance, so we don't put her in trouble. We need to wear masks, Becks, and gloves.'

Becker warmed to the thought of wearing fancy dress. 'Yeah, that's cool. I quite like the sound of that.' He thought for a moment and added, 'It'll be better if we split while we're in there. Do the job and then leave separately.'

Ches looked at Becker and nodded before replying, 'Whatever mate; nothing ventured, nothing gained.'

'You seem to be well up with this one Ches. Do you know the layout of the house?'

'I got it off Rosa.'

~~~

'So, we now have leads on several more of these gangs,' Commander Aley paused as he briefed the Tactical Support Unit commanders.

He scanned the briefing area to make sure his audience was paying attention before continuing. 'It looks like they're a motley collection, but it seems there's no more than fifteen people involved in the kidnapping and extortion racket. Most probably all of them have previous, including links to various outfits involved in extortion and terrorism.' Aley carried on talking about the evidence relating to some recent kidnappings of politicians before changing tack. 'At the same time there could be a link between these criminal elements and a more politicized group, but this is where we need to do a lot more work. There are groups whipping up violence at street level, as we all know. They're deliberately dragging the country down, but these are not just the one-off summer riots that we normally get. These people are organised and clinical, whereby several hundred militants turn up and wreck an area, always hitting a target, and nearly always involving arson and theft of high value goods as well. The money seems to be going back to a central fund, but we don't know who is doing the stealing most of the time as the ones at the centre of it all are never there. We can't get easy visuals on many of the militants as they wear balaclavas and use concealment as well.'

He paused to drink some water and check his notes before continuing. 'However, we do have forensics on some of the fences now. They're having to go further and further afield to get rid of the stuff. The militants are even getting their relatives or loved ones to take the stolen gear abroad. We could start pulling them in. But we need the ringleaders.'

'Sir, how do we know that this is political?' one team leader asked. 'If they're sending the cash abroad anyway couldn't this just be organised crime?'

'Good point, but this is more than just a hunch – it's what everything points towards. We're starting to get some good leads on the political angle, and we know that there are some old hands from Northern Ireland involved. Looks like some of them are linked to Europe and the Middle East. The Irish are in bed with the Arabs, and we'll have to take them on first, but we do know some of the figures are home-grown. We can't get people into the Arab gangs, as we don't have the people who can do it, and they know that.'

'Sir, how about we extend stop and search?' another team leader broke in. 'We could bring in a lot more, and quickly.'
~~~

'Yeah, we're working on that, but if we keep alienating parts of the community then we'll get nowhere.'

After the briefing Jake and Chris grabbed a coffee.

Jake was annoyed, quietly stating to Chris once they had sat down 'We're just messing around mate. We need to shut down these networks completely. There're too many gangs roaming the streets; it's like Northern Ireland in the bad old days but on a bigger scale.'

'Jake,' Chris replied casually. 'The politicians have screwed us over so we can't control the streets because we don't have the manpower. So, the problems are wider than even Aley claims. He's a politician as well, don't forget. Or at least he reports to them. The riots are just a smoke screen, and we just have to ride it out. We'll get there in the end, but it'll take some time, so we've all got to be patient.'

'Meanwhile Rome burns, and we all look like numpties.'

'We have no real choice, Jake.'

~~~

'You know Jez, you can be quite cynical sometimes,' Declan asserted as he took a long sip of his pint of lager. Declan and Jez had just finished work for the day at the industrial unit in North London and were in Camden Town for a night out.

'I know Dec,' Jez replied. 'But I wouldn't be your blood relative if I wasn't so damned cynical, now, would I?'

Declan laughed while Jez pointed at the TV screen above the bar and commented, 'You know I used to think it was Scotland, Wales and Northern Ireland that were holding England back but now I realise it's the other way round. England's a complete mess.' They both stared at the scenes of major rioting across English cities from the night before.

'Some of these places look like they've been bombed out,' exclaimed Declan.

'Yeah, I see it Dec,' Jez replied, shaking his head.

'Where's Gav?' Declan asked.

'Oh, he's just disappeared with a girl for the evening.'

'Good for him. So, we're just finishing off now then?'

'Yeah, looks like it, a general builders' clean. But I'm glad we are busy.' Jez took another sip of his pint, adding wearily, 'Even if it is knackering me out.'

Declan nodded, replying, 'So am I, totally knackered. But you know what I hate most Jez? It's working every hour, with hardly any breaks.'

'I know, but the grass is always greener elsewhere. Isn't that what they say?' Jez paused, adding, 'But packing it all in is not for me, I've tried it. And I've no choice anyway, not with the family.'
~~~

'I know, been there,' Declan replied sadly, before slowly adding, 'Look I have to be honest with you about something.'

'Can it wait, Dec? I need a slash.'

Declan wanted to tell him about the meetings he'd had with the police and the fact Gavin hadn't been the real target the night he was attacked. He wanted to talk about the fact that he seemed to be on a rollercoaster back to the past, now he was helping the Met without even being asked. In reality he knew that he had to keep quiet for all their sakes. Jez walked off towards the toilets.

~~~

Ches and Becker arrived on the gravel drive of a large Edwardian house on the edge of Grantham. It was a warm Saturday night, but they were heavily made-up and dressed as two vampires. Rosa would turn up, as agreed, an hour later. No one at the house party would know them, other than Rosa.

Ches had only met Rosa once, and briefly, six months before at a party in nearby Stamford. It was Danny who had mentioned the safe and how to get to it, Rosa having describd the layout to him. Rosa and Danny had lived in Grantham for only a few months and couldn't easily be connected with anyone else locally. As far as her boss was concerned, she had never even mentioned Danny to him.

Rosa had got all the invites for the party and briefed Ches and Becker about the layout of the house. She wouldn't approach them during the evening so any CCTV footage wouldn't show them together.

They entered separately and on entry the first thing Ches noticed was a river of beer flowing down a stainless-steel channel in the main hall. They both decided they would indulge in a couple of beers to build their confidence. Their masks stayed on while they drank but they kept away from one another.

Rosa arrived, on cue, at 10:45 P.M. and immediately distracted the host. He knew her well enough by then and trusted her implicitly. Ches and Becker would hit the safe some time after 11:00 P.M. and they would stay at the party for another hour before disappearing separately. They hoped that any hidden cameras wouldn't pick up their exit. The key to the first-floor room with the safe had been copied by Rosa using plasticine the week before, and she had checked the new key in the lock without any problems only two days before.

At 11:15 P.M. Ches and Becker managed to steal their way to the room at the end of the first-floor corridor. Ches had pretended to the woman he was talking to that he was going off to score some cannabis from someone else at the party. Becker had managed to extricate himself from a Goth girl called Gail who was becoming more attractive the more he drank.
~~~

Rosa had told them which painting the safe was behind and Ches carefully removed it from the wall as Becker stood guard outside. Ches didn't need to take off his gloves as he merely had to pull the door open. Rosa had mentioned that there was no actual alarm system, just the boxing to act as a deterrent.

Inside Ches found several manuscripts, which he left, and what looked like £100,000 in used notes. There were also two Rolex watches. He decided that they had probably been awarded the host as payment for a game show he hosted and were therefore traceable. He left them in place.

He closed the safe, putting much of the cash into a plastic bag and then tapped the door gently. Becker entered. They quickly split the cash, securing it in the tight waist belts they had worn for the purpose, under their voluminous vampire costumes. Becker rejoined the party. Ches then positioned the painting exactly as he had found it, exited and locked the door to the room. They rejoined the party.

Becker went back to find Gail the Goth. He apologised for not scoring any drugs and then proceeded to get to know her a lot better. At 12:30 P.M. Ches slipped past the swimming pool at the rear of the house. He climbed over the wrought iron fence and then saw a path heading off across what looked like open common land into the moonlight. He could see a public footpath sign and decided to follow it.

He had reasoned that if Becker stayed behind at the party it could be a good cover, at least for Becker, as the girl would vouch for him if the robbery was discovered that evening. However, he doubted it would be discovered immediately, as everyone was too far gone on drink and drugs to take anything seriously. Moreover, there were no security guards.

He started walking briskly along the moonlit path. Ches also reasoned that the cash in the safe was only small change for someone like the host and, judging by the size of the house and the wheels outside, it wasn't going to destroy the man's livelihood.

As he walked, he thought about how the facts might be unveiled. The minor celebrity would appear in the papers saying he had been robbed, much like any other celebrity with a property in the recesses of suburbia. It would be a small headline in the news, a few days or weeks hence.

The police would have a job identifying him and Becker from all the other revelers, if indeed the CCTV cameras were functioning. The security had been so lax Ches felt almost obliged to tell the host how he could improve it.

'I'm in the wrong business here,' he stated to himself as he headed across open moorland in the moonlight. 'I should be advising people like him about their security. Not taking these risks.'

After another ten minutes of stumbling through mud he found himself sliding alongside a metal fence. He saw dark figures silhouetted about three hundred yards away on the other side of the fence. They looked like they were spaced equally and holding rifles. He saw flashes and cracks as the figures appeared to be attacking an old derelict barn, and he soon realised that he was on the edge of some kind of military training area. It was more a case of déjà vu as he suddenly recalled his years as an infantryman, which had come to an abrupt end soon after his second tour in Afghanistan in 2009.

He dropped down into the undergrowth and could see a path leading into woodland away from the fence. He was sure that the figures hadn't seen him as they appeared to be focused on the target they were attacking in the distance, so he slipped down the path.

The sound of cracking gunfire carried on for a few minutes as he headed down the trail. He saw the occasional lights of cars in the distance indicating that he was now moving towards a road as the trail widened out. He guessed the main road could be anything up to a kilometre away and decided that he would try and follow it back towards town and then work out his bearings from there.

He didn't want to draw attention to his vampire costume if anyone passed him, so he smudged his face as best he could, hoping it would make his skin appear a lot darker in the bright moonlight. Ten minutes later he picked up a wide B road that had a paved edge and headed down towards what looked like the bright lights of Grantham below in the distance.

The road headed straight past the entrance to a very large army camp, and he had no choice but to walk briskly past the gates. He crossed the road, turning his back on the camp as best he could. It occurred to him that, if he had been spotted, the only CCTV that would have picked him up was at the gates. However, the money belt didn't create any profiles on his body as he was still in his flowing cape and costume. People might notice his appearance, so he kept his head down even when a vehicle passed at speed with lights on full beam.

'I bet Becks shags that bird tonight.' The thought appealed to him. 'Lucky bastard, at least he has an alibi. So long as she doesn't ask about his waist belt.'

He carried on down the road and saw a right turn after a petrol garage. He figured it would take him along one side of the town and back towards the flat. Ten minutes later he was inside. He had passed no one as he walked.

~~~
~~~

CHAPTER FIVE

'What a case,' exclaimed Jake. 'You do realise that this report shows we have enough to bring Sinclair in, Chris?'

Chris looked up from his desk 'I think we'll just have to work with it for now mate. After all it's only a high-level profile of the guy. The man's clearly just another narcissist, Che Guevara type, or maybe just a Walter Mitty depending on your point of view.'

'Maybe he is, but we can pick him up regardless.'

'I think his lot might be about to do something big, so we need to get everything straight with Aley and not just go steaming in.'

'And what about that guy we pulled in for the Holloway attack? Are you still certain he's part of the Harrow network?'

'Yes, I am, but if you look at the legal procedure he could be out again in weeks. Luckily his own lawyer can't stand the sight of him so he probably won't get any breaks. But some of the evidence is flimsy.'

'Well, I hope we'll have that bastard set in concrete before long. We need to get him on a decent charge as well.'

'According to forensics he may have had several years in Latin America and some Arab training camps, due to his skin damage. He probably did more bloody military training than you did! All the same we need more evidence, and we need to pick up these networks. Surveillance hasn't given us much so far.'

'I think we should get in there ourselves Chris. We can't trust some of these rookies.'

'I totally agree but that's up to Aley at the end of the day.'

~~~

'I think what turned me off soldiering in the end was the push-button type of warfare that came along after 2010.' Declan lifted his pint glass in mocking salutation of his own career in the British Army, motioning it towards Gavin and Jez in the front bar of the Islington pub. 'By my last few tours, it had taken over. Boy soldier to colour sergeant; that was me.'

Gavin grinned. He'd always enjoyed listening to Declan's stories. It was a Wednesday in late August and early evening. The pub was filling up and overflowing onto the street.
~~~

'But I don't know where you were or what happened to you at points in your army career. The rest of us had no idea where you were.' Jez looked at Declan quizzically.

'That was the idea. You weren't supposed to know.' Declan had drunk too much, and he knew it. However, he was sick of the lies he had told over the years, and so he decided to reveal more to his cousins about his past than he ever had before.

'It's simple Jez. They snatched me off an upgrade course and then asked me if I wanted to do something more interesting, along the lines of military intelligence. They then gave me my upgrade anyway. I ended up covert in Northern Ireland.' He paused for a few seconds. 'After a while I'd had enough of that, so I got a posting to help train psychotic Khmer Rouge fighters in Cambodia. I was in support of specialists and had no idea what it was all about in reality. I then went back to actual soldiering and did a couple of tours in Bosnia, and then, later on, one in Iraq and two in Afghan. You know about those anyway. In the end I just stuck it out to get the full pension.'

Declan stared at his glass and then at the people enjoying the early evening warmth on the street.

Gavin responded quietly, asking, 'So how many people actually knew about what you were doing?'

'No one, not even my ex-wife, knew what I was up to.'

There was silence eventually broken by Jez. 'I don't know anything lads about all this, but I think a lot of people don't have a clue what's going on in reality. You put your arse on the line Dec for those bastards in Westminster. That's all I know.'

Declan replied quickly, 'You're right Jez, people don't have a clue. Cambodia was a mess. We were training child killers. When I found out what was really happening, I told them to stick the damned job and demanded to go back to proper soldiering. They had only wanted me there because I had a decent knowledge of weapons and ammunition. As far as I'm concerned, we helped the wrong side out there.'

Declan cut off. He took a swig of his pint and continued, 'Look lads there's a lot of stuff happening that you just don't know about. You don't want to know about it.'

Gavin nodded, asking quietly, 'So Dec, who were those rebels?'

'They were the Khmer Rouge; the same psychos who butchered several million of their own people just over a decade before I got there. And we were helping to train them just because they happened to hate the Vietnamese, in other words the same people who had kicked the Yanks' arses. It was a proxy war because the regime in Cambodia was backed by the Vietnamese who had taken over much of the place after 1980. There was eventually a coup in 1997 and Pol Pot, the Khmer Rouge leader, died. The whole thing was just a game, and a game that cost around 250,000 lives from 1980 onwards. We should keep out of these games. But we never learn.'

The three of them stared into space.

'What do these politicians expect?' exclaimed Gavin. 'They messed up our economy, spent all our cash on wars, created yet more terrorists as a result of their failed foreign policies, and then bring in millions of foreigners when our unemployment is sky high. Then they wonder why it is that the rest of us have had enough.'

Jez nodded, replying, 'I must admit, for me they've had it coming for a long time; and the writing's been there on every wall. It was just a matter of time. It's hardly surprising, as the politicians don't give a monkey's armpit about this country. There is such a thing as payback.'

Declan looked sideways at Jez, commenting, 'I served this worthless political establishment for too bloody long as a soldier and did their dirty work for them. I could have taken a bullet for those corrupt bastards at any time; *'cos that's the job.*'

'And you only realise that now?' Gavin responded.

Two hours later they went into the lounge bar as the city workers had started to disperse, and some tables had become available.

They sat down and said nothing for a minute. Then a man's voice caught Declan's attention. He looked deftly over his shoulder towards a figure sitting two tables away.

The voice spoke in low tones into his phone whilst staring at Declan. Declan froze. It was unmistakeably that of a Derry man whose voice Declan recognised. Declan turned back and stared into space.

Gavin got up to go to the toilet. He passed the seated figure as he walked into the toilets. Declan noticed that the man didn't look up. He was late middle-aged, bald on top, with grey edge hair and a rounded red face.

While Declan knew that he recognised him he also had a flashback to the night that Gavin had been attacked. He kept one eye on the man to see if he was about to make a move. When Gavin came back Declan gestured to him and Jez that he was leaving and grabbed his jacket. The three headed for the door.

Outside Declan turned round, exclaiming, 'Look lads I'm going to take my time walking home.'

Jez was concerned, asserting, 'After what happened before Dec, I think we should make sure we all get back OK.'

'Don't worry about me. You both hop in a taxi, and I'll text you when I get back to my flat.'

Jez nodded.

Gavin hailed a taxi for him and Jez. Declan sauntered off but then walked back past the main entrance of the pub, standing hidden in a shop door nearby. Forty minutes later the man from Derry walked out of the pub and headed up the road. Declan watched him, still hidden in the darkness of the doorway.

He followed at some distance and was relieved to find that the man obviously lived locally, as he wasn't going to board a bus or get a taxi, instead entering the concierge of a block of flats. Declan seized his chance and, running the last fifty metres to get to the door before it closed, he entered the lobby as the man was about to get in the lift. The lobby was empty as Declan slammed him into the lift car, punching him in the stomach three times. The man cowered on the floor without a fight.

Declan shouted, 'Now, who the hell are you? Do I know you? Answer me or you'll get it. That's a promise not a threat.'

'I don't know what you mean.' The man made no attempt to get up and was holding his head in his hands.

'You look like you knew me from somewhere. I've seen you before.'

'Maybe I'm your bloody guardian angel pal?'

'What does that mean?'

'What I say Declan.'

'How do you even know my name?'

Declan punched the man in the head, and he let out a scream. The lift was now stopping. Declan kicked the man hard in the ribs and said quietly, 'Now this is what we are going to do. We're both going to go into your flat nice and slowly and have a little chat.'

Exiting the lift Declan followed the man to the door of the flat. The man turned the key in the lock. It clicked open and they walked ponderously into the lobby without saying a word. Declan could hear muffled voices coming from a room further down the corridor.

'Who are they?' he scowled at the man kicking him hard in the shins such that he let out a yelp.

'And keep your mouth shut or I'll kill you,' Declan stated in low tones. The noise in the front room had stopped.

'Is that you Tommy?'

'Aye,' he replied.

'What're you up to?'

'I'll be going to bed guys.'

'Don't be daft, come and play cards with us.'

'OK boys.'

Declan rushed past Tommy as he entered the room and stormed into the centre from where he saw three figures bent over a table. He jumped on the first, throwing him into the second. A gun fell to the floor. Declan picked it up and checked the safety. It was an old 9mm Beretta 92 with a silencer. He pointed it at the furthest man, clicked off the safety, turned and then fired one round into an empty armchair. He moved back while ordering everyone to lie on the ground in front of him.

'How any more are there in here?' Declan shouted. 'Tell me, or I'll kill all of you.'

The man who had spoken to Tommy replied, 'There's no more here. The others are out somewhere.'

'Where; exactly?'

'What, are you some kind of copper?'

'I told you once I'm not screwing around. I want to know why you lot are on my case.'

'There's been some mistake pal. We're not after you anymore. The boss realised you weren't working for the government and was calling it all off tonight. But Tommy here got too close. It was a mistake; a big screw-up. That's all it was.'

'So, who the hell are you people? And why does Tommy here know my name?'

'If we tell you that we ...put it this way; it's just not worth our while telling you. We're far too low down the chain if you know what I mean. We just do what we're told and then we get paid.'

Declan felt a cold chill running down his back and it suddenly occurred to him that these men weren't criminals.

'You're the real bloody deal, aren't you? I should have guessed.'

He moved back as fast as he could and exited the flat. With the weapon pointing down he ran down the stairs and out of the building, concealing the weapon, having fixed the safety. He ran down the street and crossed over towards Upper Street. When he had got far enough away, he immediately rang the number given him by Chris Kane.

An operator answered, 'TSU desk, can I help?'

'I got a hide for you. It's located at...'

~~~

Becker slumped further down into the sofa in Ches's flat. He and Ches had finished a bottle of malt whisky to celebrate the recent trip to Grantham. They had got most of the way through another as they divided up the spoils of the Saturday night a week before.

Becker had been explaining to Ches what he had got up to in Grantham after Ches had left, mainly with the Goth girl he had met at the party.
~~~

He continued in the same manner until asking, 'So how the hell did you get home that night Ches? I thought you'd been arrested.'

'What did it matter to you? You copped off with that bird.' Ches answered abruptly.

'Yeah, I know. I don't need to go on about the sex again mate, but I will anyway. She rocked.'

Ches couldn't hide his lack of interest but at the same time he didn't begrudge his friend, as well as a good cover story and alibi.

'So, do you think he's even found out that he's been robbed yet?' Ches asked.

'I'm hoping not, at least not for a few more weeks. He looked like one of those people who never checked what he had in his safe, or bank accounts, and that means he probably won't be able to pin it down to the night of the party. If he asked the police, I bet they'd tell him he could have been robbed any time.'

'That's sweet, and we had masks and gloves on. That means none of our prints or DNA will be on the safe; or anywhere else for that matter.'

'Yeah; except on my girl,' Becker replied, and both men laughed.

'I doubt he'll even bother reporting it. He's loaded, so a hundred grand is loose change to him.'

'No, I know. So, let's not kill ourselves worrying about it.'

~~~

'This is a nation that claims to be all about peace and love.' Brandon Sinclair was briefing his closest associates in a small industrial unit off Mare Street, Hackney. 'That's while it sells weapons systems to the highest bidders. It's a corrupt state at every level and we have to deliver justice. That means taking the fight to those in power. We'll destroy them, along with their media and celebrity cronies. But only the complete eradication of this corrupt establishment will work, and nothing less.'

There had to be a gear change as far as he was concerned. After months of riots, he had finally decided that it was time to bring things to a head and stage attacks on government buildings.

He continued, 'We have all sat back while British politicians have bombed their way around the world in recent decades. Just by voting or not voting we've all had some kind of impact, but by not asking the right questions of the politicians we're also guilty of criminal negligence. That negligence has aided and abetted this country's corporate-led criminality against innocent people across the globe. Ours is a tyrannic state; a gangster nation selling weapons systems to the highest bidders and searching in vain for cheaper fuel and
~~~

energy to power our overcrowded island. It's now the time to fundamentally alter this nightmare we all live in. Moreover, we've allowed our problems on this island to become global problems and that has to be dealt with once and for all.'

Sinclair stepped back from the podium. He had wanted to state many other things, but he held back, as it was time to let the younger members take the helm and have their say.

There was to be an indirect press release in expectation that the government, desperate as it was, would then approach him in order to negotiate a settlement with all the militant groups. Once those talks broke down, as inevitably they would, further actions would be propagated, not through general street violence, but via much more accurate targeting of political and security agencies.

There would be simultaneous raids on government offices, security headquarters, ammunition facilities and other installations. As militants were attacking targets across the country, there would also be coordinated and sporadic unrest across many towns and cities. The politicians would be forced to negotiate, but on his terms. He didn't need to say anything further for now, as his own commanders had taken care of organising this next phase. The only real aim was to motivate the street activists and get more people to join in.

One of the other speakers stood up, Klaus, a veteran of street battles across Europe and a good friend of Sinclair. He spoke clearly. 'The militias will be expanded as more fighters have now been trained, and they can be brought into the fold. When the fighting commences many more will join us until thousands are taking part in attacks. The authorities will be overwhelmed; they simply don't have enough trained personnel to cope with a full insurgency. They will have to give into our main political demands, and some of those demands will have to be met before any negotiations can take place.'

The next speaker mentioned the fact that they were planning to link up with some of their key allies within other countries, but that it had to be done methodically to get maximum effect.

Sinclair still didn't trust some of the other newly associated groups to keep their mouths shut and feared they would give his plans away. Therefore, it made sense to only reveal aims on the eve of the day when they wanted an action to take place. Thus, just a few people at any point in time needed to know what was happening. It was a process that called for tact, duplicity and clarity at the right moments in the right measures. However, he didn't trust many of his own people to execute such a strategy. He would maintain strict control partly through Jay Saxby.

To that end, Sinclair and his closest associates had sent out a decoy dressed as himself who had been 'captured' by the security forces a few days before.

Sinclair knew that, since the decoy was now being held in police custody, the TSU had become emboldened. It was being fed a stream of misinformation as it attempted to find out where safe houses were located. It wouldn't be too long before it rumbled that the man in custody wasn't the real man. But while they searched pointlessly Sinclair could act, as it gave him the space he needed to plan and carry out some decisive raids.

Saxby, as Sinclair's most senior female associate, stood up to speak. 'We have to put any recent setbacks behind us. Together we're stronger than the sum of our parts and when we look at the calibre of comrades we have amongst us then we have nothing to fear. We have the capability to destroy everything in our way. It will only take a few thousand to take on the state apparatus, to create just enough confusion and mayhem. We'll crush the TSUs while the riots are in full swing. By the time we've finished there'll be a provisional authority with real power in our hands. We'll achieve all our objectives, as we will always have the upper hand.'

The gathering murmered approval and Sinclair and his associates got down to dicsuss the next targets.

~~~

'If the English had any real guts they'd start their own bloody revolution,' Jez exclaimed loudly in the bar of the East London pub.

Declan smiled. 'You know Jez you might have hit upon something mate.'

He was still smarting from his recent brush with danger but was only too aware of what he had stumbled upon. He was in no doubt that the flat had been both a staging post and a command centre for some kind of armed group. However, the men he had happened across had cleared out long before the Tactical Support Units had arrived. He was not going to be visiting that area again any time soon.

All he'd ever wanted was to get away from the life he'd once led, but that was now impossible. The TSU had been impressed by his actions and one senior officer had called him to suggest that he could now be paid for his services regardless of the accidental nature of his street intelligence.

Jez started up again but was drowned out by another voice more powerful than his own. It was that of a late middle-aged Dublin man called Finn, whom Jez had known for several years, and who had joined them for a drink. In the past Finn had provided Jez with many contacts for finding construction work. Declan and Gavin had never seen him before but had heard everything about him, especially his reputation for getting hopelessly drunk.

The Dubliner spoke proudly, but not about construction contracts. 'All the British politicians have ever done is turn British people into strangers in their
~~~

own land just like they did with my country. That's what's at the heart of these riots. They've all messed up, Labour, Liberal, Tory. My advice is to get rid of the public-school morons and start again. That's all there is to it and that's no less than what this country, and its truly decent working-class people, deserves.' He was on his sixth pint of Guinness.

'And that will be closely followed by anarchy Finn,' Declan replied loudly.

He threw a sideways glance at Finn as he continued more quietly. 'That's all that was happening in Northern Ireland, criminality. That's why they had the peace process, because terrorism and violence wasn't working any more, as it wasn't controlling the streets. And that's what will happen here in England. Everyone'll be fighting each other. It's bad, I give you that, but things could still get a lot worse.'

Jez put his pint down and intervened, 'Anyway lads what about another round of drinks. And then, Finn, we can talk business. Those station platforms don't re-lamp themselves you know, and I need to know who to talk to at the goods yard.'

He took a final swig and then continued in the same vein. 'Sorry to be a nuisance but we need some contacts boys. It's not what you know, it's who you know. Isn't that right Finn? Same again?' He got up and walked towards the bar.

~~~

'Look mate, I've spent most of my life trying to get off with posh birds and have sadly failed. I'm only going for fat, ordinary, chicks now, if that's OK with you.' Ches had opened his emails and was showing Becker the notifications he was getting from one of his internet dating sites.

His tone suddenly altered. 'Becks, I have an email here from one of those psychos you were involved with. Why are they emailing me?'

'Ah, I must have included you in some of the forwarded links. I think I could have forwarded an email, and they must have checked out the previous ones in the chain. Sorry mate.'

'Thanks for that, I owe you one,' Ches replied sarcastically.

'Just delete it, they'll go away. They were just a bunch of freaks. We've got our own work now Ches.'

Ches deleted the email and opened up a news story. 'Look at this, there's going to be a series of massive protests across the country.'

'What a waste of time! Let them get on with it, I couldn't give a damn.' Becker looked genuinely disinterested.

'OK, but think about it mate,' Ches replied. 'That means that the whole police force will be stretched to breaking point, and some of those celebrity properties will be up for the picking, my friend.'
~~~

'We don't know that for sure, and we don't even know if we got away with the last one yet.' Becker was concerned as he could see danger in Ches's renewed eagerness to target more properties. 'You need to slow down Ches.'

'Look, Rosa is still going there to look after the place. The guy hasn't even mentioned it to her. Maybe he doesn't want to lose face, or he knows that the stuff is long gone, and he'll never see it again. Either way, please just stop worrying.'

'So, he wasn't insured Ches. That's why he's not bothered. Plus, he knows the filth don't give a damn about him or any other celebity tossers. But that doesn't mean we got away with it.'

'Forget it. This is a perfect storm for us, as we can hit more places while these riots and attacks are in full swing. We could do loads of places while there's still time.'

'Ok, calm down mate, you're going way too far. And by the way, please don't accidentally tell anyone about any of this. I don't want anything bad happening, especially where the other outfits are concerned. All they ever cared about was their own world. I got next to nothing for what I did but I still don't want them to know what we're up to.'

Ches nodded. In a more conciliatory tone he added, 'I know Becks you don't need to tell me again. Anyway, I reckon a lot of those are heading for a tough time. They choose poor targets, breaking into cash tills or doing over places with CCTV. As you said it never pays, and they might have all got onto candid camera if you know what I mean.' A thought occurred to him. 'Do you think you were ever caught on CCTV mate?'

'No, that was the good thing, as me and the other lads were always in the back of the van. That's why we got next to nothing. We did the driving, radios and sorted all the logistics. But that was as far as I got.'

'We still have an advantage then don't we.'

'Yes, if we plan things right.'

'So, let's see what we can do within reason.'

~~~

Chris was looking at what had been left in the Islington flat after it had been raided following the tip-off by Declan. The scene in front of him was, he had decided, low worth in terms of evidence.

He turned to Jake, asking, 'How did they get away?'

Jake looked up from his corner. 'They look like professionals. Everything must have been pre-packed and then taken away before our team arrived, a quick exit. They left very little with their own DNA on it. They must have other places like it.'
~~~

'I reckon they're all living out of a vehicle Jake, or several vehicles. They're much too mobile. We need to check the whole area for CCTV on all routes. We'll check with forensics but it's a vehicle that'll lead us straight to them.'

'Chris, I thought the boss was demanding results, like yesterday. We probably haven't much time for all that.'

'Tough, that's what we need to do right now.'

While Chris's team was going through the apartment, Commander Aley was listening to a specialist briefing by an intelligence chief in Portcullis House on countering the terrorist threat. It was targeted specifically at radical militant groups. The male speaker was tall, bald and in his sixties. He looked more like an academic than a member of the security service.

His voice was pedestrian. 'Operation Emerald is, as you all know, a counter terrorist operation geared mainly at preventing subversive organisations attacking specific sites. It's our job to take the fight to them, to search them out and bring them to justice. What we're looking at here is a total mobile shutdown, and to that end you will operate via base stations only, so all networks are coordinated. For much of the time you will be dealing directly with a specialist signals unit.'

He paused to look up through his reading glasses before continuing. 'The kidnapping of politicians is a strategy that's been mainly seen in the Middle East until now, and only until quite recently I might add. Now it's increasingly being employed in British cities to undermine confidence in the security services. We have to deploy units to target this strategy, and we therefore require TSU to be fully on board with us. This calls for a new kind of leadership, and I do not mean by the politicians.' There was a ripple of laughter through the audience of around twenty chiefs drawn from the various security services.

He continued, slightly raising his voice. 'The essence of leadership should, in many respects, be like any other. That is to take disparate people and forge them into one force, whether for fighting, logistics or otherwise. And that is what these networks have been good at doing themselves in recent months.

'In general, the security services are failing, as there hasn't been a decent counter-initiative. At least not one that could help galvanise the rest of the country against the networks. The public out there generally regard us as being part of the problem, as we are seen as being solely on the side of an unpopular government. Don't forget, the public know that successive governments have spent hundreds of billions of their pounds on failed wars and conflicts, some of them apparently illegal. They are not in the mood to forgive.'

He paused to drink water before continuing. 'However, our job is not to protect the politicians from public scrutiny. Our job is to protect the public. That means we do not intervene unless we have to. If certain politicians are being arrested and detained, as they could be deemed criminals themselves, then we may have to stand aside in order to protect the peace. That may be difficult for some of you to get to grips with. But this may be the only way of defusing situations, as if we don't allow such actions then we will become targets ourselves. Right now, we don't have enough allies out there on the streets.' Those assembled remained in silence for a few seconds and then there was a ripple as they discussed what had been said.

Commander Aley then got up and left abruptly. He headed for the TSU briefing room in another office in Westminster. From there his broadcast would be seen by specialist units across the country. He gave a cut-down version of the same briefing but leaving aside some of the more controversial content.

Afterwards, in a break-out area at their HQ, Jake looked at Chris and said quietly, 'If only my mates from my old regiment could hear this right now.'

Chris tried to control his grin but couldn't. They then poured themselves coffee and took a sandwich each. They were just about to start a long night shift.

Another member of Chris's team, Jeff, a Scouser, came over.

'What was all that about? I mean we've had some dodgy briefings but that one was just taking the piss.'

Jake replied, 'Jeff, didn't you ever have poor briefings when you were a soldier?'

'Yeah: come to think of it. Well, we had O groups and all that in Iraq and Afghan. But they told us the opposite. Anyone who threatened us in any way was a potential target. We had to use our honest belief and all that in order to win the conflict. But they said we would win in the end. Commander Aley seemed to be telling us that the rioters and criminals out there are possibly right, and that we should go easy at times. And that the politicians are all bastards. Maybe times are changing quicker than I thought.'

'To be honest I think Commander Aley has a point.' Chris interjected. 'We're alone now in the middle of all this crap. There is no system anymore. We should all remember that when we're aiming our weapons at potential targets. We're on the streets of our own country here, and we can't mess up.'

Jake looked out the window. His own experiences as a soldier in Afghanistan, Iraq and the Balkans had left him with a deep dislike of politicians, but he had always respected his fellow soldiers and commanders in the field. The time he had spent in such challenging environments had been the right thing to happen to him at that time in his life. However, this conflict within the UK was now the wrong experience at the wrong time, as he had no interest in the carping politicians. There were no real objectives, just more failed policies and violence as a direct result of an incompetent political establishment. He looked at Chris and Jeff and closed his eyes.

~~~

Three hundred people had crammed into the disused commercial site near Turnpike Lane, north London. Most were drawn from diverse organisations that had decided to work together in order to coordinate militant activities against the government. For many there was something surreal about sitting next to former political enemies, but at the same time entirely logical.

Above the sound of the crowd Brandon Sinclair asserted his presence. 'Welcome to everyone here. Let me start by saying that our collective actions are now prevailing because the government is weak and, above all, Britain is basically bankrupt. The entire political and economic system is collapsing, and ordinary citizens are coming over to our side now. For them we're already the difference between law and order in many parts of the country. Only a small percentage could even be bothered to vote at the last election, so there's no longer any confidence in the politicians.'

Ches was reclining near to the back. He had decided to go along having seen a small poster about the meeting in a café that morning. It intrigued him and he had little else to do.

Sinclair continued. 'All the time we hear the politicians, both left and right, talk as if they're in a bubble. All they've ever done is to rape this country, selling off the nation's assets, giving all the profits to corrupt middlemen and corporate entities who creamed off all the wealth. Ladies and gentlemen, now's the time to take it back, to overthrow this rotten regime, and deal with those inside it once and for all.'

There were loud cheers as Sinclair paused to take a drink of water before continuing. 'But this will be the first year of a new era. This is *Year One* comrades.'

Near the back, Declan stood beside a column that was located on one side, giving him an oblique view across the gathering. As he scanned the area, a small camera attached to the top of his jacket moved with his gaze, taking images of the people in front of him. He had been approached by the TSU to carry out surveillance, based on a recent government initiative to allow former soldiers to work directly for the security services once they had been given security clearance. The camera had been provided by Chris Kane. As he turned, he suddenly made out out Ches's features and concentrated on him for a few seconds. He made a mental note that he had seen his old mate from his days as a soldier.

Meanwhile, Ches was mulling over what he had read in the newspaper that morning. The celebrity, whose house he and Becker had robbed, had announced that he was leaving the country. However, he hadn't so far revealed the fact that he had been robbed. Ches muttered quietly under his breath; *I bet that bastard had a lot more hidden away.* He then also recalled what Becker had
~~~

said a few days before, *If you want my advice mate, don't stick your cash in a bank just yet. Convert it into dollars. I heard rumours that the pound is going to be devalued.*

The speaker continued, stating that parts of the media were actively calling for the arrest of senior politicians for a range of crimes. He stated that nearly all politicians now lived in guarded communities unable to go anywhere and were effectively under house arrest. There were loud cheers from the area around Ches and Declan. He then encouraged those assembled to gather in more disenfrachised people to support the ultimate cause, the overthrow of the hated establishment.

At the end of the meeting Declan followed Ches at some distance to the exit. He then saw a man confront Ches momentarily, with Ches pushing past to get out of the building. Declan also forced his way out and followed Ches for a short while until breaking off and turning back.

Declan's only reason for attending the meeting was to see if he could spot potential militant commanders, as Chris Kane had specifically requested him to do so. His specialist training, dating back to his time spent working covertly in Northern Ireland, meant it was easy for him to blend in with everyone else. He was not so surprised that so many people were at such a meeting, as he knew there was widespread disillusionment amongst the general population.

Once the place had emptied the doors were locked and one of the speakers got up and lifted several automatic rifles out of a container. The man was addressing the small number who had stayed behind. They didn't seem to notice Declan as he stood by the door and assumed the posture of a guard.

'If I could have your attention, please,' Sinclair requested politely. 'We need to stop talking and start acting. Those of you still here will be assigned as area commanders and you will be responsible for taking over local command. You will soon be shouldering these weapons.'

Declan had noticed that most of the people left were dressed in matching blue-grey outfits that appeared to have a light combat DPM. One such man, standing at the back, then revealed a lot more holdalls behind a row of stacked benches. He then talked for ten minutes, going over weapons drills. When it was obvious that the meeting was finally over, Declan exited and walked to the outside street and then into a side street. He kept walking and within a minute he was on the phone to the Tactical Support Unit control room, *Chris Kane, please.*

As he waited, he checked his camera to make sure that all the shots were clear. He didn't want to be accused of providing poor quality evidence. *Hi Chris, I think we need to meet.*

~~~
~~~

CHAPTER SIX

The guard drew near the heater, away from the autumnal wind sweeping in through the permanently open door of the guard hut. The government listening facility wasn't shown on any map of East Anglia, and it wasn't even referred to as an MOD site on any local road signs.

The guard was near the end of his shift, and he was looking forward to the comfort of his sleeping bag for the rest of the night. Another, positioned at the gate, stared blankly into the pitch-black night, his eyes never quite adjusting to the darkness as the light from the floodlights on the fence constantly dazzled his vision. He couldn't see the darkened figures moving through the surrounding forest. A CCTV monitor flickering inside the hut had momentarily shown the figures, but no one had looked up to check them.

An elongated white transit van pulled up outside the gates, and four men dressed in standard army combats stepped down. The guard stared through the narrow opening in the gate but couldn't see their faces as they seemed to be turned inwards. One of the men approached the gate. He showed his ID through the aperture and the guard pulled the gate open. The van drove in.

Then ten men burst through the gates. The guard was only able to notice that they were all carrying rucksacks. From within the group one man burst forward towards the guard with a silenced 9mm automatic pistol, shooting him in the shoulder. Another two sprinted forward, into the hut, overpowering the second guard. The bulk of the group then carried on towards the gates to the central control station inside the camp. Three men remained to secure the perimeter gate.

Meanwhile another van pulled up at the second perimeter gate one kilometre away on the outer road. The eight men demounted quickly and overpowered the guards. The two teams then converged on the four central control buildings, breaking through the inner set of gates to get to them. They then placed demolition charges on the four separate units of the intelligence facility. There were only three people inside and they were physically removed to a remote part of the site and tied up.

While the charges were being prepared most of the men made their way back to the two sets of outer gates, in their original formations, in case police units started appearing.

Once the charges were set, each with an allotted firing channel, all the attackers returned to the vehicles and sped off to a point overlooking the camp a couple of miles away. All that remained was for the man initiating the explosives to find the correct channels on the remote firing device, one for each building.

Several seconds elapsed between each explosion, creating shockwaves up the hillside. Human nature would prevent anyone in the vicinity from venturing out for a few minutes. That gave the two vans time to speed off towards a clearing in woodland eight miles away where everyone transferred to other vehicles.

~~~

'Watch out mate; that stuff will make you dump like an elephant.' Chris ignored Jake's expert observation and continued to pile chilli sauce onto his kebab. They were in their unmarked vehicle, a black Vauxhall Insignia, staring at a house fifty metres away on the other side of the Bayswater Road. The trees lining the street were dense with summer foliage so as to obscure their view of the house. Moreover, the small area of window they could see was blacked out by thick curtains. After another hour had passed two men left the house and started walking slowly up the street towards central Bayswater, away from Chris and Jake.

'Jake mate we're on. You jump out and then I'll follow you.'

'No probs Chris,' Jake stated clearly as he checked his UHF radio and stepped out of the vehicle.

Chris eased the brake, and the car moved off, his right hand brushing his holstered gun as it came up to adjust his sunglasses. When they were ten metres behind the men Chris slowed the car.

'You are getting me, Jake?' Chris asked under his breath into the small transmitter.

'What's that, mate?' Jake replied as he sped up to get closer to the two men as they walked towards along the pavement.

'Radio check.'

'Check Chris, we're on.' Jake was moving swiftly, and it was clear the two men were heading for the underground station.

Chris, I'm going for a ride.'

'OK mate, I'll hang back and stay near the house again. Just check out what they're up to and don't overstretch yourself.'

'Will do.'

~~~

Ches and Becker were walking up Brick Lane towards the junction with Bethnal Green Road. Ches could see that Becker was slightly agitated and remained silent as they walked.

Becker was the first to break the gloom, quietly. 'Ches, I just want to make some cash. We're doing OK, but we don't want to screw ourselves in the process.

'I agree Becks,' Ches replied softly.

'I'm thinking of getting away, out of this area, to somewhere safer for a while. But only if push comes to shove mate.'

'Do you think things are getting out of control?'

'I just get a feeling that we need to go a bit slower. There's a lot of stuff happening right now.'

'Yeah, but we're doing OK.'

'I wouldn't bet on it.'

'We aren't terrorists. We've just robbed a few worthless bastards.'

'Whatever. I don't want to get caught. I've got other stuff to think about now. To be honest, mate, we've plenty of cash. I wouldn't mind just pissing off abroad right now.'

'Well, that's OK for you mate. I'm worried about my own family; my mum's getting on. She hasn't got anyone but me and my brother. We have to stay here whatever happens.'

'You got a point, but there is another way of looking after your loved ones if everything falls apart.' They stopped walking and looked obliquely down the road as they stood outside a shop.

'Yeah, what's that?' Ches asked.

'Get heaps of cash and go away. Go somewhere there isn't anything happening.'

'That's OK if you've got somewhere to go.' Ches paused. He reflected for a moment and then continued. 'Actually, I have to be fair; Ireland, seeing as we're from Galway.'

'Lucky you mate,' Becker replied. 'You'd better get ahead of the stampede.'

'There's been enough Irish in England over the decades so why not a few English over there? It's safe so why don't you come as well. After all we've a lot of cash stashed away. It'll do just as well in an Irish bank. We could lie low there. Get your girl to come over as well.'

'I don't know Ches. I'll think about it.' Becker paused. 'But it's time to start thinking about these things mate. This place may be going down the tubes. Let's take what we can and bugger off, while we can still walk out of here with it all.'

~~~
~~~

'Sorry Chris, I lost them near Victoria. They must have jumped in a taxi.' Jake was on his radio outside Victoria Station.

'It's OK we'll get the CCTV and find where they went,' Chris replied. 'We'll get uniform to do it.'

'Anyone turn up at the address?'

'Nah, I think it's just them there. I'll get a team in when the boss gives us a thumbs up. What we really need is weapons, any explosives or detonators. We know they're up to something, but we need a link to some of the stuff that's happening.'

'I heard they made several arrests after the raid on that place in north London a few weeks back. Some things were traced.'

'Yeah, but only clothing and equipment that was dumped. They will still have all the weapons they took. There's probably enough forensics on the stuff. But it'll take some time.'

'I know. It's not something we have much of.'

'Oh well, the next team is coming. Get back here. We'll need to brief them.'

~~~

'Excuse me, mate.' The hand was large and clumsy as the man pushed past Declan and then headed down into the cargo hold. The ferry was fast approaching the dock and, ever since boarding at Stranraer, Declan had been close to passing out. He had hardly slept at all in three days. The previous week he had been briefed more times than he could remember and then taken on as a full-time operative by the Tactical Support Unit. He was now heading to west Belfast to check on a group of suspected militants.

To the intelligence services it had been obvious that the assailants who had recently attacked several military installations had known precisely when and where to go once inside the various establishments. It was only a matter of time before those who had fed information to any groups involved would be tracked down, and that included former enemies of the British based in Northern Ireland.

Declan had been briefed that there was a likely connection with a group in west Belfast. As the ferry docked, he wondered how, having left the British Army years before, he was now working for the security services in a part of the world he thought he had left behind a long time ago.

'You can check out but never leave,' he muttered to himself. 'Jeez, maybe I should just jack this in before I get too deep.' He thought of his son and his ex-wife. If anything was to happen to him, he wondered if they would ever know.

The dock was a place he recognized, and it was somewhere he had never wanted to go back to. And until now he had not. Going back to work
~~~

undercover felt like failure. He thought of some of the people he had helped put away in the past and the fact they had all since been released. 'I wouldn't be surprised if I get slotted out here.'

~~~

Ches was wandering along the back streets towards the centre of Brixton having stayed at his mum's flat near Loughborough Junction for a few days. His ultimate destination was a pub on Acre Lane. In terms of making prior arrangements, she was ahead of him and had already made plans to go and stay in the Irish Republic with one of her three sisters for a few months. It was somewhere he hadn't been for many years.

Ches had joined the British Army in 1994 and the fact that he had relatives from the Irish Republic meant that he had been required to have security clearance. He knew the MOD had run background security checks on him and had kept track of his whereabouts especially when he had been visiting the Irish Republic. Like all other serving personnel at the time, he had to inform the military whenever he visited his relatives there. However, while there had never been a problem with visiting back then, he wondered if his name was still on a file somewhere.

Soldiering was the only thing he had wanted to do when he was a child and since he had left the military, he had felt empty. But it felt somewhat ironic that if his personal records were still on file from his time as a soldier they could now be used to track him down for any recent illegal activities, what with joining Becker on his latest nocturnal crime wave. It also felt odd that he could now be seeking refuge somewhere abroad in his late thirties. He never really wanted to leave London.

And then there was the money. His best bet, while the banks were still functioning, was to set up a new account in a bank abroad, perhaps with his mother as power of attorney. That way they would at least have access to money and shouldn't run into any financial problems. But then again, he could just take a load of cash and live abroad for a while. As he walked, he resolved to rethink the whole thing through. His mobile phone went off.

'Yeah, it's Ches. Who's that?'

'It's Craig. You remember me from the meeting the other week?'

'How did you get my number?' He recalled the man and the fact he had tried to get him to stay behind and join the gathering. He also recalled the sneering expression on the man's face, the main reason he had ignored him and walked out of the building. He suddenly felt a bolt of fear run through his body.

'One of your friends gave it to me. I have a little proposition for you.'
~~~

'To be honest I'm going abroad soon, and I don't know when I'll be back.'

'This would only require a short period of time. It's just looking after something for us. You'll get paid for it.'

'What sort of stuff?'

'How about we meet up later today? I can tell you all about it then. Meet me at seven at Streatham Hill Station.'

Ches had little or no intention of doing anything for the man, but he reasoned that he had nothing to lose and could use some more cash. He did in fact want to do another job with Becker but there wasn't anything on the horizon.

'Ok Craig, I'll be there.'

~~~

The man in grey-blue combat clothing was sitting on the floor as he stripped and cleaned an AKM automatic rifle. He was training a group of thirty people in weapons. 'Make sure you follow the sequence as I've shown you. Remember the safety catch is also the fire selector; unload the weapon before cleaning and ensure the weapon is safe, with the safety in the up position before it's cleared. Always hand a weapon only when it is clear to another person, as we don't want any accidents.'

Brandon Sinclair moved around the outside of the group. It was largely made up of those who had been on the fringes of the movement but had recently decided to respond to the problems created by the economic and political meltdown. He viewed the weapons instructor as having a critical role within his organisation, listening intently as the man put the weapon back together, explaining the simplicity of the mechanism and how superior it was to most other weapons.

When he had finished Sinclair assembled the group and started a briefing. 'Don't believe a word the politicians tell you. Look at the track record of all British governments; they've done nothing for the working classes. Those clowns in power are screwing the country just as they've been doing for decades - so this is the time to kick all these corrupt idiots out and get some decent people into power. People need real work, not just jobs in fast-food outlets, and that means proper paid jobs leading to decent lives and proper careers. This is what this fight is about; building a decent society.'

The group listened to what he was saying and took in every word as they cleaned and oiled the weapons. Sinclair intended those present to become commanders of small groups of militants themselves. He knew that it didn't matter that much to anyone what politics actually meant. Many of those present became unemployed after being thrown onto the economic scrapheap
~~~

in recent years. Where the money would actually come from to pay their theoretical wages in the future wasn't a question Sinclair cared to ask, but for now they seemed motivated enough.

For him it was the political result that mattered more than anything else. It was something that had to succeed; *Otherwise, none of this will be worth the effort.* They would be the ones who would inherit the future they were about to fight for, and no one would be able to take that from them once it was all over.

~~~

'Forget about the information you've been given Declan. It's like all the old information; irrelevant.' Declan was sitting in an empty café near the entrance to Queens University, Belfast, chatting to Cathal, the last of his old contacts. He was a man in his late fifties, pale, stocky and red-faced with a deep scar under his left cheekbone. He had seen more than his fair share of violence, political or otherwise.

'It serves no real purpose other than fiction. You see once a story passes through more than one person it gets changed, embellished, embroidered and it becomes just that: a story, nothing else. And that is precisely what we have here; just a story.'

'So, what are we actually looking at then?'

'I don't actually know Dec. Anyhow you've leaned on me too many times in the past so why're you coming back here again to pester me?'

'I know these people are involved in something; and you know they're involved as well.'

Cathal struggled to keep his voice down. 'Do you want the bad old days back again? Do you really want that? Because that's where this is going.'

'They already have the bad old days back again, on the mainland.'

'Screw England! I mean it. We've had it quite peaceful here the last two decades and I'm not going to be the one to ruin that for the younger generation. Screw the English and let the corrupt bastards in power die. Let the militants kick their fat, worthless arses. They've had it coming and you won't find anyone here from any walk who would tell you any different Declan. They'll get what they deserve, right, they will.'

Declan finished his tea and got up to go. 'You know where I am.'

~~~

As the selected members of the security services took their seats, a uniformed general from the Joint Chiefs of Staff of the Armed Forces, took the pen from his mouth and began speaking. 'You should all know who I am, General Brydon to those of you who don't. What I'm about to tell you is not to go beyond these walls, ladies and gentlemen. I mean that emphatically. So, if you do conceal an interest in leaking this information then think again.

When you hear the statistics, you start to begin to understand the situation. Suffice to say that the political establishment has reduced the Armed Forces from 250,000 in the late 1990s to around 160,000 now including all three services. That's not enough to control our own streets let alone someone else's. They have quite literally been playing roulette with our security and we're all paying for it. Moreover, we have large numbers of young people who've been denied opportunities in life and are therefore turning to either organised crime, militant activity, or both.'

He paused, sipped from a glass of water and looked up at those assembled before continuing. 'Do you know why they're doing this? I'll tell you why, because it pays, because there's nothing else for them. We aren't sitting on a powder keg any more, as the keg has already exploded and we're all being thrown skywards. We're the ones who are supposed to be keeping the peace but that can't be done. This is all down to the collective failure of our politicians, some of whom deliberately committed criminal acts and should therefore be brought to justice. I will remind you of one thing; *we are not here to protect them.*'

One of the security service chiefs interjected, 'Are you saying we should leave them to the militants?'

'No, I'm not saying that. But as far as we're concerned some of our so-called leaders stand accused of committing war crimes. After all they started wars that have created the biggest refugee crisis in our history and more militants on our streets than at any time in living memory, and then they still try to blame everyone else. I can see a time when we'll all be involved in bringing them to justice. That time is nearly upon us.'

'But our job is to restore order,' a female chief replied.

'What we need is someone with an ounce of leadership to come along and restore the balance in this country in the long term. And that's what ordinary people want. They want us to protect them because they're afraid. That's our job isn't it; to restore a balance, to serve the public and re-create some kind of status quo?' There was a murmur of approval from around the room to the general's question.

He looked around the table. 'Have you considered that the lives of many ordinary people are being torn apart by insecurity, crime and corruption, every minute of every day of every week? And what do the BBC and the media report? That it's the militants who're responsible, when we all know the real responsibility for the failure to govern rests with the politicians. They've allowed these communities of hate to grow as a direct result of their failed policies. We'll have to restore order on our streets, whilst calming nerves and explaining to them that we're on their side and not that of the failed authorities. But we may have to make some kind of deal with the militants. That's how these things actually work. Not through propping up tired regimes that have had their day.'

A chief of security interrupted, 'General, we'll have to be damned careful not to create confusion about who we order our personnel to go after. Many ordinary people are simply out to protect their families and property and quite frankly they will have to, as we have nothing like enough people for that job amongst all the others we have to do. We're no longer a thin blue or red line but an opaque one.'

'I agree. But where we can, we'll make a difference and gradually we'll turn this around. I say this to all of you: do not lose faith even if it looks like we're losing this country.'

An intelligence chief interjected. 'I know what you mean general, but we're not going to have an easy time of it are we? This isn't just a military coup that we're talking about. We are facilitating the end of an entire political establishment.'

'No, it isn't a coup,' General Brydon replied. 'It's just an extension of ongoing operations against terrorism and failed states. You thought your tours of duty in the Middle East were the end of it, but they weren't, they were just the beginning. We will lose this country unless we adopt this approach. This is about regime change. Nothing else will work.'

~~~

Ches walked up to the entrance of Streatham Hill station and nodded at Craig who stood just inside the ticket area. Craig then turned on his heel and gestured for Ches to follow him. The two men then crossed the main road and walked up the hill opposite the station.

'So, what's this small business you have for me then?'

'It's a delivery. When we get to where I want, I'll show it you.'

They crossed a few more streets and then turned left down a side road, towards some old garages.

'My lockup's down here.'

Ches didn't say a word and just followed Craig as he lifted an old garage door and went under. He pulled the door down behind them and then opened a few boxes, revealing a number of handguns in the dim light of the garage.

'So, what's it you want me to do with these exactly?' Ches asked nervously.

'Distribute them?'
~~~

'Where, exactly?'

'We'll let you know.'

Ches now realised that he had seen too much and couldn't walk away easily. At the same time, he didn't want anything to do with what he was looking at.

'Not so sure about this. I don't have the contacts to do this.'

'You don't need contacts. We'll sort that out. You just deliver.' Craig paused and picked up one of the pistols, his hands gloved. 'As a test you can take this to the address and person on this note.' Craig handed the piece of paper to Ches.

Ches held the note in front of him. He knew the name on it, that of Barry Ledcot, a Mancunian living in Stockwell. Barry was someone he had bumped into in local bars, and his nickname was Daffy. He was well known mainly because of the activities of his brother Dave.

Daffy had been a face in the area for a couple of years, but Ches had always been wary of him. On a few occasions Becker had helped Daffy fence the odd item. Daffy and Dave had a cousin serving life for a contract killing a few years before. It was common knowledge around South London.

Daffy was a simple man of twenty-nine years but had a mental age of less than fifteen. However, he had a knowledge of the streets that was impressive. For Ches he was precisely the sort of person who should never own a weapon of any kind. However, it was the same reason why Craig wanted to make sure that Daffy would receive one, because he could be manipulated and controlled easily.

'I not only want you to get this to Daffy: I want you to show him how to use it properly. We've some jobs for him and this is important Ches.'

Craig knew that Ches had served in the British Army. He also knew that Ches cared a bit about people like Daffy and that he would try to make sure he wouldn't kill himself or anyone else for that matter. But it was too much to ask as far as Ches was concerned.

'I'll buy it off you Craig; along with all that ammo.'

'No way: this is the deal. You take it to Daffy. Daffy's my man now, you get me?'

Ches could sense the evil in Craig's voice and decided to play along with him. 'OK Craig; I'll get it to him.'

'And there's a neat *Oner* in it for you, once we know he's safe with it. You read me bruv?'

Ches nodded but a cold shock traversed his body into the pit of his stomach. Craig unfurled a bundle of cash. 'Two hundred now, and we'll let you know 'bout the rest.'

'Make it two fifty Ches. I'm a bit skint mate.'

'OK my man,' Craig replied eagerly. 'We look after our boys.' He was quietly relieved that Ches had seemingly accepted the deal. He unfurled some more notes and gave them to Ches.

'I'll take it over later.'

'No, you won't, you do it now bruv.'

Craig bundled the weapon into a holster and then into a small rucksack Craig had provided along with the ammunition. The two walked out of the garage and after Craig had locked up, they walked towards a rusty old VW Golf parked ten metres away.

Thirty minutes later Craig dropped Ches by a block of flats in Stockwell. 'As I told you pal, make sure he knows what to do with it. We'll do the rest. OK?'

Ches nodded and walked towards the block.

~~~

Declan was walking through Belfast's Ormeau Park on the way to a park bench, one that he had chosen for the meet. The informant's name was Robbie.

'Good to see you Declan, where've you been? I haven't seen you for ages?'

'The USA, Scotland, England. Usual places.'

'What're you up to now?'

'Well, believe it or not, I'm doing paid work here; just not the kind where you sit behind a desk,' Declan replied sardonically.

'Hope it's interesting.'

'If I told you you'd die of boredom anyway.'

Robbie stared ahead and nodded. Declan spoke clearly. 'What I need is to get some heads up on various people you already know about. I can't tell you why exactly, as it's an ongoing business. I'm sure you've guessed that already.'

'OK Dec: that I can handle. But the unrest in England is getting out of hand. That's the reason you're here isn't it, or at least something along those lines?'

Declan nodded and stared ahead.

Robbie added, 'Don't forget Declan that I know one of the reasons we're here is to try and help sort out all the crap that's going down. But I wouldn't assume anything where I'm concerned.'

Declan was slightly surprised at the statement and paused before he replied. 'I know that, Robbie. Do you think I don't know that?'

Robbie ignored Declan's question and carried on. 'So, what is it - the small matter of certain politicians who've gone missing? Or tracing some weapons?'

'No one gives a damn about the politicians. It's irrelevant. I'm here to trace a network. That's it.'
~~~

'Think again Dec. You're probably looking in the wrong place. You think it's something to do with Belfast or whatever; but it's not. Look, most people from these parts are just hired hands these days doing dirty work for someone else. It's all just part of the economics Declan.'

Declan smiled and couldn't see the point of talking any further if Robbie didn't know anything. He knew that there wasn't much hope of getting a good lead anyway. He stared blankly across the park.

Robbie was slightly bemused at the leaden silence. 'So, come on Dec; what are you really doing here? I thought you said once you'd never come back.'

'Maybe it's unfinished business Robbie. You might be able to help if you can keep your mouth shut for long enough. I'll find you if I need you. Thanks for coming today.' Declan stood up, turned sharply away from the bench and walked off, the dry heat stinging his face in the bright autumn sunshine.

~~~

'So, is he still claiming to be Brandon Sinclair?' Chris looked up from the folder on the table and smiled at the attending officer and the duty solicitor. 'He had us on the go for a while, as we all thought he was genuine until the DNA finally turned up. We thought at first, he was just being quiet, but he genuinely doesn't speak much English.' Chris laughed and turned to the man sitting next to the duty solicitor. 'Good likeness though. You were selected well weren't you mate; threw us all off the scent you did.' Chris stared at the man in front of him and then nodded at the glazed screen, with Jake on the other side.

'So, we know who you aren't, but not who you are. And quite frankly we don't give a damn as it's of no interest to us. That you were once active in various parts of Afghanistan and may have been involved in street bombings in India over the last few years may be the case. By the way, the Indians share their DNA. How nice of them! But it's not our concern right now. We're going to send you back to the Middle East as we have some friends there who can deal with you.'

At that the solicitor went into overdrive. 'I'm sorry, officer, but that won't do.'

'He'll be going under the new legislation. There's no argument about it.' Chris paused and looked at the man again.

In a lowered tone Chris continued. 'We don't even want a confession as we have enough evidence, but we do need some names and we're going to get them. Even if it's the last thing we have to drag out of him it'll be names. Every single one. But for now, we're sticking your man back in the cells.'
~~~

The solicitor shook his head, replying, 'Not unless you have a very good reason for that. My client is walking free and there's nothing you can do about it.'

'Do you read the news every morning Mr?'

'Creasey. Daniel Creasey. Why?'

'Because if you had you'd see that the government has approved unlimited detention periods for the foreseeable future; as of now.'

'We'll see about that.'

'Good day, Mr Creasey.'

A few minutes later Jake and Chris were in a custody suite with coffee and chocolate bars.

Jake stuttered, 'I never thought they'd work that guy out. It's obvious now. He was never Sinclair in the first place. He genuinely didn't understand a damned thing we were asking him.'

'He certainly fooled me!' Chris replied dejectedly.

'I mean he's a ringer for the man.'

Chris sipped his coffee and then replied caustically, 'Well we certainly wasted some days on this guy, thinking he was the big man. How many more decoys will there be?'

'I remember one time I had to guard Taleb fighters in Bastion and some of them looked like westerners. If you took their clothes off and put them in jeans and taught them a few things Britsih they would've got away with it.'

'Yeah; that's because some of them were Jake,' Chris laughed. 'But you know some of these people trained with the IRA in the desert years ago, and it's been going on for decades, so it's not difficult to see a few of them trading identities.'

'But we still don't know much about the structure of the network, do we Chris?'

'No, but we do have a few aces up our sleeves. We got a few possible plants ourselves.'

~~~

Ches and Becker were dressed in black, with balaclavas pulled tight over their heads. They let their mini headlamps dangle round their necks, turned them off until they needed them. They cut an opening in the fence surrounding the mansion and then ran across the open ground to the external walls of the heavily timbered edifice. The night sky was bright enough to plainly see the upper window they had targeted as a point of entry. As there were no cars in the drive, they figured the owners were away. They had already seen that there was no CCTV on the outside.
~~~

Ches climbed up the side of the house. Only a few days before, he had looked at street views of the exterior and worked out where the best footholds were located. He pushed up the sash window and climbed into the large upstairs bathroom. He guessed there was no PIR or security alarm in that area. He then secured a rope around the radiator and dropped the rest to the ground outside. He placed his headlamp on his forehead and then turned it on. Becker soon followed, with a small bag of tools.

Ches had briefed Becker about how he thought the place was laid out and where the main alarm panel would be located. He slid out of the bathroom around the partially opened door, along the upstairs corridor, and found the panel at the top of the stairwell. He then disarmed it and looked around. There didn't appear to be any independent PIR systems, but he checked anyway.

He then found the master bedroom. His enquiries had shown that a company had installed safes in the area over the previous five years. Normally they were set inside bedroom walls, especially where people were retrofitting ensuite bathrooms.

Ches made his way back to the bathroom and he and Becker then waited to see if they could hear any movement in the rest of the house. There was nothing.

Becker whispered, 'Any idea where the safe is Ches?'

'Down the corridor; follow me.'

He slowly opened the door to the full width and poked his head out; nothing could be heard. They groped their headlamps, pointing them downwards, and made their way slowly down the corridor.

Once inside the master bedroom Ches found the safe and then went to work on the mechanism. After several minutes it was open. Inside they found around thirty bundles of fifty-pound notes and three bags of gems as well as a large manila envelope. They bagged it all and made their way back to the bathroom where they had made their entry. Becker, with the bag of tools over one shoulder, slid down the rope and onto the gravel. Ches untied the rope, dropped it out of the window and then climbed down the outside the same way he had climbed up. They put the rope in the tool bag.

They had just got to the tree line when a large saloon car pulled up at the entrance. They slipped through the hole in the fence. Hearing laughter coming from the house they knew that it would only be a short while before someone would discover the robbery. They crossed through the woods following the Ordnance Survey map lit by Ches's head torch, now turned to red.

Both men moved quickly. The van was in a clearing near the road but partially hidden behind brambles. Once inside they sped off down the lane.

After thirty minutes they got to the secluded parking area where Ches's car was parked. Ches got into his car, and they then drove separately through the Northamptonshire countryside along different roads towards the A1.

~~~

'People need answers as to why their social, economic and political systems have been wrecked by corrupt governments over the last fifty years. The politicians have squandered all our collective wealth, and now is the time to take it back.' The tall, hirsute man was addressing the crowd of demonstrators in Clissold Park, Hackney. In his early thirties, he had recently organised demonstrations against various political targets. As a result, he had been put under surveillance by the security services.

Chris Kane's undercover operative was a young newcomer to the TSU called Elaine. She seemed to be enjoying her alias as Jan, a first-year medical student. She shouted louder than anyone else and had already caught the eye of the young demagogue. As soon as his speech was over, he came over to greet her.

'Hi; I thought I'd seen you before but forgot your name?'

Elaine smiled as she replied, jokingly, 'Why do you want to know, are you following me?'

'If you want me to then yep, I'm following you. Maybe I can buy you a drink along the way?'

After sleeping with him all night, and several fake orgasms, she had all the information she needed from him by the morning. That included the names of all his associates, their hideouts, organizations, and even the foreign powers that were backing their activities. Chris and Jake knew she wouldn't blow her cover, but they stayed nearby just in case, as the surveillance car had tracked the happy couple from a local bar to the charismatic insurrectionist's Islington flat.

Later that morning Elaine was feeling upbeat, despite the previous night's activities. She stepped into the front passenger seat of the unmarked TSU vehicle in Highbury Fields.

'You would never guess; he supports Palace!' Elaine stated, as she cradled a creamy, flat white, takeaway coffee given to her by Jake in the driver's seat. 'Isn't that a joke? It's my dad's team. A revolutionary! He's just another spoiled suburban prick.' Neither Jake nor Chis wanted to point out that she seemed to have been enervated by the previous day's exigencies.

She continued; her voice even louder, 'And another thing, his mother's got a big pile in Kent somewhere near Tunbridge Wells. If only the idiots buying his bull knew that!'
~~~

'Yeah, yeah Elaine,' Jake replied. 'We thought it'd go something like that.' Her youthful exhuberance had made him feel suddenly, and prematurely, middle-aged.

'These things usually get started by rich, jumped-up pricks,' Chris explained. 'Even the most ardent radicals are often just middle-class fakes, Che Guevara included.'

Elaine looked slightly confused, 'Who's that?'

Jake laughed as he sipped his takeaway coffee. He couldn't help smiling but he was secretly jealous of the fact the erstwhile revolutionary had bedded the young woman. He also didn't like the obvious conclusion that he and Chris now appeared to be more like protective uncles than specialist police officers.

Chris, from his position in the back seat, could sense that Jake was getting a bit green-eyed and changed the course of the conversation. 'Elaine, did he say anything about their latest activities? This is serious. We need to know as his comrades may have been dishing out pistols to kids.'

'All he said was that he was glad he wasn't an MP in Parliament. I thought it was a bit of an obvious comment.' Elaine's blank expression didn't help the situation.

'So, what does that mean exactly?' Jake asked, somewhat forcefully. 'Did he say anything else?'

'Nope, nothing much. He talked a bit about what they'd do if they got to be really powerful. But it sounded like bollocks really. Anyway, I got all the info you wanted. Didn't I?'

'Yeah, you did well Elaine, really well,' Chris stated loudly. 'You'll be off the gig for a while, but make sure you put everything in the report, including his address.'

'But he keeps texting me,' Elaine replied. 'Shouldn't we bring him in anyway?'

'No, tell him you're away for a while,' Chris replied. 'He can't do anything about that, and we'll take it from there.'

'OK, Chris.'

Jake sat back and stared at the street, before placing his coffee in a holder and turning the key in the ignition.

~~~
~~~

CHAPTER SEVEN

Declan sat in the hired Vauxhall Corsa looking at the side doors to the club, located in west Belfast. He had been there over an hour but to avoid suspicion had driven off and come back to the area a few times by different roads, just in case anyone had been employed to overwatch the street. He had been informed in an email sent the day before that the main suspect in the group liked to spend much of the day in this particular place, so Declan knew he was in for a long haul.

'When's this bastard going to show?' Declan had a 9 mm SIG P-228 pistol postioned under the car seat. The magazine was loaded. It had been provided courtesy of the security service.

'I really don't want this any more,' Declan muttered. 'Oh well, patience is a virtue and all that.'

He steadied himself with the knowledge that he would be getting paid handsomely, and that there weren't many other ex-servicemen who could do, or be relied upon to do, the task in hand. However, he also felt slightly guilty as, in order to cover his tracks, he had told Jez and Gavin that he was doing a short work contract in the Middle East.

'I'll do this job and then that's it.' Declan felt calmer, frowned slightly, and then carried on reading the newspaper. His role was only to report what he observed. He was not supposed to be following every move by the target. A second later the side door to the club opened and two men walked out. They got into a VW Passat and drove off.

Declan followed them at a distance for a couple of miles but then decided not to carry on. It was becoming too obvious, and his job wasn't to create security issues. He had plenty of video footage of the men, so he made for the safe house. It was obvious that he needed an extra pair of hands and eyes for the job and wasn't interested in what anyone else had to say on the matter. If the security services didn't want him to continue that was fine, as long as they paid him.

'How did I get back into all this crap?' he asked himself again over a cup of tea once he was back in the safe house. The answer came back swiftly: he had never been able to work regular hours in a regular job. Even working on building sites had been too structured for him.

'Maybe I'll get a job on a country estate somewhere. At least it'd keep me out of trouble and that would be more my scene anyway, with a shotgun. Life's not so bad, I've got an army pension. I just need a new start.'

He wondered how long he would have to stay in the province carrying out surveillance. He figured another week at most. His mind drifted back to the event, weeks before, when he had been on his first surveillance job for the TSU at the political meeting. He thought about his old army buddy Ches and what he was up to. 'What the hell was he doing there? How weird was that?' He was aware that Ches had probably seen him when he had stood by the main entrance door at the end of the meeting, pretending to be helping with security.

Could Ches be a member of the militant group? 'Nah: it's just not his style. But he's up to something else; no doubt about that.' Declan paused and sipped his tea. 'Maybe he was looking for a swift buck somehow.' And then a minute later, 'Those anarchists must be paying Ches to distribute weapons or something.'

~~~

'So, tell me again about these evil foreigners whose weapons you say you found in an alleyway.' Jake was questioning a teenage male who had been caught in possession of three small handguns. 'They're not the only ones who run guns and never give up their seats for old ladies or pregnant women. There's a bit more to it than that; isn't there? What part are you playing at, son?'

'Excuse me?' The duty solicitor looked coldly at Jake and Chris. 'My client should not be subjected to leading questions. If it happens again I will be going to the Police Complaints Commission, do you understand officer?'

'And what, exactly, can they do about it?' Chris looked coldly and blankly back at the legal aid, a grey-haired, overweight, middle-aged solicitor.

Jake smiled, continuing his questioning of the suspect, 'I want an answer; where do you fit in? Why are you supplying pistols to kids out there on the steets?'

The boy looked sheepishly around the walls. He had no idea what to do or say. He just stared at Jake.

The solicitor interjected again. 'That's irrelevant. My client has no proven relationship regarding organised crime.'

'I'm not suggesting he has a relationship with organised crime,' Jake replied. 'These guns are likely to be used for possible terrorist activities during which time innocent members of the public could be killed or seriously wounded. Do you understand that?'

'Officer; it really isn't relevant.' The solicitor's voice raised an octave.
~~~

'I'll tell you what's actually relevant,' Jake replied. Jake drew up his muscular frame in the chair and stared at the shaking solicitor. 'But in the meantime, don't get in the way; or you could be detained for perverting the course of justice.'

'Is that a threat officer?'

'No, it's a promise. We know where the goalposts are boy 'cos we put them there for a reason.'

Jake was from the West Country and habitually used the term *Boy* in conversation. But to Chris, who enjoyed hearing Jake say it, it always sounded hilarious.

Chris curtailed his smile and then motioned towards the solicitor, asking, 'You know I've never met a solicitor like you before. Where did you say you're from again?'

The man was now feeling subdued and fell silent at the smirking policemen. The fact that Chris's side arm was poking slighty out from under his jacket helped prevent any attempt at a quick retort.

'OK, let's get on with the questioning. We haven't got all day,' Chris asserted loudly.

'Thank you,' Jake replied loudly.

~~~

Ches and Becker had been staying several nights near Southwold, Suffolk, at the home of one of Becker's aunts, a formidable woman called Bella. They looked out of the kitchen window, and across the rolling countryside, as they ate breakfast.

'You know Becks, I enjoyed that one,' Ches said pointedly. 'It went really sweet and always nice to do over a rich bastard's place, especially if they're a politician.'

'Yeah, I was up for that one as well. Not a bad haul. What'll we do with the rocks?'

'Don't know, I'll check them out.'

Becker had no reason to doubt his friend, as over the past fifteen years Ches had never conned him, at least knowingly, out of a single penny.

'But Ches, that envelope. What was it exactly?'

'I don't really know. It looked like cash to me, that's why I took it. But actually, it was a bunch of documents. Someone's probably going to want them back.'

'What sort of docs?' Becker asked.

'Official ones. One was titled *Actions in the Event of Civil Emergency* and it's full of statistics.'
~~~

'But these days everything's on the computer.'

'This looks like it's about how many people the politicians will kill, if they have to, in the event of an insurgency. Or allow to be killed.'

'What do you mean?'

'What I said, they'll kill thousands if they have to deal with mass unrest and social upheaval. It's serious stuff. The newspapers would love to get hold of this. It's probably worth more than the actual gear.'

'Who could we sell it to?'

'No idea, but let's just keep hold of it for now.'

~~~

Jake and Chris had got all the names they needed, including some of those who had supplied the weapons. There were still some unaccounted for, based on the information they had gathered from the teenager, but Chris was confident his team would pick up the rest before they were used.

'These jokers are bloody amateurs anyway,' Jake exclaimed, as he thumbed through the file on the weapons.

'Are you sure about that Jake?' Chris replied.

'Yeah, I'm sure.'

'OK, but what about all these hits around the country? We don't know where they'll go next. Amateurs don't do that kind of thing. It looks like a network.'

'Yeah, all very well, but it's not this lot who're doing it. We don't know who it is yet, but this bunch of idiots aren't going anywhere except prison.'

'Well, I think some of these groups are connected. They may not have all met each other yet, but they move in similar circles. Remember *Smirnoff*; our middle-class revolutionary friend that Elaine got to grips with? Well, we've just brought him in. He thinks he made a name for himself.'

'He'll probably write his freaking memoirs next week,' Jake snorted.

'Yeah, and he'll have plenty of time for that while he's inside for ten years; for plotting terrorist offences.'

'Good riddance!' Jake stated. 'I suppose you're right in that there're a lot of groups out there and some of them know each other. They might share a bit of info even if they don't have the same aims.'

'True, but the only ones that really stump me are the occasional kidnappings. No ransom is ever asked for and no one knows where the people have gone. They could be dead for all we know.'

'Some of them probably are Chris, but I doubt they're being held in the UK anyway.'
~~~

'I guessed that much. They're probably all in some foreign hole I expect.'

'No, I suspect they're already dead. We shouldn't be pre-occupied with them. They are history, and therefore not important. Whoever took them got what they wanted: probably justice for what happened somewhere.'

'But there's a lead, as they all have one thing in common.'

'What's that then?'

'They were all once serving cabinet members, so there could be a link with some of these armed gangs if there's a political edge. There could even be some foreign outfit involved.'

'Yeah well, like I said, they probably deserve it.'

~~~

Ches had dropped the van off at a mate's garage on Green Lanes in Dagenham. It would now be scrapped and the parts sold or disposed of. The tyres would be taken to another yard and stuck in a pile with hundreds of others. Nothing could ever be traced.

He was still surprised at how well the job had gone, but also unsure as to what to do next. He knew that he was heading into a danger area, conscious of being a little too confident. He and Becker had accrued plenty of cash, and the latest jewellery would be fenced, but he didn't care what it all fetched, as long as they got a reasonable amount. He hated jewellery and just wanted to get rid of it, the only good thing being that stones and gems were easy to conceal and even easier to get rid of.

He had told Becker to go away with his girlfriend for a few days, while he sorted out the cash. Becker and Gail had taken a ferry to France in preference to taking Eurostar, or a flight, so it wouldn't look too flashy. Moreover, a holiday in France was never very obvious, at least not in mid-autumn.

He, on the other hand, just wanted to relax and avoid any potential hassle from overzealous police officers. Relaxation required time, and he intended to give himself as much as possible. However, he was also aware that so far, they had been lucky, as they had left no prints on anything and there had been no CCTV cameras involved. But it wouldn't always be like that. So, maybe now was the time to take a long break and re-evaluate.

And then there were the weapons he had taken to Daffy. He had been paid well for delivering the weapons and no one could trace them to him. But he still felt uneasy about it, and he knew that he should never have done it in the first place.

He tried to rationalise for his own benefit whether a firearm could really help resolve anything in life, but he couldn't see how it would. He reasoned that when he had been a soldier the weapon had gone with his job, in the way
~~~

a bricklayer uses a trowel, or a schoolteacher a pen. You couldn't get away from them and they just became part of everyday life. As a soldier you learned to live with weapons, all the time, and even sleep with them.

But now it would be a complete pain to try to conceal them, from just about everyone, and he wouldn't want to ever have to use one again. Just owning one was enough for someone to be sent to prison for years. He resolved to never provide another weapon as long as he lived. It was then that he thought of Declan.

He'd know what to do to stop everything that's going down. If I explain, he'll understand. I need to stop Daffy getting into trouble 'cos of that dickhead Craig.

He thought back to that night when Craig had bullied him into carrying the guns. 'What was I thinking? I must have been off my head going there.' But the thought of seeing Declan again filled him with confidence, even if it had only been at a distance. 'So, he's a doorman now. That makes sense; he's probably with a security outfit.'

He remembered that a few years after he had left the army he had met Declan in a pub in Islington. Declan had said that he would often be drinking there if he ever wanted to meet up for a chat. But that was over five years ago.

That night they had gone over their time as infantry soldiers serving in the Balkans when Ches had been little more than a recruit and Declan was already an old hand. It was Declan who'd got him through that freezing winter in Bosnia, living in an ISO container. They had also done a spell in Kosovo in 2001. By then Ches was a corporal, driver and signaler, and Declan was a warrant officer. For Ches it had been a great time, with loads of laughs, and something he would never forget.

Unlike what came later in Iraq, where both men had hit a wall; clearing body parts after IED blasts and generally not knowing whether they would make it home in one piece. Ches eventually left the army as a two-stripe corporal soon after his second tour in Afghanistan. His thirteen years as a soldier had at least got him a half-pension and some great memories. An officer had tried to get him to join the reserves, but he could never do that. It was all or nothing; the same for Declan who had left not long after Ches. Declan had been one of the main influences on his life. He'd know how to stop weapons hitting the streets.

~~~

Declan met up with a new agent, Stefan, who was sent over from London to help with information gathering. That evening they pulled up outside the
~~~

block under surveillance in west Belfast and Declan decided to have a brief look around under the cover of semi-darkness before entering.

Before getting out he gave a small camera to Stefan, stating, 'See if you can get this thing to work mate. You're obviously better than me at this kind of crap. If you see anyone you don't like, then take a shot. Send me a text if anyone comes along. My phone's on vibrate.'

He jumped out of the car and walked past the block of flats for a hundred metres. He then turned and walked briskly up to the block. The front door wasn't locked, and he went straight up to the flat under surveillance on the first floor. Listening at the door he heard nothing. Slipping on some thin latex gloves and a balaclava he took a slim metal plate and eased the lock of the door open, giving it a swift smack. The door sprang ajar, and he walked in. Checking his step at first, he looked around to sense the atmosphere. Realising there was no one there, he went to work. The tiny device fitted neatly under the coffee table, which luckily was made of wood and not clear glass.

He headed for some filing cabinets and, after checking the drawers, he then looked at a few financial documents, mainly bills and bank statements. The statements showed nothing other than some earnings, but no evidence of large payments to bank accounts. He took a few pictures of the statement details on his phone.

There were too many files to go through, but he flicked open a few. He placed a bug at the side of the cabinet and was taking some shots of the contents of a file when the phone vibrated in his pocket. He closed everything up and shot out of the flat, securing the lock. He then went up two flights of stairs and sat down on a landing near the roof access.

Two men approached talking too quickly to be comprehensible, Declan hearing only a muffled, 'Forget them is all I can say.'

Declan couldn't make out any more of the conversation as they went into the flat. However, he knew that the listening devices he had planted would probably give a clear enough account of whatever they were saying inside the flat.

He left it a couple of minutes and then walked swiftly down the stairs to the lobby, quietly opening and shutting the main door. He then got back to the car.

'Did you get them?' Stefan asked absent-mindedly whilst checking his phone.

'Yeah, no probs,' Declan replied.

'London's not wrong then.'

Declan wasn't interested in what the man sent over from the mainland had to say. As far as he was concerned, they would be doing things his way, or no way.

Stefan carried on playing with his phone, adding disinterestedly, 'Did you find much?'

'Not much: some contacts, names and dates. There were some boarding pass stubs as well. Anyway, let's get the hell out of here.'

At that point they saw a car pull up a hundred metres down the road near to the block. Stefan looked at Declan and gulped, 'They might have CCTV in there.'

'I'd have seen it. I checked the stairwells as well; nothing.'

'It's a trick dealers use a lot. Seen it in Leeds, Manchester, you name it.'

'OK, well I didn't see it here.' Declan was getting fed up with the man's questioning attitude. The occupants of the car stared down the road in their direction.

Declan added, 'Don't pull away just yet.' The way the streetlights were positioned there was no way the two men could tell if there was anyone in their car, as Declan had checked when he had walked down the street the first time and there was too much glare. The men got out and walked towards the entrance to the small block of flats. After they had disappeared inside the block Stefan reversed the car, slamming it round and pulling away much too quickly.

'Look mate it's not bloody Miami Vice. Do you understand what I'm saying?'

'Yeah: sorry. I'll go a bit easier.'

Declan felt like hitting the agent. He'd give him the slip as soon as possible. The best route for him was to go to the airport that evening and take the first flight, anywhere.

~~~

'Be very careful. I'm in a gestation period.' Jake raised his right eyebrow as he spoke.

'That sounds painful,' Chris replied, but didn't look up from the newspaper. Instead, he lifted his coffee mug towards his face.

'I'm only quoting what my pregnant missus said to me last night. I mean what am I supposed to do? She's going ballistic at times.'

'Don't know mate; although mine's going to be exactly the same.'

'How many weeks?'

'I don't keep count pal.'

'Jeez! Don't say that to her, whatever you do. Just don't.'

Jake and Chris shook their heads as Commander Aley walked into the briefing area. Aley spoke first, 'Sorry, I didn't realise you ladies have some kind of mid-morning brunch going on here, but please don't let me intrude.'
~~~

'It's really quite OK sir; really it is,' Chris stated a little too politely.

'Oh, that's a bloody relief,'Aley replied with a grin on his broad, red face. The sound of the man swearing surprised both Chris and Jake, although neither showed it.

'Well, it looks like your man, Declan, has done us a favour. He's found us some useful leads in Northern Ireland. He got into a flat and found some evidence that some suspects have been going to the Middle East regularly.'

'Where is he now, sir?'

'He's back in London but gave us the brief earlier today. Apparently, he's not happy with the agent who was sent out there. I agree with him. He has contacts and doesn't need any rookies with him. It's not on, and I'm having words with a few people.'

Aley turned and walked out.

Jake smirked and said quietly, 'Like it matters.'

'Well, it does to that guy,' Chris replied.

~~~

'England is a sterile, suburbanised, sanitised country where media and state control is everything – where control has to be everything, as the country is only ever one step away from implosion. But the truth is that the politicians do not hold any real power any longer.' Brandon Sinclair was psyching up his inner circle, in what he called his war cabinet in the office of a disused Croydon warehouse. His aim was to get them ready to lead some real urban fighting against the government.

He continued. 'This is a nation without a real centre, at least at the present time. The politicians don't give a damn about any of us, and they have shown that often enough by telling us that what they really want is a giant labour camp with lots of cheap foreign labour. They are now close to getting that but it's our job to stop them. That requires us to destroy any notion that there can be some kind of deal struck with them. They no longer have a hold over us. So, there will be no deals.'

At that point Sinclair let Jay Saxby take the stand. She thanked him and spoke assertively. 'Brandon is absolutely right. We need to hit them soon; not in six months, or even six weeks for that matter. We have to strike much sooner, before those corrupt bastards start to organise themselves.' There were loud cheers of approval from the thirty commanders gathered around the table.

She continued. 'As far as the politicians are concerned if you haven't got any money then you can get lost. There's no welfare state anymore. Everything that people fought for has been destroyed by the three main parties over the
~~~

last forty years. This is no longer a *United Kingdom*. Moreover, all those bastards in Westminster have ever done is to export a vicious kind of anarchy: the same brand that sold weapons to Saddam Hussein whilst training and supporting various other psychotic regimes around the world. They did more to encourage terrorism than any other state on the planet, even more than the United States or Saudi Arabia. And now they claim that all those wars had nothing to do with them and in fact nothing to do with this country. So, people: this is where we stop history – right here.'

Sinclair looked on, happy in the knowledge that Saxby was fast becoming the rising star of his movement. She finished. 'We no longer have any right to territories overseas or the resources of other peoples. This overcrowded island and its trash culture has no right to anything in this world; not anymore. The whole rotten deck of cards is about to come crashing down, and it will be down to us. We are going to finish this business.' The crowd let out a chorus of *Huah!* punching the air.

This was the build up that Sinclair was searching for and secretly he knew that only Saxby could provide it. He then went out of the office to phone his militia commanders in five chosen locations around London. They were positioned close to ministerial and security buildings, including the Tactical Support Units. Over the course of the following two nights several hundred of the trained and armed militants would turn up across the five locations and attack specific targets. This was a major step-up from the rioting on the streets that had occurred so far.

Whilst the commanders prepared their plans of action, Sinclair and Saxby were to be kept informed at all times about what was happening across the area. The moment Sinclair's militants started shooting at the police in the early hours, situation reports would have to be sent in.

~~~

The recently refurbished office in Moorgate reminded Ches of the deck of an ancient slave ship, with rows of people all pointing the same way and looking miserable. 'All they need are oars and the place would be a galley mate,' Ches quietly quipped, as they walked over to Becker's workstation through the lines of silent workers.

'Step into my palace,' Becker retorted, grinning.

'Why should I?' Ches asked under his breath. 'Why would anyone want to work here pal?'

'Do you think I want to? I have to. I was ordered here by the dole office. Anyway, what's it to you? All jobs are rubbish at the end of the day and I'll get the sack from here, as soon as, mate.'
~~~

Becker was talking just loud enough so that those around him could hear – he didn't care. As he'd been forced to take the job, he was also looking forward to being fired for bad behaviour, or, at the very least, a bad attitude.

Becker looked at Ches who had raised an eyebrow. 'Relax Ches, it's lunchtime mate. Let's go for a stroll.' Ches smiled at an attractive young woman sitting opposite Becker. She looked away.

In a café on Whitecross Street Becker and Ches waited for their food. Becker spoke above the noise of the café. 'I've always hated the City of London. I can work anywhere within reason but not here. It's full of dickheads in suits, money grabbers, desk jockeys and all their bitches.' He added, quietly, 'Mate: what's next? I'm bored out of my head and want to do another job.'

'Not here, Becks. We don't talk about it in a café, remember? We'll go over it later at my place, but I have something.'

He then recalled something else he had on his mind. He had to try and find Declan.

~~~

The first shots were fired somewhere near Harlesden. Several unarmed police had been targeted by an armed gang. Two were shot dead and several others were injured. An armed response unit arrived too late.

After hours of other targeted attacks, intense fighting continued across London between the police armed response units and militants. Both sides suffered many casualties. Tactical Support Units were then deployed with a shoot-to-kill policy. By 5:00 A.M. armoured police vehicles were out patrolling the streets, on which lay many bodies.

The government was informed of the growing numbers of dead and injured as well as the sudden change in tactics. It was clear both the methodology and the rules of engagement were now changing.

~~~

Declan was back in his flat in Harrow watching footage of an assault on a police station on his laptop. 'This is really happening.' He thought it somehow ironic that, in comparison to England, Belfast was completely peaceful. He also knew that his recent trip to Northern Ireland had been a complete failure in most respects. The raw intelligence hadn't been of much use. He had, after all, only discovered one single outpost.

He got up, put on his jacket and stepped out into the cold November air in the direction of his local newsagent. He opened the door, bell rattling as usual, the stifling atmosphere making him forget the cold. He walked in, looked up at

Gian, the old Sikh shopkeeper, and remarked, 'You OK, Gian? Maybe you should shut up the shop, with all the mobs out there attacking people. They won't be buying the Daily Mail any time soon.'

'I don't care, Dec,' the old man stated proudly. 'I've seen far worse rioting in Punjab. There's been a war going on out there you know, it just doesn't get reported.'

Declan had lived in the area for a number of years and he had never heard the old man speak so assuredly before. He replied in an upbeat way, 'Well mate, if you have any problems with gangs trying to steal from you send me a text. I'll come down here pronto. I'm only around the corner.'

'That's really good of you Dec, I'll remember that. I know what a good man you are. I appreciate people like you.'

'No problem. But I mean what I say, OK?'

'Here, take the paper Dec. I don't want your money today.'

'Come on Gian; I want your shop to survive. I insist. Give me freebies some other time.'

'OK, next time then Dec.' Gian smiled as Declan gave him the money. He then shouted after him, 'Look after yourself mate.'

'I will mate,' Declan called back.

His main fear was that he would be forced to leave London by the TSU, even though he was sure that he hadn't been seen by any of those he had pursued. None of the places he visited had, to his knowledge, CCTV cameras, either inside the buildings or outside. However, whilst not totally sure of the situation, he was equally past caring.

'Enough people have been killed already, so what's my bloody life worth anyway?' He rationalised that after so many years as a soldier he was lucky to be alive. He thought of his son, thankfully now living in Australia with his ex-wife.

He found a café that was still open. It was empty and he turned to the front page of his newspaper. *Slaughter on the Streets*; the headline ran next to the pictures of the bodies of several police officers. The paper carried in-depth analysis of the urban fighting as well as of the recent kidnapping of three former, high-ranking politicians. There were images of places in the Middle East where they were believed to have been taken, possibly by fast yachts moored on the south coast.

The editorial seemed to connect the upheaval on the streets with the kidnappings. It stated the one link that had tied all the kidnappings together; that the politicians had all served in the government as cabinet ministers and had all sanctioned military action in the Middle East. They were also heavily involved in the sale of weapons systems to regimes now propped up by the British and US governments.

The editorial itself didn't make any other wild assertions, but instead just stated that the breakdown of law and order was essentially a symptom of the fact that a great number of people no longer trusted the political establishment. It blamed many decades of political failure for the widespread economic, social and security problems.

'No surprises there,' thought Declan.

In the world news section, there was an article claiming that a Middle Eastern TV channel had interviewed several of the supposed kidnappers, who were threatening to kidnap and behead many other western politicians. In one shot there was a window behind the man being interviewed whose face was covered by a shemag scarf. Declan stared at the background. It wasn't Baghdad but looked very much like an area of Basra he had visited while serving in Iraq in late 2003.

'I'd recognise that place anywhere. They really messed up here. Those terrorists aren't going to be happy bunnies, as every intelligence agency out there will be able to work out where this place is.' He got onto the phone and rang the number he had been given by the Tactical Support Unit.

'Put me onto the TSU control please; Chris Kane,' he asked quietly, as the café owner brought over his roast lamb lunch.

'He's not here, sir. There's just a few in, right now. I'll get you the duty officer.'

After introducing himself Declan went into some detail about where he believed the building could be located. At the end he paused, exclaiming, 'You know, if it were me, I would act sooner rather than later.'

'We know sir – we're doing our best. But thank you for what you're doing for us.'

'It's nothing!' Declan replied.

He put the phone down and stared at the food on the table.

~~~

The voices on the vehicle radio were still animated.

'Tango Alpha, this is Zero, state location, over.'

'Tango Alpha: now at RV, packet safe; over,' Chris's armoured van driver replied.

It was Saturday morning and with a lull in the fighting Chris's thoughts turned to Annie, who was now so obviously pregnant he needed to turn the spare bedroom into a nursery. However, the radio chatter kept getting in the way of his personal thoughts and his exhaustion, after two days of urban patrolling, was now taking a grip. He longed for a normal radio broadcast as
~~~

he thought it might help him understand more about what was happening on the streets.

He looked at Jake, who was using the laptop, and was about to tell him to check the main news when Jake interjected. 'Chris, we've had some more info about what Declan was up to. NI Police need to share some details, and they just sent them over on an email.'

'OK, lay it on me then.'

'Well, there's a transcript of part of a conversation from a flat he bugged. It seems it gave a lot of info, including details of likely attacks. That was all the police needed in order to move in. There were full admissions by all the men in the flat of their activities, including potential strikes on government targets.'

'That's excellent.'

Jake paused. 'I also heard that he was worried his cover was blown by one of his contacts. Apparently, they didn't follow protocol.'

'Sorry, you're ahead of me there. Does that mean Declan's cover has been blown completely?'

Jake hesitated and then replied, 'I don't know; it might be.'

Chris thought through his exhaustion, trying to take in what Jake had said. 'To be fair this is small fry. The militant groups are all too busy planning the next phase of their operations. We just need to connect the various dots mate.'

Jake replied with a sarcastic tone to his voice, 'I don't really think we're talking about dots anymore, do you?'

Chris replied wistfully, 'No, we'll just have to connect the cracks. But we have people in custody, and everyone breaks under interrogation eventually. I reckon some of them will give full accounts of what's happening and where the rest of the networks are located. We just have to wait, that's all.'

'I don't know about that Chris. Things seem to be constantly shifting from one place to the next and we have no idea where will be next. Do we actually have the luxury of waiting?'

Chris shook his head and sighed.

CHAPTER EIGHT

'Right, this is what we know.' Commander Aley was addressing the Tactical Support Unit commanders in a large *O Group* meeting. 'Weapons have now been distributed throughout the four main radical groups and are in circulation. There aren't thousands out there, but there are enough to do some considerable damage. They will be used on our officers. We now have some army support units patrolling the streets in major towns and cities. We believe there's a mixture of new militants and established radicals, as well as some foreign groups. It's a kind of unholy alliance.'

'But one that knows what it's doing,' Jake muttered under his breath to Chris, who stood motionless.

'We have ten TSU teams in London, twenty officers in each, supported by Mastiffs in each pod. And all of you will be carrying weapons from now on. Very little work is to be done from here. Take sat phones, extra ammunition, water and whatever else you need to get the job done in your designated areas. We will be fully tactical with mobile coms, so UHF radios should be taken as well. You'll all be linked in the Mastiffs to Control with continuity support at different locations. Some militants will be reccying, so be aware of that; don't set patterns and don't get cornered, but don't be afraid to return fire. The public are scared, and they want results and they're looking to people like us. You are there to stop bad things happening ladies and gentlemen. Go out there and get results.'

The TSU officers checked their kit and said very little to each other. It reminded Jake of the times he had been a soldier on mobile patrol inside armoured vehicles in Iraq and Afghanistan.

~~~

'All we ever get is the constant re-shuffle of deadheads; the same tired bunch trying to re-invent itself without any actual positive change. The country's totally screwed.' Declan couldn't help but hear the man who was chatting to his friend sitting next to him, as they watched a TV news report in a Camden bar showing yet more rioting from around Britain.

The man's friend replied loudly, 'So what's this crooked lot going to do now, carry on blaming previous leaders like they usually do? I hope the army
~~~

takes over soon.' Both men seemed to be jaded, and Declan felt sorry for them, as he did for anyone who had to live right next to the violence.

However, from what Declan had observed, most other people in the bar were annoyed only because the evening's football matches had been postponed due to the lack of police manpower, as most of the available police officers were either on riot or civil contingency duties.

Declan mulled over where he fell in the scheme of things. He had been paid well for his recent activities and was relieved that there didn't appear to be any more assignments in the near future. He didn't know if the militant networks were on the back foot after the recent clashes with the TSU, but equally he didn't really care that much. Like everyone else he just wanted the violence to end.

As he clutched his pint of lager an old and familiar face stared at him from the other side of the bar. The man came wandering over with a pint of Guinness.

'Ches, you scared me, you old git,' Declan exclaimed, embracing his old friend. 'I didn't know you lived over this way. Where've you been hiding?'

'I don't live round here, Dec,' Ches replied, releasing himself from the bear hug and shaking Declan's hand firmly. 'I just happen to be in the area. Mate of mine stays up the road.'

'So, you're stalking me mate.'

'Totally, Dec; of course, I am. You know me, the boys always called me *The Creeper* on account of my nocturnal habits.'

'Yeah, being around you was like being in a constant freaking horror movie.' They hugged again and laughed.

Declan had a sudden and warm recollection of the times they had shared in Bosnia in early 1996, during Ches's first tour of duty with their regiment. Ches was usually at the centre of the laughter that had helped get them all through the winter, spent partly in a freezing ISO container.

'So, now you found me, what're you up to?'

'Oh, this and that; and quite a lot of other stuff, not that it's your problem.'

'Is there a problem?' Declan sensed slight hesitation.

'Recently, yes, there's been a problem.'

'Anything I can help you with?'

'Actually, there's something you might be able to help sort out.' Ches's voice went much quieter. 'But I can't discuss it here.'

Declan nodded. 'Tell you what mate, let's finish the beers, grab some kebabs and go round my flat. I've got some decent malts on the go.'

'Nice one Dec,' Ches replied. 'That'd be great.'

Two hours later, they were both slightly worse for wear, and Ches decided it was time to open up. 'It's a simple thing Dec. I took a gun off a young lad a little while ago. Some faces had been giving them out on the streets.'

'And how can I help?'

'I bought it off him to stop him killing himself. But I didn't let on to the face.'

'Good plan - you did well.'

'Yeah, except the boy got taken in and questioned for other stuff. So, I'm not going to the police with it, as they'll arrest me, especially with all this politics going down at the moment.'

'And you haven't done anything with it?'

'Of course not, not my style at all, you know that. Keep the guns in the armoury, every time. I just want rid of it, so I don't get done as well.'

'Yeah Ches, I see that. But I haven't seen you for ages mate, so I don't know what you're up to, do I?' He thought. 'Tell you what, let's get hold of it and we'll both deal with it.'

'Cheers Dec; I appreciate it.'

'On one condition: help me find some of the other gats out there.'

Ches paused before answering. 'Well Dec, I got one back. But there's got to be loads out there. It's a tall order.'

'I know but it's only one condition. And you don't have to do much, just tell me what you know.'

'Why Dec: what're you up to?' Ches immediately felt uneasy and despite their renewed acquaintance wasn't about to let his guard down.

'Nothing mate, let's just call it, continuing duty. We're both trained soldiers so let's do our country a favour. What do you say mate?'

Ches nodded, replying, 'You're right, we should give something back.'

'That's more like it, Ches,' Declan paused. 'You know things could've been different in every sense. We were lucky after all those scrapes, don't you think? Others weren't so lucky.'

'I know what you mean. We got around enough: the Cob, Musa Q'aleh, wherever.'

Both suddenly recalled just how scared they had both been at times during their tours of duty. Ches's main recollection was that Declan had been the senior. He had got him, and many others like him, through all those tours. 'Remember that Chinese 107 that landed near us Dec?'

'Of course, mate. And all those patrol bases we manned and any number of CLPs. You were a lucky charm Ches.'

'Why do you say that?'

'Well, you were a *Gooner*: gooner do this, gooner do that. You were always like that, always had a plan of some kind.'

'Guess I did Dec.'

'You spent most of your time on exercise attacking the rest of us. In truth I thought you'd mess your life up, but you seem to have your head screwed on.

Good luck to you Ches. Although I always thought you'd end up on a boat, living on a barge on a canal somewhere. Don't know why exactly.'

With that Declan raised his glass. Ches stared back at him and raised his own glass, not sure what to say.

'Here's to old times Ches.' Declan raised his glass again, adding, after a sip of whisky, *OK, so give me the details.*

~~~

Jake was leading his team through a disused industrial area near Tottenham Hale, his Sig Sauer MCX rifle raised as he checked his stride. 'Ray, you take the other side: you and Pete.'

The two men ran across some open ground and three shots rang out. Ray fell. More shots poured into the stricken man. Jake sprinted to Ray's aid and, with Pete's help, dragged him away as several more bullets sped past.

'All units, officer down,' Jake shouted into his mouthset. One round hit the magazine on Jake's weapon, ricocheting into his right leg. He screamed in pain and carried on, dragging Ray until they were all behind a wall. Once behind the wall he shrieked for help. Other units came forward and got a fix on where the gunmen were located. The team sniper went to work and after about twenty seconds the exchange of fire ended.

Ray was immediately on his way to hospital. Jake was propped up against the wall and was soon triaged and strapped up by a team medic who pumped morphine into him. It took another minute to get Jake loaded onto the back of an ambulance.

An hour drifted past and the realisation that the militants had registered hits was now starting to sink in. At the same time the adrenalin of the team members started to subside. They left the industrial site as others came in to replace them, but the two militant gunmen were now dead.

'Ray didn't make it then,' Chris said quietly to himself in the Mastiff on the way back to HQ, after hearing on his secure line that the TSU man had died on the way to hospital. On arrival there would be a debriefing over what had happened.

Once back Chris's team slumped dejectedly into the seats in the briefing area. Naveen, one of the younger team members but already bloodied after days of urban warfare, wasn't afraid to voice his concerns to Aley above those of the other team members. 'Sir, some of the lads are a bit shaken. We felt we were left out in the open a bit. We feel we need to use effective cover, not expose ourselves.'

Chris nodded in agreement, said nothing, and looked up at a TV monitor that was showing a debate from the House of Commons. The sound was
~~~

switched off but the sight of MPs debating at Westminster seemed to be quite ironic considering what was happening out on the streets. Chris sat back and reflected on that last gruelling shift.

Commander Aley attempted a reply, 'Of course you should be using effective cover...'

'I'll sort all that Nav,' Chris interrupted. 'We've a lot more to do and we have to keep going. Some of us will just have to learn on the job.'

'What happened to the specialist firearms units?' Naveen asked unreservedly.

'They're still coming down, but at least we have the sniper now,' Chris replied. 'But we need people all over the place at the moment, including other parts of the country. We all know that it'll be an uphill battle to control the streets.' He wasn't about to let emotions get hold of his team and he wanted to keep a firm grip on them now Jake was hospitalized. The surgeon had operated to remove the fragments, and he had been told Jake would make a full revovery.

'And the soldiers?' another team member asked.

'They have specially trained units out there as well,' Chris replied assertively. 'But they're not about to unleash hell. We don't want any bloodbaths; not where ordinary rioters are concerned. We're only going after the actual gunmen, so it stays with us for now.'

The following morning Chris was at Jake's bedside. Jake was in good humour despite the wound to his thigh, stating loudly, as Chris approached, 'Now don't take advantage of me big boy, not while I'm lying prostrate like this.' Jake wagged his index finger at Chris.

'Is that all you ever think about?'

'What, promotion? I'm not actually feeling very upwardly mobile at the moment.'

'What're you reading?'

'It's the latest sequel to Pride and Prejudice.'

Chris picked up the novel sitting on the bedside cabinet. It was by Lee Childs.

'Bollocks it is. You know you were lucky you weren't shot in the balls.'

'You're right. I'm going to wear combat nappies next time.'

'You are kidding me, combat nappies?'

'No, I'm not. We were issued with them on my last tour in Afghan. I sneaked a pair home. I never actually wore them out there, but I think I will here. At least the rest of you will have a laugh.'

'I am already - just the thought of it.'

'Let me know about Ray's funeral by the way.'

Chris said nothing and just nodded.

~~~

A government minister was being interviewed on the radio as Ches was driving his van. The man spoke passionately. 'What we are seeing out on the streets is the vanity of young men with the adolescent desire to despise authority for the sake of it and commit acts of violence for no real reason. Such seeds of hate are born in societies where elements of the youth have never learned where the goalposts are, mainly due to the influence of the left-leaning liberal establishment. That is the root cause of the problems we are facing.'

The radio presenter was uncompromising in her response. 'But the argument the militants are putting forward is now well-publicised and surely should be taken seriously: that the political establishment is corrupt and violent and has started wars around the world in recent decades whilst bringing our economy to its knees. They also state that it has encouraged violence within society as a result of failed social policies. These are just a few of the latest statements from Brandon Sinclair, the leader of the militant groups, and they do seem unambiguous. What do you say?'

'I'm not going to even credit that with an answer.'

Ches laughed, shouting, 'You just don't get it. Look at the lot who were kidnapped; they were all bloody war criminals anyway. I don't care what happens to any of them.'

Declan looked over at Ches clutching the steering wheel, and stated, 'I agree mate. It was our lads who got blown up because of some of those bastard MPs and their bogus deals with defence companies. Do you remember Rave and Dazz?'

'Yeah, of course I do. Don't forget that kind of thing Dec.'

'So where do you think this is all heading?'

'I don't know. I suppose the establishment is getting a bit of a kicking. But the families of all these people being killed and injured on the streets don't see it that way.'

Declan nodded, adding in a sombre tone, 'The world's full of nasty bastards and most of them probably deserve to die. That's the only political philosophy I've ever known.'

Ches stared out the front window of the van. They pulled up at Daffy's council block and went up to the fourth level. Ches knocked on the door and Daffy answered.

'Alright mate, how're you doing?' Ches walked past Daffy and into the flat as he spoke.

'I'm OK Ches. Who's this?'

'Oh, he's a mate of mine; Dec. Mind if we sit down?'

'Yeah, no bother.'
~~~

After five minutes Declan and Ches had the names of five other local youths who had been given weapons that Daffy knew about. Declan revealed a considerable amount of cash and gave a wad of it to Daffy in return for the information.

'Thanks man,' Daffy responded eagerly. 'You know Dec I've never been interested in guns. I'm sick of the sight of them.' What Daffy didn't reveal was that he had already been so helpful to the police that they had struck a deal to keep him out of the youth justice system. The deal involved the eventual capture of Craig, and Daffy had passed everything he knew about him onto the police, without snitching on any of his other local friends.

After a cup of tea, and a brief chat about football, Declan and Ches left the flat.

'Well, that was easy Ches. I wish all such things were as simple as that,' Declan said as they got into the car.

'Yeah, but I wish the TSU behaved a bit more like the police did with Daffy, instead of shooting people up.' Ches then looked at Declan sharply, before asking quizzically, 'You're not working for the Met, are you?'

'Not exactly Ches.'

'What the hell does that mean?'

'It means what I say: not directly. I work for myself.'

"What like some kind of PI?"

'Yeah, at the moment I am a bit like that. I'm kind of freelance Ches.'

Ches snorted and grimaced, shaking his head and snorting, *Dec, why didn't you tell me. I hope it's a good earner.*

'It is mate. And by the way I will sort you out for this. You've done very well indeed. That Daffy is a good lad, and lads like him are really useful for stopping crap happening. He may look daft but he's not, is he?'

'Nah, he isn't daft, you're dead right there. But remember Dec: you're doing me a favour, remember? I came to you.'

'Yeah, you did, and for the right reasons. That's why I'm going to make sure you get paid Ches, just like Daffy.'

~~~

Commander Aley wandered across the floor of the ward, looking at all the medical paraphernalia. He slid up to the bed.

'So, how long before you get out Jake?'

'Well, they have to make sure there's no infection first, sir. It's healing OK. So, it should be soon. But I can't put too much weight on it.' Jake paused, adding, 'So how's it going out there, sir?'
~~~

'Crap generally. Loads of gunmen are still running around. We don't have any real breakthroughs yet.'

'What happened to that Irish guy?'

'Not heard from him too much recently. We gave him a rest for a while, but I heard he's still, at times, coming up with the names of suspects.'

'He's doing our jobs for us. Maybe he should have my spot sir.'

'Are you joking Jake?'

'No, I'm serious. If he gets results, get him in. He knows what he's doing; doesn't he? I heard he did surveillance as a soldier for years.'

'Yeah, and that's why he's been useful. On the flipside he's been breaking down barriers and storming in. Not a great approach generally.'

One hour later Chris was at the Tactical Support HQ near Ealing where he was listening to a briefing to the TSU squad leaders by Commander Aley. 'Forget about third hand information guys, we need first-hand. Whatever importance you have attached to bad intel is irrelevant; only pursue the stronger leads.'

Chris's phone vibrated. He was half-obscured behind a partition wall, so he took the call. He moved away from the group.

'Hi, what's up Declan? I thought you were having a rest; a well earned one by the sound of it?'

'I've got some more names for you.'

'Can't you take it easy?'

'No.'

'OK, shall I call you back? I'm in the middle of a briefing.'

'I think we'd better meet. I'll come up there. Or we can meet in a bar I know in Finsbury Park if you're OK with that. I need some more cash though.'

'When, exactly?'

'How about tonight: 8:00 P.M.? It's important.'

'OK. What's the bar?'

~~~

'You know if all this crap carries on for much longer England will just end up like the Bosnian Republic: a pointless little entity.' Declan stared at his pint of lager.

It was 7:50 P.M. and Declan was sitting in the Finsbury Park pub. He had not failed to notice a tall bald man with glasses standing at the bar. Every now and then the man would look over in his direction, as he held a pint glass and spoke to another man.
~~~

Declan soon realised that they were two plainclothes police officers, who had probably been sent by Chris ahead of his own arrival. He then went to a different table in a side bar, allegedly to watch a football match on the TV screen. Chris arrived and sat next to him.

'Thanks for tailing my cousins by the way,' Declan said quietly to Chris.

'That's fine. We just want to make sure they're safe.'

Declan nodded at Chris, continuing, 'You could have saved their lives without knowing it.'

'No problems Declan. We do what we can to protect people. That includes you as well.'

Declan slipped an envelope into Chris's pocket as he got up to order some drinks. The envelope contained the list of names of those who had been supplying lethal weapons. When Declan came back with the drinks Chris handed him a newspaper, inside of which was a plastic bag containing £20,000 in cash.

Two hours later Chris was sitting with Commander Aley in the TSU briefing room and listening to what he had to say about the worsening situation on the streets. 'Given a choice most people will walk away from violence; it's only human nature. But we still have to get more units out on the ground to break this down.' Aley paused for a moment as if he was pondering what changes in tactics might be made to improve the worsening situation on the streets.

He continued, 'Something just turned up Chris and I'd like to run it past you. Apparently, many of the senior service chiefs cannot put up with the political situation any longer. They just don't want the politicians in charge. They would rather have a bunch of generals running the show. The thing is - it's now almost official. But this is strictly between us at the moment, OK?'

Chris was slow to respond at first. 'Yes, sir. But what are we expecting to happen now?'

'What is being tabled is that we ask for some kind of liaison with the militants, especially people like Sinclair, or one of his lieutenants. Whatever, we need to put the public first and avoid more casualties.'

'But that's not really for us to decide, is it, sir?'

'Well, I think it is - on a practical level at least. The politicians are running scared. Many of them now refuse to come to London for fear of being attacked, and that's all the parties. They seem to want to get soldiers out on the streets and not us. But from what I can gather the generals don't want to support the politicians anyway, which means they have effectively cut themselves off. They are therefore forcing this situation upon everyone else and making things impossible for the government.'

'Well sir, to be fair, we all know how corrupt the politicians are. But it's still very odd.'

Commander Aley looked at Chris and grimaced, before replying, 'Chris, our duty is to the public and to the Crown, and not to these scab politicians.'

'I've never doubted your judgement, sir, and neither have the men. We will follow your orders no matter what happens.'

'Thanks Chris. Do you know in all my thirty years in the force I have never seen anything like this? The politicians have been trying for too many bloody years to turn us all into unquestioning robots while they made cock-up after cock-up. That includes the massive reductions in personnel in the security forces, while encouraging totally open borders. All they've done is to effectively destroy security in this country.'

~~~

Brandon Sinclair and his senior commanders were gathered in an industrial unit in Harlesden. The debate was an open forum so that anyone could be heard, and as long as they stood up and spoke their opinion had to be considered. It was Sinclair's intention that everyone should all be allowed a say on how to coordinate attacks on the government.

One scarred and stocky Yorkshireman stood up and spoke loudly. 'Time and again we've been forced into pointless wars by the scum in power, and these are wars that have wasted the lives of decent young people. They are the same filth that tell us that we no longer have any say in how our own country is to be run. We've been destroyed as a nation. Now we have to hit these bastards hard and destroy them before they cause the country any more damage. We hit them now. That's my view.' There was a chorus of approval from those gathered.

Another man, a Mancunian, stood up and spoke. 'What's also true is that we're being called terrorists in our own land. We have to take it back and this is the time to strike. We'll never get another chance.'

The fifty or so gathered carried on debating the general political situation for twenty minutes until Sinclair decided to direct the debate towards actions that would target the machinery of power. He stood up and declared loudly, above the din of the discussion, 'This is all fine, but we need to answer some basic questions about our network. For example, how many trained people do we now have? How many weapons do we have? Without answers to those questions this is a pointless debate.'

One of the commanders replied. 'We reckon around 1000 semi-automatics; 300 pistols; along with 8 grenade launchers and around three thousand people who are trained to some degree.'

Sinclair thought for a moment before replying. 'It's not enough. But if we used our resources wisely it might be enough to make some kind of impact.
~~~

But that's only if we strike in the right places and with support in the form of mass action.'

He paused, thought, and then spoke again, 'We need a mass of people to march on Westminster, just as a smoke screen. The real business is to get to the high-level civil servants so we can strike a deal to avoid further bloodshed. We can pretty well ignore the police, but the TSU will never give up. They have hundreds of officers and have recently expanded. From what we've seen they have some of the best intelligence officers. They have also taken out a number of our own people. But we can hit them harder and in more places. Take out a few more of them and the commanders will start to think about negotiating.'

One of Sinclair's commanders then asked, 'But what about the generals? We seem to be ignoring them.'

'They're largely on our side. Up north serving soldiers have been openly telling our people that they'll not get in our way and will come over to us at some point. In the south there are fewer soldiers, but they are the same as the northerners. They won't intervene. Moreover, the generals are still angry about what the politicians have done to the Armed Forces over the years, so they don't support them anyway. Truth is we've already been given the nod by them.' He paused, looked around and sensed a growing confidence.

He continued, 'We'll strike harder now and take control of the situation. The media is still on the government's side, so we'll need to be far more robust. Don't forget our line: that we'll be delivering justice for those devastated by corrupt policies and that's exactly how the rest of the world will see us. Therefore, we have no choice but to take power by force. But there'll be a legal case for what we're doing.'

One commander interrupted, 'Even if we win, we have no government in waiting, so how are we going to govern?'

'I know. We'll need to appoint a transitional authority. It's easier than you think, as Scotland, Wales and Northern Ireland already have their own state ruling bodies. The generals, if they do eventually come over to us, can secure the borders and act as general administrators where required. If really necessary, we can ask the UN to form an interim government. This sclerotic, stupid establishment will finally be brought to account, whatever it takes.'

~~~

'So, that's where we are, we're going out to round up the rest of the gunmen, without any real idea where they're located.' Chris was trying to explain to Jake the new standing orders along with some of the rules of engagement from the most recent briefing. 'We'll be easy targets. And if necessary, we may have to negotiate because the boss doesn't want any more civilian casualties, and
~~~

because our politicians are likely to be forced out of power some time soon anyway. They'll possibly get charged as war criminals and gangsters. And then an unelected government will take over commanded by the generals who are rather tenuously in charge at the moment anyway.' Chris paused as Jake rolled his eyes.

'It's a bit like Northern Ireland in reverse,' Jake replied. 'Except this time the criminals are not going to be elected to power. They're already in power and are about to be forced out.'

Chris said nothing but stared out of the window of the north London flat Jake shared with his pregnant wife. All Chris could see were months of further upheaval. Jake had described to him what years of conflict had done to people he'd met in the Balkans and Iraq and all he knew was that he would fight to the death to prevent such a situation occurring in Britain.

Finally, Chris replied, 'It's a bloody civil war. That's what these useless politicians have done to us. They've destroyed our country and started an actual civil war.'

'I know,' Jake responded icily. 'But we have to do what we have to do. Maybe Aley's right that we shouldn't fight if we can avoid it.'

'Perhaps he thinks we can dig in and then let the militants burn themselves out. That way there may be fewer casualties and some kind of transition to something better.'

Jake stood on his crutches and stared dejectedly out of the window. 'Yeah, I suppose that might work. It's probably the best strategy, come to think of it, even if it seems weak. After all, it's us the militants are actually scared of, as they know we'll fight to the end. Even the Armed Forces don't want to get involved. But we can do the job.'

'So, it's not up to the politicians, or even the security services, anymore. Basically, this is last chance saloon for all of them and if we can't sort it then it'll be total anarchy. And they know it.' Chris paused before continuing. 'But I don't know who's really in charge any more than Aley does. Quite frankly I don't really care. These decisions are mainly high-level, intelligence-led ones. It's also about containment and our teams are charged with that task.'

'Where's that leave us if it all goes tits-up Chris?'

'I don't know mate. I'm not going there.'

'And I can't walk properly, let alone run. This is killing me pal.'

'I know it is. I would be the same in your shoes, you know that. But when you come back you will be there with us. Make it soon, I need you.'

'Yeah, too damned right. I'll be back with you lads sooner than you think.'

'I know that, Jake.'

~~~
~~~

'You might be wondering why we called you here Declan.' Commander Aley was briefing Declan about the role they had given him within the Tactical Support Unit. 'I'll cut to it; we lost a good man recently from this team and we want you to take his place. We see that you are weapons-trained, from your service record. But you'll need a short period to get back up to speed. You'll have to be proficient and pass a weapon handling test. We'll also brief you up, so you'll be able to slot into the team. Your skillset and knowledge, that's what we need right now. How do you see it Declan?'

'No problems so far.'

A few hours later Declan, having received a number of briefings, was put into a training programme that would last many days. The sessions included specialist weaponry, urban warfare, evasion and extraction, medical evacuation drills, cognitive testing and spatial awareness testing.

After two days he received his personal weapons, a SIG Sauer P226 pistol and Steyr RS-556 rifle, and then given expert coaching by firearms instructors. Later that afternoon he was thrown into a real-life scenario and given clear objectives concerning what he had to achieve, and the recommended methods involved. It was up to him how he employed them.

He soon found himself moving round a vehicle in a simulated training area covering his arcs with small movements of his pistol. However, 9mm pistols had never been amongst his favourite weapons as they kicked, rendering at least two principles of marksmanship almost redundant; that of maintaining a firm position and hold and firing without undue disturbance to the position.

Declan had always believed that, in order to be accurate, you also had to be within close range of your enemy. Pistols could therefore be both dangerous as well as indiscriminate unless one was at close quarters, which was a rare event for most soldiers. He reckoned that if he hadn't enjoyed using them whilst in the British Army then he wasn't about to start now, especially as he had only ever fired a rifle, not a 9mm pistol, on operations.

However, targets started popping up left and right and instinctively he had to decide whether they were innocent or a threat. Declan was getting it right every time and the attending staff could see that he was a natural marksman.

~~~

'Whoever wins this fight will have to understand that in the long term it will be the victors that get the blame.' Jay Saxby was addressing several hundred trained fighters in a disused warehouse in Hillingdon. 'The blame not only for the violence - but what comes after as well.'

She continued. 'The media are saying that we shouldn't be attacking the establishment. That's after all the damage and destruction the politicians have
~~~

done to this country and many others, including millions of deaths across the Middle East. They don't seem to realise that most citizens of this country are now on our side and that there's no democratic system left. But we're the ones doing something about it.'

'Too right,' shouted one bearded, tattoed man. 'They're all bloody criminals, so kill all of them.' The man had to be calmed down by some of those around him.

Brandon Sinclair intervened and pointed straight at the man, stating, 'You're right, and we all have a right to be angry. This is a righteous conflict, and we all know it. So, some of us will die, and I truly thank all comrades, just like you sir, who support us and are putting their lives on the line so that others can have a better way of life in the future. I am proud to be here with you, with all our brothers and sisters, as I am proud to be a part of this movement.' There were loud shouts of approval from those present with many punching their fists in the air.

Sinclair continued. 'The government filth went on the TV late last night and do you know what they said? They said that they now regard us as the main threat. Did they ever stop to realise just how much of a threat they have been? Just how many lives they have destroyed. Did they ever realise how many innocents have died as a result of their wars and the weapon systems they have sold to garbage regimes around the world? We are now putting all that right.'

The crowd started chanting, 'We will kill, we will kill…'

Saxby took over, 'Thank you comrades. Never forget - there is no compromise with corruption. The world is divided between those who are a part of history and those who make history. We're the ones making it right now.'

More cheers engulfed the warehouse as she continued, 'Let's destroy this filthy establishment. They are the ones who've murdered innocent people across the world, all in our name. We have to get this country right once and for all.' At that she hesitated, looked around, and proclaimed, 'Comrades; we'll destroy every last one of them.'

The chants rang out, 'Kill! Kill! Kill…'

Thirty minutes later two snipers armed with Heckler and Koch PSG-1 rifles moved onto a rooftop overlooking the approach to a government ministry building near Waterloo. They moved swiftly and picked positions. They then took clear shots on the targets below, killing outright two junior cabinet members who were standing at the entrance to the building four hundred metres away. Their job done, they escaped down a steel external stair and onto the street, straight into a waiting van.

~~~
~~~

Jake was back at work but confined to office duties. He was using one crutch, having ditched the second as it seemed to be getting in the way of his concerted attempts at restoring his own mobility. Chris was holding a mug of coffee in both hands as he sat and stared, somewhat disbelievingly, at Jake.

'So, they said you would need months of therapy, seeing the OT everyday?' Chris asked. 'So how did you manage to swing coming back to work so soon?'

'I saw the top man and said I had to get back soon as. It was doing my head in, as was the wife. I mean I know she's pregnant, but she doesn't need me on my arse at home. It was a bloody nightmare.'

Chris laughed, snorting a reply, 'So, did you claim it was damaging you mentally, being stuck at home?'

'Something like that. I just signed a few disclaimers; that I would stick to light duties, whatever. It was a piece of piss. What's the crack with you then?'

'Yeah well, me and Annie had a bit of an argument the other night. She said something like, *you won't be happy until you're dead.* I think she'd rather I did some bone office job and earned more money.'

'It's not you mate – she knows that deep down. I told my lady that I was coming off the TSU completely. Complete lie. I even embellished that with a story that I had been told I would now be working with some intelligence graduates, the types who are good at problem solving. I was thinking that would never happen anyway, even while I was telling her.' Both men laughed.

'To be fair, it's actually tougher on them,' Chris replied. 'They're both preggers, and they don't know what the future holds. And let's face it you were nearly killed, and one of our mates is dead. I get what they're saying. I wouldn't want to be with them if the roles were reversed. It's just too bloody stressful.'

'Yeah, it kills me to think about what happened to Ray as well. We are running the risk of getting hit every day. Those insurgent bastards are blowing the hell out of this country.'

Chris didn't look up immediately. Jake could sense a certain guilt as Chris replied somewhat sheepishly. 'I'm not sure if anyone really cares any more about protecting politicians. Do you think anyone here does Jake?'

'No, not politicians. They're always in it for themselves. I served this country for years as a soldier and I don't know why, or for what exactly? Maybe this bunch, or the generals, the ones that are trying to take over, are worth a go; whoever they are. Let them have a crack.'

'I can't believe you're saying that. You always seemed to be such a massive hater of the militants.'

'Well, maybe we should all think twice about serving those morons in power. Some of them will get what they deserve.'

'Some of them already have.'

'Yeah, I've stopped watching the news mate. We don't have it on in the evenings; far too depressing.'

An hour later they were sitting in a small group room with Declan. He was explaining how he had come to do undercover surveillance work in the British Army. 'Well, it was basically a case of having done everything in the infantry, so I fancied a change. I was doing OK. The wife was still around, and my lad was at school, so it was extra money.'

'And a bit of a career change then?' Jake asked.

'Yeah, whatever that means.' Declan paused before continuing. 'A few things recently have made me think about things. One involves this lad that I know. As a young Tom he screwed up everything he did. I remember one time we were doing an exercise setting up a village with booby traps. You know, the ones we used back then were done with combination switches, and they came in small tins. They were difficult to use especially when your fingers were cold. I mean I hated showing the lads how to set up these booby traps, but it was my job.' Declan stopped, took a swig of coffee and then continued. 'This one time he was taking hours over it and I could see he just wasn't into it. I had to take over and show him how to do it, except we were using a small amount of PE, just for effect really. I set it all up and we all went back a safe distance. The idea was to get the lads together and get one or two to smash their way in, to the killing zone, but away from the switch and the small charge. We called them confidence charges. They would trip the wire, but it was still some distance from the detonation.'

Declan took another swig of coffee and continued. 'Anyway, this silly bugger goes steaming in with blank rounds going like nobody's business, but in the wrong place from where I told him. He was much too close to the PE. And the bastard thing detonated. It nearly killed the silly twat. He got blown over. He tried to blame me, but I had told him exactly what to do. It taught him a lesson; he never did anything like that again. He ended up a good soldier. I did tours with him later, and he was a top lad, reliable, disciplined and a good laugh. It was great to see him turn his life round.'

'Sorry Declan,' asked Chris. 'Why are you telling us this?'

'I bumped into him recently. He was over the moon to see me.'

'Where exactly?' asked Jake.

'It was when I found out they were dishing out weapons. He was there. Turned out he was checking on a young lad who had got hold of one of the guns.'

'Good plan. But what did he do with the gun?'

'We paid the boy a visit. My mate thought I could get rid of it.'

Chris looked annoyed. 'Declan, why didn't you tell me?'

'You didn't ask. And anyway; I was undercover, remember? I wasn't coming running back to you to tell you everything. I wanted to pick up more of the things in my own time. Another boy had already been questioned by the Met.'

'Oh well, it looks like we're too late,' replied Jake. 'But we could have picked up the lad.'

'You are joking, aren't you?' Declan gave Jake a dirty look. 'He's just one kid. There're hundreds of gats out there. What do you think is going on?'

'Calm down Declan,' Chris said assertively.

'Don't try to talk me down pal.' Declan shouted back. 'I'm doing your dirty work; just like I did for the surveillance wing. You people are going nowhere, take it from me.'

'Look, we know what we're doing Declan,' Chris replied assertively.

'No, you don't, not if you're relying on people like me. You can't just blaze your way through all this. I'm too long in this game, OK?'

'OK, so the militants and criminals they work with have got weapons. We know that most of them are well-trained, so we have to play this game until we can bring them in.'

Declan scoffed and shook his head, replying, 'You've got a lot to learn, that's all I can say.'

Jake suddenly felt a surge of hatred for the man, stating loudly, 'Look we've just lost one good man recently and I'm out of the game, so who do you think you are?'

Declan looked away from Chris and Jake towards one of the long, blast-protected windows that formed part of the front of the building. Chris stood up, stating categorically, 'Come on Declan, if you want to carry on in this outfit you'll have to change your attitude.' Declan got up and left the room without saying another word.

After a moment of silence Jake turned to Chris stating loudly, 'Don't let that jerk near me again. And that's not a threat; it's a promise.'

'Yeah, I know but he's right in a way. Taking out the likes of that young lad will do bugger all,' Chris asserted. 'The top people are the ones we need. Not the rank and file.'

Chris then thought of the officers who were either dead or injured. 'The lads in our teams may as well enjoy themselves while they can 'cos things are about to get a lot worse Jake.'

~~~
~~~

CHAPTER NINE

Ches was sitting in his flat near Loughborough Junction watching TV, as Becker and his girlfriend walked in. Becker shouted, above the din of a reality show, 'Ches, why are you in your skids? Put some shorts on will you.'

Ches didn't look up but retorted, 'Piss off Becks, it's my flat.'

'Have some respect Ches, there's a lady present.'

'Why, you had a sex change at long last?' Ches replied lazily, adding, 'You could have told me you were bringing your woman over.'

'Mate, my woman has a name.'

Ches looked over at Gail before replying politely, 'Sorry Gail, I'm still hung over.'

'I can see that Ches,' Gail replied softly. 'Don't worry, Becks is going way over the top. I don't give a toss that you're in your skids, babe.'

'You see Becks?' Ches said slightly too loudly for his hangover. 'You exaggerate, again.'

Becker smiled and then stated caustically *You've obviously seen plenty of guys in their pants Gail so that's nothing knew.* She didn't reply, but instead slapped Becker cleanly across the face.

Ches laughed loudly. 'Hell mate; I'm liking her already.' Ches laughed a bit more as Becker held his arms up shouting, 'I surrender, I surrender.'

Gail gestured to Ches, 'Do you always watch TV like that?'

Ches nodded, whilst grinning and chewing the remnants of a sandwich. He then choked, coughed and carried on watching TV.

When Gail had gone to the bathroom Ches turned and looked at Becks. 'Mate, I've got another target for us. This one's a lot more interesting.'

~~~

The TSU bomb disposal team had been working on the device in a derelict, concrete shopping mall in the centre of Luton. The mall had been another victim of the recent economic downturn and was due to be demolished.

There had been a tip-off from a payphone to the local police station the previous afternoon. All they had said was that the device was going to detonate the following morning after the market traders were due to open up outside the mall. Chris and Jake were sent there to check any weapons forensics and gather
~~~

any information they could. That included talking to members of the public who had been there over the previous two days. Jake wondered if it had really been worth the risk to the lives of the team, as the place was due to be demolished anyway. He reasoned that it could have been detonated in-situ.

'Why did they decide to make it safe Chris?' Jake asked testily. 'It was only about thirty kilos, and the public around could have been kept away. They should have just blown it.'

'Yeah, Jake, but the place is still being used by a few businesses, so it still has commercial interest. We would be accountable for any damage.'

Jake saw it differently. 'My mate was EOD. The Royal Engineers used to carry out live blasts on old derelict shopping centres, but late at night. He did one at the old Tricorn place in Portsmouth back in the early naughties. It was about 20 kg.'

Chris didn't care. He just wanted the forensics, and any local intelligence and CCTV footage, so they could track down those who had planted it. He guessed that most of those involved had been on camera at some point whilst walking around the area.

When he got back to the vehicle he saw a web link back to HQ in London. Commander Aley was speaking to a team in the briefing room. 'I've been asked a number of times: *What are the profiles of the senior militants? And what are their backgrounds?* As far as we know they're a mixed bunch and hate everything about this country, especially the political establishment.'

One TSU commander shouted back, 'So there's nothing new there then, boss?' There were a few jaded laughs from the assembled members of the unit, some of whom had been out on continuous patrols for days, with hardly any respite.

Aley replied tersely, 'True, but it's not for us to judge the situation. However, it is for us to prevent the militants causing yet more violence. We all know people who've been hit in recent weeks, and we have to fight on. For the politicians this is a losing battle, and they cannot expect a victory in the conventional sense of the word.' He was then conscious that he had probably said too much.

He paused and then, in a more sombre tone, 'Many people now feel very remote from the government. Thankfully most members of the public out there still support us, but we will have to expect the worst from now on.'

Declan was sitting on the far side of the meeting area. He wasn't at all interested in what Aley had to say. He turned to another man and said quietly, 'What is that guy crapping on about?'

'Buggered if I know mate?' came the muffled response.

Aley continued, 'So remember we're dealing with a lot of very frightened people. They're terrified about what the next few months, or even years, may hold. So, let's not frighten them even more. Yes, there are some violent groups out there, but they're few in number and nothing we can't handle.'

At that there was another ripple of laughter mixed with disbelief.

~~~

'To be honest with you mate I don't believe in England, or any other country for that matter.' Ches was talking to Declan, whilst sitting on a bench in a graveyard just off City Road. The weather was surprisingly warm for a Tuesday in November.

Ches continued, 'As far as I'm concerned, I wasn't serving this country when I was a soldier in the Balkans, Iraq or Afghanistan. I was serving with my mates, and the rest of the British Army. In reality England's just an overcrowded dump, and a lot of the people out there are just deadheads, cheats, fraudsters, whatever. We have every type of moron and freeloader living here; so, screw them. That's where I am in life. I'm not against the militants either. At least they know what they're doing, and that's a lot more than anyone can say about the politicians.' Ches had agreed with Declan that he would help track down some more people to see if any more weapons could be located.

Declan knew that Ches wasn't really part of any organised gang, but he was slightly surprised at his general attitude and outlook. He replied, 'The way I see it is that most countries are just motley collections of dirtbags, corrupt bastards, cowardly politicians and minor league celebrities. Those who *actually* do the work, as well as the fighting, are in the minority mate. They're people like us.'

Declan then adopted a slightly heavier tone in his voice, which reminded Ches that Declan had been much more senior to him when they had been serving soldiers. 'Actually, in some ways I do think you're wrong. Some people are worth fighting for.' He paused and then added softly, 'It's odd, but as soldiers I think people like us had more in common with the enemy than we ever did with most people in our own country. At least the people we were fighting had values; they believed in something. But they were actually fighting for their own people, and I was fighting for mine. Do you see that?'

Ches nodded. He couldn't be bothered to get involved in any politics. He didn't know that Declan was trying to prevent him from saying anything that might incriminate himself. All he wanted was some hard facts, as the conversation was being transmitted back to Chris and the team. Declan also didn't want any more diatribes from Ches, just plain evidence. He needed to steer the conversation away from politics. The deal wasn't that Ches would be taken in. As far as Declan was concerned, he hadn't done anything wrong, and he had been responsible for taking at least one lethal weapon off the streets.

'Yeah Dec: I see what you're saying,' Ches replied, after thinking it over.

Declan paused before he spoke again. 'Have you come across any more kids with guns Ches?'
~~~

'Yeah, I have Dec. But I can't get to them. They're hidden away. But I can get a couple of mates together and, with you, I reckon we can sort them all out.'

Declan smiled and winked at Ches, 'OK mate, let's sit down and work out how we're going to get those guns back. Just like old times; disarming people in the Balkans, Iraq wherever. That was our job, wasn't it? Except now it's here and it's not really any different.'

Ches nodded. For once he felt like he was of some use.

~~~

'One side of the establishment goes on about the other all the time; but they have all been busy selling weapons systems to dictators around the world without any questions asked and regardless of the consequences.' The meeting in the empty industrial complex in Croydon was in full swing as one of Brandon Sinclair's lieutenants, an ex-soldier with a thick beard and bald head, continued speaking in a monotone voice to the assembled militants.

'And then it was people like me who were sent to sort out all the problems our own politicians had started, while the bastards were trying to start new conflicts somewhere else. Our politicians are the real enemy. They radicalised a generation of innocent people in wars that have cost millions of lives, messed up the economy, and all the while the workers have had to foot the bill. I say good riddance to them.'

Brandon Sinclair had little interest in the proceedings. His main concern was starting the next phase of the operations against government targets. He had shared this with his inner circle of commanders just before the meeting, and they had all agreed that they should now concentrate solely on the real issue, the final phase of hostilities.

Sinclair stood up abruptly, announcing, 'Thank you for that comrade, I'm sure that we're all in agreement here. That's why we're here after all: to try to sort this country out and stop future wars being perpetrated. However, let's not go over any old ground. We have to think about the next phase, and we need to get our heads together. We could be close to taking power in this country. Just think about that.' The hundred, or so, assembled murmured their approval.

Sinclair continued, 'We have five more targets; and this time we're taking them out separately. We're forming heavily armed teams in order to do this. By changing our tactics we'll start to put the Tactical Support Units on the back foot.'

He pointed at the table in front of him. 'The team leaders, and those working with them, are named on each of these envelopes. Every leader will get the envelope explaining exactly what they have to do and how they're
~~~

going to do it. We cannot deviate from these timelines or actions but if there's any major concerns then get back to us. I suggest to all team leaders that you get your eyes on and get your people on board immediately. We're sorting out the logistics and we'll let you know when we're ready. But there shouldn't be any issues. Are there any questions?'

There were none and the team leaders picked up their orders.

~~~

Gavin picked up the newspaper in the Finsbury Park pub and read out the headline, *Senior Minister took Bribes*. The damning front-page news was about the arrest of the Foreign Secretary, as a result of the exposure of his close links with a defence procurement company. The article highlighted his disregard for parliamentary procedure, as well as the fact he had been taking kickbacks whilst ensuring the company received inside information about government contracts.

On the TV monitor on the wall opposite the debate from the House of Commons was entirely about the same subject. An opposition leader was talking from the benches. 'I'm glad he has finally been brought to account. There has to be an end to these corrupt practices, especially taking kickbacks in return for giving out contracts. Moreover, it's a well reported fact that some of the companies awarded contracts overseas have sold weapons systems that are now known to have been involved in the massacres of innocent people. However, it's a little late in the day in his case, as he should have been stopped by those around him, especially the Prime Minister.'

Declan shook his head and said to Gavin, without looking up, 'How many innocent people do you reckon have died over the decades because of what people just like that have done?'

'Maybe defence is an inappropriate word in his case, as no one is actually being defended any more,' Gavin replied. 'Not the civilians who've died, or the troops lost or the civilians after years of slaughter.' They looked at the TV screen. The Prime Minister sat motionless on the front bench of the government ranks, staring into space.

On Declan's mind was the fact that his cousins might be getting exposed to potential dangers as he got more and more involved in security matters. He knew that he was still on a list of some kind himself and certainly didn't want them involved.

He didn't look up as he spoke again. 'This sort of thing has been going on for decades. It's all part of what the government does so why the big fanfare now?'

Whilst he felt exposed, he had other things to take care of as well, and had just finished briefing Chris's team about all the information he had gleaned
~~~

from Ches. Of equal concern was that the TSU would now try and pick up all the faces he had provided, which could blow his cover. He didn't know what else to do but could only trust Chris to act according to his own instincts. They were hopefully astute ones.

'Are you alright Dec? You look far away.' Gavin looked at Declan intently as he spoke to him.

'Fine mate; just tired that's all.'

'Things getting you down, are they?'

'Yeah, some things prey on my mind. But it's my problem.'

'Something to do with that work you did in the Middle East?'

'Something like that Gav.'

Gavin nodded and looked up at the TV monitor again. Declan took a swig of his drink and added, 'Everyone has to be careful these days.'

'I know you. You'll try and keep everyone else out of trouble if you can.'

'I wish I could.'

There were few people around them in the pub. They looked up at the TV monitor and the caption now read, *New corruption allegations against senior ministers.*

~~~

Brandon Sinclair stood in a room in the Croydon safe house and reflected on recent events as his main lieutenants chatted around him. Most of the conversations were about the channels of procurement that had recently opened up with delivery notes, chains of custody and transfer documents from port authorities for all kinds of equipment. It was all heading towards his burgeoning network. It meant that someone inside the security service would have most likely now got hold of this information, and it would point straight at him and those around him.

He also knew that recent activities would have exposed them to much greater scrutiny, and not everyone inside his network had been that careful in covering their tracks. But at the same time there was no real need for being candid anymore. He had narrowly escaped arrest a few times and as new avenues were opened up by the TSU his people got better at closing them down. It was an exercise in accepting losses whilst moving on with the campaign.

He had been remarkably lucky so far. But as he stepped back to see the bigger picture it was becoming apparent that some of those in power didn't actually want to take action against him and his militants. The facts linking him and his people with violent actions could now be proven, but something seemed to be protecting him and his higher-level associates. He just couldn't put his finger on what exactly.
~~~

He waved his arms in the air at the dozen or so of his closest lieutenants present, signaling for the meeting to commence. He began. 'We now have the basis for a negotiation. The draft includes the following. First, the immediate suspension of parliamentary activities; all MPs are to return to their constituencies. Second, UK membership of NATO and the UN ruling council to be terminated, and personnel returned to the UK. Third, all serving and former cabinet ministers of the last twenty years are to be arrested. Fourth, all UK borders are to be closed indefinitely, except for exit-transit through the main hub airports by tourists and those on business. Fifth, all British troops are to be confined to barracks.'

He paused and looked around at the subdued group, before continuing. 'These demands are non-negotiable. They have to agree totally to them, or we will release all our fighters onto the streets and continue the fight until all the government forces are crushed.' He stopped himself going any further for now. They were clearly now in a full-scale confrontation.

Jay Saxby then confidently picked up the chair. 'OK people, we are now entering the final phase. The government will be running to catch up and as a result will be hopelessly out of touch. This is the *End State* comrades: the end of decades of political failure, lies, corruption and war crimes by the politicians of this country. We are going to annihilate the political establishment, once and for all.'

~~~

'She's probably a hooker,' Becker exclaimed. 'It must be part of the job description; getting tied up by a politician.'

Ches and Becker were about to break into the opulent Derbyshire home of a senior banker, and member of the House of Lords. Through the late November mist, they noticed light emanating from a downstairs window. Ches, clutching a small bag of tools, had crept closer and could just see through the lit rear window of the mansion from his position twenty feet away. In the ground floor room, a young woman had been tied to a small bed. He gestured to Becker to come towards the side of the building, and he moved forward.

'Stay near to the wall mate,' Ches said quietly. 'I'll get in and give you all clear. He's probably cleaning his dick, so I'll sort him out and tell the girl to keep quiet. Then I'll open the rear door. OK?'

Becker nodded.

Ches crept along the wall and tried the back door. After a few moments working with his screwdriver on the lock he was in. He slid along the corridor and could hear the muffled sound of a male voice. He was sure it was that of the banker.
~~~

'Just wait, my dear. We still have one hour to go, remember?'

Ches got a large wrench from his bag and moved towards the door opening from where the sound was coming from, edging along the fabric-covered walls. The door was slightly ajar. He looked gingerly, careful not to make any sudden movements.

The man had his back to the door and was standing naked except for a leather mask, gimp outfit and a pair of black boots. Ches wasn't immediately sure if the apparition could see or hear anything, so he moved back into the shadows of the corridor.

He wanted to make sure that there were no mirrors positioned strategically within the room which would give him away. Only by moving back could he check the interior. He then stole forward near to the architrave of the door. He could see the outline of the man again, who appeared to be fumbling with a large black object. It was clear the figure was fully pre-occupied and hadn't noticed anything happening behind him. The young woman was sprawled face-down and motionless on the bed with her arms and legs tied to the corner posts. She was almost completely naked except for a thin bra and panties. There were no mirrors in the room.

'What a bloody pervert!' Ches thought.

He swiftly lifted the wrench and, moving quickly but smoothly into the room, he brought the wrench down on the figure's leather-clad head. The man crumpled to the floor and Ches hit him again, hard across the back of the head, to make sure he wouldn't get up. He looked about and noticed on the top of a set of drawers a handy blindfold and several short lengths of tough twin-core cable. It took Ches less than a minute to apply them to the man's hands and feet and blindfold him. He left the gimp mask in place. Ches noticed that the outfit made the man look inhuman, like some kind of pot-bellied crow. He had no reservations about hitting him again if necessary.

The girl on the bed had been blindfolded and lightly gagged. Ches wanted to be sure she couldn't see or hear him and, although he fully planned to let her go, he also knew this wasn't the room where valuables were kept. The politician would never risk keeping anything where he played his parlour games.

The girl was unmoving, and a horrible thought entered Ches's head. He looked down at her and, noting that her skin was a pale blue colour, he saw that there was a ligature around her neck. She appeared to have been strangled. Ches ripped it off her neck and slit the rest of the bindings with his personal knife. He then ran back to the rear door, opened it, and beckoned Becker over with a raised hand signal. Becker was there in seconds. Once back inside the room Ches turned her over, exclaiming, *Quick, let's get her breathing.*

Ches put two quick breaths in her throat, and she choked and coughed, putting her hands to her throat. They sat her up.

'What is happening?' She said in a clipped Slavic accent.

'Well, I guess your friend thought it would be a good idea to tie you up while he got into his outfit.'

'Where is that bastard? I did not agree with this.'

'Well love, don't worry, as he is flat-out unconscious.'

'I hope he dies. He is pervert.'

Ches put one of the sheets around her shoulders. Becker went off to look for some water in the kitchen. When he returned, he gave the girl several sips. Ches had already dragged the comatose man to the side of the room nearest to the door.

'I'll get him tied up tight,' Ches stated as he started unfurling more cable. 'That will scare the hell out of him when he eventually comes round. He'll think he's lost his senses.'

'By the looks of him he'll enjoy it, Ches,' Becker quipped. 'But not too tight. We're not trying to kill him, just rob him.'

'Does he have money?' The girl shouted.

'Calm down love,' Ches replied. 'That's why we're here, as he's listed as one of the wealthiest in the Lords. So, he'll have some cash somewhere.'

'But where is the money?' The girl asked.

'That's our problem love,' Becker replied. 'But there's going to be a safe in this house somewhere.'

'I heard him talk about attic to a friend on mobile,' the girl said.

'OK, let's start there then,' Becker stated.

The girl got up and went to look for her clothes. A minute later she was back.

'My name is Mila.'

'I'm Ches, this is Becks.' Ches was surprised at how formally she had addressed them but found it somehow sweet at the same time. He smiled at her and held out a wipe he had found on a side cabinet.

'For your face, Mila.'

'That is nice of you, Chezz!' She smiled back at him.

The three went up the stairs, soon climbing a spiral staircase to what they assumed was the attic. The door at the top was locked. Becker tried it a few times, finally exclaiming, *A sure sign. The door would only be locked if there were valuables in there.*

'If we smash door, you think anyone hear?' Mila asked.

'Who cares; let's do it,' Ches replied, picking a lump hammer out of his tool bag. He ushered them back and smacked the lock with the hammer. Nothing happened. Ches and Becker had enough space to get both their boots onto the door, and, after a number of hefty kicks, they knocked the door off the latch.

They walked into what was a study, but a study like no other. There were pictures of films going back over a century, including posters and black and white stills. There was a particularly large, framed, still of a man hitting a Morlock on the head with a wooden stave. The Morlock was moving back through the air towards the viewer.

Becker pointed at it, stating, 'The Time Machine, Ches, by H. G. Wells. It was a brilliant movie.'

'I think you'll find it was a book, originally, mate,' Ches retorted. 'But you're right. It was totally amazing.'

Ches was impressed by the array of memorabilia, and momentarily almost forgot why they were there. He stopped himself. 'Come on guys, let's find the safe.'

After ten minutes searching the three of them stopped, somewhat exhausted. Becker suddenly had a hunch. He flipped up the picture of the Morlock. 'There it is, guys, behind the Morlock.'

Ches went to work. Five minutes later the safe was open. Inside there were bundles of used notes and a number of jewel-encrusted tiaras and broaches.

'Must be some kind of collection,' Becker commented, looking over Ches's shoulder.

'More like an inheritance mate,' Ches replied.

'You think they're his?' Becker retorted.

'Never mind mate,' Ches replied.

He turned to Mila. 'What we'll do is split the cash love. But the diamonds we'll have to put through a fence.'

'What is fence?'

'Oh, jeez, we don't really have time to explain. But I'll take the jewels, OK?'

'Yezz Chezz, I hate jewels anyway.'

When they had finished loading everything into a bag Ches turned to Mila. Look, you're welcome to come with us. We'll give you your share. But don't tell anyone about this.'

'Yezz that is nice; I understand, thank you,' she replied. 'This is better for me Chezz and just get my jacket.'

The van was parked up by the side of a lane two miles away. Mila cursed the first two hundred yards in her heels and then took them off. She fell asleep in the van while Ches drove it thirty miles east to the Lincolnshire border. He carried her into Danny's flat in Grantham at three in the morning.

'Why did we do this mate?' Becker snapped, pointing at Mila, as they dropped her on a bed. 'We should have just dropped her off somewhere.'

'Are you for real? She's probably forced to live in a brothel, as most of these girls are slave labour. Do you get that? The MPs are all in on this. Just look at that gimp bastard back there. And you think we should just dump her somewhere.'

'Not my problem mate.'

'Well, it is now Becker; so, start to grow up a bit. That girl of yours up the road might appreciate it if you showed her some balls for once.'

Becker was too tired to fight back and just went and slumped on the sofa.

~~~

Chris and Jake were stripping their 9mm pistols having just done their personal weapon handling tests. Both had passed easily. Jake had been part of his regimental shooting team as a soldier and had always scored high in competitions. He had been so good early on in his military career that his senior officer had wanted him to go forward for specialist marksmanship training. However, he hadn't wanted it at the time and shooting just became an enjoyable exercise as a result.

'What's next boss?' Jake asked.

'Let's grab a coffee with Declan after this.'

'OK boss. Fill me in with some of the latest if you have any.'

In the briefing area twenty minutes later, Jake noted that Declan initially looked subdued and slightly guarded. It was no doubt a hangover of their bust-up a few days before. He also knew that Chris had already seen the report about the weapons on the streets that Declan had filed and guessed that the senior commanders were impressed with Declan's work. However, it was largely academic, as there was so much happening that a few less automatic weapons wouldn't make that much of a difference. At the same time Jake couldn't be bothered with any more run-ins with Declan. The three of them shook hands and went and sat down in the small staff lounge off the briefing area as Chris went and got the coffees.

'So, Declan. This man, Ches, was in your regiment and he's a good lad you say. He's already taken a few guns off the streets. What's the plan now with him?'

'Leave him with me and don't let any of your boys get involved. I'll handle it and I'll track down more guns. Just let me do it. If you send in another load of goons, well it'll just ruin everything. And frankly most people out there are sick and tired of what's happening, or just plain scared. It's getting like freaking Baghdad in some areas no thanks to what the TSU has been doing.'

'Yeah, I get your point,' Jake replied. 'I have problems with some of the tactical stuff as well. But don't forget that some of our guys have been getting hit recently. So, we all need a bit more diplomacy if that's possible.' Jake paused. 'By the way, keep your voice down a bit round here. It's just an observation. Some of the lads have been pushed to the limit.'
~~~

Declan nodded gently and looked up at Jake. He then noticed that there were a few TSU officers in earshot, but they hadn't appeared to hear the conversation so far.

Chris arrived back and placed the drinks on a coffee table. He looked up, commenting, 'Looks like you two have been exchanging views. So where are we Declan?'

'I'm meeting Ches again tomorrow,' Declan replied. 'I'm going to find out everything he knows, especially about these armed gangs. That's everything from the start, and then I'll get back to you tomorrow evening. If anything comes up, I'll let you know. It could be that this Craig creature and his comrades-in-arms are planning something spectacular. But it could also be they are just part of something else.'

Chris swiftly drank his coffee. He realised that the poitical situation was far more fragile than most of the commanders, or anyone above them, would have anyone believe. If they had to rely on information from people like Declan's friend Ches, then something had gone badly wrong.

~~~

Ches, Becker and Gail were in a café on Whitecross Street in Islington. When Gail went off to get some drinks Becker started explaining to Ches why his relationship with her seemed to be going the course. Most of the girls he had dated in the past had left him after a few months. But the girl he had met at that party in Grantham, months before, was now firmly part of his life.

'And she is female at least,' Becker added.

'No, she's still breathing mate.'

They both laughed very loudly, so loudly that people nearby turned to look at them. Becker waited until things had gone quiet again and asked softly, 'So, what about this Mila?'

Ches stared back at him, before replying quietly, 'Honest mate, Mila's a goddess. She's perfect. It's the real deal.'

'You're screwing with me Ches. You mean it?' Becker replied.

'Yeah, I'm screwing with you, but yeah, I mean it. She's totally perfect. And she'll be here in a minute.'

'Well, I'm happy for you.'

Foremost in Becker's mind was that he had recently bumped into one of the members of the *Outfit* as he called them; the group he had once been a part of and with whom he had carried out armed robberies on a regular basis. The man had suggested he got back with them and Becker had said he would think about it. However, he also revealed details of a potential new target, another rich politician.
~~~

The prospect of yet another hit intrigued Becker. With Ches he had already many thousands of pounds in cash and there were still items left to fence. But he felt that they needed to make some more money before calling it a day. Mila suddenly appeared at the table.

Ches looked up at her and smiled, 'Hi Mila.'

After a pause Becker added, 'Hi Mila.'

Ches grabbed a chair for Mila to sit on and ordered her a flat white coffee.

Becker whispered, 'I saw one of them yesterday, Ches. They've got another one lined up.'

'Do you know who it is they're after?' replied Ches swiftly.

'Yeah, some mega-rich politician; name like Harneck or something. He's made money out of everything and everyone, and he's got his fat fingers into some defence company that's been minting it because of all the wars.'

Ches immediately recalled someone with a similar name that he had once come across. He tried to shake it off but couldn't, and then replied, 'What would it involve?'

Becker seemed slightly shocked at the speed of Ches's response. He had noticed how positive Ches had become in recent months about taking on more jobs, but he was still surprised. 'To be honest I haven't given it that much thought, but we'd have to be careful with this one Ches. I know where the place is, and I know it would be difficult.' Becker continued, 'Why don't we go over there and do a reccy? We could get in ahead of that mob, so let's check it out first.'

Ches nodded, replying, 'Fine, we may as well just have a look at the place. That's not going to cause any problems.'

He then smiled at Mila. Sorry, love, we've been ignoring you.'

~~~

Brandon Sinclair and his associates were in the Croydon hide discussing the planned action about to take place across London. However, Sinclair was tired and his voice betrayed signs of doubt as to whether all their objectives could be achieved. 'I think the politicians will have to accept that they need to negotiate terms very soon. And we will need to be ready for that.'

Saxby was the first to respond. 'So, Brandon, could that mean that we actually stop fighting and start negotiating?'

'Not exactly Jay. I'm not saying we will meet with them. After all, we do have some items that are non-negotiable.' His reply seemed somewhat sheepish.

'So why negotiate with those bastards at all?' Saxby replied. 'We can take everything we want.' Saxby seemed animated, such that Sinclair was on the back foot.
~~~

'You're missing the point, Jay. We have to be clever. We can't run this network properly, let alone the rest of the country, and we'll need some allies if we're going to carry on with all this. We'll only have enough weapons and ammunition for a short period of time.'

One of the commanders interjected. 'Why don't we just waste those bastards in the TSU? That will send out a clear message that we're not messing around.'

Sinclair replied angrily, 'Because we don't want to look like a bunch of criminals ourselves. Some of them may be psychos but if we're ever to be taken seriously this has to be done the way I'm saying. We can't start a killing spree. We won't achieve anything if we go down that path.'

'And what, exactly, are we achieving?' Saxby asked, clearly annoyed.

'We're trying to give people out there a real choice. We'll arrest the most corrupt politicians. We'll put forward our agenda legitimately, but not as a bunch of tinpot gunmen hell-bent on revenge.'

'But we're not a party,' another commander replied assertively. 'We're a paramilitary outfit. We don't have policies.'

'We do now; and we'll all decide on them.'

Saxby responded tersely, 'We're fighting the state and we're winning. We don't need an election to legitimise what we're doing. Let's just take over and then tell people what's happening. As soon as we negotiate, we'll be on a downward spiral.'

The others murmured approval, but Sinclair stood his ground. He raised his voice above the chatter. 'No, it doesn't work like that. We need a functioning group that can take over running the country otherwise we'll have chaos. We have to provide security but at the moment we're too few in number to control this country. We have to have a proper political organisation. That's what people want and it's what they'll get. Not chaos; not in my name. Do you people understand?' A strained silence came over the meeting table.

~~~

'Frankly Ches I'm tired of pretending that this country is worth fighting for. It's basically run by gangsters.' Declan broke off. He and Ches had arranged to meet in Finsbury Park, and they were sitting on a bench in the winter sunshine. 'The fact they don't carry bloody Thompsons is neither here nor there. They're still gangsters.'

Declan stared across the park, watching a few families strolling in the park.

'So, what exactly are you fighting for now, Dec?' Ches replied. His low voice was getting under Declan's skin.
~~~

'I serve no master. We're all on our own. Bollocks to the politicians, and the police. They're all in it for themselves. I've done enough of their dirty work over the years.' Declan paused before continuing, 'Did I ever tell you what I did for a while in the army, when I first started?' Ches shook his head.

'I snooped; first of all, in Belfast, pretending to be a young Irish lag drinking in bars. I did a similar thing later on but in other places. I wasn't a troop sergeant at the time.'

'You never told me that Dec.'

'I couldn't tell anyone. But I had enough of that kind of existence a long time ago. Why do you think the country's falling apart? It's because of the total lack of understanding of what's actually happening on the streets of this country. The entire political establishment is basically a club, a bunch of public-school drips and phonies. I've been around some of them, and I know how they behave and who they are.'

'So why are you leaning on me to get the rest of the weapons back?' Ches asked abruptly. 'Like we have any real chance anyway?'

'I'm not. I don't give a damn about the weapons; especially if the militants use them against the politicians. But I do care if they're used against innocent people on the streets. Do you get me Ches?'

'We can't control what happens Dec. We're not soldiers anymore. It's each to their own, as you said.'

'Well, I just don't want to see innocent people getting slotted.'

'I don't disagree Dec – it's just that we're only two in number. We can't police the place.'

Declan nodded and stared across the park. His thoughts went back to a previous existence, as a young NCO sitting in a base in Northern Ireland, having some porridge at dawn, one cold March morning. He was chatting to a young soldier. It was the man's first tour and Declan had been assigned as Duty NCO that day. Later on, Declan heard a number of explosions and some fighting near to the base. It was normal. He found out soon after that the man he had been chatting to at breakfast time had been killed. That was a normal day in Belfast back then.

~~~

Jake was back on the team, no longer assigned to light duties. He and Chris were watching scenes of chaos and violence, from towns across Britain, on a TV monitor high on the wall in the station canteen.

'What's happening out there?' Jake exclaimed as he stirred his cup of coffee. 'Have we lost control?'
~~~

'Not yet mate,' Chris replied. 'But I know they're calling up some reservist troops under the Civil Contingency Order.'

'Left that a bit late, didn't they?'

'Yeah; quite frankly my patience is wearing thin, especially with the security chiefs.'

'Yes, it was one of them that once told us we had to face down potential militants and radicals on the streets and then cut the number of officers by half. So, he managed to wind up half the nutters out there and they gave us fewer people. The man was a total twat.'

'I know. I think I know the one, Aley gave him a dressing down in front of a cabinet minister.' Chris went and poured another coffee from the heated jug on the counter.

Jake found the right moment to ask the question he had been waiting to ask for several days, deliberately avoiding any references to Declan. 'How are we getting on? Have we got hold of any contacts again?'

'No, it seems they've all gone underground recently.'

Jake nodded and sipped his coffee. 'And what about our crew, are we at full strength?'

'More or less, but it's the strategy that's wrong. Too many short-term directives, and no real planning.'

'Hasn't it always been like that?'

'Maybe, but it's not the way to deal with this situation. We need to be ahead of the game.'

Jake nodded and paused before he spoke. 'Have you thought about your own future?' He was careful not to speak too loudly as other officers were standing and sitting nearby.

'Yeah, all the time Jake,' Chris replied quietly. 'But not just yet. Transferring right now isn't going to make me any friends with things the way they are at the moment.'

'True; and you'd miss all the fun.'

'You maniac,' Chris grinned. 'We'll see. Anyway, you're fit again now. You're my number two; I need you.'

'Thanks for that.'

They looked out of the window. Smoke was billowing over the rooftops on the horizon.

~~~
~~~

CHAPTER TEN

The decapitated body of the man was dragged through the streets in a part of town that has seen a greater share of violence than most over the last twenty or soyears. Onlookers screamed abuse and threw objects at the bloodied remains of the man. The shaky, but gruesome, video was being trailed into homes around the world on the back of a TV news story from the Middle East.

The TV report continued. *The body is believed to be that of Sir James Hay, one of the main architects of British foreign policy over recent decades. He had been visiting Baghdad for a weapons fair when his vehicle was hijacked in the south of the city more than six days before.*

Few people in the café looked up, continuing with their conversations. Meanwhile Ches and Becker discussed the next hit they were going to carry out, with Becker stating quietly, between mouthfuls of chips, *Look mate; it's just you and me, no one else.*

'That's OK,' Ches replied. 'We don't need anyone else's help anyway. So, it's not an issue.'

'Yeah, but I really think you need to get some distance from that Declan guy, Ches. I know he's your old pal and all that, but I get this feeling that he's not what he says he is, if you see what I mean.'

'Yeah, I get that. But I can't just walk away. He's an old mate and a good guy. And anyway, he may still have some use.'

'I think that's how he feels about you mate.'

Becker seemed to be suggesting that the likes of Declan wouldn't normally be seen dead in the company of Ches and Becker. Ches looked at Becker, stating assuredly, 'Whatever Becks, let's just do this one. The target's a dirtbag and I want my hands on the bounty.' Ches said this with a smile on his face as he rolled the final words.

Becker replied after a slight pause, but more positively, 'Yeah, well, he sounds like he's one of those twats who got lucky in all those wars, doesn't he?'

'Too true, but he only got lucky at everyone else's expense.'

~~~
~~~

'Look, I can handle the pressure on my own life but not anyone else's, that's why I usually work alone Chris.' It was 3:00 A.M. and Declan had a meeting with Chris close to the railway station in Harlesden.

Chris wasn't in any mood for compromise after many days of leading his team in the hunt for illiegal weapons and intelligence on the militant networks. He was losing patience.

'Look man; it's not right. You can't just ignore the rest of the team. You're supposed to be working with us.'

Declan was slightly surprised at Chris's dismissive tone and replied irately, 'But it's my decision Chris, and anyway I've got used to the way I do things. I've always been like this. But I can still help operate as your eyes and ears. I'm not sure I should have been involved as much as I have, but I guess I'm in this too far now to get out.'

Chris stared blankly at Declan. He recalled Jake's raw dislike for Declan and tried to shake it off. As a professional he couldn't let his personal feelings become evident.

Declan broke the silence again. 'Look Chris, I didn't come here to pass time and how I work is my business. I have a few leads, and that's all I can say. But I'm concerned that you're leaning on me. I'm not the Met and I'm not the Tactical Support Unit. You need to develop some other contacts it seems to me – but I will carry on regardless.'

'Yeah, I know all that Declan.' Chris stared into the blackness of the street. He needed another breakthrough. Moreover, he didn't really want Declan to try to gel with the rest of the team. Now Jake was back, Chris needed him to operate freely and having Declan around would create a bad dynamic. Ever since Jake had been off, they had been performing badly as a team, so they didn't need Declan's presence creating tensions.

There was also the fact that one of his men had been killed and two others injured. He looked at Declan. 'OK, Declan. You do what you have to and fill us in at regular intervals. You've got the secure net; and you know where we are anyway so just let me know what's going on, please.'

As Declan walked away into the night Chris wondered what had gone wrong in the man's life. His service record was exemplary, even if some of the years seemed to be missing off his files. He seemed socially inept, in some respects, but he wasn't shy or awkward. It didn't stack up. He also appeared bored with life, like none of it really mattered and he was just a passenger.

He wanted to quiz Declan more about his knowledge of the political situation. Whenever anyone mentioned the recent violence Declan had little to say. Chris sensed that he understood far more than he was letting on and wanted to question him about some of those who had worked with Brandon Sinclair in the past.

Chris also knew that Sinclair had once been released from custody due to a lack of evidence connecting him with any of the attacks on political targets. He pondered *was there a reason for that I don't know about?* It seemed that Declan was avoiding such issues and was only interested in his own way of working. *There has to be another piece to the jigsaw.*

Chris shook his head and turned back towards the waiting police car, an unmarked black BMW.

~~~

The Right Honourable Dick Harnack was one of those politicians who liked to use pejorative terms about others all too frequently. Words like *coward* or *scrounger* were such a common part of his vocabulary that it was quite apparent to a seasoned observer that the man had certain preconceptions about society.

More than once, it had been suggested that he only used such terms because he was concerned that others had accused him of exhibiting such qualities himself. Such comments, as well as his views about other MPs, had featured in national newspapers. They had never won him any friends in high places, especially within his own political party.

Ches was aware of the man's unpopularity as well as his connections with various defence companies. One of them had been known to both him and Declan when they had been serving soldiers. Like all soldiers they had handled ammunition, and in their case a great number of mortar rounds. The initials stamped on the fuse of each round were of the same company where Dick Harnack was a director, receiving an annual stipend of £150,000. His promotional work around the world had won contracts from the House of Saud to Indonesia and beyond.

As Ches was parking his black and battered VW Golf on a side street in Hampstead, the years in which he had been an NCO in charge of a mortar team came flooding back. There were both good and bad memories. He remembered the occasion when Harnack had visited his regiment before they deployed to Iraq in late 2003. He recalled the way he had spoken to them, like he owned them.

He could never have imagined that he would one day be pulling up near the man's house with the sole intention of robbing him. Ches also recalled that Harnack had been an arch backer of successive military campaigns in the Middle East. Those were campaigns that had taken the lives, well-being and sanity of a number of Ches's mates. So, he saw no reason to feel any revulsion at what he was about to do.

Becker had never served as a soldier, but he did know that Ches was usually right about people. And Ches had told him that the politician in question was
~~~

not really a human being, but *just another scumbag making money out of misfortune.*

They sat in silence in the car. On the radio the news report was about a British businessman who had recently been kidnapped in the Middle East. He had gone to Iraq with the promise of a large defence contract. However, he had been enticed away from the main business event by a small group who turned out to be militants.

'None of it makes any sense,' Becker stated loudly. 'No one can be that stupid.'

'You'd be amazed how stupid people are where money's concerned Becks.' Ches remained impassive as he listened to the rest of the news report. A grin of disgusted indifference soon formed across his face.

'Let's get on with this mate,' he said loudly, switching off the radio.

~~~

Declan and Gavin were waiting for Jez in an Irish bar near Russell Square underground station. It was 5:00 P.M. on a cold Saturday afternoon and they were in the mood for some convivial drinking. Jez arrived twenty minutes later. Declan stared at Jez as he sauntered over to their table clutching a pint of Guinness and a bag of crisps.

'Those bastards never leave you alone, do they Dec?' Gavin stated as Jez sat down.

'Yeah; too right mate, you can check out but never leave,' Declan replied.

'The police have no right to lean on you like this,' Gavin added. 'They know that it could screw your life up anyway – but they just keep on going.'

Declan had never actually wanted to reveal the recent events in his life, but he no longer saw the point of being reticent. He had therefore relayed what had been happening over the last few months. His cousins had been only too aware of Declan's absence from the construction business, but the fact that Declan had been involved in police work didn't really surprise them either. However, Declan was surprised that they now seemed to regard themselves as part of his life with no obvious desire to leave him to an uncertain fate.

'It may not be so bad you know,' added Declan in a much quieter tone of voice. 'I'm getting paid after all. By the way, I appreciate the fact you two still don't mind talking to me about all this.'

Jez replied softly, 'I don't give a damn about any of the mad bastards running around out there. But I do care about you Dec. And there's no point in living like mice again.'

'Yeah, too damned right,' Gavin added.
~~~

Jez recalled the time he had fallen asleep in the taxi and Gavin had been nearly jumped from behind. He then suddenly realised his last comment was hardly of any comfort. 'Sorry Dec, I didn't mean that you have been living like that.'

'We know what you meant Jez,' Declan replied. 'Like I say, I appreciate that we can all still meet up for a beer. It proves to me that I have you guys around me and that's all I need in life, not the bloody police or the security services for that matter. The whole place is probably going up in smoke anyway.'

'Indeed,' Jez sighed. He felt jaded after a week on a construction site in north London. 'But let's talk about more positive things.'

~~~

The Right Honourable Dick Harnack lay sprawled on the floor, having been beaten around the body with a baseball bat. Ches knew he hadn't inflicted lasting damage. Whilst serving soldiers Declan had once demonstrated to him the art of restraint when it came to a beating. He had said at the time that anyone could dish it out, but few knew when to stop.

Becker didn't understand. He thought the only point of being there was to get the combination to the safe out of Harnack, *So why the beating*?

Ches had stopped and was whispering something in the man's ear. Becker couldn't make out what he was saying, just the odd word. He realised that they were running out of time.

He decided to intervene. He grabbed Ches and shouted, 'What's going on mate? Let's get everything and get the hell out of here.'

Ches stood up and kicked the spreadeagled form in the stomach. Becker took out a ligature.

'No, you don't,' Ches stated.

'But…'

'No: I'm dealing with this man. Here's the combi; you deal with the safe this time.' Ches had written it down.

'You already got it from the bastard! Why didn't you…'

'Just open it! Leave me alone with him.'

Ches seemed both aggressive and remote. Becker had never seen him like that before and went off to open the safe. Inside he found papers as well as money and jewellery. He bagged the contents and left the documents. A few seconds later he heard a door slam. He put the cash and jewellery in a black holdall.

Ches appeared almost immediately and looked inside the safe. 'Take the docs mate.'
~~~

'Why?'

'Just do it! I need them. They'll go in the bag.'

As Becker was putting them in the holdall a newspaper clipping flipped out of one of the folders. On it was written the headline: *Two killed on army exercise.*

~~~

Jake was sitting in a group room surrounded by colleagues. One of them, a young officer, who looked like he hadn't slept for months, stated abruptly, 'I'm glad you're here Jake - we need some old warriors like you. It's getting like the Middle East out there.'

Commander Aley walked in accompanied by an assistant. He looked even more stressed than normal, but managed to say, 'Great to see you all.'

Jake stopped himself from making a facile quip in return, managing a guarded response, 'Well we wouldn't want to be anywhere else right now, sir.'

Aley gave them all a short briefing on how the rioting had swept across many British towns and cities and how the Tactical Support Units were now the last line of resistance. Normal policing wasn't possible in many areas and there had been constant callouts for firearms offences. He then exited swiftly with the assistant.

'Who's that, his nurse?' Jake said a bit too loudly once the doors had only just closed behind them. The other men laughed loudly, Chris more than any of the others.

Jake continued, turning to the young officer, 'Well to answer your question mate the last time I was in the Middle East I had to get granola bars sent out as the NAAFI didn't stock them, but at least we don't have that problem here.'

Chris interjected loudly, 'Just for the newer members of the team I'd like to point out that Jake's main strength is in thinking laterally.' Chris grinned and there was a low ripple of laughter from the other squad members as Jake grinned back.

Jake knew that Chris had recognised his obvious reference to the Middle East, that he was referring to military operations. It was a subtle mechanism for priming the newest members of the team, some of whom were confused by Jake's comments but were about to get a baptism of fire.

Chris added, 'Lads, if we need any granola bars, Jake here will sort you out.'

'Yeah, no probs boss,' Jake smiled. He knew he was truly back where he belonged. Chris and the team would be out all night targeting a potential safe house in Lewisham.
~~~

'Guys, listen up.' A voice boomed across the floor of the open plan office next to the group room. Chris's team filed out into the main area.

A tactical commander was standing by the main screen. 'We have three addresses we need to hit tonight. Chris's team will lead in the first. Once you have all been briefed by your team leaders get your waepons prepped. Don't forget forensics have to get involved as soon as we find any residues of explosives or ammunition.'

~~~

The white passenger van pulled up at the gates of the munitions research facility at 4:00 A.M. Ten men dressed in combat gear got out and the first showed his pass to the guards.

'We're here for a reservist weekend, working in the facility. Sorry we're so late; got delayed up north on the M6.'

'You'll all need to book in, inside guys,' the guard responded. 'He'll tell you what blocks you'll be staying in.' He opened the gate and let the van through.

The van parked on the other side of the guardhouse. The occupants jumped out, immediately overpowering the guards. They took their weapons and tied them up. Two of the assailants then occupied the same positions as the guards, with one on the gate and the other behind the desk.

The rest of the men got back into the van and travelled across the facility to the inner gates. They smashed through the Abloy locks with boltcroppers. They then went onto the first of the bunkers after re-securing the gate.

They smashed their way through the locks of the sliding doors of the first ammunition building and once inside they checked the ammunition. There was a limited number of high explosive ordnance, with a few 60 mm mortars, but nothing of any greater magnitude. The next store was packed with 81 mm mortars, HE grenades and 105 mm artillery shells. The next held shaped charges for bridge demolitions and boxes containing slabs of PE7.

They took many of the grenades and exposed some of the munitions, moulding plastic explosives across various artillery shells and mortars. A commander quickly linked up the various detonators in the three stores to the detonation circuit. The latter was connected to a remote firing receiver. Another man got back in the van and sent a UHF message to the two men in the guard house.

The men in the guard house reported that the second van had pulled up at the rear gates, overpowered the guards, ready to block anyone attempting to get into the facility. A base protection patrol had been sighted but had not yet appeared at either gate.
~~~

With the detonators, circuits and explosives in place the forward party climbed back into the van for the return drive to the front gates of the facility. Once there the commander leaned out of the window of the vehicle, shouting to those guarding the gates, *Open the gates and then radio the guys at the rear gate to bug out and then get in the van.*

Once through the gates the van stopped and the men who had been in the guard block jumped on board. The van then made its way along the narrow country lanes. After going just over a mile, it pulled up on a ridge overlooking the valley from where they had just come. The other vehicle had gone off in an entirely different direction.

The commander said nothing as he got the remote firing device out of its pouch. He had pre-set the channels before the journey that evening. He got the unit up and running and then pressed the keys in sequence to find the right channel. He held his breath, pressing the two firing keys together. Three seconds later there was a loud crack and then a deafening rumble. They felt the shockwave come up the valley towards them. Once it had passed over, they started off again.

~~~

Declan had a 4:00 A.M. meeting with Chris and Jake inside the TSU vehicle compound. He wasn't in a mood for compromise. 'So, you've been tailing me all this time,' he stated loudly in the darkness. 'You don't trust me or my methods, do you?'

'It's not that Declan,' Chris replied. 'We just need to know all the people you're dealing with; that's all.'

'I told you that the lads I deal with are bright and switched on. You've likely screwed it all up and blown my cover.' He paused, adding, 'You know my old mate isn't just clever. Clever is about just getting what you want. Skill on the other hand is getting what you really need and then delivering it. This lad has it in bundles.'

'I didn't say he hadn't.'

'But that's what you thought; and it's how you've played it. You couldn't trust me.'

'Look, I'm sure he's a really talented lad. And that he's your ears and eyes but...'

'Chris, you still don't get it. Without people like us you've lost already. So far, I've been straight with you guys but all you've done is thrown it right back in my face. Even my cousins have seen your lads tailing me and put two and two together. You people are desperate, running scared. So, for now, it's over: there's nothing more I can do for you. If my cousins have it all worked out,
~~~

then the various groups out there watching me have also got it sorted.' Declan went off into the night.

~~~

A man stood on Parliament Square, in front of the House of Commons, and unveiled a large sheet with text on it. It read *NO FUTURE,* and it was the last thing the few politicians assembled inside the House of Commons would have seen on their way through the security check earlier that evening.

After an hour of debate, over the worsening security situation, one opposition MP stood up and asked the front bench of the government, 'Having just reduced the numbers of operational armed police, yet again I might add, there now seems to be a growing insurgency within the UK. So far, you've managed to avoid criticism by keeping the worst of the attacks off the front pages. But let's be honest here: what does the government propose to do now?'

Brandon Sinclair was watching the live debate on his phone as he sat in a restaurant barely a mile away in Green Park. As he ate, he also studied the editorial column in the broadsheet newspaper in front of him. It raised the question as to why government ammunition facilities had only recently been targeted by militants. After all, they had been poorly guarded in recent years due to extensive cuts in defence spending and that had been common knowledge. Taking out such facilities would have had a major political impact on the government's ability to wage war against the militants. The conclusion was that they had actually been lucky to escape such attacks up until now and last night's events were therefore hardly surprising. He smiled. Sinclair asked for a filter coffee and watched the activity within the House of Commons. The Prime Minister's speech was being drowned out by choruses of *Failure* from both the opposition ranks as well as his own backbenches.

One opposition front bench spokesman then got up and made an outspoken attack on the government. 'This is a disastrous establishment, presiding over an exhausted country with a flat-lining economy. We now have a compromised and disjointed society because of the failed policies of successive ministers. It may have escaped your notice, but we also have large pools of completely disillusioned young people; and some of them are quite handy with weapons and explosives, or so it transpires. Add to that the violent and aggressive nature of our youth in general, as well as the marginalisation of whole communities, and this is where we find ourselves. We're not on the verge of civil conflict, we're in one.'

The Prime Minister burst back, 'And for how many years did your party fail this country? It was your party that started the rot; your party that failed to close the borders; your party that failed over the Middle East..."
~~~

One voice from the back benches became clearer as the debate got more heated. It was that of a Scottish Nationalist. 'Many of the MPs of this house have been supporters of the kind of decadent and failed policies that have helped bring this situation about. This entire building is now just a liability in the eyes of the great mass of people, and we have all helped to create an ungovernable and corrupt society. This is precisely the kind of situation most failed states have on the eve of revolution. Our collective decadence, ladies and gentlemen, and our mutual mistrust, has cost our nations. We have all failed. We have failed every single person in our nations.'

~~~

Declan flicked through his newspaper. The TV monitor above his kitchen worktop left the confines of the debating chamber of the House of Commons and a picture of a man came on the screen under the headline: *Former cabinet member found in a coma.*

It seemed that while the injuries inflicted were those that would normally have been suffered in a fight, no forensic evidence had yet been found. The man's property backed onto Hampstead Heath but there was no CCTV footage of anyone breaking an entry. No neighbours had heard any noise or shouting. Declan had a mild flashback to his conversation with Gavin and Jez a few evenings before. He then thought of Ches.

What followed was a related news story about an ammunition incident over ten years before that had taken place because a manufacturer had put cheap, imported components on several hundred shoulder-launched weapons. One had then misfired and exploded on an army exercise seriously injuring several infantry soldiers. The man found in a coma, Sir Dick Harnack, had been a director of the company and he'd played a crucial role in selling the weapons to the British Army.

Questions had at the time been raised over the manufacture of the weapons and the checks that should have been put in place. All others from the batch at the time of the incident had been taken out of service and examined, with many found to be faulty, due to poor componentry.

Declan then recalled the incident that had happened to his own unit with the faulty mortar. The two men killed were personal friends. A thought suddenly crept over him. He put the piece of toast down and stared blankly out of the window. 'Stone me! That's what the bugger's really been doing all this time. I thought he was up to something.'

~~~

'He looks a bit glassy-eyed mate; do you think he's dead? Or just no longer gives a monkey's?'

'Probably the last one mate.'

The two black-clad and heavily armed militiamen stood over the motionless body in front of them. It was that of a senior executive of a commercial bank based in the heart of the City of London. His name was on a list of those targeted by Sinclair's militants, not only because his yearly earnings were of a stratospheric nature, but also because his bank had been donating large amounts of money to individuals within government circles in exchange for kickbacks. These had given access to government contracts. It was Sinclair's policy to only go after those deemed to be acting corruptly and in favour of the government. This was just such a man.

Sinclair's network had also been trying to help those communities hardest hit by the economic downturn that had been washing over the country for several years now. Some of the proceeds from robbing corrupt public figures were therefore being given out to the poorest families in the country. However, while many of his supporters viewed themselves as latter-day Robin Hoods, to Sinclair they were not just about the redistribution of wealth, as they were only one way of getting quick cash for his cause.

To Sinclair, there were no illusions as to the ultimate aim. Such activities were mainly about moving the country towards the *End State*, as he called the final phase of activity. They were nothing other than a declaration of civil war.

'Shall we?' one of the militants asked his comrade. It was a polite enquiry as to whether they should continue moving through the vast Holland Park property.

'Not yet,' the other replied. 'I want to see what he has to say about the people he's been involved with. This one's skimmed enough off for himself.' He then lifted the sprawled figure's head up off the floor. The man seemed beyond help. The two militants then decided to ransack the property.

Meanwhile Brandon Sinclair was with his commanders in the Croydon safe house, away from the violence that was sweeping the capital. He turned to one of them, a weather-beaten ex-soldier, asking, 'We have a few more targets tonight, so, how's it going for you?'

'Truth is Brandon we don't have much control over it,' the man replied. 'We thought we'd better just get on with hitting some of the minor targets; and the ones that give us a bit of a cash boost if you know what I mean,' he said with measured assertion, coupled with a grin.

Sinclair wanted to be seen to bring order to the streets after the petty thieving. He would then abruptly call off the attacks, suggesting perhaps that he was the one in control of the general situation. Not even those closest to him would be allowed to know all his real intentions for the future.

He jumped back into a pro-active mode. 'OK, let's get on with it guys, we need to prepare for the next phase. This meeting with the command group has been organised to discuss the coordinated attack on the security forces across the country.'

After a further hour of talks Sinclair gave a final briefing and then sent out a UHF and texted message. 'All Call Signs: move to Amber State.'

~~~
~~~

CHAPTER ELEVEN

Annie pulled her distended figure off Chris. She was sweating and exhausted and slumped to his side. 'Wow I didn't realise that making winners could be so tiring,' she exclaimed ironically.

'Well, you should do love, you've got one inside you,' Chris replied. He was tired and motionless due to the demands of the long shifts he had been putting in. He then capped his left hand over her buttock. She groaned.

He could not be completely preoccupied with his domestic situation, and he re-focused his thoughts on what was happening out on the streets. He recalled the ill-tempered meeting early the previous morning with Declan. He was concerned that Declan had forced him to accept a bad situation and one that he had no ultimate control over. But there was no one else that could do the job of getting guns off the streets as few officers were connected to local communities. There were other potential undercover operatives, but none as experienced as Declan. Moreover, in such a dangerous and fluid situation there wasn't time to get anyone else up to the same standard.

Two hours later he was sitting in an unmarked police car with Jake and staring at the front door of a Victorian house fifty yards away along a road in Balham. Jake was still happy to be back doing surveillance work with Chris and the team. In recent weeks there had been some limited success in arresting militants and Commander Aley had decided that he needed the best teams in place around the clock to find out what more could be done.

Other law enforcers in towns and cities across Britain had come to the same conclusion, that this was now the time to get heavy with the networks and to go on the offensive. It had clearly rattled many of the militants as they were hitting back even harder and were out in the open, which was where the Tactical Support Units wanted them.

'You know Jake,' Chris observed. 'I've been digging a bit deeper with regards to our friend Dec and a few things have come up. He has gaps in his service records, and it would appear he spent quite a while in South Asia in the early nineties according to his regiment.' Chris sipped coffee from his flaskmug.

'I thought this was the guy who did tours in Iraq, Northern Ireland and the Balkans,' Jake replied, slightly confused. 'How could he have done all that and still been in Asia?'

'Because he did stuff other than the things he claimed he did. He didn't mention anything to us, and I guess Aley didn't care about the gaps.'

'Maybe he went for selection, and then went out there, to Asia.' Jake replied.

'Selection? For what?'

'Special Forces.'

'How would that relate to Asia?'

'I think some of them were training anti-Maoist guerillas at one time, possibly in Cambodia or Laos. But I don't know.' Jake paused before adding. 'It could have just been a break from soldiering. Have you looked at that?'

'Yeah, I had a brief scan; but he was still being paid by the British Army.' Chris paused. 'There's a report done on him as well. In brief it states that he's a rare combination of someone who can think, who can motivate and who can fight; all to a very high level. Whoever was writing the report seemed to think that the man is so good in all three respects that he had an incendiary and explosive side to his personality. It seems to be suggesting that he could be a threat as much as an asset.'

~~~

The TV monitor high up on the wall of the Islington pub displayed a brief statement denying the accusation that Sinclair's network had been engaged in terrorist activities. Few people in the pub noticed. The accusation had been sent out two days before directly by the Prime Minister, with Sinclair and his supporters officially labelled *terrorists* by the State. It then flicked over to show images of burning police cars in various English cities.

'Looks like we're entering an end game,' Declan commented, as he turned towards Gavin. He saw Ches sitting a few tables away and acknowledged him with a barely perceptible nod. He had asked Ches by text not to come over but instead sit nearby.

'What do you mean, Dec, an end game?' Gavin replied.

'These militants are going for broke. They're probably going to stage a massive attack.'

'You're kidding, aren't you?'

'Nope.'

~~~

The parliamentary enquiry into the failure to control the spiraling violence on the streets had started, and Sir Digby Bill, Chief of UK Homeland Security, was being called to account by a front-bench opposition MP. 'So, Sir Digby, we all seem to be paying for the screw-ups by your department. What have you to say on the matter?'

Bill stood up and, looking directly at his questioner, answered threateningly. 'If we'd had the right resourcing and the right kind of people we could have made earlier inroads into these networks. But they were never made available, and the militants seem to be set on destroying society no matter what. So, there's little else we can do apart from wholesale intervention and martial law.'

The chairman intervened. 'The situation in our towns and cities has helped undermine the stability and authority of our government and the very stability of society. Do you realise just how many people out there are now feeling completely scared and isolated?'

'No, I don't,' replied Bill. 'But I don't accept that it's my department alone that is to blame for the failure out on the streets. The failure is due to the political establishment with the history of both poor accountability and management at a higher level than mine. My colleagues and I will not be used as scapegoats.'

'I will stop you there,' the chairman started, but it was too late as Sir Digby Bill had stood bolt upright to his full height of six feet two inches. He stormed off.

The committee chairman called after him, 'You're being suspended pending further investigation into what you and your people have been doing while you were in charge.'

The chairman then turned to the others in the panel and commented, 'I think we can use this situation to some advantage.'

~~~

There were loud cheers from the hundred or so militants gathered in the south London warehouse. Several stood up and applauded. Jay Saxby, now Brandon Sinclair's official second-in-command, continued speaking. 'They just don't get it, those corrupt morons in that so-called parliament. They think that we all live for TV gameshows and sporting circuses, and that we don't see the bigger picture of what they've been doing. They think that they can cajole and bully the world, having denied us all what's ours by right. Such control freaks are in all parties. They're the same filth that spent billions on wars that should never have been fought. They will always think they can attack and destroy whoever they want; that's why we have to destroy them with the limited resources we have. No prisoners and no surrender. Remember that people - this is a fight to the death.'

Saxby went over to shake hands as the militants applauded. The noise from the assembled crowd grew louder, *no surrender, smash the state*! For several minutes it drifted outside to the surrounding streets.
~~~

Sinclair was in his Croydon safe house watching the proceedings on a webcam. He could also see other demonstrations happening simultaneously across the country.

Meanwhile a crowd of several thousand militant sympathisers had gathered in the streets around Tooting Broadway, engaged in a stand-off with Met Police units. By the end of the night the area was ablaze and there was fighting with the police and security forces in towns and cities across England. Sinclair's call to step up the attacks was being answered, and he was happy with the response so far.

~~~

'So, Ches. Got any ladies in your life?' Declan asked as he and Ches stood by a bar in Camden.

The week before Declan had asked Ches to come to an Islington pub but not to talk to him. The reason had been simple: to see if the TSU were following them both. They weren't. Declan now wanted to give Ches his share of the cash the TSU had sent him for his own services. He also wanted to tell him to go away for a while until everything had blown over.

'Yes Dec,' Ches replied quietly. 'Mila.'

Ches grinned. He looked slightly askance at Declan, before continuing, 'I'm not the lad I once was. Neither are you, mate.' He paused before adding, 'So why did you really get back in touch with me? Was it just to see if you were being followed?' Ches asked the question in a matter-of-fact manner rather than implying any real concern.

Declan stared back but didn't answer. He shrugged and frowned. There was a tired look on his face, and he ordered a pint before answering dispiritedly. 'I don't know Ches, but I can't do any more gun-chasing. I have some things I have to take care of. As for guns, they're now someones else's business. Besides I just want to give you this cash mate.'

Ches looked down as Declan passed him a brown bag hidden in a newspaper. He guessed that Declan hadn't arranged to meet him in order to enlist any more help. However, while he didn't believe that it would be the last time they would ever meet, he also knew they would not be moving in the same circles again for a good length of time.

Declan continued. 'I'll give you some advice Ches. Take care of yourself and those closest to you. Things are turning really nasty pal and I'm out of it now.'

Ches forced his own gaze and met Declan's as he squeezed the bag. 'Yeah, you too mate. Thanks for this Dec.'

~~~

Assault rifles were being handed out along with magazines of ammunition. Jay Saxby was going over the last of the key preparation points. She had organised three teams of twenty for the attack on the government complex and two teams in support. Each of those had twelve men. The main aim wasn't to kill the personnel inside but instead disable the machinery which dealt with intelligence and the processing of forensic information. The plans of the facility and much of the information about the security systems inside had come from various sources including a recent mass hack on government websites.

Saxby turned to the team leaders. 'We've made sure that those running the remote surveillance of the facility in recent weeks and months were well briefed as to the type of info we're after. They've done a great job as we now have a good picture of what we're up against.'

So far, she hadn't been very impressed by the assorted combat skills of the men on show. They had been practising in a muddy and wooded area that afternoon when a grenade pin had been pulled out by one of the men. He had then thrown the grenade without much concern about where it went. Luckily it landed in some deep brackish water that had taken the impact of the blast. But it had never been the intention to waste valuable ammunition or to endanger those involved.

While Saxby knew that the planned attack might not go well, they had to carry it out to prove that they were now serious about attacking state security infrastructure. They had to keep the momentum going even if it meant they would take many casualties.

She got together all the fighters, in their dark grey uniforms and body armour, and then stood over a model of the complex with all the surrounding routes. The first two fire teams would subdue the guard houses and then the third would head into the facility. The two other teams were going to keep any patrol units at bay and act as reserve in case they were needed, as well as covering the egress routes.

Once inside the occupants would be evacuated and then explosive charges would be positioned so as to take out the main buildings. Saxby had estimated that the whole operation would last around forty to fifty minutes. Extraction would be along the same routes as they had entered.

Saxby went over all the timings and extraction. If there were any problems a sixth team located two miles away was on standby to help but only if more firepower was required. They also had two extra vehicles, five miles away, each with a team of five. The radios were then tested and call signs checked. All the fighters cleaned, oiled and loaded their weapons.

At the ame time, a TSU team was laid up in a small convoy just off the M40 in Oxfordshire. They had been tipped off about the attack only two hours before and the sixty heavily armed officers had been cobbled together from various outfits at the last minute.

'All we know is that the government listening centre is about to be hit so we'll fan out in three teams.' Chris sent the message to the various call signs. 'Wait out for further instructions.' He clicked off the handset on the vehicle radio.

Jake sat next to Chris without speaking. He had a bad feeling about this one, as it was likely there would be no warning until just before events turned kinetic.

Chris turned and looked back at the rest of his team who were having a break behind the armoured vehicle. He and Jake got out and walked round the Mastiff to the foot plate where the men were gathered and the rear door was ajar.

Chris interrupted their conversation. 'So, guys; according to the boss it looks like we've all been misinterpreting the situation. The militants are obviously just a bit misunderstood and really just enjoy starting riots and killing people for jollies. So, we aren't reading them correctly – as if we did, we would be doing a whole lot better apparently. In terms of management technique, it seems to me that there's good old *top-down* Victorian and then there's something I call *Brazilian*. Does anyone know what that is?'

Jake let a smile creep across his face, as he looked at the other members of the team. 'You don't have to answer that one guys,' he stated.

One of the younger officers replied first. 'Yeah; isn't that some sort of a dictatorship method of managing?'

'Dictatorship?' Chris replied. 'Brazil isn't a dictatorship, you maniac! No: it's when you get your arse shaved by the boss when things are going tits up. That's a Brazilian!'

The team fell around laughing, Jake louder than anyone.

Once the laughter had died down Chris continued. 'Our boss seems to think we aren't working hard enough. All I can say is that if I find who it is that's been arming those cocksuckers out there, they'll be getting far more than a bloody *Brazilian*. We help each other today lads, so look out for your buddies.'

'Huah!' shouted Jake, followed immediately by a chorus of *Huah!* from the rest of the team.

At that moment the radio operator shouted down the vehicle. 'Sir, Commander Aley's on the net.' Chris nodded at Jake and walked off, Jake following behind.

'I hope you're keeping the lad's morale up Chris,' Aley enquired.

'Well, someone has to, sir,' Chris replied drily. He then added, 'Don't worry; the lads are fine.'

'I know that, Chris. You're someone we can rely on.'

'Thanks, sir. What's the problem?'

'We need to talk about your man, Declan. Is he still working or has he jacked it in?'

'The truth is I don't know. He doesn't want to meet us as he's concerned about his cover. At the same time, he seems to be avoiding all the secure channels we've given him.'

'What does that mean?'

'That we're not getting anything from him at the moment.'

'Too bad, as we'll have to find those weapons whatever, as well as any others.'

'Sir, those weapons could be orbiting the planet for all we know. They're gone and there's little Declan could have done about it anyway. They'll probably be used; either against our lads, or for robbing. But we can't do anything until we get more officers. Maybe forensics can give us some leads?'

'I checked Chris – nothing at the moment,' Aley replied. He paused, adding, 'We do look weak you know.'

'I know we do, sir.'

'Over the last few months, we've been getting weaker, and the militant networks have been getting stronger. The politicians haven't been leading. They're just about managing; badly as it's turned out.'

'That's because none of them have ever been in a uniform, sir. If they had they would look at the world differently.'

'You think I don't know that? Our own boss has been kicked out, forced out by a bunch of Whitehall morons. The new guy had better hit the ground running is all I can say. And those tossers had better start listening to what we're telling them; pretty damned fast.'

A crackle appeared over the UHF radio and Jake picked it up.

'Go ahead control.'

'We have contact at grid…' the sound of gunfire could be heard clearly across the woodland and the team lifted their eyes.

Jake nodded at Chris, who was looking up at him.

Chris stated clearly, 'We'll move to location, and then wait out.'

Chris took over the radio. 'All call signs listen in – move to RV now, repeat move to RV.'

He then went back to the satellite phone. 'Sir, we have to move fast.'

'Understood Chris, good luck.'

The team got back in the Mastiff and the patrol stormed off. One vehicle split off to cover the rear gates of the government facility. Within a minute the remaining four vehicles arrived in woodland several hundred metres from the outer gates of the complex. Chris ordered the engines to be switched off and looked through his binoculars from the gun turret. The militants were attempting to break through the outer gates and into the facility.

Chris clicked on his handset. 'Jake, get your guys into position.'

Jake took three men, running low around the fenceline, until they were within two hundred metres of the gates and behind the attacking gunmen. He checked the frequency on his UHF radio, and then shouted, 'OK guys, down on the ground.'

In the dim late winter light, they could see targets clearly through their optics. OK lads, on my word of command I'll take two to the right, Brad take centre two, Paolo take left side two. Robbo, you hold back mate and see what else you can find and then hit them. Is everyone clear with what I just said?' The team grunted *Clear* in unison.

A few seconds passed, but it seemed like ages to the men.

'Fire!' came the word of command.

Within seconds the six militants leading the attack were down. After a couple more seconds had passed Jake could see that there were other shapes near the fence.

'Stop firing lads. Watch and shoot.'

The shapes were in disarray. Their inexperience showed as they pulled back hastily, not having expected to be shot at from behind. One more fell.

'Cease firing.'

Four hundred metres away another TSU team was now hidden in the trees. Chris then saw another attacking group of militants who had got through the outer fence and clicked on the handset; 'Bravo, take out the main force.'

The squad then went to work picking off those attacking the main buildings. Chris didn't want to let his adrenalin rush get the better of him, but he couldn't stop the confidence building within him. 'This may be a long day, but we're going to win this one,' he thought, as he gave another fire control order over the UHF. 'All call signs, watch and shoot, watch and shoot.'

~~~

Ches kicked a can into the street as he walked with Becker along Bethnal Green Road towards Shoreditch overground station. 'Screw that bastard,' he shouted.

'Yeah, OK, I heard you.' Becker was fed up with Ches's outbursts and was only there because he wanted to clear up any loose ends from their last robbery.

'We should have taken a step back and thought about what we were doing. It's my fault anyway. I just went after the cash. I didn't think.'
~~~

It was now obvious that the recent hit on the home of Sir Dick Harnack had attracted far more media attention than they had expected. It was also obvious that their activities were attracting a lot more police attention.

'What was his name again, Harneck was it?' Becker asked.

'Harnack,' Ches mumbled in reply.

He knew that news of the attack had probably been kept out of the public realm just long enough so the establishment could try and hide the past business activities of the victim. But the repercussions were still evident, as a sharp-eyed journalist had latched onto the story about the robbery. Ches had been told by a trusted street contact to lie low for a while. They had at least managed to split the cash.

Becker was harbouring his own view that Declan may have had something to do with the enhanced interest in their activities, but he had no desire to corner Ches over it. He realised that this was now the time to split, while they were both ahead, and while they still had a reasonable amount of cash behind them.

He recalled that they had been in the pub a few weeks before and Ches had told him not to look at Declan; like the man was being followed. His personal feelings at the time had been uncompromising but he had kept quiet nonetheless and took some comfort from the fact that they had both made a lot of cash in a relatively short space of time without any help from Declan, or anyone else for that matter. They could therefore afford to lie low for a while.

Becker broke the gloom. 'Look mate, I think I'll bugger off up north and stay there for a while.' Becker was assuming that Ches had not been expecting that but, in reality, Ches had hoped that Becker would lead on breaking away for a long period of time.

However, a cold sensation now overcame Becker as he walked along, beside his reticent friend. 'You didn't give any info about me to Declan, did you?'

Ches replied casually, 'Becks, who do you think I am, a freeking supergrass or something?' He paused, adding, 'Well, anyway; that's the best idea you've had yet mate. I'm looking at going over to Ireland with Mila and my mum. Let's stay in touch though. I'll get the final load of cash out to you but then let's have a decent break, Becks.'

'Yeah, deal.'

They shook hands and parted company.

~~~

A man with a Yorkshire accent and a scarf wrapped round his face appeared on the TV. Declan looked up from reading the newspaper and stared up at the screen above the breakfast bar in his flat.
~~~

The man in the scarf started to talk. 'The British politicians have sanctioned the torture, bombardment and slaughter of innocent children, women and old people across many countries for many years, so now is the time for justice. Centuries of persecution will now stop. The days of access to cheap oil are coming to an end; and the era of supporting compliant dictators to keep the oil flowing is over. We're going to keep attacking until their world has been destroyed, replaced by our way of life.' The camera drew back from the man, showing him cradling a Dragunov rifle, with two men in black balaclavas standing on either side. One of them held a large knife against a hooded man's neck.

The transmission immediately switched to a studio with a newsreader. *It is believed that the man who was executed was Sir James Stern, a former government minister who had been one of the architects of the Libyan War. A body has not yet been found. He is the fifth former government minister to have been executed over the last two years. Meanwhile, new leads have been found into the attack on another former establishment figure, Sir Dick Harnack. He was found beaten and tied up in his home two months ago. Police officers are still putting together forensic evidence from the events of that night...*

Declan scowled at the TV screen, shouting, 'I wish they'd done the same to you, you bastard.' He laughed when he recalled that he had suspected Ches of carrying out the robbery and attack on Harnack. 'Who cares who did it anyway? It was Harnack's crap ammunition that cost the lives of two of our guys. He's lucky to be alive.'

He then recalled meeting him years before when he had been selected to carry out specialist training of so-called *friendly forces* in Cambodia. Harnack had been on the Select Committee at the time. 'Slimy bastard,' he stated loudly.

'Jeez; that was a terrible job. Training those vicious little bastards because the likes of Harnack thought it was a good idea; just so they could go out and kill innocent villagers who happened to disagree with their brand of politics. What the hell were we doing there anyway? How many years did I do that for? How many innocents got slotted because of people like him?'

~~~

Ches was walking along the alleyway coming out of Tulse Hill station, straight into the path of two youths who were smoking skunk. One of the two shapes caught his eye. It then blocked his path, shouting, *Bruv, give us yor wallet.*

Ches didn't say anything but in a swift movement caught the boy underneath the chin with a deft uppercut. He then moved back as the other youth lunged at him with a knife and caught the boy's arm turning it round, so the knife pierced his side. Ches forced the blade in as far as he could and then
~~~

threw the boy across the alleyway. He rifled their pockets finding an assortment of other peoples' IDs and cash and cards. He took them all and then kicked the two assailants for good measure.

'Having a bad day are we, you losers?' he said as he strolled away. 'And screw the police as well,' he said to himself.

~~~

'This is a complicated fight.' Commander Aley had just started a briefing session with his TSU commanders. 'On the one hand you have the leftists and their various militant groups. Then you have Sinclair who, put simply, has a programme for taking over the whole country. Then you have other groups who have separate agendas. What's also true is that many of these people are now working together. They're turning increasingly towards sporadic violence and whipping up local grievances against the police but more especially they are against mainstream politics.'

'Excuse me sir, if I can interrupt.' Chris spoke loudly, interrupting Commander Aley. 'I'm not clear on what's now classified as mainstream these days?'

Chris didn't normally interject at briefing sessions, but he had grown tired of the monologues from Commander Aley and had a wager with Jake that he could interrupt at an early stage in the proceedings with a bone question. Jake nodded his approval at Chris's question, but only so as Chris could see.

'Can I get back to you about that Chris?' Commander Aley was slightly dismissive in his tone.

'And on top of that we now have a situation…'

At that point a desk sergeant broke into the briefing area, exclaiming, 'Excuse me, sir. If I may, can I have a word?'

'Oh, is it necessary?'

Aley was clearly angered by the intrusion but moved towards the door alongside the sergeant, who replied, 'Yes, it is, sir. The PM has asked for a briefing.'

'Is the media officer briefed yet?'

'Control want to run things past you first, sir, but we can go now if you want.'

'OK, sergeant; lead on.'

~~~

The vehicles were back at the safe house and the militants were unloading, checking and cleaning their equipment. Saxby knew that of those that had managed to get away safely most didn't seem too overawed by what had happened. Moreover, none had actually used assault weapons in anger before the operation, so they were now well blooded. It had gone well only in that part of the facility was now in tatters. They had suffered three dead and twelve wounded but had ultimately managed to fight off the TSU by bringing in the back-up units.

It wouldn't dent the security services capabilities too much, but it sent out the very real message that this was not some amateur organisation. However, both Saxby and Sinclair also knew that the message to the politicians was clear in that there would be a long struggle ahead, potentially a very bloody one.

If they didn't fight on, then they would lose everything; and fighting in itself wasn't a guarantee of success. But that was all they had left. They had to hit back, for the real country, that great mass of people being disenfranchised by the corrupt establishment. It was down to people like those who had attacked the facility that day. Moreover, this was a clear message that the street fighting was now well and truly over. The TSU was facing an organised insurgent force with a command structure. As far as Sinclair was concerned, they had no choice but to continue the struggle.

Saxby gave a quick debriefing about the success of the attack and what they were going to do in the coming hours. They would split into separate vehicles having changed into civilian clothing. They would then make their way to the various designated safe locations. Some would go to a farm in Scotland and others would head to the Welsh border. They wouldn't meet again for a couple of weeks, during which time they would be paid by couriers. They would not leave their locations until they were advised by central command.

~~~

Ches dumped the bags in the corridor of the old stone cottage. He had forgotten how beautiful the drive was across the Cheviot Hills to his aunt's home in a small hamlet a few miles south of the Scottish town of Kelso, just over the border with England. The bright spring day had helped build his confidence as he sought the inner strength required to support Mila and his mother.

His life had changed now that he had met Mila. He knew that nothing could ever, or should ever, be the same again. He didn't care about the collapsing world around them, nor about the recent acts of robbery and violence that he and Becker had committed. Neither did he care about Declan, the TSU or the security services. The only thing he cared about was the survival of Mila and his closest family.

His mother and Mila would be staying there with his aunt, Caitlin, for as long as possible. On the journey up they had noticed others heading for
~~~

airports and ferries, so it was obvious that the exodus from England had now begun. They had decided against going to Ireland to stay with his other aunt, at least for the time being. Caitlin's cottage had plenty of spare space and anyway the place was much bigger than the oldest sister's in County Kerry.

As he and Mila crossed the threshold Ches sensed a certain familiarity, perhaps due to the odour emanating from the old walls. But he wasn't sure exactly what it was. On his way up to the entrance he had recognised the old schoolhouse next door in which he had stayed as a child after his parents had gone their separate ways. Following the split his mother had taken him and his sister from London up to Caitlin's village to start over. The schoolhouse in those days had recently become empty and his mother had been able to rent it for several years, far away from her former life at the hands of an itinerant and alcoholic partner.

Ches recalled that the yard at the back of the schoolhouse had been home to all kinds of weird contraptions and metal tanks. In some of them, dead rats had floated. Ches remembered their black bodies with pink snouts and tails flailing. The colours and shapes were now so vivid he could touch them. But everything now seemed smaller than it would have been back then, judged through the prism of a child's eyes.

He then realised that his childhood was now just a distant memory. But the sensation of being drawn to an earlier time was somewhat reassuring, even if that period of his life had also been one of upheaval.

Ches called out to his mother, who had entered the house having hauled in some more of their belongings. 'I have to head off mum.'

He turned to Mila. 'Don't be afraid, love. And ask Cat or my mum for whatever you need.'

Mila smiled and hugged Ches *OK baby, as long as you come back soon.*

Ches and Mila cuddled while his mother walked in. She waited a moment before shouting *Ches, get in the kitchen. Cat needs some help. I want a quick chat with Mila.*

~~~

The detonation had damaged the outside of the Interior Ministry building and sent shrapnel across the area. Twelve passers-by were injured. The minister in charge, once informed, felt strangely out of his depth. He had arrived fifteen minutes after he got the call but hadn't yet contacted the security service and it had been one hour and forty-five minutes since the explosion. He went over the events leading up to the bombing with the attending officer, as Chris and Jake listened in at the door of the incident control van. It was one of a number of police and TSU vehicles that had responded to the call.
~~~

‘So, what do we know?’ the minister abruptly asked both the building’s security officer and the team assembled around him.

‘Well, sir, there’s no real need to panic. No officers or senior figures have been killed or injured. The injuries to others were light.’

‘Yes, sir,’ a media officer interjected. ‘This was just a political act; one only to remind us, what we are dealing with.’

I know that the minister retorted, scornfully trying to grasp back control of the situation. ‘Far more damage has been done in real terms by the other recent attacks.’

The security officer interrupted him, ‘But, sir, we do know that the bomb was placed by two men on a motorbike seconds before it was initiated. The police control room saw them and was in the process of sending a team, but it was too late.’

‘Just as well they were late,’ Jake muttered to Chris.

The security officer continued, ‘Sir, we have a lot of shots already of the bike. It was just an old Suzuki SX 250. Plates will be fake, and colour as well. We have roadblocks but we’re looking for a truck as these bikes get ridden into the backs of other vehicles and then that’s it, gone forever. We have to look and think laterally. It went south just after the explosion.’ The minister turned away for a drink of water.

Chris turned to Jake and said under his breath, and well out of earshot, ‘You know for him a disaster is really just having the wrong wine with a meal.’ Jake smirked and nodded.

‘Well, OK!’ The minister seemed dazed and awkward.

‘Sir, if we can shut down the routes effectively, we may get them,’ Chris responded, joining the debate. ‘We suspect there will be a safe location.’ The minister looked into space and nodded.

Chris and Jake then waited for a further briefing and headed back to HQ. Commander Aley wanted a briefing about the situation and Chris relayed what had happened.

Two hours later, and with the next TSU shift ready to go out, Commander Aley finished his own briefing about the bombings. ‘We therefore need to form up the teams and get out there on the trail of this network. All hands for this. It will be a long shift people.’

It seemed government buildings in London were now being targeted directly and the rules of engagement were therefore changing. Chris, Jake, and the rest of the teams and their members got their equipment and headed to the vehicle park.

~~~
~~~

'What they said could only happen in the Middle East is now happening here, and we're not just edging towards revolution anymore, we're in one. The security services are completely pegged back.' The Minister for Homeland Security stopped talking, twitched, and then sat back and stared at the rest of the senior cabinet members assembled around the table.

The Prime Minister sat motionless. After massaging his temples he responded, much to everyone's relief. 'History is just a series of lies that no one questions. Do you know who said these words?' The ministers looked at each other and they all shook their heads.

'It was Napoleon Bonaparte, to an aide whilst in exile on the island of St Helena. And no, I'm not comparing myself to Napoleon. But I don't intend to be the first British PM to be exiled because of the lies of others especially at this time. We need to show more initiative. Moreover, we're not prisoners here and we'll not be blackmailed. We are the elected cabinet, and we have been elected by the people of this country who are now looking at us to provide solutions.'

Those gathered around the table looked at each other, slightly bemused at this outpouring of emotion from a man who had engendered little passion during his time in Downing Street.

He continued, unphased, 'For decades successive governments have been seen to be corrupt and lacking in the basic fibre that is required to do this job. Those politicians failed the people of this country. This is why we now have a war, a real war, within our own borders. History will judge all of us to be cowards, because that is what we are, unless we do something to change this situation and not let down the great mass of people out there. We need to defeat these militant groups and take back this land and govern it fairly; not unjustly as has been the case.'

~~~

Ches had returned from Scotland. He was in his flat going over the files he had taken from the safe of Sir Dick Harnack. They were spread out on the low coffee table in his lounge. He hadn't wanted to take them, and he didn't know whether to sell them to a media group or just burn them. However, together with the papers from the previous robbery, which were also marked *Restricted*, they made a formidable collection.

'There's enough info here to convict the last three governments,' he stated to himself. 'I don't think anyone can trust anyone after reading these. It looks like Harnack teamed up with some crooked London-based import-export merchants to strike deals over everything from weapons sales to trading human flesh. He must have kept the documents in his safe to act as future
~~~

blackmailing material. They were obvious bargaining chips in case he wanted to lean on someone.'

Ches wondered if the militant groups, rather than the media, would be interested in buying them. 'It would do their cause a lot of good, especially if they got it all out into the papers.' He shook his head. 'Ah, I don't know.'

In his phone he still had the mobile number of Craig, the man who had tried to get him to distribute guns. He gave him a call and explained what he had, without explaining where he had got it.

Craig thought for a moment before replying. 'Yeh, I know someone who could help. She's called Saxby. I'll give them your number if it's OK with you Ches.'

'Yep, that's no problem.'

Jay Saxby was quick to follow up and phoned Ches twenty minutes later. 'So basically, Ches, Craig filled me in with the details and, well anyway, it seems that politicians from all the last three governments had a hand in these deals in some way. And you have quite a few of these documents, is that right?'

'Yes, I do. So, what happens now?' Ches replied.

'It would be good if you gave them to us. We'll pay you, of course.'

She seemed both persuasive and anxious. Ches guessed that she was probably keen on scoring some kind of media coup, or, at the very least, selling the material to the highest bidder.

Saxby continued, 'Tell you what Ches; if you want us to have it, I will ask my boss and see what he says, and we can organise a time to meet up. But I will call you back soon, OK?'

'OK, no problem,' Ches replied, somewhat sheepishly.

Ches put the papers back in the document holder. He didn't want them anymore. Then a feeling crept over him. He didn't want to get involved with anyone like Saxby, mainly because he didn't want to run the risk of getting into the crosshairs of a TSU officer, or anyone else for that matter. He phoned Declan. It took him thirty seconds to explain what he had.

Declan was assertive in his response. 'Look mate, I want you to do the right thing here. But for now, that means giving all the documents to me. And then get the hell out of it. It's kicking off everywhere now and it would be best to just go away if you can.' Declan's reply was more like an order, but Ches knew that Declan meant what he said.

'The likes of this Saxby character are extremely dangerous, and not to be meddled with mate,' Declan added.

'OK, just tell me where and when we can meet Dec.'

~~~
~~~

Jake sat down next to Chris in the central meeting area, ready for another briefing by Commander Aley. The room was nearly full of officers.

Jake quipped to Chris, *you know Chris, I always come back to this place feeling rejuvenated and ready to take on the world.*

'I wouldn't tell the wife that mate, she'll leave you,' Chris replied.

'You've got a good point. I don't think she wants to stay in London for much longer.' Jake wasn't joking and Chris looked at him, raising an eyebrow.

Commander Aley walked into the room. His presence struck Chris as being like some noxious gas as he drifted past the seats and looked around. His voice was terse, that of a man under immeasurable stress, who hadn't slept well in recent days. 'Listen in. There are now some strong leads on the latest bombers. That is being dealt with by various agencies and means that we are going after a number of groups. I won't waste any time, so here are the orders for each team.'

He put the open documents on the table at the front, adding, 'And by the way I hope you all realise that you'll have your work cut out tonight.' He walked out of the meeting area.

'You know that man has all the subtlety of an epileptic bloody elephant,' said Jake, out of the side of his mouth, as he picked up the team's orders.

'Yes, I know what you mean Jake,' Chris replied.

~~~

Declan was sitting in his car one hundred metres from Ches's flat. He had watched and waited in the twilight after Ches had walked down the road ten minutes earlier. This had allowed sufficient time to see if Ches had company. He opened the car door and walked towards the entrance to the flats. Ches had given him the code. He entered, went up the stairs to the first floor and knocked on Ches's front door.

'Dec, you could have texted me first,' Ches stated as he let Declan in. 'I mean I didn't know what time exactly you were coming.'

'Maybe I could but I wanted to surprise you.' Declan paused. 'Maybe I just didn't know what to expect here. I'm a bit worried about who might show up on your doorstep.'

Declan could see Ches still clasping a small kitchen knife in his left hand, evidence that he was clearly worried about who might show up. 'So am I Dec,' Ches replied.

'Calm down mate, I'll take care of it all for you.' Declan sat on the sofa. 'I'm sorry about not texting you. I just wanted to be sure - and then jump them if I had to. If they knew I was coming, they could have ambushed me.'
~~~

'It's just as well you are here. Take a look at that file.' Ches pointed to the low table in front of Declan. 'That proves that a certain cabinet member this guy Harnack knows was screwing everyone over. It shows how much he was getting paid to take bribes on behalf of defence companies and ease transactions with government military contractors. You recall we all had to shake that bastard's hand when he came to visit our regiment? He was standing next to Harnack. You remember that?'

'You think I don't?' Declan replied, almost shamefully. 'It was his friends that supplied the dodgy ammunition that killed our lads. He probably knew it was dud as well; him and Harnack.'

Declan picked up the files and Ches went off to make some tea. He flicked through the loose documents. After a couple of minutes Ches came in holding two mugs of tea and placed them on the table.

'Where are you up to Declan?' Ches asked.

Declan didn't look up as he replied. 'None of these surprises me Ches. By the way I split from the police. I know I came here to stop you striking a deal with any of those nutcases like Saxby but I'm not sure what side I am on right now. My head's a bit messed up anyway mate.' He paused, adding, 'But I thought you'd gone away Ches?'

'I did Dec. But I came back to sort out this crap and clear the flat. I'm glad you jacked it in. To be honest you seemed to me to be supporting those corrupt bastards in the TSU, and that's why I was happy to see the back of you.'

'The only real reason for what I've been doing is for the families of lads like Daz and Rave,' Declan replied forcefully. 'After all, what have they got left now? They lost their dads for no good reason. Whether it was an ammunition accident or in wars in the Middle East it makes no difference now. What exactly was the point of what we were doing as soldiers Ches?'

'You tell me mate. All those wars ever did was line the pockets of scum like Harnack and his mates. But we all know that now.'

Ches pointed at the documents. 'Anyway, I'm giving you all that crap. I've no further use for it.' Ches sipped his tea. 'I suggest you take it all. I don't need it. I just want to clear this place out in case anyone comes here while I'm away.'

Declan said nothing but nodded at Ches. He picked up the folder and then walked towards the front door of the flat. 'If you decide to stay in London let me know. Try and stay in touch Ches.' He opened the door, waved and walked out.

~~~

Commander Aley was one of the few senior personnel who had been asked to attend a government briefing about the worsening security situation. He joined
~~~

the various heads of agencies and chiefs of staff around a table in an underground office in Westminster.

A political analyst, a bespectacled woman in her late thirties, was the first to speak. 'Let us all be clear at the gravity of what we're now facing. We have failed to prevent the flow of weapons onto the streets and the police and security services have now lost control in a number of key areas of our towns and cities, most notably in Manchester, Leeds, Birmingham and London. Armed groups are now claiming that they run these areas, and the police have been either penned back or driven out. The choice we're faced with is either a full mobilisation of the army or the continuing use of Tactical Support Units. Before we go round the table let's hear from Commander Aley of the Met Police Tactical Support Group.'

Commander Aley stood to his full height of five feet ten inches. 'There are just a few points I would like to make. Firstly, we are holding the gunmen at bay. There aren't so many of them as first thought, given time our teams will break them down. The insurgent forces initially had the advantage, as they used surprise and momentum, but they know that they do not have the strength to hold ground. Moreover, they cannot secure any means to acquire control or governance. This is of critical importance as it means they have limited time to achieve any aims they may have.'

Several of those around the table nodded. Aley continued. 'Calling out the entire army may work, but I would suggest that we only use those units that have real experience of urban warfare. We do not wish to make enemies of innocent people and the main lesson of our involvement in certain overseas arenas is that we need the support of local communities. The soldiers concerned have to have far more restraint than they do willingness to engage with the enemy. That's why we need experienced NCOs as well as field commanders. Please remember that our Tactical Support Units are disciplined and well-organised and we have not had any incidents where members of the public have been killed or injured. That is something I'm very proud of.'

At that there were more nods of approval from around the table. Aley looked up. 'Moreover, we have exceptional commanders, and we know they can be relied upon to lead in the field, so we don't want anyone else upsetting the good work achieved already. If you use inexperienced troops, you may get a bloodbath which will play into the hands of the radicals. In addition, history has shown that a lot of these militants don't have the stomach for a long-term fight. They will run out of money, motivation, support and even food and ammunition. We hold the ground and always will, so it's really just a matter of time.'

One voice, that of a security chief, piped up from the far end of the table. 'Commander Aley, I bet there are a lot of ex-dictators in the Middle East and elsewhere around the world who felt that they held their own ground once: Mubarak, Gaddafi, Assad, even Saddam Hussein. And where are they now?'

Commander Aley looked along the table and, noting that the question had been put by the chief of MI6, replied hesitantly. 'That's a fair point, sir, and of course I'm not saying this will be easy. But we are a democracy and that is the main strength we have. The radicals are not elected and nor are they electable, and they know it.'

Another voice interrupted; that of a senior cabinet official. 'Yes, I completely agree with Commander Aley. But the militants have support from much of the general population who are angry at central government and the failures over the economy, as well as wars that have helped bankrupt the nation. Mass immigration has put impossible pressure on our society, much of it as a direct result of those wars. Recent polls show that for the greater majority of the populous the main political parties have had their day; and one could say that we have failed. This is much bigger than the Met Police and it's not your job, Commander Aley, to engage in politics. We just need the security briefing from you and that's all.'

Commander Aley sat back in his chair and said nothing. The politician was called Sir Gideon Ambrose, a liberal cabinet member who had made his living sniping at other politicians and public figures. He was someone for whom Commander Aley had little respect.

A chief of staff interjected, in an irritable voice. 'We understand all that, but the point Commander Aley is making is that the militants cannot continue to hold these areas, so therefore we have to hit them now. We can't let them entrench. That is why we need soldiers on the ground as well as armed police units. However, Ambrose, I don't expect anyone in politics to understand this situation as it's your failure that has put us here in the first place.'

There was a murmour of approval from the uniformed members present, with the Secretary of State intervening, 'Please, let's keep a modicum of civility here. This isn't a blame game. We're all responsible for this situation and we all have to work together. If we don't, we are lost.'

A chief from another branch of the security services followed immediately with a question. 'So how long have we got to take down the militants in real terms?'

'Two weeks max,' Commander Aley replied assertively. 'We need to mobilise some specialist army units and the rest of the TSUs up and down the country. We will also call up the more experienced army reservists under the Civil Contingency Plan. But we have to do it now before it's too late.'

Those assembled around the large table looked at each other in grim silence.

~~~
~~~

Declan was in his flat with Gavin and Jez watching the response by the Prime Minister to the demands being made by Brandon Sinclair and the National Revolutionary Council on the TV screen above his breakfast bar.

When it was finished the channel relayed Sinclair's written response to the government's request for them to hand in their weapons. 'We're not negotiating. They obviously want to learn the hard way and that is how failed establishments always learn, *the hard way*. Our demands are not negotiable. We're going to exact justice for those who died from the years of atrocities committed by British governments. They're the real terrorists and the real enemy of every man, woman and child on this planet. Whatever they have decided is of no relevance to anyone. We will win; make no mistake about that.'

Declan turned to Gavin, stating, 'I think that Sinclair guy was past the point of debating a while ago.'

Gavin laughed, replying, 'Yeah, there's no doubt about that.'

'Shame really.' Jez interjected. 'I thought we'd lost all the Irish ranters way back.'

'Well, some of them never actually learned to shut up, did they?' Declan replied.

'You have a point,' Jez retorted. 'Maybe us Irish are just a breed of sociopaths.'

The three men laughed, and Declan placed a movie in the DVD port.

~~~

'Well Ches,' Becker asked, as he paused to sip his coffee. 'What have you been up to the last few weeks mate?' They were sitting in Ches's flat.

'Oh, not much Becks, but I was up in Scotland for a while visiting relatives. You remember Mila?' There was a distinct pause as Ches qualified himself. 'She'll be staying up there for a while at my aunt's place.'

Becker recalled that Ches had offered to put her up in his flat, much to Becker's amusement at the time. He was mildly surprised that they were still together and equally surprised that she was now staying with Ches's extended family.

He decided that it would be better to move onto another subject. 'Thanks for sorting out the rest of the gear mate. Me and Gail are pretty happy right now.'

'Aren't you going back to Lincs with her permanently then?'

'Yeah, looks like it. We've got enough to get by for now.'

Ches just stared at Becker blankly. The events of the last few weeks and months had left him jaded, not least that he now seemed to be responsible for
~~~

the welfare of an illegal immigrant, even if he had fallen in love with her. Not that anyone was about to come looking. And Ches wasn't complaining. The last three jobs had gone very easily for them, and they could now afford to lie low for quite a while.

'It's good to see you again Becks.' Ches toasted Becker by raising his mug of tea.

'Here's to happier times mate,' Becker replied, lifting his coffee mug in reply.

On the TV the face of Brandon Sinclair appeared on the screen with the caption, *Militants Attack Security Service HQ*. Neither man spoke, each lost in his own thoughts.

~~~
~~~

PART THREE

CHAPTER TWELVE

Commander Aley was briefing TSU personnel in the HQ near Ealing after a heated meeting with senior service chiefs. He spoke assertively. 'Our main duty is to protect the public. Op Emerald is being rolled out and it could mean that the best course of action is not to fight on the streets but to negotiate. It seems we cannot wholly support the politicians any longer. Indeed, we may have to allow the arrest of certain politicians as some of them are accused of crimes stretching back over twenty or thirty years. It's not our job to get in the way of due legal process but, on the contrary, to help deliver them to an international tribunal if that's what's required under international law.'

He paused and scanned the men and women in front of him before continuing. 'So, let's all act extremely carefully when dealing with what is a very sensitive situation. Most especially, do not stand in the way of an international arrest warrant. Find out what you're dealing with, on an individual basis, as we cannot afford to make any more mistakes. Do not prevent politicians being taken into custody by those with the right jurisdiction. That means ask for ID, by all means, but don't contradict any kind of arrest warrant if it's obviously authentic. This is a very sensitive situation, so use your discretion.'

A TSU divisional commander from Birmingham took over. 'The National Revolutionary Council, as the militant groups are now calling themselves, is in control of large swathes of the country and the notion that we can still apprehend people just for carrying a weapon has now evaporated. All any of us can do is to play a holding game until some attempt at bringing order can be made. However, if fired on, we can fire back. The fact is that few politicians seem to understand the severity of the situation but remember we're not here to protect them; we are still here to protect the public. Those are two very different things.'

Aley had required that all his personnel listened to the briefing. Chris and Jake listened, at first, in semi-stunned silence. However, much of it confirmed what they had already guessed, or interpreted, after many weeks of turmoil. When it was over they donned their body armour and weapons and headed out to the Mastiff armoured vehicles, as many other units did so in almost every other major town and city across Britain.

Jake knew that the large hulk of the vehicle was protection against most types of missiles, especially those of the shoulder-launched variety. He had an immediate attack of déjà vue, having last been in a Mastiff on his final tour of duty in Afghanistan in 2012.

He had always felt secure in them, at least in Helmand Province, but he pondered on the irony of the fact that they now needed one in order to travel on English roads. However, he also felt guilty. His civilian friends were struggling to get food and fuel but he and his partner, along with their new-born son, were given preferential treatment. There was food delivered, alongside household and medical supplies for all TSU members. And there was also the security that came with his profession. And then it occurred to him, 'For how much longer?'

Many of his former army comrades had been left on the scrapheap by successive governments and he knew that a lot of them had sympathies with the militants. How they and their families would be coping was something that concerned him above all else.

Chris, as unit commander, had to relay his own briefing to the men under his command once they had got into the holds of the Mastiffs. He picked up the transmitter and started talking. 'Remember, much of the country is now in a state of emergency. There is no effective governance across large swathes of it and fighting is going on in many different areas for whatever reasons. All we know is that chaos currently rules on many streets, and it's our job, and the job of others like us, to bring order to people's lives. Forget much of what you've been told today. Our only interest is in wrestling control of the streets back from the gunmen.' He then went round to the rear and stood on the backplate of the open rear door.

'So, this is where tolerating political corruption gets you in the end,' Jake stated quietly to Chris as he settled into his seat at the back of the armoured vehicle. He continued, 'What a bunch of useless bastards those politicians really are. Or, should I say, were.'

Chris said nothing but just nodded in reply and then went to the front and relaxed into the vehicle commander's seat. Chris wanted Jake to sit and chat to the younger members of the team in the back to make sure they wouldn't get overly anxious. They had to stay calm. However, the noise of the engines made talking difficult.

All the men had their rifles loaded but not made ready. Each carried eight full magazines of ammunition with five stun grenades, five smoke grenades and enough rations to last twelve hours in case they had to stay out on the ground for any length of time. On board there was more boxed ammunition, fifty stun grenades, thirty smoke grenades, as well as extra rations and water.

Chris briefed all six vehicles in the patrol through their headsets. He again reminded them that they were fighting for what was left of the country and to restore order to people's lives. He joked about the fact that all tourists, foreign businessmen, many members of the aristocracy and various celebrities had now all sought refuge abroad.

He knew that the exodus had happened slowly at first and then, over the last few days, it was as if a human tidal wave had gripped the country with airports crowded by fleeing families. Parts of the media had been locked down as the security services started issuing 'D' notices, mainly to stop panic being generated as a result of the exodus. But it was also a pathetic attempt to try and restrict the flow of information, to prevent news filtering through to the militants.

With regards taking into custody potential political criminals Chris had no direct orders yet, and he circulated the fact to the men. He also explained that it was *unlikely they would have to implement such orders if they did come through*. He stated that the most important thing was that everyone under his command had to listen to his fire control orders, as well as any others he issued.

~~~

Declan, Ches and Becker stood on Hampstead Heath and listened to the speakers. The initial address had been by Brandon Sinclair and his message related to the intensification of activity against government targets. It was designed to permeate through all the subsequent speakers' words.

Jay Saxby then spoke. 'The politicians have always expected the great mass of people to fall in line with their way of thinking, but we have gone too far now, and the momentum is with us, and we cannot compromise. Towns and cities are behind us, the National Revolutionary Council, and we will bring justice for the countless killed as a direct result of the meddling by British politicians across the Middle East and beyond.' Saxby stopped for a moment and surveyed the crowd of around thirty thousand who had assembled. She then looked at the view across London.

She continued. 'UK politicians have been sponsoring state-led terrorism around the world for far too long, and that means that many dictators have been armed and aided by the Britsh. In Iraq, Cambodia, Indonesia, Saudi Arabia and beyond, warlords and psychos have been trained and equipped by British politicians. They even gave them aircraft with which to bomb innocent people and land mines to kill them on the ground. Make no mistake – we are living in a country that has supported terror across the globe for decades.' A loud murmur grew from the crowd. To Declan it sounded like a groan from the depths of hell.
~~~

Saxby continued. 'We are a nation of war criminals, as we all stood back and let the scum we elected do this to the rest of the world. You may die in the civil conflict that is engulfing our country, but you will be remembered for destroying corruption, just as those who destroyed previous corrupt systems around the world are remembered today. Today we kill but tomorrow we build. We will build this nation on the fundamental precept of freedom, and not the lies and smokescreens we tolerate now. We will build, not by using their divide and rule tactics, but by means of the rule of real democracy and the laws of this land.' An enormous cheer went up – it seemed to lift the entire landscape off the ground, sending a shockwave along the hillside. 'We will also bring revolution to other regions of the world. Make no mistake, many will die, but the future will be far better for all of us.'

Saxby concluded. 'The few people in this country who make up the ruling classes do not live in our world. They didn't go to serve in pointless feudal wars in foreign lands and see their friends blown to pieces or lose their limbs. Not a single member of the present government ever served in the conflicts in Iraq and Afghanistan. They never struggled to bring up a family on a low income or no income. But they have done terrible things and more to our country and others. It is the politicians of this land who are the real enemy. Go out and destroy them.'

The crowd screamed their approval. However, the spectacle reminded Declan only of a somewhat lacklustre music festival or pop concert, especially as it had now started to spit with rain. The three stood and listened to the rest of the speakers, Declan noting that Sinclair remained silent throughout the proceedings.

~~~

Jake got out of the Mastiff holding his rifle and looking through the sights to scan the area around him, checking for both militants and ground signs. It was a perfect spot for an ambush, and he wondered why they had stopped in this particular place, between buildings in an open area where there seemed to be no other people.

Chris jumped onto the tarmac and walked over. 'Get two of the lads out of the vehicle and meet me by that wall,' Chris stated, pointing at a small embankment ten yards away. Chris got to the low embankment wall. It had a link mesh fence above it. There was some movement one hundred metres away on the other side of the wall in a small green swathe of grass.

It occurred to him that it was most likely some innocent scavenging for food. The Mastiff had a few extra rations to give out to those most in need, although people generally backed off when they saw the armoured vehicles.
~~~

He felt slightly ashamed as it wasn't the best way to approach groups of terrified, hungry people who had been exposed to upheaval for weeks on end.

Jake and two officers got to the low embankment. He felt sick to the stomach. They had been mobile patrolling for three days now and, while the objective had been to deal with armed gangs, they had, so far, achieved nothing. Suddenly three shots hit the top of the wall next to their location, and they all fell to the ground.

Jake shouted, 'Effective fire, stay low.'

'Someone, get eyes on.' Chris shouted. The other members of his vehicle took up positions and the teams in the other vehicles did the same.

One man from the second vehicle shouted out, 'Seen; three hundred metres quarter right, top of wall to right of tree.'

'OK hold fire,' Chris shouted back. He then turned to Jake, away from the radio. 'Jake, put two aimed shots on that location.'

'OK boss, will do.' Jake immediately fired two aimed shots as ordered.

'Wait out guys,' Chris stated into his mouthpiece so that the other teams could hear through their headsets. 'Only return fire on my order.'

Several minutes went by and nothing happened.

'Jake, have you got a visual on what's happening around that area?'

Jake scanned the area.

He replied, 'I have my eyes trained on that area but nothing's moved.'

'OK mate, we'll give it a bit longer, and then we'll all get back in the vehicles. We can't go flying over there. That's exactly what they want.'

After three more minutes Chris gave the order, 'Everyone back in the Mastiffs.'

He came back to the side of the vehicle. The rest of his team members had stayed near the Mastiff, using it as cover, in case any more shots came their way. The top gunner had the heavy machine gun trained on the tree and wall.

'OK guys let's get back in,' Chris shouted to his team.

Through his headset he then stated, 'All vehicles confirm status.' The other Mastiff commanders then confirmed that everyone was back in their vehicles.

Jake felt agitated. He was also hungry and opened a box of rations. He took out the chocolate, sharing some of it round.

'Here you go guys. It'll help with the adrenalin rush. Well, it'll make it worse anyway.' He laughed as he gave it out.

Chris looked at him and shook his head, 'You're just full of it mate, how can you be eating now?'

'Chris, when have you ever seen me not eating?'

The explosion was deafening. The top-gunner fell against the side of the cabin as the men reeled. An RPG round had detonated on the external armour.

Chris and Jake dragged the gunner onto the floor as a second round hit the side of another Mastiff. The other men secured the rear door as Chris shouted to the driver, 'Give the order. All call signs reverse now.'

The vehicles screamed off in reverse, away from the onset of three more RPG rounds, all of which hit buildings and targets aimlessly. Chris knew that they would need a much bigger patrol before they could come back to the area.

'Sod this,' Jake stated loudly, as he checked the gunner over. There were no obvious injuries. 'Think you're just winded I reckon.'

Each man was left with his own thoughts as the driver swung the Mastiff round to face the direction of travel. Chris picked up the transmitter and radioed the rest of the patrol. 'Emerald 3 call signs: RV at Location Two. Confirm, over.'

Each vehicle commander radioed back that they would meet at the designated point. Ten minutes later the vehicles pulled up and the commanders exchanged stories about what they had seen. They were then told to sit tight by Chris until further orders came in from HQ.

Jake sat aloft at the top of the vehicle and looked through the optical sight of his weapon. He could see plumes of smoke rising over London and every now and then he could hear shouting and screaming, and gunfire. He got down from the turret and spoke to Chris who was in his seat sipping coffee from a flask.

'Why on earth are we not down there where the real fighting is Chris?'

'Orders are orders Jake, you know that.'

'Can you hear it?'

'I know; believe me, we won't be here for long.'

The order to move came within minutes. They got to the edge of a suburban precinct and formed up with several other TSU patrols, scores of vehicles and hundreds of men. Chris knew that other such groups were converging on locations around the London area. He also knew that they were finally getting their act together after months of indecision and top-level failure.

~~~

The man's face was almost completely shrouded by a jade green and black Shemag, as he appeared on the Arabic TV news channel. His eyes stared intently at the camera. He began speaking eloquently in a public-school English accent. 'Life is really just a collection of experiences; it's not at all about material things. All the objects we collect in life are meaningless. Only actions and beliefs have meaning. That's why many regimes around the world are falling apart, as they have spent so much time pursuing consumerism, they have missed the point of life itself. They thought that consumerism would keep
~~~

people happy. But it doesn't. Their houses are built on nothing and are about to collapse. This is what's happening right across the western world. People are tuning out and trying something different: civil conflict, the overthrow of corrupt political elites and breaking the chains that hold them back. This is no different to what the Middle East has been going through for the last fifty years. One corrupt establishment after another has been exposed; lies, cowardice and hypocrisy. Decent people are now taking the law into their own hands.'

The obscure media channel then showed the latest news clips of the London skyline in flames and soldiers and security forces battling gunmen in a number of other cities, as Declan and Ches watched on Declan's laptop. Such things had long since been banned from mainstream TV by the British authorities, but they had no control over global media.

It struck Declan as mildly ironic that for many people the only way to receive news was on an intermittent foreign website, often in a private bar or small club where screens would show events when they were unfolding. The main British networks, on the other hand, now only showed what the politicians allowed. Few people watched them.

Ches and Declan remained transfixed to the Arabic channel, especially as to where the gun battles were taking place. The security advice on the radio was to not travel unless it was to hospital or in case of urgent need, including evacuation from those areas where the fighting had grown too intense. No such information was forthcoming from the mainstream British TV media channels.

~~~

'We had a phrase in the army; *Combats are not for ironing; they're for dying in*. Well Chris; that's what it's all about now.' Jake spoke as he sat cleaning his rifle, without looking up.

'Shut up, muppet. You'll scare the younger lads.' Chris scowled at Jake. Six days on the road with the men had tested Chris's resolve. He had never served in the army or the reserves and hadn't yet got to grips with the privations he was suffering.

'They're going to get a blooding mate,' Jake grinned. He knew that Chris still had to get past some of his own fears.

'Yeah, too bloody right they are Jake; and you'll get one in a minute. We need them to watch our backs, so don't scare them.'

The rest of the team had deployed outside of the Mastiff, and they were now covering the area with the sights of their rifles from various vantage points.
~~~

'They'll be fine Chris; have some faith. They're all trained, some of them by yours truly!'

'What you mean Corporal Jones?'

'Don't knock that generation Chris.'

'I was joking.'

The comment lifted the gloom but only slightly. Chris's patrol had been ordered to penetrate closer to where the militants were based. Plumes of smoke were still rising above the rooftops. Jake was second-in-command, but Marek, a former Polish Army Intelligence Officer, had been appointed to lead another section of men and Chris was starting to rely on him.

Ten minutes later Chris and Jake jumped out of the Mastiff. Chris shouted, 'Marek; you take two men and go forward twenty metres to that large doorway up ahead. Cover the street from there.'

Chris signaled up the road to an old Victorian building that had been set on fire and was now a blackened shell. They had been instructed not to enter any buildings as the TSU had lost too many personnel in ambushes and at the hands of snipers.

'No problems boss,' Marek replied. After the Polish Army he had served in Iraq with the US Marine Corps and then gone to college in the USA. After that he decided that a career as a London policeman suited him better and he had moved his family over. Chris could see he was astute and the best man he had next to Jake. He was also a superb marksman.

Marek got to the doorway. He used the scope on his rifle to survey the area. He turned to his personal radio. 'I can see movement; 300 metres quarter right, maybe five men moving around. They're carrying assault rifles.'

'Check on and confirm,' Chris replied.

'Confirmed; enemy boss.'

'Can you get a clear shot down?'

'Just about.'

'Hold position. They're likely to have high power rifles at least as much as ours, PKs or AKMs.'

'I can go round a bit if you want and get a clearer view.'

'Yeah; that's OK Marek. We'll move up and take over your current location.'

Within seconds of Marek moving forward gunfire came down from a rooftop above him and the other two men. They were soon pinned down under heavy and sustained fire. One of his team members was wounded in a leg. Jake didn't hesitate. He lept forward with another officer, cleared the ground and got to cover near to Marek.

Jake then returned fire on to the position from where the shots had come. The firefight lasted about thirty seconds during which time the position was subdued. Jake then fixed his sights so as to keep any other snipers' heads down.

Two men pulled the wounded man back to the Mastiff. Chris had already radioed for the Medevac to come up and it soon shot down the road, reversed so the back doors were opposite Chris's Mastiff. They then bundled the man into the back. He had a severe arterial bleed from his thigh and was taken away immediately.

As Chris gave a Sit Rep more shots hit the side of the Mastiff. The top gunner unleashed a withering salvo of fifty calibre fire in the direction of where the shots came.

After another minute went by, Chris shouted *stop firing* into the radio, not wholly confident that the gunner had a clear target indication. He then got on the radio.

'Jake; check the target area with your sights. Top gunner: give me a target indication will you.'

'OK boss.' The top gunner scanned the area using the side of the turret as protection.

'I think I have located his last: but he's now moving around the roof tops.'

'OK everyone: watch and shoot.'

The men on the ground moved slightly from the Mastiffs, as to be shielded by whatever cover they could find as the seconds then ticked away.

'Everyone: hold fire until you get a clear indication,' Chris stated through his radio.

Chris decided to order the patrol to move back one hundred metres to a safer location, also so they could cut off a possible escape route. At the same time, he could see other TSU vehicles moving through the surrounding streets. Control would have to establish how many areas had now been cleared before they made any further moves. Chris then ordered his team back to the vehicles.

'This is going to get a bit harder if we lose any more people Chris,' Jake stated quietly once he had crawled next to the commander's seat at the front of the vehicle.

'Yeah, I know Jake,' replied Chris. 'But it's what we have to do as no one else will do it for us.'

The vehicles then moved off up the road.

~~~

Declan, Ches and Becker walked along with the crowds towards the Houses of Parliament, where an enormous demonstration was taking place. Many troops had refused to fire on the thousands of protesters, and some had openly joined the protests. A *No Mans Land* had formed between the protestors and the
~~~

security cordon. No one stepped across it apart from a few reporters, evidence of the reduced media presence.

Two small helicopters hovered over the crowds, one disappearing behind the parapets of buildings as it scanned the Westminster area. Several salvos of gunfire suddenly came out of the blue from an unknown source. No one moved.

Ches had managed to copy and scan all the important documents from the safes of the politicians they had robbed. Becker had sent some front-page copies to an Arab news channel. He and Ches had reasoned that if they wanted the rest they would pay, as it wasn't clear if the British media outfits would be functioning normally for much longer.

Declan secretly believed that the documents were not that important, as the political situation was eclipsing everything else. What really mattered was what was happening out on the streets and that could go either way. Still, he clutched them, as they were the only bargaining chips left.

'You know someone once said to me that, aside from family, whatever most of us regard as important in life is usually not that big in reality.' Declan didn't turn to look at Ches and Becker as he spoke. 'I suppose it's all just a question of how life goes and how we react.'

'What brought this on Dec?' asked Ches.

The events of recent months had now caught up with Declan. He had never cared in the past about the people he had fought, no matter how brutally. But he was now jaded and worn down by the constant upheaval. It felt like some kind of punishment. He'd had enough of the daily despair but more importantly he was concerned about the future for his own family and friends. The phone networks were down, and he knew that they would all be scared and concerned about him, as he was about them.

Declan didn't reply but stared at the chaos ahead of them. He suddenly realised that they had to get the information out there, if anything to show just how corrupt the establishment had become. One of the documents clearly stated that the government would happily sacrifice two million people in the event of civil conflict and that emergency powers meant that any member of the public could be executed. He had been trying to hide from the truth in his hands, not least from the fact that the documents contained page after page of inventories showing how senior politicians had gained secret payments from armaments' manufacturers.

This included Harnack's own dealings with so-called defence procurement companies, including the one for whom he had tried to hide the real reasons for the deaths of the soldiers on exercise on the Scottish borders some years before. Harnack had managed to keep it out of the House of Commons and out of the mainstream newspapers. Declan now felt that they owed it to the families of their former mates to expose the lies that surrounded their deaths.

There had been other ammunition incidents and misfires on operations, and no one would ever know how many or precisely why they had occurred. But the fact that they had all been covered up by politicians like Harnack went very deep with Declan. As far as he was concerned Ches, himself and many others had given everything for the country just so a bunch of spineless political gangsters could turn a profit for their business friends.

Moreover, some in the corporate world could both give and take payments after striking deals inside the government's complex web of military procurement. That was all that Declan knew, and while he didn't want to be taking action, alongside Ches and Becker, he reasoned that he had no real choice. They had to see this through.

A unit of riot policemen on horseback attempted to charge through the throng of people but it was met with a volley of objects and petrol bombs. One woman shouted, 'Don't harm the animals.'

A man close to where they were standing shouted back. 'What about the bloody animals on top of the horses?'

Ches laughed, stating, 'How about that! There's still a sense of humour out there despite all the crap going down.'

Declan and Becker smiled. Some baton rounds rang out as a Tactical Support Unit tried to force the crowd back. One man in his late sixties fell nearby, trampled by people fleeing the shots. Once they had passed Declan ran forward to help the stricken man. He marshalled Ches and Becker to help carry him to a side street.

However, fighting seemed to be breaking out with what Declan then realised were plainclothed police units and they had to force their way out of the area.

'Look lads,' Declan shouted. 'Let's drag the old boy up to that corner. I know it's not much safer but there might be some medics up there.'

They got the man to the edge of some railings. Ches ran over to where some nurses were helping people injured in the fighting, and grabbed one by the arm, exclaiming, 'We've an old chap here who's been trampled. Looks like a fractured skull.'

'We'll get to him,' the woman shouted. The old man was moved gingerly into their small perimeter. The three men then removed themselves to an area just in front of the railings.

After another ten minutes the street fighting subsided enough for a few people with loudspeakers to get their message across Parliament Square. 'A ceasefire is requested so that injured people can be evacuated.'

After a few more minutes it became apparent that general mayhem had ceased, and people were standing around in groups. Some of those who had appeared armed a few minutes before now seemed to have concealed any weapons for fear, at the very least, of being picked out by the stealthy surveillance footage. The police units withdrew to form a line by the carriage gates in front of the House of Commons.

Ches, Declan and Becker managed to walk towards the front rank of the police lines. Declan did the talking. 'We'd like to see someone in authority. We have some important documents. They relate to national security and what's been happening.'

There was no response from the police, many of whom were exhausted and not in any kind of mood for diplomacy.

'OK, let's put it another way. If you don't go and get someone from the security services, then we will authorise the sale of copies we have made of these documents across the Middle East.'

One officer shouted over, 'Who are you people?'

'We're former servicemen. These documents relate to the sale of weapons systems by politicians.'

A gap opened in the police ranks and the three walked through. They carried on walking towards the gates and were stopped abruptly by a rank of men armed with assault rifles. They were dressed in black overalls of an unspecified security service unit.

Declan had guessed that the seats of government had been vacated for days although he knew that many in the crowds still believed that the politicians were still debating. He didn't really care what was happening behind the walls of power. Whether they were discussing the arrests of militants or the price of cheese it made no difference to him. The men were ushered through to meet one of the commanders.

'So, what's this incredibly exciting new take on events you can give us then?' While the senior policeman was being sarcastic the scars across his face shone in the light. They were old and well indented in his brown complexion. It took Declan a while to work out what was wrong with the man's face. It had been slashed down one side so that the ear was distorted as a result. He realised that no knife, no matter how jagged, could have done this. It looked more like a shrapnel wound.

Ches spoke first. 'We have a lot of information here on government ministers receiving cash from various defence companies, as well as other potential cover-ups. We have documents that conclusively prove that weapons systems were sold to violent regimes overseas with the full backing of the British government and that various politicians colluded in the procurement of weapons systems that hadn't been tested properly. This was something that resulted in the deaths of British soldiers as well as others. It was all covered up, as these docs prove.'

The senior officer looked at them and remembered what had been said in the briefing a few days before: *If anyone turns up claiming politicians have committed crimes of any kind then they need to be taken seriously.* It meant that if the situation could be defused in any way, then it was worth consideration.

'Ok, we'll allow you guys to talk to a liaison officer. But bear in mind it will take time. More than one person will want to look at your documents. And you will have to give some kind of statement. Do you understand that?'

The three men nodded. They followed the officer towards an armoured police van, as more fighting erupted in front of the police lines and petrol bombs came overhead. Declan recalled some of the dark days he'd experienced as a British soldier and muttered to himself, 'Did they ever really go away?'

~~~

In another part of London Chris's team was backed up in a side road along with two other Mastiffs and all three vehicles were exchanging gunfire with unknown assailants who were firing from surrounding high walls.

'We need to concentrate the fifty cals on the higher levels – put that out, that all call signs are to do that,' Chris screamed to the vehicle's radio operator.

The young signaler had been struggling to cope with his nerves as rounds were flying around the vehicle aimed mainly at their location. What bothered Chris was that the escape route they were going to use looked like it was about to get cut off. If they took any more casualties, they would not be able to guarantee themselves a safe passage out.

Chris then shouted out, 'Give me that radio lad.' Donning the headset he continued: 'Right all call signs listen up. We're getting cut off; I repeat, we are getting cut off. We need to pull back to the high-level bypass about seven hundred metres back. We cannot match their firepower – not at this range anyway.'

As he spoke a rocket-propelled grenade hit the side of the Mastiff, exploding against the set-off armour, but still throwing the men around who were inside.

'All call signs: move, now!' Chris shouted.

The three armoured vehicles sprang into action and, as more RPG rounds landed, they forced their way through the burning and devastated landscape. Chris knew that they were being beaten. They hadn't slept more than a few hours in five days and couldn't go on without reserves. But there wasn't any, as no army units had appeared. They were on their own, running out of ammunition, food and willpower.

~~~

'We seem to have a major problem.' A security chief was speaking to the assembled heads of various government departments at a location in a disused underground station in central London.

He continued. 'I have it on reliable evidence that we are losing the streets and that the militants are defeating the TSU. We are outnumbered and outgunned. Where soldiers have been deployed, they are refusing to fire on militants and many units have stood down. The security services will be making a joint announcement shortly.'

One high-ranking cabinet minister, one of only three who were able to get to the location, finally lost his modicum of reserve. 'You people were told weeks ago that the police tactical units couldn't handle this, but you refused to listen. That's the real reason the country is lost. Or it will be unless a miracle happens.'

A chief of staff scowled at the politician. 'Who are you trying to kid? You and your crap government have been systematically screwing this country for long enough. Is it any real surprise that your failed policies have led to this situation?'

Another member of the cabinet intervened. 'Please. There's no time for this. There's no point – we have more pressing concerns.'

'At least you're right about something at long last!' the chief of staff replied. A ripple of cynical laughter broke out around the table.

The security chief interjected, exclaiming, 'Right we've heard enough. What's left of the security service will be assuming control of this country over the next forty-eight hours. The police have clearly lost control and are unable to bring order to the chaos around us. We'll bring in martial law as of midnight on Thursday and then make an announcement on behalf of the government that we'll start negotiations with some of the rebel leaders. We'll also ask for a ceasefire.'

He looked around, before adding, 'We request that support teams, backed by armed police units, move into those areas where the fighting has been heaviest to help and support the local population and restore order. And, by the way, I sincerely suggest that all the main political parties keep quiet, for the near future at least, as we'll manage the transition.'

~~~

Mila opened the small dormer window in the attic bedroom. She looked out onto the Cheviot Hills. The unexpected whiteout had taken them all by surprise. She lit a cigarette and turned the radio on. There was a broadcast for more blood donors to come forward, as supplies were running low owing to the heavy casualties in England. She wondered what had happened to Ches, not having heard from him at all for the last three days.
~~~

The newscast reported on fighting in many areas. However, no one could confirm what was happening overseas as many media networks were operating under a general ban. Most newspapers had stopped production altogether, mainly because no one wanted to buy them.

She stared at the pile of photocopied documents wondering why they were so important. It was the last thing Ches had said to her; *Please don't let them out of sight love.* She had thought it would be easy enough to wait for his return, especially as there was plenty of food and drink in the house. But now she was worried and impatient, and the sight of the documents was a painful reminder of his absence.

Part of her was still amazed that she was no longer being forced to have sex with strangers, no longer being told what would happen to her family back in Moldova if she didn't turn tricks. She also knew that the gangmasters had long ago decided she was dead. Anyone who just disappeared like that must have been killed as far as they were concerned.

They had dropped her off at the politician's house that night and, after waiting outside for hours, they must have eventually stormed in. She reasoned that, as the house looked so impressive, they knew the man was an important figure. They would have guessed that he was keeping her there for a reason and written her off.

It was only when his face started appearing on news reports that they would have started to fill in the blanks: that he had been attacked by professionals. And they would have assumed that such criminals would likely kill any witnesses, taking the body away for disposal.

As Mila pondered what the gang would have made of events, she also recalled that she had never been back to the brothel. She had never contacted her friends there, although she ached to know if the girls were alright, especially her closest friend, Vanta. She was so young and decent. She should never have been stuck in such a pitiful existence in the first place.

At the same time Mila was glad the British politicians were getting what they deserved. They had nothing but contempt for girls like her. The politicians actually seemed to encourage trafficking; after all they had never lifted a finger to stop it. It was one thing all the British political parties did seem to agree on, that foreign prostitutes were great for the economy. Even if the girls themselves had never actually wanted to become sex workers in the first place.

She looked out across the thick fall of snow. 'Where is Chezz?' she asked herself. 'I hope that stupid friend he spoke about hasn't put him in any danger.' She lit another cigarette to calm her nerves.

~~~
~~~

From the turret of the Mastiff Chris could see smoke billowing across London from his vantage point on Primrose Hill. Large crowds were merging below, and he had no doubt that by the time they reached their destination they would be swelled by many more angry people.

A sudden feeling of failure overtook him. Helicopters were flying a long way above the crowds, powerless to change the reality of the situation on the ground and underlining the fact that millions had assembled across the country in a single attempt to overthrow the political establishment.

An order suddenly came over his headset. 'All units stand down until further notice. Do not engage with the militants. Repeat *do not engage*.'

Chris stooped down into the cabin. 'Jake. We lost mate, no more fighting. It looks like they're about to negotiate a settlement.'

'Well,' Jake replied. 'I guess if we don't give up now then we'll just be repeating the same mistakes we've made before. Then there'd be even more crap. Just like all the other bloody groundhog days.'

'I can see that now mate,' Chris responded, emotional and exhausted. 'We've all just been bloody martyrs for those morons in power. They got so many good people killed for nothing.'

Jake nodded and grinned resignedly, before replying, 'Too right Chris, *screw the politicians*. Maybe they should let the army run the show for a while.'

At that moment two shots came across the top of the Mastiff, skimming and then ricocheting off the top-gunner's nest. Chris recognised that they were probably just to remind them who was there. He jumped down into the vehicle commander's seat and got on the public address tannoy.

'Whoever just fired that be aware there is now a general ceasefire – we are not firing back unless our lives are in danger, and we will not attack you. There is about to be an announcement, so we appeal for calm. The emergency services need space to operate so please respect this ceasefire. If you don't let them through, we are still under orders to protect them. Be aware of that.'

Another shot came across the vehicle; just one solitary round amongst all the violence that had been occurring.

'That was just a *bollocks to you* from them mate,' laughed Jake. 'Let them stew for a while.'

Chris then ordered the vehicle back another hundred metres. He then took a message on the vehicle radio. 'Listen up guys. New orders are to be issued at 1300. I'm guessing after the top brass have tried to strike a deal.'

'Yeah, and I know exactly what they're going to say,' Jake replied. 'But these guys are not backing down. They want them all out, *every, last, one,* and then a provisional government put in their place. I just hope we find a settlement otherwise this situation will get even worse.'

Jake and the other men in the Mastiff shared a stony silence. They could hear, above the sound of the radio chatter, the chants from the crowds marching not so far away. They got out and stood by the vehicle. The other teams did the same.

Ten minutes later Commander Aley arrived in an armoured convoy and looked around at the teams as they stood, exhausted and propped up against their vehicles. He stood to one side and started to address them. ‘First thing I’d like to say is how grateful we all are for the sacrifices that have been made. Many people will be in our thoughts.’ He paused before continuing. ‘I’ve had a less than rewarding time with the ministers. They seemed to underline the fact that there is no real plan of action. It is now all about damage limitation.’

‘Thanks for letting us know,’ Jake uttered under his breath to those immediately around him.

Aley continued. ‘We’ll need to exercise greater judgement and restraint. This is critical, as a lot of people will now try and take advantage of the situation. We need to stop them. We’re now the only real resistance against anarchy, as well as the failure of the politicians. But one day people will thank you, and don’t forget that.’

‘You watch,’ said Jake quietly. ‘He’ll be off like dirt off a shovel in a minute.’ Chris nodded imperceptibly and smirked.

Commander Aley finished his impromptu speech. ‘Unless you have been in some kind of conflict zone before it’s not easy to explain what’s happening. But we’re all in it together and we have to continue to do our jobs. There’s no choice. Some have paid the price in full and will be honoured. Do not let them down.’

Once Aley had left Chris turned to his team. ‘I think what he actually means is that we’re already past the separation stage where the politicians are concerned. I think it’s now the divorce stage.’

‘Too bloody right mate,’ replied Jake loudly, and the rest of the men groaned in agreement.

~~~

Ches stood with his back to the ranks of police and security forces and started talking to Declan. ‘So, let’s get this straight Declan. We’re actually going to march in there and give these documents to the politicians? That sounds like we’re going to give them the hard evidence of corruption and then they’ll just bury it. Shouldn’t we just sell it to the foreign media?’

‘Yeah, let’s flog it,’ Becker added assertively. ‘It might be worth something.’ Becker was confident enough to look Declan in the eyes as he spoke.

Declan stared at the entrance to the Great Hall of the House of Commons in front of him as he clutched the attaché case to his body. The three of them
~~~

had been held there for over an hour. Suddenly Brandon Sinclair, flanked by two bodyguards, came up to them and looked straight at Declan.

'So, you brought the documents with you, I take it Declan?'

Declan raised the small attaché case. 'Yes, Brandon. The documents are also scanned to several discs and memory sticks.'

'I think it's time Declan,' Brandon Sinclair replied. He gestured towards the entrance. Ches and Becker stood in amazement as the two men walked alone through the police corridor and on to where the heavily armed members of a Tactical Support Unit lined the route into the buildings, under the watchful gaze of the tower of Big Ben.

Scores of other armed police and personnel guarded the area. They were not about to let the militants get anywhere near the inner sanctums of the House of Commons, but at the same time they couldn't get beyond the boundaries of the immediate area themselves. It was a type of stalemate, and Sinclair had seized his chance to finally walk into the corridors of power.

He gestured at the first officers he could see, shouting, 'We need to get into the House of Commons and talk to some politicians.'

One of the TSU officers scowled back. 'And who are you, the Queen of Sheba?' Other officers laughed at the two men.

'As far as you're concerned I am. I'm the reason there's a bloody war going on around here and I'm the only person that can stop it. I'm Brandon Sinclair.'

An armed TSU commander stared at Sinclair for a few seconds and then recalled the briefing he'd had that morning. He also recognised Sinclair as the most senior militant commander.

He then visually checked both men in front of him to see if they were hiding anything. Despite the cold weather they were not wearing thick clothing and neither appeared to be carrying weapons. In fact, the man standing next to Sinlcair was not carrying much apart from a small attaché case. He then ordered two of his men to search them, shouting, 'You can't come in here with weapons. So, we'll have to check you over. Give us proof of who you are as well.'

'That's OK,' Sinclair replied. He and Declan unstrapped their belts to show that nothing was hidden. They then opened their wallets and produced their IDs.

Ches and Becker had stolen away from the gate and were walking back towards the front of the police lines. They had agreed that they didn't want anything more to do with the political wrangling.

Declan knew that the only hope for a real end to hostilities lay with the evidence in his hands which would convict several serving and former politicians. He also knew the real reason Sinclair and the security services had struck a deal; so that justice could be seen to be done and help defuse the tension on the streets. Moreover, at least as far as the various chiefs of security were concerned, Declan could still act as a liaison with the NRC, the main militant group. They had Aley's approval.

He was glad he had still retained contact with the former C.O. of his old infantry regiment, Major Tilbrook, who had gone on to become Lord Tilbrook at MI6. It was a conversation with Tilbrook several hours before that had cleared Declan and Sinclair to appear at the Houses of Parliament. *Thank God for old acquaintances,* reasoned Declan.

However, Sinclair and his allies would never settle for liaison alone and Declan knew it. Sinclair had made it clear to Tilbrook in their conversation that they wanted all British politicians implicated in war crimes to stand trial. His last words on the matter were clear: *So many millions of lives have been destroyed by the actions of various British political regimes that it's time for justice - for all the victims of failed foreign policies.*

There had been a belated attempt by some politicians to force the dissolution of Parliament. This was mainly to help buy some time, so they could find escape routes. However, a slight majority had realised that this was in fact the time to come clean and they wanted to see the terms about to be put before them.

'The dead have long memories,' was one headline on a banner across the square. A man with a loudhailer was the only voice that could be heard as Sinclair and Declan, flanked by two TSU officers, waited to go through the main entrance. The man spoke steadily, 'We have fought our way across this country and we have won. We are dictating terms to you – the scum of this country protected as you are by the state troopers. This is the end for you criminals. We're taking control. We are taking back what is ours, our country, for the working class. And we'll not let any of you off.'

Several petrol bombs came flying across from the crowd and into a section of heavily armed police. A cheer went up: *Kill, kill, kill the filth.* And then louder cries: *Smash the State, Smash the State.*

Chris's armoured vehicle finally arrived in front of Westminster Underground station at the head of a small convoy. Jake was standing in the turret and using his binoculars to get a closer view of what was happening, both in the crowd and at the entrance to the House of Commons. His jaw dropped as he suddenly saw the two figures standing by the entrance. He shouted down into the vehicle.

'Boss; take a look at this.'

Chris looked up quizzically and struggled into the turret beside Jake who gave him his binoculars. 'Yeah, seen. Nothing surprises me now. The informant seems to have become a revolutionary, and there's nothing we can do about it.'

Chris had a sick feeling in the pit of his stomach. He suddenly realised what had happened. 'But how did he get to be standing there? He must have been with them all along.'

'Like I've said to you before mate,' Jake replied. 'I've spent enough time on operations and nothing surprises me. Guys like Declan; well, they're in their own world mate.'

Chris kept staring, with a feeling of raw hatred welling up inside of him. 'He was playing both sides while our guys were being killed.'

Jake looked up. Chris had lifted his rifle and was easing his left hand over the cocking handle. Jake pulled Chris's left wrist away from the rifle. *Chris, let it go.*

Jake continued. 'The politicians are getting what they deserve. Those creeps have had it all their own way for long enough, so we may as well kick their useless arses out of power. That's where it's at, so don't let any personal stuff get in the way.'

'Yeah: I get it,' Chris relented. 'But that bastard will get....'

An explosion rocked the square. Jake could see that the shockwave was traversing so fast people were going down as the head of it passed. There was a surreal pause before the screaming began. Medical personnel were there in seconds, but Chris and the rest of the squad could see bodies lying about. As he turned back, he saw that Declan and the other man had already disappeared into the lobby of the House of Commons.

He shouldered his rifle and scanned the square for more potential bombers. The TSU teams then demounted and started spreading out, pushing the crowds away from the wounded, with everyone now mollified and compliant.

~~~

'We've had enough of the wars and the politics of hate that you people have practised over the years.' Brandon Sinclair was addressing those politicians who had remained, in the Great Hall. 'We've also had enough of the destruction of our way of life and of the raw capitalism that has, for too long, suffocated and dislocated our own country. That's why we're at war with you. You have committed every social injustice possible against the people of this country. You're not fit to be in this so-called parliament.' He stopped briefly and looked around him. The real debating chamber had been declared out of bounds to all, and he could see that he and Declan had effectively been prevented from entering there.

He continued, shouting, 'This is no longer a house of representatives, as you have turned it into a place of corruption, of power by default. You have thrown the future of this land away, on failed policies. But today we are bringing this to an end.'

Declan stood in awe, staring at the surrounding walls and ceiling. He then noticed that the few remaining politicians, whatever their political colours,
~~~

were nearly all from the older generation. They were the redoubtable men and women who would not let their seats become occupied by those same revolutionaries who had been attacking them.

'So have you come here to negotiate with us?' one MP piped up.

Sinclair fixed his eyes on the unfortunate. He walked calmly over and looked the man square in the face. 'Do you really think that you and your government, or what's left of it, are really in any position to negotiate?' The man writhed slightly.

'You've let the war criminals, casino bankers, corrupt politicians and financiers off the hook. This is judgement time, not a time for negotiation. Many of you should be under arrest for war crimes and crimes against the British people and others across the Middle East. What's more, we have some of the hard evidence here with us.'

Sinclair took the attaché case off Declan and continued. 'The evidence of government corruption is clear enough from what's in my hand.' He held the case aloft. 'There's no point in maintaining the status quo any more as the people of this country don't benefit in any respect from your failed government. It's time for change.'

Sinclair paused and smiled, before continuing. 'I have forty thousand fighters ready to storm this area. If any police or armed units put up any kind of resistance they will be crushed. Some of you are to be arrested and tried for war crimes. Whoever is left is to be physically removed and put under house arrest. We will then build a new political system. This is final and there is no negotiation. Think of it like this: this is good and exciting for ninety-five per cent of our population. But for the five per cent who are, like you, utterly corrupt, it's a total disaster, but of your own making.'

Sinclair realised that the few political stalwarts left had collectively taken on an air of defeat. After another ten minutes his commanders had finally forced their way into the building. The politicians were rounded up briskly and dragged outside to their uncertain futures.

A sniper based on a roof overlooking the square picked off a few of Sinclair's men but he was soon overwhelmed with gunfire and eventually his body could be seen hanging from a parapet. Chris and Jake and the rest of the TSU teams had been forced back and had taken up positions on the south bank of the river. A ceasefire was then called.

~~~

Ches and Becker managed to break free of the crowd once the police had lifted the cordons. They then started walking towards St James's Park. Becker wanted to make his way back to Grantham and, after an emotional hug with
~~~

Ches, he ran off towards Green Park. The underground had stopped working but there were still the occasional buses somewhat bizarrely ferrying people around the West End.

The events of the last few days had not quite sunk in for Ches and he didn't fully understand what Declan hoped to get out of it. He just knew that his part was now over and all he wanted was to get back to Scotland and Mila. There were still a lot of gunmen around, but he wasn't bothered as anyone could see, without a second glance, that he was neither part of the machinery of power nor a militant, as they were wearing blue-grey overalls.

As he strolled along, he was more concerned that he would run into an armed police unit, no doubt of the kind that Declan had recently been part of. However, it had also occurred to Ches that he didn't believe that a man like Declan could ever throw his lot in with the police. He had a nagging suspicion that there was something else behind Declan's logic. 'Perhaps it was just a ploy to get near the politicians, or a way of getting back at the people behind the scam that cost the lives of some of our mates. Anyway, I doubt I'll ever know the truth.'

Ches smiled and muttered, 'Thank God for people like Dec. At least they can be bothered to do something.'

He was suddenly on the ground staring up at the sky and had no idea what had just happened. The next thing he felt was the searing pain in his legs, and he looked down and along his body, unable to flex. The round must have ripped through his left leg, the bottom half of which was pointing at a strange angle, and then travelled through his right. Both wounds were just below the knee. He knew that the injury was severe and called out for help.

He came round with a large paramedic looming above him. He passed out again, but not before the paramedic heard only one word, *Mila*.

~~~
~~~

EPILOGUE

Three months later Brandon Sinclair's face was still beaming around the world. In order to ensure that society wouldn't break down completely he had struck a deal with the heads of the various security services. Together they would allow the civil service to operate freely, as they had before the overthrow of the politicians, so as to form a transitional authority and thereby ease the formation of a new political structure.

However, some of the militants had turned against the NRC and decided to carry on the fight. Chris, Jake and the Tactical Support Units therefore found themselves fighting yet more sporadic battles with militant splinter groups. These became known as the National Revolutionary Brigades. Meanwhile the NRC threw their hat into the political ring completely, forming a new party and embracing a wholly democratic approach. There was also an array of fledgeling political organisations, many of them representing smaller interest groups.

The situation wasn't helped by the fact that the US government had stated that it was about to send 200,000 combat troops as part of an invasion force to restore the hated establishment. Jay Saxby was then made a liaison officer by the US Army after falling out with Sinclair. Many media pundits were now predicting open warfare between those who supported the restoration and those who didn't, regardless of their political leanings. And no one fancied the new regime's chances of survival, as a hybrid authority, based as it was on the shaky foundations of the old.

The NRC itself wasn't completely averse to compromise. Sinclair declared a state of emergency and sent a delegation, made up of all parties, to the USA and other countries, explaining that a committee was to be set up for corrupt British politicians who would be brought to justice. Some industrialists and financiers would also be put on trial for the past sale of weapons systems to corrupt regimes around the world. The legality of the sale of such systems to states that had sponsored both violence and terrorism was being considered. Other politicians who had been involved directly in the engineering of lies in order to start wars were also arrested.

One question raised by Sinclair in the House of Commons related to the procurement of faulty weapon systems that had first been tested on British troops and then sold on the open market. This would feature at a future hearing, as the charges of crimes against humanity would now take precedence. Declan felt only slightly aggrieved at being upstaged by Sinclair but was very glad he had allowed the question to be raised in the first place.

In total almost one thousand British politicians (both serving and former) would be called upon to stand trial for various crimes over the course of the next few years after what had become termed by the media *The Battle for Westminster*. Many others, including some members of the media, were to be placed under house arrest. The transitional authority soon realised that under such circumstances the remnants of the existing establishment could never survive, and a new English Parliament was created in the Midlands. The Scots, Welsh and Northern Irish were declared federal nation states, and were to be ruled independently of Westminster. The House of Commons was thus now regarded as a relic and there were plans to turn it partly into a hotel and partly into a museum of British culture and history.

It soon became evident that real power lay in the hands of Brandon Sinclair and the transitional authority, formed as it was with what remained of the higher echelons of the civil service. Sinclair had known all along that this was where the real power lay, with the top bureaucrats, many of whom had kept their jobs. This ensured that industry and commerce remained relatively unaffected by the upheaval. It also ensured that the NRC's social and economic proposals could never be enacted, but at the same time it made good headlines to pretend that there would be sweeping changes while the country tried to settle down.

No one knew for how long the state of emergency would persist. However, the situation was mirrored in other countries, notably Spain and Italy where there had been uprisings mainly against severe austerity measures. Central Europe remained blissfully free of insurrection although the authorities there were following the events taking place elsewhere closely, such they nearly precipitated their own insurgencies as they tried to clamp down on activists.

After six months of further upheaval, and many more deaths on British streets, law and order finally returned and all the rebel groups came to the negotiating table. The police force had new commanders promoted from the ranks.

The Tactical Support Units were retained and some of the former militants even joined their ranks in order to help foster a spirit of cohesion. They were eventually formed into a new organisation called the Tactical Armed Service, or TAS for short. It was intended as a strong paramilitary response by the regional metropolitan police forces, mainly to stamp out the threat from any militant splinter groups, as well as preventing the growth of any new ones.

The Armed Forces were deployed in a general role to police borders and airports, as well as actively clearing up the mess of the previous two years of insurrection. The Royal Family returned to England and life began to get back to normal.

~~~

Six months after being shot by a police sniper Ches was taking his time getting accustomed to a prosthetic left leg, and he hadn't found the adjustment easy. Mila was his constant companion.

They soon discovered that, as several million people had left England for good, properties were now freely available across the country. They swung a decent ground floor flat in a relatively new block in Enfield. The only catch for Ches was that they had to get married quickly so they could claim they were a real couple, something which speeded up the whole process of immigration as families were now being prioritized.

After spending some considerable time not knowing where he actually belonged, Becker moved to Grantham to live with his girlfriend. He got a job as a security guard for a superstore just ten minutes walk from the big house he and Ches had robbed, all those months before.

Once there was a lull in the fighting Chris and Jake spent as much time off work as they could with their young families. Chris was soon appointed to Deputy Commander of the Tactical Armed Service. Jake became a unit commander. Commander Aley became overall commander and was answerable to the Home Office.

Of the 931 politicians arrested, 137 were convicted of war crimes and crimes against humanity by the new authority. Ultimately, they would serve lengthy prison sentences having been declared guilty of crimes ranging from the propagation of war against unarmed civilian populations to the use of tactics such as falsifying evidence in order to sell weapon systems to foreign states in contravention of international human rights laws. Of the rest many were tried for corruption, criminal negligence and fraud whilst holding office. Some were sent overseas to face criminal charges.

Amongst those indicted for crimes against humanity were some politicians and industrialists who had been responsible for the sale of weapons to the Khmer Rouge in Cambodia after 1980, as well as the training of their fighters by British soldiers. Declan, having served as an instructor in the early nineties with a British specialist training team in Cambodia, was called as a special witness, from his new home in the USA. He was absolved of any responsibility as he had agreed to act for the prosecuting authority.

The body of Jay Saxby, Brandon Sinclair's main lieutenant, was found, shot dead, in a shallow grave in the Midlands about two years after the overthrow of the government. It had emerged that for a long while she had been liaising
~~~

with the CIA behind the backs of other militants. Saxby had forged contacts with the United States well before the Battle for Westminster and by then the CIA was flying in large numbers of agents and operatives to defend their own interests. Saxby was intended to be a link with the militants and, once the weak and ineffectual British politicians had been dealt with, the Americans intended to set up a proxy government with her as a senior adviser. When that plan had failed, mainly due to Sinclair's swift actions, she had become a target for certain militant groups.

There was never any explanation as to how she was executed. Some rumours abounded that Sinclair had known for months that Saxby had been liaising with the CIA and that he had personally arranged for her to be hunted down and shot. But they were never confirmed.

~~~

Three years went by and the newly elected Prime Minister of England, Brandon Sinclair, was being interviewed by Paris Match. The interviewer kicked off with a question that Sinclair had both expected and prepared for.

'So, Mr Sinclair, you're the new Prime Minister of a free state as you have called it. What the rest of the world would probably like to know is how you managed to quickly engineer a provisional government after so much bloodshed. Surely this would have been almost impossible, as I cannot believe anyone was in the mood for compromise?'

'Well, I was the leader of the main opposition militant group, as I'm sure you know. But when things calmed down enough, we swiftly altered our whole MO to that of a democratic political organisation. It was true that some of our executives had found themselves in negotiations with the security services, but this all took place well after the fall of the government. It was not somehow pre-arranged as some are suggesting.'

'But why was there so much bloodshed? Surely a way could have been found to avoid so many terrible executions and deaths?'

'You mean a bloodless revolution? How many times has that happened throughout history? Rarely is the answer. The politicians were never interested in negotiation, and they never wanted to back down. But in many ways, it was too late anyway, as by the time the main action had started and the fighting had begun, there had been too much bloodshed by the security forces. At the end of the day, it was British politicians who made it legitimate for ordinary civilians to kill on the streets of my country; not the other way around.'

'Would you say you were unfairly blamed for the violence?'

'Absolutely, I would. We got the blame for everything because the media only ever represented the main parties. We were fighting for justice for
~~~

ordinary people, the British working classes. We were sick of the mentality of our politicians. They thought they could go on raping the resources of ours and other countries, killing their people, and ours, at the same time. We had to act so that Britain would no longer start wars overseas, and we also had to bring some of the perpetrators of previous wars to justice.'

'Would you say you succeeded in any of your aims?'

'Well, we got rid of a great many corrupt British career politicians and their cronies. We even got some justice. In February 2003 the UK effectively signed the death warrants of over two million Iraqis over the next twenty years, and many others across the Middle East in subsequent conflicts. No one can hold a different view to that. Moreover, the UK was bankrupted by that war and the others that followed, and we brought most of the architects of those wars to justice.'

'But you brought the government to an end. That means you brought stability to an end, doesn't it?'

'What people call *governance* was no longer functioning for the British people. It was only functioning for bankers, foreign businessmen, the armaments industry, the energy sector and anyone else making themselves stinkingly rich at the expense of ordinary British working-class people. The main parties didn't understand what was happening in the decade or so after 2003. It was the end of the road for them. And the vacuum had to be filled with something new; something that worked. The EU could never play that role, so we had to step in at that time.'

'But surely you had a choice, and you didn't have to declare war on your own country?'

'Well, we did. Until then the corrupt politicians had mostly got away with it - as had the financiers and bankers who'd backed them. We had no choice but to go after them. Many of them were brought to justice but far more have got away; living in South Carolina or Russia or somewhere. Anyhow, some kind of justice has prevailed upon those we could get hold of.'

'So, you blame them for the turmoil?'

'Of course they're responsible. They never sought peace but always the politics of hate. They ruined our internal labour markets and undermined our entire culture and way of life. They set black against white, christian against muslim.'

'Do you really think that's what happened?'

'Yes, and at the same time as all that was happening it was obvious they couldn't run the country properly, neither Labour nor Tory. This was despite the fact they had frogmarched our young men and women into unwinnable wars. It's hardly surprising there was an uprising. The behaviour of British politicians was off the scale. That's why we took action.'

'Would you say that British politicians were war criminals for what they had done to the Middle East?'

'Yes, I would. Many foreigners don't realise it, but we really had no choice. We had to go to war as that was all the politicians understood. That was the language of the ruling British political class. It was ironic in some ways, as it was the only way social progress could be made, through extreme violence sweeping aside outmoded attitudes.'

'So, which of the parties do you blame for what happened?'

'All of them. All the money that should have been spent on re-building our own infrastructure had been lost after 2001, either on interventionist wars, a failed social agenda, given away to the city fatcats, or the hair-brained sale of profitable British manufacturing to corrupt foreign companies. All of this was because of the failure of centrist politics in Britain. Meanwhile we had allowed everything traditional about our own country to be destroyed by the political classes and their gangster friends, right and left. So, it was both sides of the political divide that ruined my country. Then we ruined them.'

'But what about the economic damage this turmoil is doing to the British economy?'

'It's academic in most respects. We have no British-owned companies left anyway. The majority of manufacturing, energy and even construction companies are foreign and owned often by companies whose finances are underpinned by their own governments. In other words, we couldn't compete anymore as it wasn't a level playing field. As soon as a British company turned a profit it was bought out by some massive foreign corporation, or parastatal, and then stripped of all assets. We are gradually changing that situation.'

'Will there be more conflict?'

'I don't know. Fighting was the only real option at that time. Now, outside central government, things are getting better. We had too many corrupt people operating in too many towns, and now we're sorting that out. Even local authority chiefs were just gangsters, paid two or three times the salary of a cabinet minister. The whole system had to collapse in the end anyway, especially with so many angry young men walking around without stable work, along with a lot of ex-soldiers and police out of work.'

'But what's the eventual and likely outcome for Britain?'

'Apart from everything else that has happened it has ceased to be a global power and has lost all the overseas territories and bases. British soldiers will not be invading anyone any time soon. The Falklands are now the Malvinas and Gibraltar is a Spanish port. The only people who care about such things are a few tiresome old bigots who get together in small village pubs. And by not pretending to be a minor superpower we're saving ourselves a fortune. Our country is now controlled by a provisional authority, and we'll never let the corrupt back into power again, not in my lifetime anyway.'

'And what of the many politicians who have been arrested for crimes against humanity or for fraud and corruption? What will happen to them?'

'It already has, as they're now being dealt with. Either deported for their crimes overseas or serving very long sentences.'

'But what of your own supporters, are they in power?'

'Some of the heroes of our revolution are no longer around. Like my friend Declan who blew the lid on the scams over defence procurement. He now lives in Queens, New York. It was ironic that a man who had fought for the British for so long as a soldier should be hailed as a hero by both the Republicans and Loyalists in his hometown. I suppose they saw that he helped undermine and destroy the corruption at the heart of everything. He's now heavily involved in community work, and good luck to him.'

The French interviewer paused and stared as Sinclair took a sip of water.

'What is the historical lesson of all this, Mr Sinclair. What would you say is the impact of this upheaval?'

'Well, we had the right circumstances for what happened. The corrupt were taking all the wealth and too many innocent, decent and ordinary people were struggling to survive. It was a disaster about to happen, and it did because of the cowardice, short-sightedness and incompetence of the ruling classes. So, I would say that the real impact is that people now expect good governance and won't settle for less. When you consider how simple that all sounds, the price we have all paid is immense.'

'And where are things heading now?'

'We are progressing. There is now a level playing field so people can progress on their own merit. The welfare state is back. For example, young people don't need to take out mortgages for their education. It's not perfect, as nothing's ever perfect, but at least we're in control of our own destiny and no outsiders can force their policies on us either. But one thing for sure is that the small political class who ran our country badly will never be able to wield the power they once had. We brought an end to all that.'

~~~

The smell was overpowering, and it brought an immediate and terrifying flashback to Taj Ali of the Baghdad Police Forensics Team. The memory flooded back, those dark days after the fall of Saddam Hussein, and the bodies that turned up every day at the sides of roads and drainage ditches, wretched and covered in flies.

He stood by the decapitated figure of Sir Dick Harnack, the former British politician. He thought it somehow ironic that an Englishman could wind up murdered on the streets of Baghdad. But then again, after all the years of violence and upheaval, nothing surprised him anymore.

According to the Iraqi press the man had been responsible for the sale of weapons systems to Iraq's government forces as well as numerous other
~~~

countries. Those weapons included a plethora of area denial weapons, or land mines as they had been more generally known. These had been responsible for the killing and maiming of untold numbers of innocents. Harnack benefited personally from those deals, as a senior executive of the company concerned. He had been taken captive when he visited the region trying to sell a new range of devices to the Iraqi Armed Forces.

Officer Ali stood at the side of the cordon extending for many metres around the area, with the centre a protected forensics bubble at least five metres across. Children and old men lined the edge of the marked area, although many had now drifted away over the course of the day. He scanned the surroundings and thought of members of his own extended family who had been victims of the upheaval over the years, as well as colleagues killed in the line of duty. There were too many faces.

'Your execution was relatively swift and painless; unlike the pain you caused all our innocent people,' Ali stated quietly to himself, as he spat to one side, away from the forensics bubble. He could hear the other officers talking within the bubble. The victim's arms had been trussed to his rear and there was something like a blast injury to one side of the corpse. Although the head had not yet been found (and probably wouldn't be if this killing followed the established pattern) there were signs that the man had been starved of oxygen. But a full analysis was still required.

While he didn't feel any pity for Harnack he did feel uneasy, as he knew there would be other such executions, if his own experiences were anything to go by. For now, he would assist in arranging for the body to be sent back to the forensics lab.

~~~

The Long Island Railroad train pulled in at Jamaica station in Queens. It was close to midnight and Declan stepped off. He walked briskly towards the exit stairs. Out at street level he breathed in some cold and heavy January air and then stopped to look right at the sign for the Air Train to JFK Airport. Thoughts came flooding into his head, faces of old friends and flashbacks to moments in his career as a soldier. He paused for a short while and then grimaced. A feeling of disgust welled up inside of him and he turned, the wind burning his face. The apartment he shared with his Canadian girlfriend would be warm and inviting and it was only ten blocks away. He had found his home.
~~~

About the Author

James T Emry served as a soldier from 1997 until 2014, including two tours of duty in Afghanistan. He has also worked as an aid worker in various countries including Kosovo, Cambodia and East Africa.

www.ingramcontent.com/pod-product-compliance
Ingram Content Group UK Ltd.
Pitfield, Milton Keynes, MK11 3LW, UK
UKHW042346060226
467748UK00003B/79

9 781836 155195